THE BIG BAD WOLF

MY SISTER'S WAR

13 PITCH BLACK CATS

PROLOGUE: THE PUPPET KING

The brisk air didn't bother the lion beastkin as he strolled under the moonlight. Daygon looked up and stared at the three moons in the sky, embracing the silence of the night. It had been ten years since he'd claimed the position of the beast king, and yet Daygon knew he didn't deserve it.

A chilly breeze came up from behind the lonely figure, pushing his mane out in front of him. As the breeze died down, he knew he was no longer alone.

"Now, what could the noble beast king be walking around at this time for?" a heavy, sultry voice whispered in his ear. "Were the concubines I left for you not enough? Are you looking for someone with a little more endurance? I know they weren't completely fresh. I just couldn't help myself." A terrifying giggle turned into a full laugh as Daygon turned around to face the interloper.

Hovering in the air using two large bat-like wings, the most alluring creature in existence grinned at the beastkin. Her beauty was unnatural, and anyone who looked upon her knew it. However, most would be unable to deny themselves and reach out to claim such a treasure. Her perfect porcelain white skin glowed in the moonlight as her jet-black hair fell to her shoulder blades in a wispy texture. She had a perfect hourglass figure; everything was taut and youthful while on full display.

However, Daygon knew that her beauty was only skin-deep and that the demon was nothing to underestimate. He watched her dainty hands tipped with sharp, long fingernails rest on his shoulders. Her thin tail, covered in black scales, curled around and lifted his chin so that he looked the sin of lust in the eye.

"Why would I want a vile creature like you as a mate?" Daygon's voice rumbled with its perpetual growl as he glared at the demon.

The sin of lust flapped her wings to fly so she was once again behind the beast king and lazily draped her arms over his shoulders. "You call me vile, yet you never stay away from me for long. You always come crawling back to me, begging." Her voice dripped with anticipation.

"I wouldn't want you, demon. I want my mate returned." Daygon growled and bared his fangs.

"I wouldn't do that if I were you." She wrapped her arms around his neck, still hovering off the ground, but she shifted her posture so that her torso was parallel to the ground. "Remember what happened last time?" Her voice rose in pitch with each word.

The lion beastkin went deathly quiet. The memory of the demon floating behind him, summoning fallen demons to defile his mate and forcing him to watch, unable to move a muscle, destroyed his rebellious spirit. He didn't know how tense he'd held his muscles until he resigned himself to the demon. "What do you want? Why are you here?" His voice held only defeat.

"Good kitten. Remember, she is my plaything. If you behave, I might let you see her. For a little while, at least." The demon released the beast king and flew around him so that her feet were at the level of his eyes. "Kiss them."

The lion beastkin wanted to stare at the perfectly petite feet tipped with deceptively sharp triangle toenails with disgust, but he knew that would invite another punishment. The sin of lust went through every conceivable method of humiliation, and even invented a few new ones, to ingrain in him that she was in charge.

Slowly, the beast king kissed her feet as they floated inches from his muzzle.

"See, was that so hard?" She leaned over and lifted the beast king's head with a single finger. "Why so gloomy? We gave you the power to become the king like you wanted. And for ten years, you've ruled this kingdom we gave you."

"My people are starving." Daygon lowered his voice. "Ever since you arrived, food has become increasingly scarce, and no matter where we look, there is less and less. You gave me a kingdom that you're killing."

"Then take it from those less deserving than yourselves."

The sin of lust grinned as she looked behind the beast king at the source of the new voice.

"You *are* the king of the proud beastkin race. It is time you take what you deserve."

Daygon's heart skipped a beat at the sound of the angelic voice. Lust's voice invited one to act upon their carnal desires, but this voice established dominance. Daygon slowly turned to acknowledge the second demon who damned his soul.

A tall young man stood dressed in a flowing white robe next to a large tree. Two blood-red eyes looked at everything with disinterest as he walked towards the beast king. His flowing golden locks drifted in the breeze and brought attention to the two massive black eagle wings trailing him. Daygon knew better than to stay standing for long in the presence of the sin of pride. He dropped to his knees and prostrated himself before the demon he feared the most.

"There is conveniently a kingdom with a surplus of resources. They have grown fat and weak as they enjoy their peace." The sin of pride stopped three strides away from the beast king. "Take from them."

The lion beastkin quivered at the sin's words. "You want me to go to war with the humans?"

The sin of lust moved to hover over the beastkin. "Absolutely."

"Why?" Daygon didn't have time to regret his question. His world exploded in pain as he tumbled sideways, rolling until a tree stopped him. He clenched his jaw and refused to cry out in pain. Slowly, he returned to facing the sin of pride on his hands and knees.

"It's not your place to question me." The male demon's voice promised more pain should the beast king resist again. "You'll go and kill the humans. Those are your orders. I don't care how you do it, just kill them all. The sooner you leave, the sooner I can leave."

"You're no fun," the demoness purred as she twirled a finger through her hair.

The sin of pride turned sharply and walked away. "You and Greed can make all the plans you want. She said that the humans would be vulnerable. Besides, I'm only here because I was ordered to make sure this plan succeeds. You're not very grateful that I've even bother to help at all."

The sin of lust clapped her hands. "Oh, but of course. None of this would've been possible without your mightiness. You've kept the little animals in line better than a certain king I know."

Daygon flexed a single claw as he was forced to listen to the demons belittle his people. But he retracted it before the demons saw. He cursed himself for being such a coward.

The sin of lust landed right in front of Daygon while he stared at the ground. "Now be a good king and do what you're told." She wrapped her tail around his neck and lifted him to his knees. "Remember, you're not important or required. You are convenient. We can find another to replace you just as easily as you replaced the last king. Now sweet dreams," she said as she kissed the beast king on the lips.

Daygon wished he were brave enough to stand up to the two demons. Then he could at least die with dignity. But the moment he'd let them in and accepted their power, he not only damned his soul but the soul of his mate and the lives of every beastkin in the kingdom.

The sin of greed wore the appearance of an elderly woman who was quietly sitting outside enjoying a nice hot cup of tea. She wanted to be unassuming so she could watch. Her plan had many moving parts, and right now, she watched a group of armed knights walk through the gates.

She knew that her plans ten years ago were stopped by a very lucky beastkin. Everything was set up for Wrath to rampage in the city as freely as possible, but he was stopped because he became fixated on said beastkin. Then five years ago, her plans were successful, but not as successful as they should have been. Gluttony was killed by the same beastkin. But also someone had been ready for her plans. There had been enough damage to create a blood anchor at the tournament grounds, but only just.

The man known as Midas had worked against her. But this time, she had forced his hand and would kill two birds with one stone.

The sin of greed continued watching, as nobody was any the wiser of her presence. The human leading the group of five knights asked around for hunters to guide them. None of them agreed to take them. When asked why, they all said the same name, "Lucia."

"Hello, ma'am." The human approached the sin of greed in her disguise. "Could you please direct us to The Maidens headquarters?"

She put on a practiced smile. "Yes, no problem." Her voice was harder to hide in her illusion, but she softened it enough not to raise suspicion. And even if they did suspect her to be not as she was, she would be long gone before they came back to check on her. "Just head down this road for five sections, turn north for eight sections. It'll be to the east."

The human gave a slight bow. "Thank you, ma'am."

And with that the five knights walked away. The sin of greed didn't need to fake her smile as she watched them follow her instructions. Her plans were well on their way, so long as the other two kept up their end.

She got up and looked for a quiet alley and, with nobody looking, melded into the ground.

SOME THINGS NEVER CHANGE

I've told everyone time and time again, *don't make me angry. But what do they do? They make me angry.* I sat alone in my temporary holding cell, tapping my toe-claw against the wood floor. The wooden bench wasn't comfortable to sit on, but since I was already in trouble, I decided not to make things worse for myself.

I heard a familiar set of footsteps, ones I'd known would come eventually.

"What did she do this time?" my mom asked the warden, who greeted her at the door. Her voice was flat since this was the third time this season she had to pick me up from here. *And we're only three weeks into the ice season.*

"She broke both of Tanyl's arms and threw him through a door. He's only recently regained consciousness," Philibert, the warden, said as he led Mom to my particular cell, one renovated for me specifically. "Something's wrong. This is three times this week. She even dragged him here, put him in a cell, and went to her cell on her own. I've almost come to expect this once a week, but now?"

"She's just going through a phase," Mom interrupted. "She's still young, even though she doesn't look like it." I heard the footsteps stop short. "But I know my daughter. What did this Tanyl say or do to provoke her? My guess is he called her something."

You know me so well, Mom.

Philibert sighed. "She says that he called her a mutt."

"Will someone get me out of this miserable cell? I'm Tanyl Green Agate, and I'm not a criminal!" a high-pitched, whiny voice called out. *I can let you out; I just won't use the door. Also, I might not let you live!* "I demand to speak to someone in charge. Preferably someone with enough sense not to let mongrels run rampant through the streets."

"Sweetie, please be patient. I'll be back." I heard Mom storm off to another cell. *She didn't even say "hi?" Whatever.* "Please wait by Lucia until I finish speaking to this Tanyl."

"Why do these things always happen when I'm on shift?" the warden grumbled under his breath.

"Finally, someone worth talking to." *That whiny voice is going to drive me to kill him. I know I shouldn't kill people for such petty reasons, but he has it coming. Nobody will miss him. I promise I'll make it quick. Messy, but quick.* "Hurry up and get me out of here. I don't belong here."

"Hello, my name is Nora Stormleaf." Mom paused for a moment. *I would love to see that man's face right now.* "Before I have you released, I want you to answer a few questions for me."

"Whatever it takes to help you catch that beastkin who did this to me." Tanyl sighed. "So, what do you want to know?"

"You don't have to worry about us catching the girl. She turned herself in. I'm more interested in why you decided to call my daughter both a mutt and a mongrel."

I wagged my tail as I imagined the look of terror on his stupid face.

"What? I didn't say that to any elves, just that white-haired beastkin." *It's silver, you jerk.*

"She's my daughter. And she's listening to this conversation right now." Mom used the same voice she used whenever I did anything wrong.

"Impossible. How could you ever do that with an animal?"

Why is that where his mind goes first? I rolled my eyes as I stood up.

2

I stared at the metal bars that glowed a gentle blue hue. *I feel so special that they created magically enhanced bars to hold me. Unfortunately, they still won't hold me. I'm too strong. Breaking Tanyl's arms was easier than snapping toothpicks.* I walked over to the magically enhanced bars and looked down at Philibert as he moved to stand next to the door of my cell.

"Hey Phil, please let me out." I leaned against the bars. "If I have to hear any more of this, I'm going to kill him."

"Please don't." Philibert, who always told people to call him Phil, looked at me with pity in his eyes. "I know you're really a good girl, just a little overzealous. But you need to stop this acting out. You're causing me so many headaches with all the paperwork I need to fill out because of you. I know you don't deserve to be treated like that, but I can't let you out. Not until your fine is paid. Just plug your ears or something."

I glared at the human. He flinched when I wiggled my ears. "I won't leave, I promise. Let's make a deal." Phil raised an eyebrow. "If you let me out, I'll stand right next to you and use my ice magic to seal my ears. Then I swear I won't cause any trouble and never step foot in this building for two weeks."

I learned my lesson. Never use ice magic in this cell because, since everyone knows I use it, this room gets absurdly hot once I start channeling any magic.

"For two entire weeks?" he said under his breath. I grinned and nodded. "You swear?" I nodded again. "And if you renege?"

"Then you can clip my claws," I said with a grimace.

I have to make it worth his time, but why did I have to go there? Sure, it isn't permanent, but I can't go hunting for almost a week. Not like I plan on failing, though. I'm not even going to be in town all next week. Mom's taking me on another fishing trip. But he doesn't need to know that.

The warden pulled a ring of keys from a pouch hanging off the back of his belt and opened my cell doors.

"I adopted her. But I've heard enough. The moment you've paid your fine, I want you out of this city." Mom's voice was full of venom.

"I guess Mom's done with him already. That was quick," I said as I stepped out and shrugged at Phil.

I watched a tall, curvy elf woman dressed in a thick fur dress and heavy boots march towards me. Her long green hair flowed freely behind her as she glared at me.

"Hi, Mom," I said sheepishly.

Mom shoved a small sack of coins into the hands of the warden. "This should cover her fine. I'll pay for the damage when I return." *She's in a bad mood.* "Let's go." Mom placed a hand on my shoulder and led me towards the door. *I'm in a lot of trouble now.*

I hunched my shoulders as I trudged out to the street. *Even though I'm now two inches taller than my mother and fully grown, she still makes me feel small whenever she wants. Even though I turned fifteen this last wind season, some things never change.* "I'm sorry. I got carried away... again." We walked out into the street as we left the courthouse. Light flurries of snow danced to the ground. Mom shivered as I basked in the cold. Everyone wore extra layers of clothes to ward off the unusually cold ice season we were having.

Nora sighed. "I know you don't mean it all the time." She wrapped her arm around me. "And I know you have a general disregard for others, but do you want to tell me the whole story?"

That's because people almost always say something to annoy me. Why should I care about those who don't care about me? Society has nothing to offer me, so I'll only play nice enough. I have to uphold the laws after all.

I shrugged. "You know how I get after combat training, right?" Mom nodded. "I told Captain Aenwyn I needed to calm down, and that I needed to be done for the day. As I walked around, trying not to snap at anyone who even looked at me funny, I started daydreaming about our fishing vacation we're going on tomorrow. All this combat training has been making it harder for me to calm down. But when I was in the middle of fantasizing about a nice pike between my fangs, that elf yelled at me for standing in the middle of the road."

Mom sighed. "You were caught daydreaming again?" She cracked a slight smile. "And about food. It's always about food with you. But you know the middle of the street isn't the place for daydreaming."

As I stared at the ground, I drooped my ears and tail. "I know. I was just so worked up that I had to calm down. And thinking about food is a great way to calm down. If he had asked nicely, I would have moved. But he had to say something like: 'This is why mutts don't belong in cities.'" I growled as I recalled the memory. I looked at Mom with my teeth bared. "That's why I grabbed his arms and snapped them in two. And while he screamed in pain, he said some very unflattering things. So I shut him up by throwing him through the door of the closest house. I said sorry to the lady who owned it."

Mom tapped my nose with her finger. The tingle of magic caused me to flinch. "Don't growl at me. And yes, he was wrong to treat you like that, but..." Her voice dropped drastically. "You need to stop answering with violence. Not every problem can, or should, be solved that way."

I took a step away from my mother and presented my body to her. "Do you see what I am? I was literally born to kill! I'm very good at violence. Half of me says that I should eliminate all problems as soon as possible. It's really hard to disagree with her." I relaxed and headed towards home, growling. "Can we just move on from this? I want to go fishing."

"I guess this is the part where I give you the bad news."

I stopped mid-stride and turned to see Mom standing with her shoulders slumped. "Bad news?" I bolted towards her. "No. You promised me you wouldn't accept any jobs so we could go on this vacation together. You promised!"

Nora lowered her gaze as she pulled a folded piece of paper out of a pocket and handed it to me. "It isn't me who has a job to do."

I held the folded paper and noticed that the seal was broken. *Of course she would read it.* I unfolded it and looked over it.

Lucia Silverbreeze,

I have revoked your request for leave.

You are required to report for your orders as soon as you receive this letter.

This is not a request, this is an order.

Captain Aenwyn.

PS: I'm sorry.

5

I tore the paper in two.

"I'm..." Mom started to say as she reached for my head.

I shook my head and waved her hand away. "No. Just don't." I stormed off towards the base of operations for The Maidens in Aquittemia. They'd moved to a building in this city so I could continue to live with Mom. *This was supposed to be my vacation. Aenwyn said that if I was good... We agreed that I needed some time off, and this was for everyone's benefit.*

While the thin layer of snow crunched under my feet, my rage reached a boiling point. I closed my eyes and let loose a wail into the sky. As my cry neared its end, I turned it into a growl. Everyone in the street quickly distanced themselves from me. I bared my fangs at the cowering citizens as they stood at the edges of the streets, leaving most of the road open to me.

See, people here know not to mess with me. I need to have another talk with the captain. I really want to rip something apart now.

ORDERS

I shoved the door open as I scratched the ground with each step. Two people were in the entryway, and they froze as they saw me. Galla, a cute little elf with light-brown hair, scurried towards a wall to get out of my way.

After stopping, I took a deep breath and turned towards Galla. "I'm sorry for scaring you. I'm just in a bad mood."

"The captain warned us you might be." Even though Endalinne's voice carried with it an air of authority, she was a newer recruit, just like me. She walked to stand between me and Galla. Her blond hair, tied in a ponytail, blocked my vision of the small elf.

"One, I'm not going to hurt Galla. And two, she warned you?" My lips curled to reveal my sharp wolf teeth.

"Yes, she wanted me to stand here so that once you got in and I could take you to her." Endalinne didn't flinch. She was average height for a human, but that still required her to tilt her head back to stare at me. "Are you going to come quietly?"

"Lead the way." I clenched my jaw and held back a growl. *This had better be good.*

Endalinne led me through the simple yet large building that had become the headquarters of The Maidens. As we walked to the top floor, everyone was in a hurry to get out of my way. Nobody said a word to me, and all conversations stopped once they could see me.

Endalinne stopped, stepped to the side of a simple wooden door, and waved towards it. "I'm sure she's ready for you."

I don't care if she isn't. Nobody's talking on the other side of the door. It sounds like she's writing something. I shoved the door hard enough to hear something crack as it collided with the wall. A golden-haired elf sat behind a desk full of papers. Simple, essential furniture sat in the small office room. The two half bookcases that flanked the desk from behind were full of documents and extra papers, one of which was the oath I took when I joined The Maidens. There was a pair of basic wooden chairs angled towards the desk that I ignored as I stormed towards the captain.

I slammed both halves of the paper onto the table. The table sounded like it gained a new crack. "Explain!"

Aenwyn sighed. "I have been very lenient with you, given your status, age, and nature. But you are still required to show some manners and salute a superior officer." She opened her eyes and glared at me.

Growling, I stood straight, put my feet together, and folded my hands behind my back. "Happy?"

Aenwyn stood up. "No, but that's the best I'm going to get out of you right now, isn't it?" I stared at her. "Watching your ability in combat over the last five years has been encouraging. You're one of the best I've seen in all of my long years, but your lack of discipline is also the worst I've seen." She walked around to the other side of her desk. "You're clearly not ready for this, but I don't have a choice. You've fostered quite the reputation in and out of town." She waved to the door. "Follow me."

I stared down at my captain as I took a few steps towards the door. "Are you going to cut to the chase?"

"You're still young and impatient. If there's anything I've learned over the last hundred and twenty years, it's that being impatient will not only get yourself killed but others as well." *I guess it's a good thing I work alone, isn't it?* The elven captain closed the door as she followed me out. "I heard about what happened and that you caused trouble again."

"He started it," I grumbled. "People in town have finally learned to leave me alone. Why can't people who are visiting Aquittemia learn?"

Aenwyn gave me a sidelong glance. "You're expecting the whole world to cater to your needs?"

She's right. I slumped my shoulders and ears as I walked next to her.

"You've been doing better. At least ever since the incident with the Crimson Tide. And since they've been transferred to guard Bronston, Dalettoma, and Alelry for some reason, I doubt you'll ever see them again."

I groaned. "How many times do I have to say it? I didn't swallow his hand. I just don't know where it went after I spat it out."

The captain rolled her eyes. "I know. Look, they've been gone the better part of a year now. Since then, you've gotten your wish—people are leaving you alone." Her voice dropped. "Mostly out of fear, not acceptance."

"I tried the acceptance route." I threw my arms out wide. "And look how that turned out. No, that'll never happen no matter what I do. People are stupid and panicky. And with people like those from the Crimson Tide, I'll never be seen as equal." I flexed my claws, resisting the urge to drag them across the wall. "Those racists spent so much of their time in a drunken stupor saying how I was nothing more than a public menace. I never start anything, but I always finish it."

Aenwyn placed a hand on my chest to stop me. I let her. "This isn't about who's to blame. It's about how you choose to react to the issue. Nobody tells you that you have to answer bigotry and hatred with violence."

I curled my toe-claws and dug eight groves into the floor as I grabbed Aenwyn's hand. "I don't care! When laws and rules are flawed and allow someone to get away with such cruelty, someone has to take a stand. I just happen to be good at violence." I threw my captain's hand back at her before stomping down the hall.

"Waterfalls."

I paused mid-stride and took a deep breath. "Sorry. It's just so frustrating always being treated as less than what I am." I turned back to my captain. "It's just so easy to be angry, and it feels good to see people fear me. I don't have your patience to wait for change to happen. I won't live as long as you. If I want things to change, I have to make them change."

She gave me a sad smile. "You're right, if you want change, you need to make it happen." *See, I'm right!* She held up a hand. "But how you bring about that change also matters. I know it's hard, but you have to remember that the rest of the world has its share of problems too. Soon you'll have to accommodate other people's needs before your own. Especially once you have kids."

I waved my arms. "Hold on, let's not jump to me having kids yet."

The elf curled her lips. "You told me what's going to happen to you during the water season. We've made arrangements for you to stay home and deal with it, but one day you'll find someone you love and have kids. It sounds like your nature will guarantee it." *Easy for you to say.* "But we're getting off track." She resumed leading me through the building. "You have an assignment. One only you can do, apparently."

I flicked my ear towards the captain. "I find that hard to believe. The only thing I can do is hurt or kill things. I know other people can do that too."

Aenwyn stopped in front of a door to one of the guestrooms. "There's more to you than that. I hope one day you can see that." The frown on her face was almost painful to see. "A group of knights from another company requires a guide through the woods."

I nodded. "But why me? There are other hunters and trappers who know the woods well enough."

"They tell me that none of them will take them where they need to travel. Apparently, everyone says that they need your permission to go through that section of the forest." *Oh! There's only one reason for that. And they had better have a good reason too.* I flexed my claws and coated them in ice to make them larger, but still just as sharp.

"Waterfalls," Aenwyn said as she pointed to my claws.

I lifted them and shrugged, dispelling the magic. The ice shattered and fell to the ground as a fine dust that quickly melted. "Why do they need to go through my territory?"

"I'll let you ask them. They're right inside here." My captain motioned to the door we were standing next to.

I focused on my ears to try to listen in on any conversations, but I didn't hear any. *Either they're using magic or not talking.*

"Fine, I'll at least hear them out," I said right before I walked into the room.

The guestrooms weren't heavily furnished since they were just waiting rooms for people who had business with specific knights. Four people occupied the chairs in the room, while two people stood next to them.

I froze as I stared at the collection of people who were waiting for me. The first person to look in my direction was a dragoon, who stood behind one of the chairs. His golden eyes focused on me as he nearly flinched away. Blue scales shimmered in the sunlight from the window where they weren't covered by his brigandine armor. The cloth covering the plates was a dull maroon and looked freshly crafted. *Wearing armor in the middle of the day? What's wrong with him?* My blood almost boiled when I looked at his face more closely. *Isn't Phan dead? He's been dead for ten years. Is this his kid or something? He looks just like him.* He stood taller than everyone but me, and he was about three inches shorter than me. I'd grown accustomed to being taller than everyone since I grew to seventy-nine inches at the beginning of this year.

The elf sitting in front of him was a skinny woman. She sat there shivering. *She wouldn't be so cold if she didn't shave her head.* Her snow-white skin was in direct contrast to the loose-fitting black robes with a fur inner lining. She tilted her head to the side as she looked at me with her gray eyes. The confused look only made her cute face look even cuter.

"She's hot!" A human who stood next to the window stared at me with his mouth wide open. He was tall, a little shorter than the dragoon, yet just as bulky. His skin carried a light tan like he'd spent many days in the sun. He wore thick silks that swayed as he walked.

His steps were heavy, and each time his boot struck the ground, the sound nearly echoed in the small room.

I leaned back as he stopped just out of my reach. His blue eyes stared at me with fascination. "Will you marry me?" He dropped to a knee and extended a hand towards me.

That's a new one. Yeah, I don't like it.

I slowly turned my head towards Aenwyn, who was holding her breath. "Can I kill him?" I pointed to the auburn-haired idiot.

"Eh?" The human tilted to the side as he lost his balance and caught himself from falling to the ground.

"No, no, no." Aenwyn's eyes went as wide as they could as she rushed to stand between me and the fool. "No killing. He didn't mean it."

I stared at the man as his face slowly lost its color. "That's a terrible joke." I gently moved Aenwyn to the side. "What's wrong with you? You know nothing about me, and I'm guessing I'm the first beastkin you've ever met." I leaned forward and growled at him. "Why did you even think marrying me was possible?"

"I..." The human fell backwards onto his butt and slowly scurried away from me.

"Daric often does strange things." I turned to look at the other male human who was taking a few steps towards me. He spoke with a voice higher than I expected a man to have. His curly red hair bounced with each step. He was the shortest of the men in the group, barely taller than the tallest woman. He wore silks just like the other human male, but his were darker than the one on the ground. "Don't worry, he's mostly harmless. Don't be too hard on him."

And people call me immature. "Whatever." I left the sniveling man on the ground. "So, you wanted my attention. Now you have it." I flicked my tail back and forth.

A second elf woman with long brown hair cleared her throat as she sat in a chair. "We've been all over town looking for a guide through the forest to the northeast. Everyone said they wouldn't step foot in that part of the forest. When we asked why, they all mentioned the name 'Lucia.' I take it you're Lucia." Her voice was crystal clear while still being a bit playful.

"Is that a problem?" I glared at the woman. Her skin, eyes, and hair were all the same color, and her face had many sharp angles.

She shook her head. "No, I just never expected to see the famous beastkin of Aquittemia in the flesh. But since we know your name, let us share ours." The elven woman stood up and raised her left hand in salute towards me. *She's also a knight, not a captain.* "My name is Penny." She pointed at the other elven woman with the shaved head.

The elf woman stood up so quickly she hopped off the ground for a moment. "Dinar. Just Dinar." Despite her enthusiasm, her voice didn't travel much. She repeated the salute Penny gave me.

"Silverlipankeltan. You may call me Silver," the dragoon said as he raised his hand. "I understand my name is quite difficult for many."

How many of them are knights? Wait, she said this was another company. They're all knights.

"My name is Mark." The man who defended the fool gave a flawless salute. *He's not in charge?*

I looked at the last woman with long blond hair in a braid, fidgeting with the tip as she avoided eye contact. She stood the farthest from the door. "Golditress." Her salute was barely acceptable by the standards Aenwyn had drilled into me for an entire week and a half.

"I call her Goldy for short." The fool finally had the courage to stand in my presence. "I'm Daric, the leader of our adventuring party." He waved his arm towards the others. His smile spread across his face as he turned towards me.

I crossed my arms and tapped my toe-claws. "Don't you mean knight company? And you're in charge? That sounds disastrous. I would rather it be the human girl in the corner playing with her hair." I waved a lazy hand towards the one I'd mentioned.

Daric deflated. "But I'm the hero."

Hero? Something doesn't feel right. Whatever. Business first. "Where are you going after you clear the forest? What's your mission? How long is this going to take?" *I need to know what his goal is.*

"I, ah..." Daric turned towards Penny.

I rolled my eyes. "Leader, right."

Penny rolled her eyes too. "We're researching blood anchors. We're working with someone who has been studying them for the last five years since the one was created at the tournament during the prince's birthday festival." I winced. *That was not a happy day.* "We've heard of a rumor about another one and are going to investigate."

Mark squinted as he stared at me. "Were you at the tournament?"

I lowered my head and ears as I looked at the ground. "Yeah. I would rather not talk about it." The vision of Evalana's severed arm flashed through my memory. I shook my head. "So, you need me to guide you through my territory, and then what? Do I wait for you to return, or do you find your way back on your own?"

Daric looked like he was going to start talking. Silver placed a hand on Daric's shoulder and pulled him back. "Don't. Can't you see she doesn't like you? Allow me." The dragoon straightened up and performed a shallow bow. "We understand that this is going to be a long mission and we could be away for the entire season. Since we plan on packing light, we need someone who can help us live off the land. That is the primary reason we're searching for a hunter."

I growled as I turned to give Aenwyn a glare. "I really hate you right now."

"Why?" Dinar's voice barely reached me.

"Today was the day I was supposed to leave and go on a vacation with my mom. I'm guessing I have to go with them, don't I?" I continued to stare down at my captain. "You haven't left, so I guess you were here just to make sure I didn't hurt anyone. Am I right?"

"Yes, on both accounts." Aenwyn returned my glare.

"Fine." I turned to glare at the group. "But first we need to go over some ground rules."

3

FOUND HIM

"Rules for what?" Mark asked.

I pursed my lips. "As you've probably noticed, I have a bit of a temper. I can keep it under control in most circumstances, but I have rules to keep things civil." I held up a hand and extended a finger. "One, I am a person. Not an animal, a monster, or anything less. You treat me like a person, and I won't look for ways to beat you within an inch of your life." I lifted a second finger. "That leads to my second rule. I will give you one warning, then I will hurt you, and if you keep going, I will kill you."

"Why are you so violent?" Dinar held her arms close to her chest and quivered as she spoke.

I glared at the little elf. "Because, when it comes to conflict, I have a strong predisposition to fight. No matter how minor the conflict."

"Are you sure you can kill us? We could be more skilled than you," Daric said as he puffed his chest out. *Go on, test me. I'll wipe the floor with you.* "We also outnumber you."

Aenwyn placed a hand on my chest as she walked between me and Daric. "Let me dispel that illusion. She can and will have no problem beating all of you up at once. Lucia is our single most capable fighter." She turned to glare at me. "Although it sometimes goes to her head."

I shrugged my shoulders. "So what if I have a problem knowing when to stop? Some people see that as a positive trait."

"Anything in excess is dangerous." Silver's eye twitched. *There's probably an interesting story about that one.*

"The last rule is that if you hear me say 'Waterfalls,' leave me alone. That's non-negotiable." I reached for the door. "I'll meet you at the north gate tomorrow morning at sunrise."

"I'm the hero and I'm getting my very own fellowship," Daric whispered as he glanced at the ceiling.

That's it. I need to settle this now.

I opened the door. "Everyone, out." I watched everyone, including Aenwyn, jump. They looked around at each other and then back at me. "I said out!" *Why is nobody moving?*

"Come, let's leave her alone in this room," Aenwyn said as she ushered Silver towards the door. "It's better for everyone that she get it out of her system."

I watched each person as they walked past me. As soon as Daric walked by, I grabbed him. "Not you." With minimal effort, I shoved him towards the chairs. The small procession of people ceased as soon as I touched Daric.

Penny stepped towards me. "What are you planning?"

"I want to talk to him alone." I bared my fangs. "Now out!"

Mark and Aenwyn stood between me and Daric. "Whatever you need to talk to him about, you can do it with us present," Mark said as he spread his legs shoulder-width apart and turned slightly. *Not a bad stance, but pointless.*

"I warned you, don't provoke me. And you're doing that with your stance." I turned away from him and pushed Golditress and Penny out of the room towards Silver and Dinar. "I promise, I don't want to hurt him or kill him." *Yet.*

"He'll just tell us what you talked to him about after you leave anyway. He and I have no secrets." Mark never moved an inch. *Thanks for letting me know.*

"That's nice that you have a friendship like that. I have a friend like that, too." I pointed towards the door. "Out! I will not repeat myself again."

"Waterfalls. You need to calm down." Aenwyn placed her hands on my shoulders.

"What do you want from me?" Daric stood still with his hands at his sides.

"Who sent you here? Who told you to go after these blood anchors?" *I might as well confirm it. But I can't let them know. I'm afraid of what this idiot will say if he knows that I'm a reincarnator.*

"My teacher, Midas Bloodless." Daric tilted his head as he responded. "Why did you need to ask that in secret?"

I growled as I silently stormed out of the room. Everyone created an opening for me to walk through. I hated that my footsteps didn't make any sound when I stomped them. It was so much less satisfying.

"What was with her reaction?" Penny's voice trailed behind me.

"I don't know," Aenwyn whispered.

Of course that conniving, controlling, lying old fool had to be involved. I don't care that Mom loved him enough to want to marry him. After meeting him at the tournament, I made sure Mom kept him away from me. But he said he was teaching his replacement as the rein-carnator to defend the world from the demon king. But all this tells me is that Daric is the one The Voice sent after me.

I left The Maidens' headquarters and sprinted through the streets towards home. The world moved in slow motion as I dashed past everyone and out the gate. I saw our little farmhouse, which we'd bought from one of the farmers just outside the city right after Mom adopted me. The farmers still owned the land around it and farmed it. They just needed to build another house on their land for themselves. I, of course, had to help. Mom made sure of it. It was a simple little cottage, made of wood that we treated with some kind of coating liquid that smelled awful. Mom said that it would make the house require less maintenance.

I walked in, and by the smell of cooked meat, I knew Mom was in the kitchen. "I'm home."

"How did it go?" Nora walked around the corner with a plate of food in her hands. Steam rolled off the potatoes, parsnips, and fish steak. I took another big whiff. *That's carp.*

"Are you trying to make it up to me because the fishing trip is canceled?" I crossed my arms after closing the door.

"A bit." Her smile left me feeling calmer like it had done so many times in the past. "I even left you three fish uncooked and six more salted so you can take them with you when you leave. Do you want to tell me all the details?"

I stepped behind her and followed her to the small dinner table we shared. She already had my fish on a plate, ready for me to eat.

"Things have been too quiet for too long," I said as I sat down. "A group of six, likely misguided, knights are investigating the blood anchors. My orders are to guard them, guide them through the forest, and keep them fed." I picked the fish up and stared into its lifeless eyes for a moment. "Oh, and they're being led by the other reincarnator."

Mom placed her plate on the table but didn't sit down. "Are you certain?"

"He said he was Midas Bloodless's student. So, yeah." I slid a claw down the spine of the fish. "He's an idiot. The first thing he said to me was, 'Will you marry me?' Who does that?" I fileted the fish with a few more swipes of my claws.

Mom sat down gingerly, her mouth open wide. "You didn't do anything, did you?" She shook her head. "No, of course not. You're here." *Thanks for the vote of confidence, Mom.* I watched my mother's eyes suddenly grow. "You didn't say yes, did you?"

I glared at my mother.

She released a long, slow exhale. "Good. I don't think I'm ready to give away my little girl."

I arched an eyebrow. "'Little girl?' You do know that I'm taller than you, right?"

Mom half-closed her eyes and chuckled. "I know, but I still can see the little girl who was brought to the steps of the orphanage covered in an unreasonable amount of mud." *Aw, that's adorable.* There was a look in her eye like she was thinking about something, but she didn't say anything. Instead, she started eating some of her vegetables. "How long are you expecting to be gone?"

I shrugged my shoulders as I swallowed a chunk of fish. "I didn't ask. They were starting to make me agitated, so I left. Hopefully I'll be back before the end of the season. I want to have my fishing vacation before the water season starts."

Mom enjoyed her potatoes for a moment. *She never knew how to cook before. It looks like she learned a lot from Melody after she turned the orphanage over to her.* Then the corners of her mouth curled downward. "This might be too soon for you. Isn't there someone else they can take?"

I giggled. "Apparently I ruined that chance on my own. None of the other hunters and trappers will step foot in my territory. It's what I wanted, but now it's come back to bite me." I flattened my ears. "But I agree with you and Captain Aenwyn. I might not be ready for this. I still haven't gotten good at dealing with other people. A point reinforced by today's events."

Mom placed her fork on her plate and released a long exhale through her nose. "Socializing is like any skill. If you don't practice it, you'll never learn it. You come up with every excuse to avoid dealing with people and spend more time in the woods alone than anything else." There was a sorrowful frown on her face. "I've not been very good about helping you with that either. Maybe I've been spoiling you too much."

I'm not that spoiled, am I? I finished eating my fish. "You don't see the stares people have given me my entire life. Sure, I can handle them from time to time, but eventually, they get to me." I curled my tail around my waist. "Maybe I'm just being childish again, but I've never felt more alone than I do now. Evalana hasn't been able to visit me ever since she married Mr. Prissy Pants. Zenny has been extra busy bandaging the people I hurt during my training sessions. I can't look her in the eye anymore." Tears welled up in my eyes.

Mom got up and hugged me. "Shh. It's okay, don't hold it in."

I cried onto her shoulder as I suffered another bout with my depression. *Why am I so useless? Why do I constantly need someone else to help me calm down?*

I held Mom tight, but not tight enough to hurt her. "I thought that if I stayed here and didn't go with the ambassadors I could have friends, but I haven't been able to make any. Now I have to leave and go with complete strangers who are led by an idiot."

"Why don't you try to make friends with those strangers?" Mom whispered in my ear.

"Because they think I'm a dangerous freak." I pushed Mom away to arm's length.

Mom frowned. "How much do you know about them, really?"

I wiped my eyes as I shrugged.

"How much did you tell them about yourself? My guess is you only told them your rules." She raised her eyebrows and tilted her head forward.

I turned my head to look at the ground. *Why does she know me so well?*

"And it sounds like you don't know them very well either. So, if you're going to have to do this, you might as well get to know them and let them get to know you." She placed a finger under my chin and turned my head so that I looked at her again. "It won't kill you, and you don't have to tell them everything if you're uncomfortable."

"I'll try," I said as I slumped my shoulders even more.

"Alright," Mom said with a wide smile on her face. "Sometimes we need a kick to push us to do what we know we should." She placed her hand just behind my right ear and scratched.

I melted as I snuggled closer to her. *They will never know about this. This is a secret for those I trust.*

After scratching me behind the ear for a few moments, Mom got up and returned to her food. "Feel better?"

"Yeah. I'm sorry. I let my emotions get the better of me again." With a sigh, I stood up. "Is there anything you need me to do before I practice my magic?"

"I'm quite attached to my emotional daughter. But to answer your question: yes. Could you cut up more firewood? It's been freezing this week." Mom shivered to emphasize her request.

I smirked. "It isn't that cold. But I guess I could use it to practice my magic too."

Mom gave me a playful grin. "You only say that because you have a fur coat."

"Jealous?" I said as I rubbed the fur on my arm.

"Yes."

Both of us broke into full belly laughs. We ended our laughing fit by wiping the tears from our eyes.

"Alright, are you getting up early? I want to see you off," Mom said, still short of breath.

"I told them I would meet them at the gate at sunrise." I walked towards the back of the house. A thought bubbled to the front of my mind. "Are you going to have enough food without me hunting anything for a while?"

Mom smiled as she finished eating. "Who's the mother here?" She chuckled. "I'll be fine, honey. I have plenty of money saved up and can take care of myself. Remember, I've taken care of you all these years."

Yeah, where did that thought come from?

"Besides, I'll be eating salted bear for most of the season. I still can't believe you found one hibernating and killed it."

I bowed. "You're welcome." I opened the door to the back. "You know where to find me if you need me."

There was a moment of silence as I headed out. "'Prissy Pants,' really?" I heard Mom chuckle just before the door closed.

I giggled as I left to cut firewood before bed. *I don't really have to do this, because she can pull apart the firewood with magic much easier and faster than I ever could. She does this because she knows I need to practice my magic. It still feels like I take too long to form a weapon.* I practiced summoning an ax mid-swing, trying to create it as fast as possible and still be functional. Even though I could tear apart the wood with my bare hands, I used this little game as an exercise.

After feeling the signs of magic fatigue, I continued and prepared extra firewood, using my claws to pull them apart. *I wouldn't want Mom to get a cold while I'm gone.* Once I was satisfied with the amount of firewood prepared, I took a quick bath with the water Mom left me in the tub. After drying off and spending extra time brushing my fur, I laid down in my bed and stared at the ceiling.

I guess this is what they call "adulting." Being a kid again was really fun. Daric better not make things difficult for me. At least my first mission will be an easy one.

21

4

LONG TIME NO SEE

The sun wasn't up as I stared in the mirror. Daric's comment still weighed on my mind. *I guess I can admit to myself that some people could see me as attractive.* My silver fur covered me from head to toe and felt extra full since it was the ice season. The claws on my hands and feet were still just as sharp as ever as I admired them. I had grown up to be very tall, and my ever-so-useful tail was almost as long as my legs. My arms and legs were the same length because my arms were longer than a human's. My hips had widened out, making it reasonable for me to carry twins if I ever got pregnant. Their width also made running on all fours much easier. My hourglass figure continued up, and my breasts were a little on the small side for my frame, but they were more than enough for me.

I smiled in the mirror, the same smile that I always used to scare off annoying people who wouldn't leave me alone. My hair, which was the same texture and thickness as my fur, fell just past my shoulders and naturally wanted to flow behind me. All my silver fur and hair brought out my big, beautiful blue eyes. *I've heard more than my fair share of compliments about my eyes.*

I concluded my vanity session with a proper grooming of all my fur. Once I'd brushed everything to my satisfaction, I put on some clothes and started packing some things for my first mission as a knight. I paused as I saw the toy unicorn on my bookcase of memorabilia. Only two other objects sat on the shelves with the it: the rolled-up paper that said Mom, Nora Stormleaf, would adopt me, Lucia Silverbreeze, and my latest addition of a small piece of quartz shaped into an arm. Evalana gave it to me at her wedding to say thanks for saving her life.

She wants me to remember that I should never give up so long as she doesn't give up either. But it also reminds me of my most painful memories. Even though none of it was my fault, I still can't come to terms with it.

While I was packing, I heard Mom walking up to my door. "You can come in," I said the moment she stopped.

Mom walked into the room, stretching her arms. "You're up really early." She stifled a yawn. "Do you need some help to know what to pack?"

I shrugged. "Sure, I've just packed some clothes. What other stuff do I need?"

"Honey, you're going to need much more than that. Here, we need to get you a proper travel pack." She signaled for me to follow her.

After she fished out her old travel pack, we packed it to the brim with far more than I thought I would need. Somehow, everything had a purpose. That made me feel uncomfortable. *Have I really been that spoiled and taken that much for granted?*

We headed for the north gate together to wait for Daric's group. Mom made sure I wore my blue magic cloak, the one that no matter how dirty or damaged it got, would always repair and clean itself with a tiny injection of magic.

The sun had begun to peek over the horizon when the group slowly meandered their way to meet us. There was an additional person with them that hadn't been at the meeting yesterday.

Anna? "What are you doing here?" I called out.

Daric's eyes darted around. "You said you were going to meet us here. So here we—"

I growled. "Not you, idiot." I pointed to Anna. "You. What are you doing here?"

"Still a morning person, aren't you?" Anna yawned. "How are you so awake right now? I'm here as their conjuration specialist. And since I've done a lot of looking into blood anchors lately, someone thought I should come with these interesting people." She gave Daric a sidelong glance before looking back at me.

"You two know each other? I guess that saves us introductions," Penny said as she stepped next to Anna. "So, how do you two know each other?"

"We lived in the same orphanage for a time," Anna said as she reached towards my waist to pull me in for a hug.

For old times' sake, I let her.

She'd grown up, but she still looked quite cute because she was so much shorter than me. Anna's body was perfectly proportioned with gentle curves for her bust and hips. Somehow, her wavy chestnut hair was tied up so that it puffed out and covered her slightly pointy ears. *Why does she want to hide that she's a half-elf?* Her blue eyes were always a nice gem to see and brought back memories of us going shopping together. All the horrible memories of being surrounded by people shouting and reeking of sweat and other unpleasant odors.

Her clothes were brightly colored, and her shoes even looked new. *I guess some things never change. She'll always love shopping for new stuff.*

"You were both orphans?" Dinar poked her head out from around Mark. "Who did you bring with you? She's pretty."

"That would be my mom. She wanted to see me off for my first mission," I said as I pointed to the woman in question.

Anna stared at Mom with eyes wide open and mouth slightly ajar. "Everyone, Eleanah, and the others could hardly believe that Nora had adopted you. We never got the entire story." Her voice was soft as she spoke.

"It isn't interesting," I said with a slight shrug.

"You know, you could just tell people the story rather than hide it," Mom said with a look of disapproval.

"Wow, your mom is hot," Daric said as he looked at my mother from head to toe.

I grabbed Daric by his gambeson and pulled him close to give him an up-close look at my sharp teeth. "You say anything like that again, and I will castrate you on the spot. Is that clear?"

Daric swallowed hard as he nodded slowly.

"Good." I shoved him backwards.

"That wasn't very nice." Mom placed her hands on her hips. "It sounded like he was complimenting me. Besides, you said you were going to try to make friends with them."

"I'll still try, but I make no promises about this guy," I said as I pointed to Daric.

"What do you want?" Mom held out her hand.

My eyes nearly popped out of their sockets. "Seriously?"

Mom nodded.

"I want a bed made entirely out of ice that will never melt. With icy curtains and a mattress that will repair itself if I scratch it with my claws," I blurted out.

Everyone stared at me in various stages of confusion.

"Deal," Mom said without hesitating. "Now I want to hear you promise."

Is she really going to do it? I took a deep breath. "I promise to get along with everyone here."

Mom shook her head. "Not good enough. You need to promise me that you'll bring them all back safely and that you'll do everything in your power to be friendly."

I winced at the word "friendly." "I promise I will bring them all back here safe and sound. Also, I will be as friendly as I can to them."

Mom's face didn't move.

"Even to Daric."

This time, her face lit up with a smile. *You win this time, Mom.*

"What's so important about you making this promise?" Mark asked.

I turned and growled at Mark. "Because I keep my promises."

"All of them?" Daric squeaked.

"Yes." *As much as I can.* I drooped my head and took a deep breath. *This is going to be a long ice season.* "Now, do you have everything you need?"

They all nodded.

"Good, let's go. The sooner I get this done, the sooner I get to go fishing and enjoy a new bed."

"About that bed." Dinar shuffled up next to me. "Why do you want one made out of ice?"

"Because I like the cold," I said as I stormed off. "I should be off fishing, but now I have to keep all of you safe." *Why do I have the worst luck?*

"You don't need to keep me safe. I'm the hero." Daric puffed out his chest as he pointed to it with his thumb. "I will—"

"Again with the hero thing. What makes you a hero?" I turned on the immature human.

"I have two aptitudes and I was told I was going to save the world from the demon king." Daric's chest grew with each word.

"That makes you a bit more capable than the average person, but that doesn't make you a hero. And you need to defeat the demon king first. The Voice never guaranteed success." I froze as soon as I realized what I had just said.

"How do you know about The Voice?" Daric relaxed his posture as he narrowed his eyes at me.

I lifted my tail and pounced on Daric.

Mom gave me a warning look.

I dragged Daric to a wall and pinned him against it.

"I know you're reincarnated. You don't need to explain it to me," I whispered. "Now keep quiet."

Daric held his breath for a moment. "Why? You didn't answer the question."

I stomped my foot and bared my fangs. "Fine, I met The Voice too. Happy?" I kept my volume low, but the growl in my voice made my mood unmistakable.

Daric's voice quivered. "Then does that mean—"

"Yes, I'm reincarnated too," I interrupted the man. "You were sent here because of the mistake it made."

"What mistake was that?" Daric asked as he tilted his head to the side.

I growled. "Don't worry about it! And if you tell anyone, I'll hurt you." I turned around and marched away from the group. "Let's go already. And keep up."

"Is there anything else different about her that I need to know about?" Anna whispered.

"Just don't make her job any more difficult than it already is. I have a feeling that this mission will change her more than the events of the tournament did. I'm worried about what Midas has planned." *She wanted me to hear that. I love you too, Mom.*

I turned to Penny. "By the way, how long do you think this is going to take?"

Penny crossed her arms and stared at the ground. "It might take the entire season. It mostly depends on how quickly we can find the blood anchor," she said hesitantly before turning to Anna. "How long do you need to study it once we get there?"

Anna shrugged as she moved to catch up with us. "Shouldn't be longer than two or three days. I've been told to try a few things to lift the anchor, and there are a few things I want to try myself."

Eventually, I brought everyone to the edge of the forest that I'd claimed as my territory.

Daric looked at the trees with admiration in his eyes. "How do you claim a territory?" he asked without looking at me.

"Are you going to ask stupid questions during this entire trip? Come on, this isn't the time to gawk. They're trees. We're going to see a lot of them for the next week." I grabbed Daric's cloth armor and pulled him along. *There's no avoiding the conversation to come, is there?* "After we stop for the night, we can talk. Until then, I need you all to be as quiet as possible. I'm not the only predator in these woods."

Everyone followed behind me. I could hear each of their footsteps as they stepped on the frosted ground, a patch of dead leaves, or a twig. *Calm down, it isn't their fault; they don't know how noisy they are. Just because I can walk around without making noise doesn't mean everyone can.*

We walked until my stomach informed me that lunchtime was fast approaching. I heard a couple of growling stomachs behind me, too. Predominantly from Daric and Anna. "Alright, I guess we can take a break to eat," I said as I turned to point at a fallen tree. "We can sit over there."

Everyone let out a collective sigh of relief as they hurried to the log.

"Finally," Daric said as he placed his pack down and started going through it.

"Keep quiet," I snapped. "There is no such thing as safe in this forest." I watched everyone flinch.

Once I had cooled off, I decided to check out everyone's gear a little more closely.

Daric wore a long-sleeved black gambeson shirt and a brown, heavy cloak. A bastard sword sat on his shoulder. *Hero, right... Two-handed sword fighting isn't a common fighting style. Hopefully someone taught him how to use that thing properly and not cut himself on it.*

I turned to study Silver's attire. He wore the same brigandine armor he'd worn yesterday, with a black, heavy cloak. A flanged mace hung from a leather strap wrapped around his belt. He also carried a kite shield attached to his pack. *Simple and effective. He should be fine, so long as nobody jumps him too quickly.*

Mark looked like he took advice from Daric. All of his clothes and armor were the same, but he had a thinner and shorter sword. *I think that's a rapier. I wonder if it has a cutting edge. And he has a parrying dagger. If we get into trouble with an animal, he might be less useful.*

Anna wore bright-green silk pants with a matching shirt. *I think she has a few extra layers underneath, given how much her clothes poof out. But she can summon her weapons, I think, so she should be able to defend herself.*

Golditress had a bow and arrows strapped to her pack. *The old reliable bow. At least we have an archer.* She wore gray brigandine armor with a dark-green cloak.

Dinar wore more layers of dark-red clothes than anyone else, and she even had a knitted cap that covered her ears too. *Do all elves hate the cold?*

I turned to see Penny was wearing a simple dark-green gambeson and a single layer of pants. She didn't have a cloak, but she'd clamped her hair at four points with steel bands. *So no, not all elves have an aversion to the cold. But where are Penny and Dinar's weapons?*

I placed a hand on Dinar's shoulder as she chewed her dried apples. "Did you not bring a weapon?" I asked as I continued to look for one.

Her smile sent a shiver down my spine. "Oh, don't worry, I've got plenty."

Her quiet voice only made my instincts scream at me. I jumped back, well out of reach, and readied my claws.

She stared at me, confused. "What's wrong?"

Okay, she's dangerous. Somehow, she has weapons hidden in her possession. But how? I forced myself to relax. "Nothing. If you say you have weapons, I'll trust you." *But I'm going to keep a very close eye on you, little girl.*

Penny sighed. "Before you ask, I use magic." I looked between her and Dinar and noticed that their constant glows were slightly different. Penny glowed a bit brighter than Dinar, but nothing like Mom. *Mom has desensitized me to seeing other magic users.*

"Which magic?" I opened my pack and pulled out a piece of dried bear meat.

"Fire manipulation," Penny said nonchalantly.

Fantastic, just what I needed. Do I tell her? I don't know, that would admit a weakness. I should. If they're going to trust me, I should trust them too. Mom said I should try to make friends.

"Um, yeah, I don't do fire well," I said in between bites.

"Care to elaborate?" Penny gave me a sidelong glare.

"I run when I see fire," I whispered.

"Sorry, I didn't catch that." Penny leaned in closer.

I threw my hands in the air. "I'm afraid of fire, okay?" I closed my eyes as I prepared for their laughter. Laughs that didn't come. I peeped an eye open and saw that nobody had done anything. "Aren't you going to laugh at me?"

"Why?" Daric asked.

"I'm afraid of something so childish as fire. It's embarrassing." I turned and looked at the ground.

"There's nothing embarrassing about being afraid of something like fire. Fire is dangerous and being afraid of it is rational."

Is Daric acting like an adult? I turned to see him still seated.

"At least it isn't something like being afraid of clowns or anything," Daric said as he looked off to the side.

I narrowed my eyes. "Are you afraid of clowns?"

Everyone turned to see Daric tense and his eyes grow wide. "Nope! Not at all. I'm not afraid of clowns."

Anna swiveled her head back and forth between Daric and me. "What are clowns?"

"My guess is they're something from his old life. He constantly talks about things from his last life," Mark said with a dismissive wave of his hand.

"Clowns don't exist." Daric pointed a finger at Mark. *Yeah, totally afraid of clowns.*

Everyone, including me, laughed slightly. *This might not be all that bad. Maybe I'm fearing the worst for no reason.*

The snap of a twig behind me brought my enjoyment to an end. *We're not alone.*

5

APTITUDES

I turned my head slowly to glance at who or what had made the noise, and my eyes went wide.

A large white bear sauntered towards us. *It knows we're here, and it's where it doesn't belong.*

"Quiet. There's an icebear headed our way," I whispered harshly as I stood up, placing my pack on the ground.

The bear drifted to the side, and a second bear became visible behind it. *Two? That's just inconvenient.*

"What's an icebear?" Daric asked as he looked around.

I pointed to the two bears. "That."

"What do we do? There's two of them." Anna placed a hand on my arm.

I shrugged Anna's hand off. "You all can run if you want. But I need to deal with them." I crouched forward. "I'll find you after I greet these unwanted guests." I lunged forward.

"We can help!" Mark's shout almost caused me to trip.

"You want to help? Fine, be my guest. Take care of the one in the back." I pointed a finger at Penny. "Keep your fire to a minimum. If a fire breaks out, I can't put it out."

"Who do you want to help you?" Penny glared daggers at me.

The two bears were running at us as I turned back towards them. "I won't need any help." I slipped into my focused state, allowing my vision to turn red.

The world around me slowed as I sprinted straight for my target. I ignored whatever the others were saying as they got ready to fight.

The bear in front stopped running and raised itself on its hind legs. *So if this one is a male bear, I'm willing to bet a hundred coins that the other bear is female.* The bear stood twice my height as it released a painful roar. I clenched my jaw and focused on his giant paws.

As I got closer, he brought his right paw down to slash at me with his claws. I shoved my claws into his paw, just below the largest pad. I continued to run towards the bear's armpit, pulling his foreleg along with me. The bear tried to shuffle its hind legs and turn so that he could keep his balance and snap at me with his massive jaws. I followed his momentum, making his attempt at biting pointless.

Once I had his front leg pulled back, I bit down on it and brought my other arm up to break the bone. The bear bellowed as he pulled away from me. I bit down harder, cutting through all the fat, hair, and muscles. Before the bear could pull his leg back, I dug my claws into the wound I'd created with my jaws. With two deep cuts, the leg now dangled from less than half the flesh it normally did. The bear continued to pull away from me, and I from him, until the flesh ripped and we both landed backwards.

Pained whimpers were the only sounds that came out of the bear now.

You picked the wrong territory. This isn't my fault. I threw the severed paw to the ground and charged the bear as it bled heavily from the stump. It tried to limp away from me, but I rammed him and knocked him to his side.

I leaped on his throat, digging my claws in. He attempted to swat at me with his other paw, but I just kicked it away, leaving a deep gash with my toe-claws. Slashing furiously, I continued to dig through his neck until I made my way to his spine. I watched as the bear stopped moving but continued to stare at me with terror-filled eyes. The bear's once beautiful white fur was now marred by the crimson blood that flowed from its wounds.

That was almost too easy.

I took a deep breath and returned my vision to normal before I checked on the others. I turned and saw Daric drive his sword into the second bear's hind leg. His weapon stopped moving, and it slipped from his grasp as the bear spun around and swiped a claw at him. All Daric had time to do was cross his arms to protect himself.

I gasped as I watched the paw collide with the human.

His body tumbled at least an arc, maybe two, before stopping.

No! My bed!

Silver jumped up and slammed his mace into the top of the bear's skull. The bear swayed and wandered forward on all fours as I sprinted towards it and plunged my arm through its eye socket until half of my bicep was inside the animal's skull. I growled as I swirled my arm around in its brain. Once the bear began convulsing, I pulled my arm out and took a few steps back to watch it flail around in its death throes.

As everything went silent, I turned to look at Daric's corpse. "You stupid idiot, why didn't you dodge? Now I won't get my new bed. This has been an entire waste of time." I paced around in circles.

"Ow. Okay, I admit, that hurt a bit."

Did that corpse just talk? I stopped my pacing and turned to see Daric unfold himself and sit up.

"Those are much stronger than I thought they would be."

"How are you alive?" I placed my hands on top of my head.

"Are you okay?" Golditress jogged up to me. "Is your arm bleeding? Did you get hit in the face?" She dropped her bow as she grabbed my arm to pull it down.

I jerked my arm away from her and pointed at Daric. "Did you not see him get slapped by that bear and fly almost two arcs? Why are you worried about me?"

Golditress didn't look towards Daric. Instead, she reached for my arm again. "He'll be fine. It's almost impossible for him to die. If he does get hurt, he'll just heal in a day or two. Tell me where you're bleeding and I'll make it better."

I shoved the insistent girl away. "I'm not hurt. This isn't my blood."

Golditress flinched away from me. "Oh, sorry. I guess I'll just retrieve my arrows then."

I watched Golditress slowly walk away from me towards the bear. Her gaze was fixed on the ground. *I know she means well. She reminds me of how Zenny acted when I first met her.*

Silver's footsteps caught my attention. "It seems that you have some explaining to do." He pointed to the severed bear's arm. "How did you cut off a bear's arm and kill it faster than us?"

I took a deep breath and closed my eyes. *This is going to be a really, really long mission.* "I'm strong, okay? And I do this for a living." I opened my eyes and looked at the two bear corpses. "Now I have to do something about the bodies." *That's a lot of meat and hide to deal with.*

"Just burn them."

I snapped my attention to Penny and bared my fangs. "Don't you dare. They're my kills, I decide what to do with them."

Dinar poked her head out from behind one of the corpses. "Do you plan on taking them with us?"

I shook my head. "We can't. There's too much to carry. If we had a cart, maybe. But then it would be much harder to navigate a cart through these woods." *We're still close to town.* "Maybe I can at least remove their hides and take them back home really quickly. That's a lot of money. But if I do that, then it will probably take the rest of the day and make this mission take even longer." I paced as I thought out loud.

"If it's that important to you, then we'll camp here and watch them for you," Silver said as he took a few steps towards me. "You also look like you need to get cleaned up. That's a lot of blood."

"Yeah, I'm not in any hurry." Daric rejoined the group. "This is the start of my epic quest. A small delay like this won't hurt. And while you work, we can have that talk you mentioned." He walked towards all of our packs. "I have lots of questions I want to ask you."

Oh, I bet you do. I flattened my ears as I moved to the bear I'd nearly decapitated and began skinning it. "For every question you ask, I get to ask two questions."

"What kind of exchange rate is that?" Penny blurted.

34

I turned my head and growled. "There are more of you than me."

Silver stood between Penny and me. "That's more than fair. Right, Penny?"

Penny crossed her arms and looked away from us.

Silver extended his hand towards me. "Is there anything we can help you with?"

"You can stay out of the way," I said as I dragged a claw around the bear's neck. "First question: how did the wannabe hero survive? What are his aptitudes?" I continued cutting the hide with my claw down the animal's sternum.

"We didn't ask a question yet." Penny stomped her foot as she nearly shrieked.

I twitched my ear. "Yes, Silver did." I paused for a moment. "And this is my warning to you. Stop yelling."

"So, you want to play it like that, do you?" Penny clenched her jaw as she whispered.

"I can still hear you," I growled as I started to peel the hide away from the muscles and used my claws to sever anything that was stuck.

Penny's heavy footsteps moved towards me.

"Penny, please be reasonable." Dinar shuffled in front of Penny and halted her movement.

"But, she—" Penny started to say.

"Has agreed to help us and is capable of killing a bear. I don't want to be on her bad side," Dinar interrupted.

Golditress walked up behind me. "Daric has two aptitudes: durability and recovery. The durability aptitude makes his skin harder to pierce and his bones harder to break." Her voice was barely more than a whisper.

I laughed. "So he's a living punching bag."

"I'm not! I'm a hero!" Daric ran towards me, carrying all the packs.

"You've had your two questions. Now we have ours," Penny spat as she grabbed her pack from Daric. "What's your aptitude?"

"Physical," I said without turning away from my work. *No, I shouldn't hide it from them.* "And recovery."

"Wait, you're a hero too?" Daric dropped the rest of the packs he was carrying.

Evalana's face flashed in my mind. "To some people, yes." I slumped my shoulders. "But I'm not a very good one."

"That would explain the strength," Silver mused to nobody.

I finished pulling away most of the hide from the first bear. I cut off a large chunk of meat from the back and held it out for someone to grab. "Here, you can eat this today. Just cook it slowly and take small bites. Mom says it's really tough meat."

Golditress reached out for it. She looked half terrified and half amazed.

As I released the meat, she nearly fell forward as the weight was more than she was expecting. But she managed to keep it from touching the ground. Dinar moved to help her. "Silver, would you mind starting a campfire with Penny, please? I'll get this ready to be put on a spit."

"Now, what are the rest of your aptitudes?" I grabbed Daric's sword and threw it at his feet. "Don't lose that."

Daric blushed as he knelt down to pick his sword up. "Dinar's is dexterity." He pointed to the elf girl before he pointed to Golditress. "She's a bowyer and our resident healer since she can use healing magic."

Healing magic? I really hope we never need to use that. I don't want to lose years from my life. I followed the finger as it moved to point at Mark.

"Numbers." Daric then pointed to Penny. "Pyromania, also known as fire manipulation."

"I heard that!" Penny gave Daric a threatening glare.

I arched an eyebrow. *Yeah, she's a fiery one, alright.* "And Silver?"

Daric grinned. "Basket weaving."

I glared at the jester. "I haven't lied or played any jokes. Take this seriously."

"He's telling the truth," Silver said as he hung his head.

I laid the hide flat before walking towards the bear that I'd killed by myself. *Now I feel bad for the guy. Basket weaving? And he follows the wannabe hero. How much worse can his luck get?* "How far away can you use magic, Penny?" I asked as I started to work on the next hide.

"Ten arcs," Penny answered curtly.

Wow! Noted.

"You've changed, Lucia." Anna's voice nearly made me jump. *I forgot she's here.* "I feel like I don't know you anymore. There's nothing shy about you. But what I want to know is, how did you get your title?"

I chuckled. "Which part?"

"All, please," Anna replied as she walked towards me with even and confident steps.

"The short version is that while I was still at the orphanage and would go on my runs, I would run so fast that people would feel a breeze and describe me as a streak of silver. And then King Ramos gave me the title because I saved Evalana's life and spared Aurtour's life during the tournament."

"You're the one that saved my cousin's life?" Daric froze while he was unpacking a simple tent.

"And what do you mean, 'spared Aurtour's life?'" Anna narrowed her eyes on me.

"It's a long story. One I wish I could forget and that I don't want to tell." I flattened my ears. "No more questions."

6

FIRESIDE CHAT

Everyone worked in silence, setting up tents, a campfire, and a pit to dispose of the bear corpses. *It seems that everyone is willing to leave me alone for now. Maybe I was a bit of a mood-killer with those last few questions.* After I finished removing the hides from the two bears, I rolled them and tied them up with some rope. I cut some more meat off the bodies and handed it to Dinar, then moved the corpses to the pit they had made and instructed them to burn the two bodies while I was gone. Their faces were amusing to watch as I dragged the bodies. I left them as I carried the hides back to town.

My inner wolf didn't enjoy my decision to burn all the meat. The ache in my heart as I turned back and saw the smoke when I left the forest almost brought me to tears. *So much food, wasted. But we can't take it all with us. It'll go bad before we use it all, and if we took the time to dry it out or pickle it, we'd be here for weeks. This is the best I could do to take as much as we can and dispose of it so scavengers don't find a home in my territory while I'm gone.*

I made it back to the city gates much faster on my own since I didn't need to worry about others keeping up with me. I didn't waste any time finding the tanner that I frequented. He reluctantly handed me the coins for the hides. One hide was worth less than the other since it had several cuts and arrow holes in it. I ran through the crowds and back to my home to deposit the coins in my room for safekeeping. *Mom isn't home. I wonder what she's doing.*

I dropped to all fours and sprinted towards the group. I stood back up before they could see me running like that.

This might be a good opportunity to see what they're like without me around. I slowed down and stalked my way to them, making sure to stay low and quiet. They were huddled around the campfire, oblivious to everything going on around them.

"Do we really need her?" Penny said.

"I admit, she isn't anything like she was when I lived with her at the orphanage, but she looks like she really knows what she's doing." Anna rotated the spit with the bear meat on it. "She's always had a temper, it just seems like it's gotten much worse."

Silver sat down next to Anna. "She's being fairly forthcoming with us." He placed a finger on his chin before he continued. "Doesn't it feel like she's forcing it though?"

Dinar sat cross-legged on the other side of the fire, swaying gently from side to side. "I wish I had gone to the tournament and watched, but I got sick and couldn't go. Her fighting style is odd."

"Why are we talking about her like this? Isn't it rude?" Mark finished setting up the last of the four tents. "I'm sure she'll be more talkative tomorrow when she gets back. We just need to avoid talking about the tournament."

Daric sat on the ground and held a stick in his hand, drawing something in the dirt. "What happened at the tournament? Why does she keep avoiding that subject? My teacher told me I wasn't ready to go and that it was too dangerous. It was like he knew something was going to happen." He dropped the stick and hugged his knees to his chest. "Something happened that scarred her emotionally."

Anna turned to Daric. "She's still a person. And from what I've heard about the tournament, it was a gruesome event. Demons were summoned and started killing people. Maybe she lost someone close to her."

"Maybe it has to do with how my cousin lost her arm," Daric said without looking up.

"It was a sin of gluttony." They all jumped as I made my presence known. "The demon bit her arm off as she tried to save a guy who the demon killed." I sat as far away from the fire as I could while still being close enough so that everyone could hear me. "After it took her arm, I had her brother, Aurtour, carry her off to safety while I killed it."

Anna shook her head. "You killed a sin? And while you were, what, nine?"

"Ten," I corrected.

"How old are you?" Mark lowered his voice slightly.

"Fifteen. Beastkin physically mature faster than humans, elves, dragoons, and dwarves." I stared at the ground. "I have special permission to join a knight company. My mother agreeing was the biggest part."

"Who's your mother?" Penny asked.

"Nora Stormleaf," Anna answered for me. "What happened to her? How come she gave up on running the orphanage?" Her voice rose with each question.

I raised my hand and signaled for her to lower her volume. "She didn't. She just moved on once the orphanage was empty. If someone shows up now, Melody takes care of them until they find them a home. You know that her greatest wish was to start a family, right? Well, that hasn't changed. It's just that she believed that to give us both what we needed and wanted, she had to adopt me."

"And?" Dinar leaned forward. "Was it what you wanted?"

I grinned. "I wouldn't exchange it for the world."

Anna tapped Silver on the shoulder and pointed to the meat still cooking. "Daric said that you were reincarnated." *He told them. Fantastic. Now I'll have to hurt him.* "Doesn't that mean that you've lived a life already? Why would you want a mother?" She stood up and walked towards me, giving Silver room to work.

"It wasn't that I wanted a mother, more like I wanted a place to belong." I flattened my ears. "But yes, I had a life before this one. But it was cut short when I was painfully killed."

Daric perked up. "How did you die? I was killed by a virus that was killing a lot of people around the world." He stood up too, brushing the dirt off his pants as he did.

"A tornado tore me apart." I watched everyone wince as I answered. "How much do you remember of your old life?"

"A lot. Most of it I don't use, but something is going to come in handy and save the day eventually." Daric grinned. "After all, I'm the hero."

I shook my head. "Stop with the hero thing. It's annoying. What world did you come from, and were you human when you died?"

"Earth, and of course I was human." Daric tilted his head to one side. "Are you from a different world? Were you a beastkin before too?"

"Does it really matter?" *I'm going to keep the gender to myself. It doesn't matter at this point. I've lived this long as a woman. It won't change anything if people don't know it.*

"So your amnesia was just an act?" Anna asked as she held up her hand.

"Yes and no. Unlike Daric over there, my memories were shredded before coming here. My guess is that The Voice didn't give him the personal treatment like it did me. He was just a rush job to correct the mistake." I shrugged my shoulders. "So I've been learning most everything as I go. Even things I should know about beastkin."

"So, what's it like being a beastkin? Is it cool?" Daric's eyes grew wide.

I'm going to hurt this kid one of these days. "What's it like to be a human?" I raised my eyebrows. "I've lived the last ten years as a beast-kin, and I don't remember what it was like to be human. What you think is cool and weird is natural for me. From being covered in fur and walking on digitigrade feet to shedding and going into heat." I clapped my hands over my mouth as I finished talking.

Anna blushed as Daric stepped even closer. "So, when do you go into heat?" Daric asked with a shaky voice.

I growled and held up my claws as I flexed them. "Get any ideas and I will castrate you."

Golditress, who hadn't said a word since I got here, stood up and walked in between Daric and me. "Since it's getting late and very cold, we should get ready for bed."

"Go ahead. I'll make sure nothing sneaks up on you while you sleep." As I moved to find a hiding spot downwind, I waved my hand. "I don't need much sleep anyway."

"You traveled three times as far as we did. How are you not tired?" Dinar stepped towards me.

"She has the recovery aptitude. I know how effective it is," Daric said as he placed a hand on Dinar's shoulder. "Go ahead and get some sleep." He led the elf to a tent that Penny had entered just before her.

I watched Daric walk to the tent Mark had already entered. He stood at the entrance and looked back at me. He slowly went in after I gave him a nod. I grabbed my pack and found a suitable spot to keep an eye on everything without leaving myself exposed. With nothing better to do, I ate a small snack and watched Silver. He took the cooked meat and wrapped it in some large, fuzzy leaves before placing it in a spare sack.

I never knew you could do that with those leaves. Does it keep the meat from soaking the sack? I'm going to need to remember that one. I watched Silver be the last one to go to bed.

As I sat alone in the darkness, I looked up at the canopy and saw the moonlight struggling to pierce through the evergreen branches.

It's nice to see Anna again. A familiar face is comforting. I don't think Daric is really in charge. Penny acts like she runs everything in the group. I took a deep breath and felt the air stir around me. *Silver and Golditress are nice people with more common sense than Daric, the wannabe hero. Does he think this is a story and he's the main character? Does he really think that no matter what he does it'll all work out in the end?*

I enjoyed the quiet night as I watched the campfire shrink to half its size. Then I looked over to the charred remains of the two bears. *I wish we didn't need to do that to the bodies, but I'm afraid of what leaving them would have invited into my territory.*

Daric exited his tent with a few extra layers of clothes. He wandered around, probably looking for me.

I grinned and stayed perfectly still. *Let's see how long it takes him to find me, if he can find me at all.*

Daric walked around aimlessly until he heard me because I couldn't hold back my fit of laughter. "What's so funny?" he said as he approached me.

I continued giggling. "Watching you look for me. You're so oblivious."

"I found you, didn't I?" Daric pulled his cloak tighter around himself. "How are you not cold? Does your hair really keep you that warm?"

I stopped laughing and glared at him. "One, it's fur, not hair. Two, yes. Three, I told you where I was. If I'd wanted to, I could have killed you, and you wouldn't have made a sound."

Daric stood up straight. "I think you'll find my skin harder to cut than you expect."

I grinned, exposing my teeth. "And what would you do with my jaws clamped down on your throat?" Daric's face had lost all color. "This world is dangerous. I'm dangerous, but I'm not the most dangerous thing in this world either."

Daric slumped his shoulders and walked to lean next to a tree. "Midas kept telling me the same thing." He waved his hands. "'Demons are not to be underestimated. They do not attack just your body, but your mind and soul too,'" he said with an imitation of Midas's expressionless tone.

"He's right." I lowered my voice. Daric raised his eyebrows and ceased his performance. "The sin of gluttony wanted me to eat my friend, your cousin. He said that if I did, he would grant me power. I couldn't do it. But during the fight, I lost control of myself and had to stop and eat a rabbit because of his influence." I injected a slight growl into my voice as I continued. "You're not above sin. One slip is all it takes, and they'll take advantage of it."

"You really know how to kill a mood, don't you?" Daric sighed. "Did you bring a tent? What are you going to sleep in?"

I tilted my head. "You know, you aren't so bad. Maybe if you don't say stupid things and ambush people with marriage proposals, you might find a girl who's willing to marry you. You really need to work on your first impressions."

"Sorry. But once I heard about beastkin in this world, I really wanted to see one." Daric scratched the back of his head as he turned away from me slightly. "It's kind of a dream come true for me to see a furry. And since you're gorgeous, I couldn't help but try."

I shuddered. "No, just no. Not going to happen."

"Don't you think I'm handsome?" Daric turned around and looked on the verge of tears.

"Kinda. And half of me is really annoyed with the other half that wants as little as possible to do with you." I rubbed my temples. "But before you get full of yourself, that part of me only cares about one thing. It wants a male capable of reproduction because my instincts are adamant that I have kids."

Daric went from ballooning with pride to deflating in seconds. "So there's no chance, is there?"

"No." I stood up and moved away from the distraught kid. "As for the tent, I make mine every night."

I stood in a slightly open space and channeled magic to create a long and narrow igloo.

"Wait, you can use magic too?" Daric shrieked in an unmanly tone.

"Shh." I paused my magic to place a finger on my lips as I turned to Daric. "Quiet. You're going to wake the others. But yes, I can use ice magic. Although at an extremely limited range."

"How far?" Daric whispered.

"As long as I stay within arm's reach." I resumed creating my temporary shelter for the night. "It requires a fair bit of concentration, so please let me focus." *Actually, I just want you to shut up and leave me alone for the rest of the night.*

I finished making my little shelter and even made a decent layer of soft snow to sleep on too. I turned and grabbed Daric's shoulders and smiled.

He looked confused until I pulled him towards me and lifted my knee into his crotch.

Before he could scream, I covered his mouth. "Shh." I placed a finger on my lips as a whimper from the man's mouth slipped through my fingers. "We don't want to wake the others. And that's for telling them that I'm reincarnated."

I left Daric to his pain and headed to sleep. I didn't like the way Daric's eyes were glued to my butt as I crawled into my igloo. *Was I not clear enough to get through his thick skull? No means no!*

Listening to Daric pace around the camp, I didn't let myself fall asleep right away. I half expected him to try something. I almost wished he had. It would have given me a reason to hurt him again. But eventually even I needed to get some sleep.

I closed my eyes and ended my first day on my first mission as a knight. *There are so many more left to go.*

7

MISSING CRITICAL
INFORMATION

I woke up before anyone else and watched Daric start dividing the bear meat for breakfast. It took Anna waking up and agreeing with me before Daric believed that I could only eat meat. He kept going on about me being able to eat berries and other things. I even told him about the time I ate a strawberry and threw it right back up.

Once the fire was nothing more than a smoldering pile, Silver helped me bury the ashes. Everyone rolled their eyes as Daric made a comment about bears supposed to be preventing wildfires, not wolves.

Dinar and Golditress packed up the tents as we readied ourselves to continue on. I tried to wrack my brain for any reason the icebears would be in my territory. *They're way too far south. Once the ice season ends, they may not survive the heat.* Nobody else had any ideas either. Most of them didn't know that icebears didn't belong in this area.

I began my impromptu lesson on bears. "Icebears are very similar to brown and black bears. The major difference between them is that icebears are obviously white and prefer colder areas, like mountains. They also don't hibernate, and they eat more plants, like berries and stuff. But they don't turn down meat if it's available. Something drove them out of their homes and pushed them here. It could be anything like a food shortage or a dire animal invading their territory."

My small lesson on icebears gave us something to talk about while we traveled. Anna never stopped smiling as she watched me.

Our pace was terrible as we continued our journey over the next few days. Anna, while she looked quite healthy and took care of herself, didn't have the endurance to walk for a week straight. Each day, we had to take longer breaks and take them more often.

We made it to the edge of the forest after two days and were heading towards one of the smaller towns so everyone could recover and restock some.

We were taking yet another break. I couldn't stop pacing around.

"I'll be back." I didn't wait for anyone to confirm that they heard me.

My inner wolf needed something to do. All these breaks were driving her crazy, and in turn, calling me restless would severely understate my situation. *Hopefully this run will calm her down.* I went back into the forest, but I turned away from the path we'd come down and went into the thicker portion of the woods.

My silent stalking rewarded me with a deer. I carried it over my shoulders as I brought it back to the others. Anna was rubbing her feet as she'd popped yet another blister on her foot.

I stripped most of the deer down to the bones.

"Watching you focus so much on tearing apart that deer is both fascinating and terrifying at the same time," Silver said as he stood behind me.

I shrugged as I worked. "It helps me relax."

Silver hummed. "You're good at focusing on one thing, right?" He sat down on the ground nearby. "It's interesting, you're not as bad as you made yourself out to be."

I arched an eyebrow as I turned to look at him. "What do you mean, 'I made myself out to be?'"

Silver's lip curled slightly into what I could only guess was a smirk. *His facial expressions are hard to read.* "You're still a kid. I can see the childishness in how you talk. Your exaggerations when we first met were uncalled for."

I flattened my ears. "You heard Captain Aenwyn, she's seen how bad my temper gets. There's a reason I gave you the worst-case scenario." I turned to look at the meat and took a piece to eat.

"It's because you've witnessed your worst-case scenario, haven't you?" Silver sighed. "For that I'm sorry."

"And what do you care?" I growled. "The people I've killed all deserved it."

Silver's eyes went wide. "You've killed people? How many?"

I shook my head. "Wait. You didn't think I hadn't killed people already? Did you think I was bluffing?" I stood up and started walking away. "I've killed seven people, by the way."

I heard Silver stand up and follow me. "You don't look like someone who's killed that many people." He ran to catch up with me. He stopped in front of me with my mouth full of deer meat. "Your eyes hold too much innocence."

I swallowed the food in my mouth. "Because I don't feel bad about it. Maybe once I did, but now..." I flexed my claws. "Now I realize I enjoyed it." Silver started backpedaling as he put his hands up. "Don't worry. I told you how to avoid me killing you. My mom raised me better than that. Besides, I haven't killed anyone since the tournament."

I turned and walked away again. This time, Silver didn't follow me.

"That's even worse," Silver whispered as he finally left me alone.

Once Anna was ready to go again, we set off with everyone's pack filled with deer meat. I took the largest portion since I ate way more than the rest of them. Unfortunately, our travel pace didn't improve. Anna kept insisting on taking more and longer breaks. I was getting bored. And since I was bored, I ate.

The deer that should have lasted us closer to a week might not see a third day.

"Can we take another break?" Anna asked as she collapsed to the ground.

I rolled my eyes. "If we keep taking breaks like this, we won't make it to..." I turned to Penny with a hand stretched out.

"Briarford," Penny said, finishing my sentence. *I really need to get better at remembering town names.*

"But I'm so tired," Anna whined. "And my feet hurt."

Almost everyone spread out, and I heard a few grumbles from Dinar as she mumbled under her breath. Mark and Daric had sour looks on their faces as they walked away. Penny rubbed her temples with her thumbs. I let out a grunt that was plenty audible for everyone to hear.

Silver knelt down beside Anna. "What can we do to make this easier for you?" he asked as he placed a hand on her shoulder.

"My legs can't move, and my feet have blisters that are getting blisters." Anna's voice quivered. "I'm sorry. I don't exercise as much as you do. I'm not happy that I'm slowing us down any more than you are."

"Do you want a chance to take a bath?" I asked before she could reply to Silver. *I can smell you! I can smell all of you! And all of you stink!* "Of course you do. If we make it to..." I slapped my forehead.

"Briarford," Silver finished for me.

"Yes, there. Briarford. If we make it tonight, I will personally guarantee a nice hot bath with soap will be available to you first." I walked over to give her a helping hand.

Anna just lowered her head and didn't take my hand.

"We're so close. What if I carried your pack for you? Would that be enough?" Silver started to remove Anna's pack from her shoulders.

Carry? That might be an idea. But I need to check on something first. I sat down next to Anna. I forced her to straighten her back and sit up straight. She opened her mouth, but I put a finger over her lips. "I'm seeing if I can carry you without you interfering with my tail. And it looks like I can."

"You'll carry me?" Anna's eyes nearly popped out of their sockets.

I removed my pack and cloak. "Yes, but you need to have both of our packs on your back while I do. Your arms aren't tired, are they?"

"No, but I don't know how long I can hold them for," Anna said as I neatly folded my cloak and placed it in my pack.

"I can hold your stuff for you." Silver reached to lift the pack and carry it.

I placed my hand on Anna's pack. "No need. I'll run ahead and take Anna with me. You guys can catch up on your own. It's a straight shot to Briarford. I've been itching to do something since I hunted that deer." I helped Anna get both packs on her back. "You should've remembered that from when we were younger."

Anna smiled gently. "Yeah, I do remember that now. Are you sure you can do this? It won't be too much for you?"

"Believe me, I'm doing this. Because if I hear yet another one of Daric's dumb jokes, I'll throw him into a tree and leave him there," I said as I glared at Daric.

Daric placed his hands over his heart. "Calling my jokes dumb hurts. Everyone else likes my jokes, right?" I looked around and saw almost everyone shaking their heads. "What about you, Goldy? You always laugh at them."

Golditress lowered her head and blushed. "Aren't you supposed to laugh at all jokes, even though you don't like or understand them?" Her voice was quiet.

Daric held his hands over his heart as he stumbled backwards. "Et tu, Goldy?"

Your acting stinks.

Penny grabbed Golditress's hands and looked up at the girl. "No, you don't. If you don't like the joke, just say so. You don't need to feel obligated to humor bad ideas."

Everyone but Daric started laughing.

After the laughter died down, I lifted Anna to her feet, and Silver helped steady her with her more significant load. I crouched down, and Anna wrapped her hands around my chest as I lifted her legs off the ground. I made sure to hoist her high enough that my tail had its full range of motion. "Are you ready?"

Anna held on even tighter. "Is it going to be bumpy?"

I took a few practice steps, getting used to my new center of gravity. "A little, but I'll try to keep things a little smoother for you."

"Okay. I'm sorry that you have to do this," Anna whispered into my shoulder.

"Don't worry about it," I whispered back. "This could be fun."

I took off at an easy jog. Anna squeezed even tighter. *Where is she getting all this arm strength? If she squeezes any harder, I might have trouble breathing.* I lifted Anna a bit higher so that her head was level with mine. She continued to whimper. "Open your eyes." I sped up into a slow run.

Anna gasped as her head leaned back. Her grip loosened slightly yet remained firm.

The town was on the horizon, small but visible. I saw a few farms and fences in the distance. Once I was certain I could make the run, I increased my speed to run at full stride. I could hear Anna giggling. We neared one of the fenced areas and saw a small herd of goats separated into two areas.

The goats in the large pen all had puffy white wool and stood next to one another as far away from me as they could manage. *Since they all have round faces and no horns, that must be all the females.* I looked at the small pen and saw a single goat. The goat had fur rather than wool. It also sported a pair of horns, each almost as large as its square head. *Definitely a male.* The goat stared at me through the wooden barricade until it headbutted the fence.

There was a familiar tingle in the back of my mind. I turned my head away and sprinted towards the town. *I know that feeling. That goat was challenging me.*

Anna started laughing and hollering. *It's good to know someone's enjoying themselves.*

I could start making out individual people walking around the small town. *Briarford, the northernmost town in the kingdom, is our only stop on the way to find the blood anchor. I wonder how close we're going to get to the Wild Kingdom.* Dinar and Penny had said some other things about what to expect in the town, but I couldn't remember what they'd said. *Other than that calling it a town is generous, that is.* It was the size of a large village.

After we passed the farmhouse that likely belonged to the owners of the goats, it looked like we were some forty or fifty arcs away from the village proper. I came to a stop and set Anna down.

Anna leaned forward, panting, as I helped get the two packs off her back. "Wow, is that what it's like every time you run?" Her voice was high, like her emotions.

"Yeah," I said with a grin. *Welcome to a small taste of my world.*

As I got the second pack off of her, she straightened her back and took a deep breath. "I understand why you like running so much now. That was intense, and exhilarating, and just... wow." Her voice was more under control, but she was staring off at nothing, coming down from her adrenaline high.

Hunting down fleeing prey is much more exciting than that. But I don't think your heart can handle that kind of feeling.

"Hey, get away from her!" a scratchy voice interrupted us. "Get away from her!"

I turned to see who was yelling at me. There was a middle-aged human man marching towards me as he left a small, unmarked wooden building. His black hair had started to turn gray on the sides, matching his wiry beard. His clothes had several patches sewn onto them, and he carried a pitchfork. A pitchfork that he had aimed at me. *Is he threatening me with a pitchfork?*

I growled. "Put it down, old man."

"I said get away from her, you beast!" The man jabbed the paltry weapon in my direction.

Beast?

"Don't worry, little lady, we'll save you." He turned his head but kept his gaze on me. "Help! We got another one trying to kidnap a girl."

"No, no, no, no." Anna stepped in front of me and tried to push me back, but couldn't. She turned around to face the man. "Just put the pitchfork down. This is all a misunderstanding."

I gently shoved Anna to the side. *I am not a beast!*

"Lucia, don't. Please stop."

I could hear shouts and people running our way from the other buildings. Anna sounded like she was digging through one of her pouches on her pack. My vision slowly shifted to red before I lunged for the old man's weapon. He flinched backwards and tripped. I swatted the pitchfork away so hard it flew out of his hands. I flexed my claws as I growled at the now-quivering man.

"Restrain Lucia!" Anna's voice sounded slightly muffled. Before I could grab the man's leg and rough him up a bit, glowing white chains wrapped around my torso and arms. Suddenly, I was flying backwards, pulled by the chains that appeared out of nowhere.

The chains continued to wrap around me, restricting my movements but not causing me any pain or discomfort. I went flying past a being I had never seen before. A massive, glowing being, wrapped in yellow-and-white robes, held the glowing white chains in its hands. Beneath the white hood, I could see bronze skin and a hairless square face. Two majestic, pristine white wings extended from its back, and each looked large enough to be twice the size of its body, which was at least a head taller than mine.

When I finally stopped moving, I was suspended in midair, wrapped in the mysterious chains from my neck to my toes. I growled as I tried to twist and fight my way out. My efforts didn't give me any reward, so I opened my mouth to try to bite the chains.

"Please don't do that. Your teeth are so pretty. You don't want to damage them, do you?" A deep, masculine voice that sounded like a distant wave of thunder came from the glowing individual.

I stared at him and closed my mouth. *Did he just compliment my teeth?*

"All of you, stop!" Anna stood between me and a crowd of people armed with a random assortment of weapons. Her voice sounded louder and more authoritative than usual. "Cover Lucia's ears," Anna said in her normal voice towards my captor.

With a flap of his gargantuan wings and a gust of wind, the man hopped over to land right in front of me.

I growled and bared my teeth as he lifted his hands towards my ears. "Don't touch them."

He bowed as he lowered his hands. "As you wish." The large, glowing wings wrapped around me, and everything went disturbingly quiet.

"What are you? And why are you doing what Anna tells you to do?" I looked at his golden-yellow eyes. "And let me down."

"You may think of me as an angel. Specifically, I'm a spirit of control, and I'm here to assist Anna as she requested my presence."

The angel's face barely moved as it showed no emotion. "I'm sorry, but I can't comply with your request, as it conflicts with Anna's wishes."

I tilted my head. "But why did you agree not to touch my ears?"

"Because I believe she wishes for you not to hear what she is shouting at the people of this village. And since I have an alternative means of completing the task, there is no reason to make you more uncomfortable than required."

How considerate of you. "If she's shouting, then this is more so she doesn't hurt my ears." I sighed. "What's she talking about?"

"She's scolding them for provoking you. They are telling her that they were worried you were going to kidnap her since they had other beastkin attack them recently. The people here have a great deal of hatred in their hearts for beastkin. It is unfortunate that you are subjected to such treatment for simply being what you are." The spirit's face finally showed some emotion as his eyes softened and he lowered his gaze.

"Story of my life," I grumbled under my breath and flattened my ears.

His face snapped back to attention. "There is great promise within you, child. You are at peace with who you are. Now you need to conquer yourself." *What are you talking about?* "You have fought against sin and know its allure. Remember, you need to stay strong and never give in, no matter the circumstances." His voice felt physically heavier with each word. "But it seems you are free to go, so long as you promise to stay calm."

"Anna wants me to stay calm?" I asked. The angel nodded. "Fine, I will do my best to stay calm as long as nobody tries to attack me again."

He gently placed me on the ground. The chains evaporated in a shower of lights that floated upward. The angel stepped to the side and folded his wings behind himself. Anna stood facing me, and the crowd of people weren't holding their weapons anymore. They'd dropped them all to the ground.

"How about you show Lucia and I a place to eat and tell us what's been going on here?" Anna asked, her voice dropping low.

Some people quivered at the sound of her voice.
What did I miss?

CRITICAL INFORMATION OBTAINED

"Please, everyone, go back to your lives," a man in a breastplate called to the crowd as he stepped to the front. His breastplate was littered with dents and gouges, and his gambeson had been cut in several areas. "You heard the lady. This beastkin isn't the enemy," he said as he glared at me with his bright-green eyes from his plain-looking face. I noticed the longsword at his hip glowed dimly in the sunlight. *A magic weapon? A family heirloom maybe? I haven't seen one before.*

"My name is Anna, and this is Lucia Silverbreeze." Anna gestured towards me.

People picked up the weapons they'd brought and slowly dispersed. Nobody looked away from me.

The man's eyes nearly leaped out of their sockets to join his jaw, which sat nestled in the cold dirt. "She has a title?" His voice was barely more than a whisper.

I rolled my eyes. "Yes, I have a title. And I'm a knight of The Maidens under Captain Aenwyn." I crossed my arms and stared down at the man. *I will not salute this guy.* "Why did you just tell everyone that I'm not the enemy? Are there more beastkin in the area?" I flicked my tail back and forth.

Anna placed a hand on the man's shoulder. "Can we please take this someplace warmer?"

"As you wish." The man gave a short but theatrical bow. "My name is Powel. It is nice to meet you ladies." *Really? Somehow I don't believe you.* "Follow me. I will take you to my place where you two can get some rest for the night." He pointed towards one of the largest buildings in the town.

"There are six more that will be joining us later, most likely today," I said, still keeping my eyes on Powel. "Are you going to have room for everyone in your home?"

Powel looked nervously between Anna and me. "Are there any other surprises I should know about?"

"Just say it," I growled. "You're worried there are more beastkin coming."

Anna stepped in front of me. "Waterfalls." She turned to face the human who placed his hand on his sword hilt. "The answer is no. I'm going to need you to be more respectful of Lucia."

I flexed my claws as I turned away from the two. The spirit of control was still standing to the side. His chains evaporated from his hands again. I took a few moments to pace as I tried to calm down. I turned to see why Anna hadn't moved. She held up a finger to Powel, who stood silently watching me.

I took a deep breath, attempting to at least look like I wasn't going to break open some skulls. "Include some food and I'll play nice." *Comforted by food again.*

Powel released his hold on his weapon. "I'm sure we can find something for you to eat. And yes, we can make some room for your friends." He gave a slightly deeper bow than before. "I apologize for my rudeness."

Anna walked up to the angel and gave him a deep bow. "Thank you for fulfilling my requests. You are free to leave as you wish."

The spirit matched her bow. "You are kind to seek out bloodless resolutions. It was an honor to aid you in your time of need." They stood up straight together, and the angel turned to look at me. "I enjoyed meeting you, Lucia. I hope one day you can master yourself and find your true potential."

Giving out last words of wisdom before you go, how original.

He faded from our sight like he was a mirage.

We followed Powel to his home. It was a large wooden building, like the rest of the town, and stood two stories tall. I saw several claw marks on the doors and window shutters. I could also smell the faint scent of blood in the air.

If beastkin have been attacking this town, then it makes their reaction a little more understandable. But it's still unreasonable. I'm a knight of this kingdom. Just because they see a beastkin doesn't mean I'm here for murder and pillaging.

People worked around the town, fixing doors, boarding up windows, and I think someone was baking bread based on what I smelled once we stood outside Powel's home.

He invited us in, and, after explaining to his youngest daughter— a slightly pudgy girl with brown curly hair and of an average height named Christine—that I wasn't here to kill anyone, he escorted us to the dinner table.

"Christine, could you bring some food for these two? Please have a seat." Powel waved his hand to the rectangle table with a dozen chairs around it.

I stared at the chairs, all of which were solid-backed and looked uncomfortable even if I didn't have a tail. "I can only eat meat, and the less you cook it, the better."

Anna elbowed my arm. "Just bring us anything you have ready. And do you have a means of heating water here?" She clasped her hands as she prepared to beg. "I haven't had a proper bath since we left."

Christine shied away after Anna explained her body odor situation. Her eyes darted from me to her father repeatedly while she refused to open her mouth. Powel nodded to the girl, and she swallowed and stood up straight. "Yes, we can get a bath ready for you while you eat." Her gentle voice sounded a little strained, like she was trying not to cry.

Anna let out a heavy sigh. "Oh, thank you, thank you, thank you. I'll make it up to you, I promise."

I knew she wanted a hot bath, but didn't think she was that desperate. I took a quick sniff of the air. *Okay, maybe she is that desperate.*

Christine looked like she wanted to smile but held it back as she turned to leave us alone with Powel.

Powel gestured to the seats again. "Please have a seat."

Anna sat down without a second thought, while I grimaced as I turned the chair a quarter turn before sitting in it. Powel raised an eyebrow, watching me as he sat down.

Anna placed her elbows on the table and leaned forward. "What happened here? It looks like you guys were attacked recently."

Powel stared at the table. "That's correct. Two nights ago, we were attacked by a group of beastkin."

"I saw the damage and smelled the blood. How many were hurt? Did it look like they had an aim, or were they looking to cause general mayhem?" I watched the man flinch at each of my questions. "Is this a regular occurrence? Have you sent a message to anyone?"

Powel sank farther into his chair. "Three people died in the attack, and several more were injured. Two of them severely, one of which is my wife." *Things just got a lot more serious. His wife is badly hurt, and here we are, demanding food and a hot bath. Now I feel terrible.* "We sent someone to ride for Lenchester, but it will take another week before we hear anything."

Anna's cheeks turned bright red as her eyes grew wide. "I'm so sorry." Christine walked into the room with what looked like a sandwich and a pile of meat scraps. Anna stood up and grabbed Christine's arm. "You don't have to worry about getting me that bath. It can wait. Go see your mother and take care of her."

Christine's blue eyes shimmered as they went wide. She sighed as she placed the plates of food on the table. "Thank you for your concern, but there's nothing more I can do for her." Anna guided the girl to an empty chair as tears trailed down Christine's cheeks. "We set the bones as best we could, but she still hasn't woken up."

"You said there were two badly wounded. What's the state of the other person?" I turned to Powel.

Powel looked at me with a face devoid of all emotion. "Roy, a good kid who was trying to protect his flock. He was found with a fence post impaled through his leg."

I might have something that can help him. "Where is he?" I gripped the edge of the table as I stood up.

Powel nearly flipped backwards in his chair. "Why?"

"I may be able to buy him time until he can recover." *I guess that one guy at the tournament, whose name I can't remember, taught me more about my magic than I thought he did.*

"How?"

I shrugged. "It depends on what I see."

Powel hesitated but then slowly stood up. "Follow me." He walked around the table and towards the front door.

I looked at the scraps of meat. *I shouldn't kick them while they're down.* Begrudgingly, I left the meat on the table and followed Powel.

As we walked by a child carrying a bucket of water from a well, Powel asked them to go and find Carotin and bring him to Roy's farm. We continued on to the north side of the town and walked for a bit until we arrived at a decent little farmstead.

"You may want to stand to the side, out of sight, to start," Powel said as he motioned to the side of the door with the hinges.

I shrugged as I complied. *Whoever answers the door is going to freak out anyway.* "If you think you can keep them from attacking me, we'll do it your way."

Powel nodded before he knocked on the door. I heard footsteps inside. They were heavy and dragged slightly on one foot. Powel took a step back as the door opened.

"Oh, it's you, Powel." A harsh yet feminine voice sighed. I could smell blood mixed with something extra, something foul. *Do I smell rotten flesh?*

"Hello, Joy." Powel's face was full of concern. "How's Roy?"

"I'm afraid he's getting worse. His head feels like there's a fire in it, and he's sweating even more." Joy's voice broke.

Powel glanced towards me for a moment. "Listen, some strangers came to town today, and one of them wants to try to help Roy."

Joy gasped. "Really? Where are they?"

Powel held up his hands. "Don't panic and don't scream. But here she is." He waved for me to come over.

Here we go. I took a deep breath and stepped into view. I folded back my ears as I watched Joy take a deep breath. Before she released her shriek, I covered my ears.

Powel lunged for the human woman and grabbed her by the shoulders. "She's here to help. Please stop screaming."

Joy was both taller and larger than Powel. She had broad shoulders for a woman, and her braided black hair curled around her neck to rest against her considerable bosom. Joy shoved Powel with her muscular arms and turned to grab a club with large nails protruding through it. "Back!"

I shifted my vision until everything was red, then dashed through the door. Powel bounced off me as I grabbed the club that Joy held. I grabbed her throat with my other hand and slammed her against the wall next to the door.

"Drop it," I growled, my teeth inches from her face.

"Come back to finish the job, have you?" Joy said as she clenched her jaw. "Well, I won't give up without a fight."

She dropped the club and grabbed the arm that was holding her throat. I tossed the weapon away as I pulled her away from the wall, only to shove her right back into it. Joy let out a grunt as she relaxed her grip on my arm. I released her neck and grabbed her blood-speckled shirt and pulled her forward. The human tripped over the leg I had extended, landing on her hands and knees. I stepped onto her back and forced her to the ground.

"Why aren't you helping?" Joy screamed towards Powel.

I heard a sword get pulled from its sheath. Powel let out a shout as he charged me, his sword raised above his head. I created a simple spear of ice that I jabbed out and aimed at the base of his neck, stopping just short of piercing him. He stopped moving and stared at the point aimed at him.

"Drop it!" I bared my fangs at Powel.

He did. The sword landed on the ground after it fell behind his back. With a simple flick of my wrist, I tossed the spear into the air and willed it to dissolve into tiny snowflakes.

"I'm not here to kill anyone." I put a little extra weight on my leg that held Joy down. "If you don't want my help, then you can watch your kid die, painfully and slowly. You're lucky that I'm being nice. When I became a knight, I took an oath to defend this kingdom."

Joy stopped squirming under me. "I just attacked a knight?" she whispered.

"Yes, you did. It's in my power to arrest you, but since I said I was willing to help, this is your one and only warning." I removed my leg and hoisted the woman to her feet. "Have I made myself clear?" I glared into her eyes.

"Yes, ma'am," Joy said as she quivered. "But Roy isn't my child. He's my brother."

I waved my hand. *So I was wrong.* "Whatever. Where is he?"

"In his room." Joy pointed to a wall with her finger. "How can you help?"

"That depends entirely on what I see. I have an idea about what's happening, but I hope I'm wrong." With a simple gesture, I motioned for Joy to lead the way.

After Powel picked up his sword and returned it to its sheath, Joy led us through the house and into a small room barely larger than the bed and the accompanying trunk at its foot. In the bed lay a man who looked a lot like Joy, just covered in sweat and mumbling to himself. *So, this is Roy.* Blankets lay in a heap on the floor as Roy sprawled out on the bed in barely enough clothes to keep him decent. The room reeked of body odor, blood, and decay. A dark-brown bandage wrapped around Roy's thigh showed that his wound still bled, with a dark-red spot on the inside of his leg.

Let's start with something simple. "Do you have a cup he can drink out of?" I said as I turned to Joy.

Joy looked like she was fighting back the tears in her eyes. "Yeah, I can go get one."

I nodded and watched her as she scampered off.

I turned to Powel. "Look through his clothes and find the cleanest clothes you can."

"Why?" Powel stared at me with an empty look in his eyes.

I rolled my eyes. "Because he's not just hurt, he's sick." I pointed to the bandage on Roy's leg. "Does that look like a clean bandage to you?"

Powel shook his head.

I stepped over and carefully cut the bandage with a claw. A yellowish-red open wound filled the room with the smell of decay. I had to keep myself from dry heaving as I inspected it. I didn't see a damaged artery, but the entire area was dark red, almost purple. Black spots of flesh dotted the edges of the wound, telling me it was as bad as I thought. While I inspected the injury and Powel rummaged through Roy's clothes, Joy walked in carrying a cup. I thought I could hear more footsteps.

"What are you doing?" Joy shrieked.

I flinched. "He's getting something that can be used as a bandage. Your brother needs a new one."

"And who are you to say what the boy needs?" a different voice spoke.

I lifted my head and saw a man, shorter than everyone else in the room and in a dark-brown robe, walk into the room behind Joy.

I narrowed my eyes at the bald man. His face was quite round, and his clothes didn't hide his rotund stature. "Are you the doctor in this town?" *I think this is the guy Powel asked for someone to send here.*

"I am." He crossed his arms as I stood up. "What do you know about medicine?"

"My best friend, who is a human, is a doctor back in the capital. I've picked up a thing or two. This wound is infected." I pointed to Roy's leg. "It probably needs to be removed."

The little doctor's eyes went wide, and he darted to inspect the wound. After a brief moment, he turned his head back to me. "You're right."

Don't sound so surprised.

"What does that mean?" Joy placed the cup on the trunk after Powel closed it while holding a tan shirt. "What's going to happen to my brother, Carotin?"

"He likely won't survive the week if we don't amputate his leg. But that has a high chance of killing him too. I'm sorry." Carotin stood up and wrapped his arms around Joy as she wept.

No good options. "Wait a moment..." *Didn't Golditress want to help me when we fought the bears? Daric said she can use healing magic.* I growled as I grabbed my head. *Why am I so stupid sometimes? But they should be close now.* "That might work." I looked and saw everyone staring at me. "What?"

"What will work?" Carotin asked.

"One of the people I'm traveling with knows healing magic. Roy might have a chance to live. Unfortunately, we still have to remove the leg. Healing magic doesn't cure diseases and infections. It makes them worse." I put my hand on the back of my head as I turned away from everyone's stares. "Or so I've been told."

"I'm inclined to believe you," Powel said hesitantly. "If you hadn't used magic a few moments ago, I wouldn't believe you."

I guess showing off a bit does help. Now, to kill two birds with one stone. "Joy, I need you to go to the southeast of town. You should see three humans, two elves, and a dragoon walking towards town. Those are the people you need to find. Explain the situation to them and ask Golditress to follow you back here. She's the one we need. Tell her Lucia is asking for help." I pointed to the southeast.

Joy nodded and wiped her tears. "Okay. Will this save my big brother?"

"It's the best we can do," I whispered.

Joy ran out of the room as everyone watched.

"Why did you send her?" Powel asked.

"Because she isn't going to want to watch this part," Carotin said, his voice heavy with dread.

Smart man. I focused on making an ax, one that was sharp enough and dense enough to cut through the bone. I looked at the poor man, who was tossing and turning, completely oblivious to his surroundings. *There are no words to express how sorry I am. But this is for your own good.*

"Hold him down tightly." I glared at the two standing men. "I'll take care of the rest."

They nodded silently and moved to hold Roy. Powel held Roy's arms to his chest. Carotin spread Roy's legs apart and held them down as he climbed onto the bed. With a nod, they told me they were ready.

I inspected the edge I'd created one last time. I ran my pad along the edge as I focused on making it even sharper. *This is the best I can do. Hopefully it will be enough. There's no numbing the pain. I need to make sure I have enough magic to cap his leg. And if he's not conscious, I won't know if I numbed him enough.*

I lifted the ax and took a deep breath. Before I dropped it, I began channeling my magic into it. With one swift motion that had been drilled into me through countless days of weapons training, I cut through Roy's leg, buried the ax completely into the mattress, and embedded it in the floor below.

Roy screamed as he fought to flail around and grab his leg. Powel struggled a bit but kept Roy from making things worse. I focused as the world slowed down around me and Roy's screams became easier to ignore. Blood didn't wait to shoot out of the stump of his leg. I took a step forward and pulled the ax up to rest on the stump. Working as fast as I could, I willed the ice to change shape and wrap around the amputation site. *I need to freeze the blood to keep as much as possible from escaping.*

The blood that poured out from the severed leg was darker than usual. The ice ax deformed and followed my directions to cap off Roy's new stump. Then everything returned to its normal speed.

Roy suddenly stopped screaming and fighting and fell limp. His chest rose and lowered slowly yet rhythmically.

I released my breath, which I didn't know I was holding. "That was the hard part."

Carotin stared at my makeshift cap. "I didn't know you could do that." He tentatively extended a hand and touched the ice. "How long will that hold?"

I felt the pull of the magic as I fed it, trying to keep it from melting. "Maybe a quarter of a day. It should be long enough." I looked at the damaged bed and the bloody mattress. A familiar feeling rumbled in my stomach, and reflexively I licked my lips. I turned around as quickly as I could. "Take the severed leg and burn it. I have to stay here and wait for Golditress." *I hope they didn't see that. Even though I can smell rotten meat, blood still incites my appetite.*

"I'll stay, you go," Carotin said.

I heard Powel walking behind me, and from the corner of my eye, I watched him carry the severed leg out.

Carotin walked next to me and grabbed my hand. "Why are you doing this? Do you feel guilty that your kind did this?"

I pulled my hand from his grip, making sure I didn't cut him with a claw. I glared at the doctor. "No, and I'm not in the mood to talk to you about anything personal. Especially since you've only proven your incompetence."

Carotin crossed his arms. "And what do you mean by that?"

I pointed to Roy's leg. "That only happens if you neglect the wound. Did you even bother to clean it before you bandaged it?"

The man threw his arms out wide. "How could I? There were dozens of wounded I needed to care for. The beastkin took a lot of our food and clothes. I'm almost out of bandages too."

I poked his chest without my claws extended. *I can't hurt him, yet.* "Did you even think to check up on him? Were you just going to leave him like this?"

"I've been busy since the attack." Carotin's face started turning a shade of pink. "I didn't think it was that bad anyway."

"Not that bad?" My tail and ears went up. "Not that bad? He had a hole through his leg! You are literally the worst doctor ever. And I've known a terrible doctor." I pointed to the door. "Get out of my sight before I arrest you for attempted murder."

Carotin scoffed. "You can't do that. You're a beastkin."

I bared my fangs. "And a knight."

The man's face went pale as he stumbled back a few steps. "Im-impossible."

I held up my claws. "Are you willing to take that chance? Now get out."

Carotin scurried out of the room without looking at me.

The two of us, Roy and I, shared the room silently and unmoving. *At least he won't make me angry.* It wasn't terribly long until I could hear Golditress following Joy to the bedroom.

Golditress didn't waste any time getting to work. I watched as she channeled her magic and, slowly, color returned to Roy's skin. *He didn't look like he changed much, so hopefully he didn't lose that many years.* His fever was down, but not gone.

I helped carry Roy to the other bedroom and left Joy to care for him and burn the bed. Before I left, I removed the icy cap from Roy's leg to prove to Joy that he was going to make it. I pointed Golditress to Powel's house.

She magically exhausted herself to help save Roy's life. She deserves a break. I, however, need to have a look around. The beastkin responsible could come back, and I'm the only one who knows what to look for.

9

ON THE ROAD AGAIN

I entered the dining room to see everyone but Anna sitting around the table staring at me. A plate of meat scraps I'd left sat untouched in front of an empty chair.

"Where have you been?" Silver said with a small hint of worry.

I moved to the chair with the plate. "Scouting." I picked up a small piece of meat and popped it into my mouth. *Lamb, how delightful. If I'm not mistaken, this is a piece of the loin.* I savored the chewy silver skin. "After hearing about the beastkin attack, I checked the surrounding area for signs of them still in the area." I swallowed the meat. "The answer is no, by the way."

Palpable relief came from Powel.

"We have to help these people." Daric's voice filled the room.

"One, we already have a job to do," Penny said as she pinched the bridge of her nose. "Two, what could we possibly do? Stay here and repair the whole town? It looks like people already have it well under control."

Mark waved his hand towards Powel. "They said they sent a messenger to get help. And Lucia said that beastkin weren't in the area, so maybe they just wanted a quick and easy raid. Besides, if they come back, the people will be ready with greater resistance."

Dinar joined the conversation. "Yeah, we don't know what they were after. Did they take anything and how much?"

"They attacked anyone who got in their way, and they only took food and clothes." Powel twisted his face in confusion. "I never thought about what they took until now. But what does that mean?"

"That makes it sound like they're hungry," I said as I chewed another piece of fatty meat. "But why would they attack this village?" I stared at the table as I mumbled to myself.

"Why don't you guys want to help them? We're supposed to be the heroes," Daric whined.

I twitched my ear. "I already did." I looked up and saw everyone but Golditress and Powel looking at me, bewildered. "One of the shepherds was attacked and his leg was wounded and got infected. I amputated it and kept it sealed until Golditress healed him enough to begin recovering on his own."

They turned their attention to Golditress, who slouched in her chair and nodded. "Yes, so now I can't use magic for the next five days." Her voice was soft, even to my ears.

"You helped these people?" Daric's question resounded in my head.

I slammed my hand on the table, causing it to tilt as it rocked back down with a loud crash. "I'm violent, not heartless." Everyone froze. I stood up, kicking the chair back. "I thought by now you would have figured that out. But I guess you really are an idiot." I stomped to the door.

Anna came running towards me as I reached the front door, her clothes slightly disheveled and her hair still damp. "What happened? Where are you going?"

"Away." I resisted the urge to tear the door off its hinges. "I'm not wanted here, so I'll find a place to sleep outside of town. At least then it will be quiet, and I won't have to listen to anyone patronizing me."

Before Anna could say anything, I slammed the door behind me. *I'm not in the mood.* I strolled to the outskirts of town and found a small orchard that I had seen as I scouted the area. When I made my igloo, I had to make it a little smaller since I'd used so much magic when I'd amputated Roy's leg. *Anna can watch my stuff. Just when*

69

things were getting better, this had to happen. I wasn't falling asleep, so I resorted to watching the stars through the breaks in the clouds until I was bored enough to sleep.

As I watched the little dots of light filter through the clouds, footsteps were headed my way. I turned and saw Silver, still wearing his armor. *Does he ever take that off?*

I return to looking to the sky. "What do you want?"

"To talk." Silver paused. "Is that alright?"

I groaned. "About?"

"Do you mind if I sit?" I waved a hand to Silver, and he sat down before continuing. "Thank you. It's about what happened to this village. Also I have some reservations about this mission."

I perked up an ear. "What do you mean?"

Silver looked to the side. "Everything about this mission is rubbing me the wrong way. It almost seemed like we were meant to find you. We could have taken a different path here, but Daric and Dinar insisted that we find a guide through the woods."

I narrowed my eyes. "Do you have a problem with me?"

The dragoon's eyes bulged as he raised his hands up. "No, nothing like that."

I flattened my ears and growled.

"It's just things are feeling too, I don't know, coincidental?"

"I don't see it."

Silver relaxed and hummed. "I guess you wouldn't know about where the information from this blood anchor came from, would you?" I shook my head. *Should I?* "It seems like this information appeared out of nowhere. And what makes these blood anchors so important?"

"They are the, well, anchors that will be used to summon the demon king." I leaned my head back. "The idea is, I'm guessing, that Anna finds a way to lift them so that he can't come here. Nobody knows what his plans are when he gets here, but I imagine they won't bode well for us."

Silver nodded. "From what little I know about these blood anchors, they take a lot of people dying to create. Someone willing to create so many of them has to be evil. There have been two plots to create blood anchors in this kingdom, one of which succeeded."

"Are you saying that this might be another plan to create another blood anchor?" I closed my eyes as I could feel a headache budding.

Silver hummed as he grabbed his chin and crossed his arms. "Well, it stands to reason, if they are trying to summon the demon king they'll continue until he's here. We would probably know if their plan has succeeded. So they aren't going to stop now. It's been years since the attack on the tournament. The timing just feels right for them to try something again."

I rubbed my eyes to ease the pain behind them. "So what? Are we expected to do something?"

Silver shook his head. "Nah. Maybe it's something we can just keep in the back of our minds as we focus on our mission. We can't really act on anything until we have proof."

"Speaking of our mission..." My tail flicked beside me. "Why are you here? Your aptitude was basket weaving, wasn't it?"

Silver rubbed his hands. "It is, just like my father, and his father too."

I raised an eyebrow. *Are aptitudes hereditary?*

"Growing up, I never enjoyed not doing anything. Staying out of it, just to sit in a room and make baskets, it's not in me."

"So you're like Daric." I rolled my eyes. "Someone who has to 'help' because you should."

Silver's face scrunched up into an expression I couldn't read. "I'm not that naïve. No, sitting in one place for too long just doesn't do anything for me. Staying in one place builds complacency."

"You know, you do seem the most levelheaded." I waved a hand at the dragoon. "You're such a strange group. How did all of you get together?"

Silver shrugged. "We met at an inn and sort of just got along."

I flicked my tail.

"No, Midas Bloodless contracted Dinar, Penny, and I to join and keep Daric safe. We've been freelanced knights for a few years."

"And Golditress and Mark?"

"They were friends of Daric's," Silver answered dismissively.

"You're the surprise to me. Maybe Midas planned to have you join all along."

I growled. "I've already rejected him once. He really doesn't like that fact, does he?"

Silver chuckled. "Not likely. He's a bit of a heavy-handed manager. So, how did you say no to him? When?"

"After the tournament, when I received my title." I let my head rest against the ice behind me. My headache subsided. "I wanted to join The Maidens. Something about him and his plans just... I couldn't do it. My instincts crave freedom, and I doubted he'd give it to me. Besides, I've got my mom now too."

Silver stood up. "Ah, a mama's girl."

I glared at him. "This mama's girl can tear you apart, literally."

Silver crossed his arms and tapped his foot. "I'm a better fighter than you think. I've been training others longer than you've been alive."

I flexed my claws. *Fine. Maybe this will make you fear me.* "Your mace is the worst weapon you can use against an unarmed specialist like me. And your shield, that won't do anything but give me more leverage. If you used a bladed weapon you'd last longer, but once I get a claw on you, there's no hope."

Silver turned. "Maybe you're right. But you could stand to work with us a bit better."

I scoffed. *Yeah, right. I work better alone. Nobody can keep up with me. You'll all just slow me down.* But talking with Silver did calm me down a bit. So I curled back into my igloo and fell asleep.

A familiar bleating of sheep greeted me as I woke up. I shattered the igloo into dust as I stood up. With a flick of my wrist, I drew the ice to myself and coated my fur. I let the ice melt and soak me for a few moments. After I was certain the ice had completely melted, I refroze the water, then I slowly started from my head and moved down, pulling the ice off, taking all the dirt with it.

Magic is so cool.

I looked at the sky. "It's going to be a long day again, isn't it?" The sheep in the distance didn't hear my moaning, and if they had, they wouldn't have cared. My stomach growled for an extended time.

"Great, now I need some food. But first I need to finish my morning routine."

The sun tried to pierce through the clouds but failed, leaving everything looking bleak. I walked to Powel's home and let myself in. I paused for a moment to listen for anyone moving this early in the morning. Someone was walking around, and it sounded like one of the women, given how light the footsteps were. I walked to the room of the source and knocked softly.

"Who is it?" Dinar answered softly. *I wouldn't have guessed it was her up this early.*

"It's Lucia." I matched her volume. "I was wondering who has my stuff."

"It's here. Anna brought it with her when she went to bed last night." Dinar cracked open the door. "She's still sleeping, and so are Penny and Golditress."

"I guess I missed the sleepover party. Did you girls have fun?" I asked with a smirk.

The elf tilted her head. "What are you talking about?" *Okay, wrong audience.* "Though some of us slept better than others." Dinar turned and stared at someone.

I poked my head in to see who she was talking about, even though I already had a good idea of who she was annoyed with. Anna slept in the bed with several blankets covering her, but I could obviously see that she was hugging her pillow more than she was resting her head on it.

"Yeah, she talks in her sleep. She always has. It's kinda cute sometimes."

"Cute? Maybe, maybe if I wasn't trying to sleep myself." Dinar pointed behind the door and opened it farther to allow me in. "Your stuff is here, by the way."

I smiled as I saw all the other girls still sleeping. *It's been a bit of a trek. Let them get their rest while they can.*

My footsteps didn't make a sound, as usual, when I walked into the room. I collected my things to dig around for my brush and fresh clothes. Dinar waved as she left the room. I silently changed my clothes, brushed all my fur, and warned Penny as she woke up to let the other two sleep. She nodded and went about her morning routine quietly. We walked out of the room together to the dinner table.

One by one, the rest of the group congregated at the table. Powel provided everyone with a simple breakfast. A plate with a sheep's heart sat in front of me after I told Powel that it was alright if he gave me any unwanted organs. Powel's daughter left us alone to eat with her mother because she was still restricted to bedrest, but at least she was awake now. Powel stayed to answer the questions we had.

"So, what do we do now?" Dinar broke the silence of everyone slowly eating. "I doubt this town can afford to sell us supplies right now."

Powel looked down at his plate of eggs and apple slices. "That is correct. From what people have told me, if we get attacked like that again, we won't survive until the water season."

Daric slammed his fist on the table, jostling everyone's plates. "We have to do something."

"Like what?" Penny answered. "They're already working to solve this issue by themselves. Do you want us to stay here until their help arrives? Delay our payday that much longer?" She turned to Powel. "I'm sorry that they attacked you like that. I really am. But I can't afford to keep delaying our job any more. We already don't know how long it will take."

"I understand. You've already helped more than most people would." Powel's gaze barely lifted from the table. "I'm worried about if they return before we get any aid."

"I've already looked. They aren't anywhere close to here," I said as I propped my head on the table with one arm and waved my fork in a circle. "Although from looking around, I still can't tell how many attacked you in the first place."

Powel crossed his arms and closed his eyes for a moment. "By our best estimates, about twenty."

"How did they cause so much damage with so few? A town of this size has many more than that," Silver said as he finished eating.

"Because they attacked at night," I said nonchalantly.

Everyone turned towards me.

"Beastkin can see just fine in the dark. My guess is that by the time people knew what was going on, most of the damage had been done and they fled with whatever they could carry. Am I right?"

Powel nodded.

"I would rather not get into a fight with any beastkin." I looked and saw everyone staring at me. With a sigh, I sat up. "It isn't for the reason you're all thinking. It's because I don't trust any of you to remember that I'm on your side." I pointed a claw at everyone in my group.

"Do beastkin have any weaknesses we can exploit?" Mark said.

Without moving my head, I glared at the human and growled. *Did you seriously ask me that?*

The color quickly drained from his face as he shrank in his chair. "You don't have to answer that." His voice was barely louder than a whisper.

Golditress held out a small pouch towards Powel. I could hear coins clinking around inside the bag. "This should be more than enough to equate to a night in a tavern. Please take this with our thanks."

Powel held out his hand to reject the money.

"Just take the money," Mark said. "Will that be enough for you to let this go, Daric?"

Daric crossed his arms. "It's a good start."

I turned to look at Anna. "Are you feeling well enough to walk? It looks like we'll be leaving today."

Anna smiled. "Yeah, Christine gave me this wonderful cream. And she also gave me a new pair of shoes, ones more capable of withstanding the hardships of traipsing through the woods. They may look a little harsher on the eyes, but they at least feel more comfortable."

Has she had on the wrong shoes this entire time? "I'm glad you finally got your footwear situation figured out, princess." My remark earned me a glare from Anna. *Why did I say that out loud?*

Everyone decided eye contact was a bad idea and found the floor, walls, or ceiling to be exceedingly interesting.

"Anyway..." Penny broke the tension. Everyone turned to her, and once she was certain everyone was looking at her, she cleared her throat. "Now that we have everything settled, I say we get moving again."

"But—" Daric started talking, but all of us girls stared at him and turned his voice into a whisper. "Okay, let's go."

With Daric finally abandoning his protests, we packed up and left Briarford behind. We walked for a couple of days, and every time Anna wanted to take a break but the rest of us were fine, I carried her and Silver carried our packs.

After we entered another forest, Anna used some magical method to locate the direction of the blood anchor. She told me she could use the method now because we were getting close to its location.

10

FAILED HUNTING

No droppings, no nests, nothing. After I returned from another failed hunting diversion, I paced in our camp. "I'm so hungry," I moaned.

"You ate more of the deer than the rest of us combined." Penny sat on a fallen tree branch tapping her foot. "How in the world can you eat so much?"

Silver finished stacking the sticks to make a fire. "We didn't resupply while we were at Briarford. It's unfortunate, but you heard them. They couldn't afford to give us anything."

Silver motioned towards the sticks as he took a step back. I took several more steps back and turned away as Penny snapped her fingers. The subtle crackling of fire behind me told me she'd just lit the sticks.

"Haven't you been out hunting?" Mark asked.

I grumbled. "I have. But there's nothing around. It's like nothing lives here, or has lived here in years. Usually I can smell some traces of prey, but there's nothing. There hasn't been for days."

Daric sat polishing his sword. "Is that possible? This is a forest, and forests are supposed to be full of flora and fauna."

I glared him. "If you think you can do better, by all means, show me up." I waved my hand to the expanse of trees surrounding us.

Daric flinched.

Golditress walked next to me. "Do you mind if I go with you? Maybe a second pair of eyes will help."

I rolled my eyes. *Your eyes and ears are too dull to be of much help. You'll only slow me down. But fine. Because I promised Mom, I'll let you come along this time.* "Fine, but you need to be quiet."

Golditress just nodded as she went to grab her bow and four arrows. She followed me as I kept a pace slow enough for her to keep up while not making too much noise. I could clearly hear her, but then again, my senses were far beyond hers.

Things were unnervingly quiet as I looked around for anything but found nothing.

"Why are you a knight?"

Golditress's question caught me off guard. I turned to the woman. "Is that why you wanted me out here?"

She blushed as she turned her head slightly. "Yes. I believed you when you said there wasn't anything around."

I closed my eyes and relaxed. "Why the façade? Couldn't we talk at the camp?"

The woman just fidgeted with the bow in her hands. "I'm not very good with being around others." *That's obvious.* "And I noticed you don't like talking around Daric either."

I blinked. *That's not as obvious.*

"Fine." I motioned to a flat rock. "I'll answer your question if you answer mine too. You don't strike me as someone who's having fun on this mission." Golditress nodded as she moved to take a seat. I sat down next to her. "How old are you and how much do you know about what happened during the tournament five years ago?"

"I'm twenty-three," she answered. "But I don't know much other than rumors and what you've told us."

I rested my elbows on my knees and cradled my head. "As Anna said before, I was an orphan. And as an orphan, I was required to serve the military based on my debt to the kingdom. But you already know that, right?"

"I do."

"Well, I wanted to be a knight because I learned that I needed to spend a lot of time hunting too. As a knight, I would have more time to hunt. The tournament was the best way for me to find someone who would be willing to accept me." A slight ache pulsed in my heart as the memories of the tournament played through my mind. "During the demon attack, I found that I had people I wanted to protect. And becoming a knight felt like the best way to do that."

Golditress placed a hand on my shoulder. "And are you?"

I slumped even farther. "I don't know yet. This is my first mission, but all my training has done is alienate me from my closest friend since I'm the reason she has so much work to do."

"Then talk to her. If she's your closest friend, she'll understand." Golditress sounded happier than before. "I thought I had problems dealing with people."

I flicked an ear towards her. "You should try it with extra-sharp senses and a short temper. But what about you?" I turned and looked at her. "You're, if you don't mind me saying it, pretty. And you have an aptitude that makes you desirable to any knight company. You have both looks and brains. Why would you then follow an idiot like Daric? You could live an easy life with any man you want."

Golditress shook her head. "I don't find men attractive."

"Women?"

She shook her head again. "No. I'm doing this because he promised that I would see the world. It's been a dream of mine since I was a little girl." She gazed up at the canopy with a dreamy look. "Hearing all the stories of far-off places always just... It's hard to explain. But I want to see the elegant palaces of the elves, built out of crystals. See the obsidian walls of the dwarves. And maybe, one day, see a dragon's hoard."

"Dragons are real?" I shot up and turned to look at her. "I was always told they were a fairy tale."

Golditress hugged herself. "Well, nobody's seen one in at least a few thousand years. But maybe, one day, on another continent."

I shook my head. "There are other continents?"

Golditress started fidgeting with her braided hair. "Nobody knows. Any attempts to leave by sea have always ended with the ship getting destroyed by the devourers. But I want to believe they're out there and that I'll go and see what wonders they hold."

Why hasn't Mom told me about any of this? This wasn't in any of the books Zenny taught me from either. "Where did you learn all this?"

"Dinar told me." Golditress smiled as she stood up. "Thank you for indulging my curiosity. You're really a nice person, if you try to be."

"You know, you aren't all that bad either." I smirked and extended an arm in the direction of camp. "Maybe you should let your personality show with other people. I'm sure you'll do just fine. Because this side of you is far superior to that shy recluse you pretend to be. Nobody with your kinda wanderlust is that shy at heart."

Golditress hunched her shoulders. "I wish I shared your confidence."

I frowned and let it go as we traveled back to camp. *She'll open up when she's ready. But I would never have guessed she had this side to her. It almost makes me wonder what the others are hiding.*

The next day was just as uneventful as the last. Everyone else had some wild berries to eat, but me and my outraged stomach were left alone in a corner. My mouth watered as I daydreamed about food while I sat on the edge of camp.

When my eyes fell on Silver, a thought bubbled through my mind. *I know how elves taste. I wonder, what do dragoons taste like? Do they taste like lizards, or something better?*

Silver's eyes grew wide when I licked my lips as I stared at him. "Why are you doing that?" Silver leaned back as he laid down the stone he was carrying for the fire pit.

"Just a bite," I whispered unconsciously.

I heard some footsteps coming towards me before someone tackled me. I growled and grabbed whoever had decided they wanted to receive a beating today.

Daric tried to hold on to me, but I pried him off easily. Once Daric realized I had pulled him off, he tried to punch my forearm to get me to let go.

I shoved him to the ground and extended my claws as I growled.

He landed with a grunt. "You can't eat him," he said as he rolled over onto his hands and knees. "Why are you even thinking about that?"

Mark stepped towards me, his rapier drawn. "We know you're hungry, but you can't eat people. Why haven't you found anything during one of your hunts? You tell us that you're one of the best, yet you've caught nothing for two days."

I stomped my foot. "I know. It's just so hard to concentrate when I'm this hungry. Also I've been itching to hunt for something all day." I pointed my finger at all of them as they stared at me. "And just so you know, all of you look like food to my instincts." *I need to stop. This isn't playing nice like I promised.* I took a deep breath and lowered my arm. "Sorry, I'm just really frustrated. There isn't anything to hunt in the area. I didn't know that was even possible. Even edible plants have been getting scarcer recently too."

"Maybe the blood anchor has something to do with that." Anna placed a finger on her chin. "We're getting really close. Although it's impossible to know how far. But I believe we're seeing its influence on the area."

"But you need to calm down." Penny's voice tickled something at the back of my mind. "We probably crossed the border of the Wild Kingdom recently. Who knows how the local beastkin will take to us wandering around here? You can't be making our situation more difficult than it already is."

"At least you have food." I stormed up to the shorter elf. "If you think that I'm happy about this, you're wrong." I bared my teeth.

Anna shoved Penny back and Dinar pulled at her.

"Stop this," Dinar said. "Don't antagonize her."

Golditress walked behind me and grabbed my shoulders to steer me away from her. "Calm down, please," she whispered in my ear.

Anna turned her attention to me with fury. "And you." She poked my gut. "Stop thinking with your stomach. Go and hunt. Take all the time you need. We'll wait here for you to return."

I growled at Anna. She didn't flinch as she matched my glare. I leaned forward until my face was inches away from hers and growled even louder. Anna's stoic expression never shifted. Nobody else moved or said anything until my stomach made a sound that I knew they'd all heard.

"Fine. I'll be back." I stormed off in the direction we were heading.

Snow started fluttering down through the trees as I stalked through the woods. I found no signs of anything to hunt until I found footprints on the ground. *Based on the frost covering them, they may be a day or two old, but this is the first sign of life in the area. It looks like one of my footprints, but I haven't been around. A small wolf pup, maybe. I don't care; I'm so hungry that I'll eat the pup and its mother.*

The tracks were easy to follow, and they led me to other footprints. *Hoof, rabbit, bear, canine, and feline tracks in the same place? Their sizes seem all wrong. Unless these are tracks of other beastkin. And if there are people, they'll have food. Now just to be diplomatic for the first time in my life. I need to not do what I did when I met the diplomats from the Wild Kingdom five years ago.* With an obvious trail to follow, I weaved through the trees until it looked like I had walked into a clearing. A clearing with a burned-down, ruined village.

I know this village. The ruins of burned buildings with overgrown vines and other vegetation didn't hide the painful truth. *This is the village I first woke up to in this world.*

My breath caught in my throat as my heart tried to burst through my chest. Everything started getting fuzzy as my legs went weak. I dropped to my knees as the images of blood, bodies, and a cage assaulted my mind. Fear overran my instincts as I gasped for air and stared at the ground.

My chest hurt as my heart tried to break through my ribs. Every muscle in my body wanted to run away, but I was paralyzed as I remembered the flames. Their heat that I didn't remember feeling that day was very real to me now. I wanted to scramble away from the burning buildings, but my arms and legs felt tight, like ropes held me prisoner. Nonexistent walls closed in on me as my breaths turned into sharp gasps and tears streamed down my face.

No! It's not real. It's not real. My sobbing continued. I remember being unable to defend myself. Feeling completely helpless as I was dropped in the cage. My fate so far out of my hands I wished that I'd never agreed to this second life. How The Voice put me in such a horrible situation where things could have ended much worse for me.

All of the emotions crashed into me, spilling out of memories I had almost forgotten.

But I was saved. Allen saved me. He took me to Nora—Mom. There are people in this life I got to meet. Those I've come to love. This was horrible. But I survived, and now I can defend myself. I will never live through this kind of situation again. I'm stronger now, and my life is the life I choose. Nobody will put me in a cage again.

My breathing was the first to get under control. Then the tears stopped. Soon my ears weren't flooded with the sound of my heartbeat. Slowly, I calmed down and looked back at what was probably my birthplace. *The tracks led here, but who would live in these ruins and not fix them up?*

As I kneeled and contemplated the sight before me, a sound caught my attention. Then I caught wind of something or someone in the air. I focused on my hearing, and I noticed people surrounding me.

"I know you're there. You can come out now," I shouted to the people.

As I had suspected, beastkin of all shapes, sizes, and species walked out of the brush and ruins in a circle around me. One beastkin caught my attention more than the others.

"Lucia? Is that you?" the beastkin asked. "You're alive?"

Only one thought ran through my mind and out of my mouth. "Who are you?"

11

THE RESEMBLANCE IS UNCANNY

In front of me stood a near perfect reflection of myself. A reflection of me with larger breasts, and if I wasn't a primal beastkin. The same silver fur covered the wolf beastkin as she looked down at me. She even had the same blue eyes that shimmered as she took a step towards me. She wore a ragged red tank top and a black skirt that went to her knees. There was also a silver band on her wrist, just like I saw the two ambassadors wearing during the tournament.

The silver-furred woman placed her hands on her chest as she continued to walk towards me. "What did you mean? It's me, Lexia."

I stared at my doppelganger. "Who?"

"It's me, your sister." Her voice sounded just like mine as she pleaded. "I thought you were dead. No, I saw you die."

I have a sister? And she's alive?

My inner wolf bounced around inside me. It was hard to push her back as she kept nudging me towards the beastkin who claimed to be my sister. *What if she's lying?*

"Careful Lexia, we don't know her. She could be working with them." A pure white-furred foxkin stepped up and held Lexia back.

He had a sharper face than Lexia, and when I glimpsed his teeth, I could see that he was a primal beastkin, just like me. He wore clothes similar to the woman who claimed to be my sister, although they were in worse condition, much dirtier, and a dark-brown color. He was almost as tall as me, just a couple of inches shorter. But he stood with a subtle slouch to his shoulders.

"Don't be stupid, Gifford." She shrugged him off.

I stood up after a quick shake of my head. "You're my sister? How? I thought everyone was dead. How did you survive?" Something in my instincts screamed that she was telling the truth.

"You don't remember me, your sister? I remember you." She held out her arms and took a few more steps. "It doesn't matter. You're here now. Come here and we can catch up, and you can tell me about how you survived and where you've been."

My instincts kept screaming to run up and hug her, but something about the way the other beastkin were looking at me made me feel uneasy. "That's a long story." I tried to put on a friendly smile but took a step back.

"Lexia, you can't believe that this is your long-lost sister you saw die." The fox beastkin ran in front of Lexia and held her shoulders.

Lexia grabbed the male by his ear and yanked him down. He let out a yelp and whimpered as Lexia growled down at the foxkin. "You think I don't know my own sister? Well, she is. And she is welcome here."

Okay, I'm beginning to see how she could be related to me. My inner wolf pawed at my mind to push me towards her.

"Say I believe you. What then?" I asked.

Lexia turned and smiled at me with wide eyes. "Then you come back and live with us. We'll give you a home and we can be sisters again."

You know, when you say that while holding someone like that, your message might not come across like you think it should.

"I'm not alone. There's a group of people, that way, who are traveling with me," I said, pointing my finger towards the location of Daric and the others. "Are they welcome to join us?"

Lexia released the fox. He dropped to the ground, grabbing his ear and whimpering as he crawled behind her. The silver wolfkin eyed the male as he cowered before turning her attention back to me. "Of course. My sister's friends can't be bad. We can guide them here for you. It's no trouble at all. That way you can tell me about everything."

She's way too happy to see me. Although I have to admit that part of me is grateful to see her too. I just don't know how to explain to her that the sister she knew is gone and was replaced by me. Well, it looks like I'm brushing off my old excuse of amnesia again.

"You three, go find Lucia's friends and bring them here." Lexia pointed towards a male cougar, a female black wolf, and a female brown bear.

The three beastkin looked at each other. All of them looked like they wanted to say something but were trying to get the other two to say it. They kept it up until the wolf stepped forward and cleared her throat. "What do Lucia's friends look like? Also, where can we find them?" Her voice was pleasantly soft.

"Oops. That might be important information, wouldn't it?" I laughed nervously. "They're a group of seven; one dragoon, two elves, one half-elf, and three humans. And they're straight that way." I saw the shock on everyone's faces as I pointed. "What?"

"What are you doing with humans and elves? And what's a dragoon?" Lexia took a step away from me and held her hands to her chest. "Please tell me this is a bad joke."

I softly scratched the back of my head. "It's part of the really, *really* long story that I have no doubt you're going to make me tell." I held out a hand to Lexia. "I promise it will all make sense when I finish the story. But it's going to take a while."

Lexia turned away and paused for a moment. "Alright, anything else?" she said as she turned her head back to me.

"Oh, yeah." *I almost forgot about Mr. Wannabe Hero.* I turned to face the three whom Lexia had ordered to find my companions. "If anyone draws a weapon, tell them, 'If you ruin my chance at getting a new bed, I will kill you all. So be good kids and follow the nice beastkin and I'll explain everything.' And please don't do anything that can be misunderstood as aggressive behavior. They're a bit jumpy right now."

The three looked even more confused, but they gave a slight bow before walking in the direction I'd pointed.

"Alright, back to your posts," Lexia called out as she looked at everyone else gathered around. As soon as everyone, except the white fox that she'd abused, had turned to leave, she ran up to me and gave me a hug.

I froze, unable to consider any action.

"I'm so happy you're alive. Now we can be a family again." She turned to look at my outstretched arms. "You don't have a mate yet? We need to work on that."

I stared at her and made several unintelligible sounds before I shook my head. "Slow down." *Things are going too fast for me to keep up with.* "First question, how did you know my name is Lucia?"

Lexia squeezed me harder. "How can you not know that I'm your sister? I knew the moment I saw you. You should feel the same way."

"Sure, I feel something. But we can't be the only silver-furred wolfkin in the entire world. The family resemblance is frighteningly obvious, but I'm a primal beastkin, and you're not." I grabbed her arms and pried them away from me with very little effort.

Lexia's face grew a wide grin. "Now I know you're my sister. Only my sister could be this strong." I let her arms go as she continued to stare at me with an almost dreamy look. "My sister, the luckiest beastkin to be born in years. Born with the physical aptitude and a wonderfully beautiful silver coat of fur. I was always jealous of you. But it's nice that I share at least one of those traits." She gave me a playful wink.

I give up. There is no way that this is a coincidence. You win, instincts. But here comes the hard part. My stomach growled just as I opened my mouth to speak, causing Lexia to double over in laughter. "Um, before we start story time, can I get some food? I've been struggling to find any recently."

Lexia took a deep breath before she wiped a tear from her eye. "Of course. Follow me. We've also been struggling for food. The entire kingdom has. But at least now we're set for a few weeks."

Red flag!

"Hold up." I grabbed Lexia's shoulder as she turned away from me. "How many others are there here?"

The fox interrupted our conversation. "What are you insinuating?"

Lexia glared at the fox, who I now noticed wore a silver bracelet too. He flattened his ears and took a step back before she turned back to me. "Twenty, why?"

Maybe it's a coincidence. Hopefully, it's a coincidence. "No particular reason." I tried to put on a smile.

My sister glared at me. "Why are you lying to your big sister?"

She didn't buy it. Great. Now what? Wait. She may have a short attention span like me. It's time for a distraction. "Big sister? Given how similar we look, that must mean we're twins. So we're the same age."

"True, but I was born first. So that makes me the big sister." Lexia crossed her arms and puffed out her chest.

Big in other ways too. "Alright, prove it." I grinned as I mimicked her.

"As the little sister, you just need to believe your big sister when she tells you these things." Her grin matched mine.

I narrowed my eyes on my twin. "I'm certain that's an abuse of power."

My sister giggled. "What good is having power if you don't abuse it once in a while? Besides, look at you, you're the little sister," Lexia said as she pointed to my chest. My stomach growled again. "Come on, I need to take care of my sister since she's asking for my help."

Mission accomplished. Now, what was the mission? That's right, getting food. I followed my sister towards one of the more structurally sound and less destroyed buildings. The fox followed us, giving me a threatening glare the entire time. After enduring it for a short time, I stopped ignoring the impulse to growl at the man. While my sister giggled, he flinched and cowered away from me. *Good, he stopped staring at me like that. Wait, is he staring at my sister's butt now?*

The three of us walked into a smaller home that was mostly intact on the inside. Looking at all the intact furniture left me speechless.

"Welcome home." Lexia turned and smiled as she presented the building. "How hungry are you right now?"

I continued to gawk at everything. A layer of dust covered most of the floor and other unused flat surfaces. "Is this really our home?" All the furniture looked to be crafted out of wood, and I could see some of it did not take the neglect well. "How do you know all this? We were four when the orcs attacked."

"Why are you acting like you don't remember anything?" My sister tilted her head as she looked at me with a more scrutinizing gaze.

"Because I don't," I said flatly. "My first memory is waking up in the mud just before the orcs tied me up and put me in a cage. It's a day I can't forget. All the burning buildings, the bodies, the helplessness."

My sister wrapped her arms around me. "I'm so sorry that happened to you. If I'd known you were alive, I would've gone back for you. It must have been scary to be captured by orcs." We stared into each other's eyes. "How did you escape? If the orcs returned with you to their home, you wouldn't be here."

"You might want to sit down for this. It's a long story." My stomach growled again. "And I'd like to have food in me before I tell it."

"Which organs do you like most?" the arctic fox guy interrupted at the mention of food. "If you're a primal wolf, I imagine you like organs as much as I do."

So foxes are carnivores in this world too. Good to know. "Hearts and livers are the best parts. No eggs."

He looked a little deflated. "You don't like eggs? I love eggs, but I'll get you a heart. I believe I have one ready somewhere."

Is he lightening up around me? Did my growl mean something? What was his name again? I know it started with a "G." I watched him walk out of the main room.

Lexia gave a gentle smile. "To answer your question, I remember everything. I have the memory aptitude, after all." She grabbed my hand and led me towards a decent-looking chair.

There's a chair with a hole for my tail? Oh, happy day! "My best friend has that too," I blurted out.

My sister gave me a wide smile. "Maybe you remember more than you think. I'm glad to know that you were thinking of your big sister, even though you didn't know it." We sat down at the table next to each other. Lexia took a deep breath. "You were out playing, running around as you always did. You were one of the first to be caught in the attack. When Mom and I watched the orc strike the back of your head, my heart broke. They started slaughtering everyone. Mom and Dad carried me away and sacrificed themselves to buy me time to run away."

The foxkin walked in soundlessly and placed a heart on a cloth in front of me. He also placed a few strange-looking berries and a chunk of meat in front of Lexia. He sat down with a couple of kidneys in front of himself without disrupting my sister's story.

"I ran for two days before I found a wandering pack. They took me in and made sure I grew up strong." The somberness in her voice weighed down the entire mood.

I took a couple of quick bites from the heart. *Yeah, this is definitely a lamb heart. How do I make sure Daric doesn't do anything stupid? I'll worry about it later. Right now, I need to catch up with my sister.* "I have a sister. A real sister. I still don't know how to handle this."

Lexia wrapped an arm around my shoulders. "Take your time. This is a big day for both of us. I'm trying to keep it together for you. If you don't want to tell me your story right away, you don't have to. I would like to hear it eventually, but not before you're ready."

"It feels…" I sat quietly, trying to find the word to describe how I felt. "Weird. But not a bad kind of weird," I quickly added as I saw Lexia start to panic. "After the orcs placed me in the cage, I passed out. Originally, I thought that I was out for a night, but given the evidence, I don't know how long it actually was. But a group of knights from the Kingdom of Rophmna saved me. They took me to the capital city, and I was raised as an orphan. Eventually, the woman who ran the orphanage adopted me, and now I'm a knight of Rophmna. That's the short version."

"What's the long version?" the fox asked.

"My life was far too exciting for my liking." I turned to look at the fox. "I'm sorry. Who are you and why are you here?"

"Oops, sorry, this is Gifford, my mate." Lexia grabbed and nuzzled his shoulder.

"Okay," I said in an exaggerated tone. "But one thing is bothering me. What are you doing living here? Why live in this ruined town?"

"We're hiding," my twin replied with a deadpan expression. "We could use your help. And since you said you serve the human military, this may concern you too. You might be the only one I know who's strong enough to do it."

My heart picked up its pace. "What are you talking about?" I said as I took another bite of the heart.

"We're trying to overthrow the beast king," my sister said nonchalantly. "Can you help us kill him?"

I spat out my heart and watched it fly through the air, sticking to the wall, then dropping to the floor with a splat.

FAMILY BONDING

M y vision whirled for a moment before I snapped out of shock. "You're doing what? And you want me to do what? How? Why? Now? Where? Who?"

Gifford blinked several times with his mouth open, while my sister didn't look fazed in the slightest. "Will you help us kill the beast king?" she asked. "We don't want a war with the humans."

I closed my eyes as I tried to concentrate on what my sister had asked.

"I know what I'm asking is a monumental task, but I really need your help."

I opened my eyes and stared at my sister. "You're serious, aren't you?" She nodded. I sighed. "Why me? And why does he need to die?"

My sister's tail wagged vigorously as she sat up straighter. "Because you're strong. When Daygon challenged the previous king for the throne, almost ten years ago now, Daygon snapped the old king's spine by folding him backwards. That's the story that people have been telling. People say he's stronger than any other beastkin in the world. But if you're alive, that might no longer be true."

"But why do you want him dead? Who do you plan to take his place?" I asked as I flattened my ears. *Please don't say it's me.*

"I haven't thought about that yet. But I won't ask you to take his place. That would be unfair of me to ask." Lexia gave me a soft smile. "Besides, you don't look like you want the job."

"That's an understatement," I whispered as I stared at the mostly-eaten heart. My appetite flared up at the sight, so I finished it. "But you still haven't said why I have to *kill* him. Is he a bad king or something?"

"Daygon needs to be replaced because since he became king, food has become more and more scarce each year," Gifford said in a somber tone. "Instead of finding the problem and dealing with it, he's telling everyone to attack humans for food. We only did it to survive. We didn't want to hurt anyone, but we've been struggling to find food in this area. It's like life doesn't want to exist here. Animals don't come anywhere near here, and edible plants won't grow, no matter how hard we try." He placed his hand on Lexia's and sighed. "As much as I love my mate, I can't agree with her plan to send you. I don't doubt you're strong. I can feel it, but we can't afford for you to fail. If you wish to join us, I would be delighted to see my love's joy. We just need to think of a new plan. One that doesn't hinge on a stranger."

Lexia grabbed the fox's ear again, but this time, he didn't make a sound. "She isn't a stranger. She's my sister. You'll help us, right?" She turned to me, her eyes wide open and fully dilated, her lip quivering.

Not the puppy-dog eyes. We really are twins. I took a deep breath and released it slowly. Lexia released Gifford's ear as she watched me closely. "I'm with Gifford on this one. In all seriousness, I'm a stranger to you. I'm a stranger to everyone here. Unfortunately, whether or not I help you, it's not a decision I can make alone." I saw a tear form in the corner of my sister's eye, so I lunged to give her a hug. "But I'm starting to see you as my sister."

My sister returned my hug. As we embraced, Gifford quietly stood up and took what he had delivered the food on.

"It's good to hear that, at least. You sound so grown-up," Lexia whispered.

I chuckled. "Me, grown-up? In some aspects, yeah." A certain nagging returned once my emotions had calmed down. "There's something I still haven't quite grown out of just yet."

"Oh?" Lexia's tail lifted and swayed from side to side.

My cheeks grew warm as I turned away from my sister. "I still have the urge to hunt something every once in a while. And right now, I kinda need to hunt something. But you said that there isn't anything to hunt in the area. So what do I do?"

Lexia giggled. "You're so cute. But I didn't say there wasn't anything to hunt. Oh, love."

Gifford walked back to the room. "Yes?"

My sister turned to me with a wicked smile. "You can hunt my mate."

I glared at my sister. "That's not a good idea."

Gifford nodded enthusiastically. "I agree with your sister."

Lexia rolled her eyes. "You don't need to kill him, just rough him up a bit. Besides, this way you can show Gifford what you're capable of."

I eyed Gifford. "Hunting him won't be that hard. It probably won't satisfy me."

Gifford glared at me. "You aren't that good."

I clenched my jaw. "I am. If you're so desperate to see otherwise, then we'll go with my sister's suggestion. I'll even give you a twenty-count head start."

"You may want to only give him a ten-count." Lexia placed a hand on my shoulder. "He's better than you think."

"Fine, I'll give him a thirty-count," I said with a growl. *Why don't I start now?* "One." I could smell a delightful scent of fear coming from Gifford, as his eyes grew wide. "Two."

Gifford clambered out of the room and jumped out a window. He started running on two legs, but quickly shifted to all fours.

"This looks like it will be fun," Lexia said with the barest hint of a playful growl. "I'm going to enjoy watching."

I continued counting as I stood up and followed my sister to the back door. *I'm not some frightened prey. Why would I jump out a window when there's a perfectly good doorway available?* While I counted, I carefully examined the place where he'd landed after he jumped out of the window and let my vision slowly shift to red. I found, memorized, and honed in on his scent. Once I reached thirty, I bolted off in the direction I saw him run, following his scent. As the world blurred ever so slightly, I heard my sister shriek as she failed to keep up with me.

I slowed down enough to analyze his footsteps to see how he was running. *He's going to be so easy to catch.* I grinned as I recognized him running on two legs. As I shifted to run on all fours, his scent got stronger. Following his scent made the hunt much easier until his footsteps led straight to a gigantic tree. The massive oak tree was easily ten arcs tall, and that little cheat had run up it.

I went around to the other side of the tree, attempting to catch his scent on the gentle breeze. The wind didn't carry his smell, which forced me to look around for him.

He had to have changed directions. But which way? I focused on my ears, but the only thing I could hear was my sister panting as she ran to catch back up. *If she's tired, then he can't be too far.* I looked up into the branches but didn't see him.

Lexia stopped short, likely to catch her breath and see how the hunt would continue. *There's no way he stayed up in the trees. He had to come back down. There weren't any signs that he doubled back, so he had to have gone left or right.* I contemplated my options before an idea popped into my head. *I can't climb up since I promised Zenny I wouldn't climb trees anymore, so I just need to look for his claw marks.*

I went around to the other side of the tree and easily found his claw marks, proof of him climbing up. But after two arcs, the claw marks stopped. I noticed the last mark from his right hand was angled slightly to the right. *He went right!*

With a new direction, I bolted to the next tree and followed his path of him jumping from tree to tree. Gifford was more agile than I'd given him credit for. After following him for several trees, I saw the claw marks he'd made as he descended. The area was thick with his scent. *He's definitely tired now.*

I focused on my ears again, and this time I heard more than the rustling of leaves and my sister panting as she tried to keep up. I heard another person panting. *Gotcha!*

I sprinted towards the sound of Gifford's heavy breathing. The sound came from the other side of a wide tree. When I crested the tree, Gifford turned to look at me.

"Found you," I said with a wide grin.

He scrambled backwards, never taking his eyes off of me. I leaned forward and pounced at him. My outstretched arms grabbed nothing as Gifford rolled to the side. Digging my claws in, I slid to a halt and growled as I grinned. *Yes, please resist. It's more fun when they resist.*

The fox stood up and raised his claws in a sloppy fighting stance. He bared his teeth as he growled at me.

I rolled my eyes as my vision returned to normal. "You're putting too much weight on your lead foot." And to demonstrate why that was a problem, I kicked his ankle. His leg buckled, and he fell to one knee as I rolled to my feet. "And your hands are too far out. You won't be able to defend against a quick jab to the inside." I kicked him in the chest, knocking him to his back. He reached for my leg, but my leg struck him and returned out of his reach before he could touch me. "Who taught you how to fight?"

The fox placed a hand on his chest as he slowly turned and rose to his feet. "Nobody. I've had to learn on my own." He turned and glared at me. Without provocation, he swiped his right hand, claws extended, in a wide arc towards me.

"Don't attack so wildly." I leaned back just out of his reach and stepped in as his hand passed me. "You leave yourself far too open and defenseless." I grabbed his hand and pulled him forward. Once he was off balance, I kicked his trailing leg behind his lead foot, tangling his legs together.

The fox gracelessly flopped on the ground with a grunt. He tried to push himself off the ground, but I slammed him back to the dirt with one hand. I dug my claws into his back, drawing just a touch of blood, and leaned next to his ear. "Killing you would be so easy right now."

"You wouldn't dare." Gifford turned his head to glare at me.

I stood up and removed my claws from his back. "My sister seems to love you. So I'll play nice." Before he could move again, I grabbed his foot and dragged him to his mate. Once Lexia could see us, her face lit up with a smile. I continued to drag my prey to my sister, and once we were close together, I lifted the fox by his foot and presented him to her. "I got you a present."

"Oh, you shouldn't have. He's perfect." Lexia clasped her hands together and nearly squealed, her tail wagging back and forth. "Can I keep him?"

I looked down at Gifford. His fur was a mess. Dead leaves, small twigs, and dirt decorated his disheveled fur. And his shocked expression was priceless. "If that's what you want. You can do whatever you want with him. You're an adult." I shrugged as I dropped my sister's abused mate.

"Don't worry, we're going to have lots of fun, you and I." Lexia scooped up the foxkin and whispered in his ear. "Right now, if you would like. A reward for pacifying my sister."

The fox had a wide grin as he wagged his tail. *Have at it, lovebirds. Just please wait until I'm out of earshot. I have no interest in listening to what you're about to do. We aren't that close of a family yet.* The sounds of the two behind me shuffling out of their clothes gave me all the motivation I needed to run back to the village to see if the others had arrived.

I continued running back to the ruined village. I entered the clearing and saw a dozen beastkin standing in front of the group I was traveling with. Daric was in front, hand on his sword hilt, standing over Anna, who was kneeling on the ground. Her hand was flat against the ground, and her eyes were closed. *You have got to be kidding me.*

I sprinted towards my charges.

13

MAKE ME

"Leave her alone." Daric tightened his grip on his sword.

"No magic." The foremost beastkin, a black bear, spoke in a deep, rumbly voice. He stood head and shoulders taller than any of the other beastkin surrounding him, and they were all around the same height as Silver. While his clothes looked heavily abused, like all the beastkins' here, they almost looked too small for his massive body and limbs. "I don't know what you're planning on doing here, but no funny business."

He's a primal beastkin. This is about to get violent, isn't it?

"We aren't doing anything funny. There's a blood anchor here. Can't you feel it?" Penny threw her arms wide as she presented the surrounding area. "Our mission was to find it and investigate. Don't get in our way." I watched Penny draw in magic.

"I'm not doing anything dangerous," Anna said as she continued to dig through her pack.

"I think you made that up. There is no such thing as a blood anchor." The bearkin crossed his hulking arms. "You're here because Lexia permitted it. And..."

I slid to a stop in between Daric and the primal bear beastkin.

"Lexia?" Before I could say anything, he took a few sniffs of the air. "You aren't Lexia."

"No. Wrong sister." I flexed my claws as I bared my fangs. "And you will not touch them."

A female badger beastkin stepped towards me. "Why are you defending them?" Her high-pitched voice caused me to twitch an ear. "You're one of us. Shouldn't you agree with us?"

I glared at the badgerkin. "Because it's my job. And even though I'm a beastkin, that doesn't mean I'll immediately agree with everything you say." I pointed a sharp claw towards the woman, and she flinched backwards. I turned back to the bear. "And as for you, there are such things as blood anchors. If this lady says there's one here, I believe her."

The black bear didn't move.

I turned around to face the group and saw a grin on Penny's face, so I stepped towards her and pointed my clawed finger inches from her face. "Stop! You don't need to provoke them. We're their guests. Play. Nice!"

The magic Penny was holding dissipated as she released it. "Fine. The sooner we get this done, the sooner we can go home." She turned on her heel and walked away.

The beastkin didn't start walking. I turned to look behind me and saw the bear beastkin staring me down. My instincts knew what was coming next. I could see it, too.

"You aren't Lexia. You aren't in charge. What makes you think you can tell me what to do?" He took a step towards me and held his arms out wide. "You smell wrong. You're an outsider like them. You should leave."

I grinned. "Make me."

The bear's roar nearly deafened me.

I'm going to bury you. A constant ringing sound droned in my ears as he led with a wide swing of his left arm, claws extended. *Going for blood? Good! Hopefully he has more fight in him than my sister's mate.* I ducked the obvious attack and struck the back of his hand with my claws. The bear stepped back as he inspected the blood that soaked his fur.

"You will pay for that," he growled.

"Make me." *He is way too eager to attack. I can just fight defensively and counterattack each time he swings.*

The bear stomped towards me. I could feel the ground shake slightly with each step. He lowered his right hand, and with an upward slashing motion, reached for me. I sidestepped to my left to dodge his attack, then took a step forward.

My opponent must have learned his lesson about overcommitting to an attack, because he swung his right arm towards me.

As his arm collided with my torso, I wrapped my arms around his barrel-like forearm and dug my toe-claws into the ground.

The bearkin's eyes went wide as I stopped his arm. He growled as he brought his other hand around towards my face. I turned and pulled his arm over my shoulder. A wail of pain from the bear followed the sickening snap of his elbow dislocating behind my head.

I released his arm and ducked around to grab his leg. My opponent cradled his disfigured arm as he continued to scream.

"Stop screaming!" I shouted as I grabbed his leg and pulled it out from under him.

The bear landed on his back with a hefty thump and a grunt. I jumped onto his chest and dug my claws into his thick black, and surprisingly soft, fur. We growled at each other, and the bear slammed his left hand into my hip. The attack dislodged me from him, and my claws took some flesh and fur with them as I tumbled away.

I groaned as my hip burned with pain. To block it out, I slipped into my rage-fueled state. Everything turned red as I limped towards him.

Did he crack my bones with one hit? If my hip bone was cracked, I wouldn't be standing right now. Either way, I can't let him hit me again. That hurt! Time to make him hurt.

I ran towards the bear beastkin, but as I did, a figure jumped between us. Daric held his sword in his hands. "Stop, both of you. You're both hurt, and this isn't necessary." Daric turned his back to me as he watched the bear slowly prop himself up on his good elbow. "We aren't here to hurt anyone. We're here to help save the world from the demon king."

"You're making that up," the bear said in between deep breaths. "There's no such thing as the demon king."

"There is, and—"

I grabbed Daric's shoulders while he was speaking and flipped him over my head. "Out of the way, idiot!" As Daric landed on the ground, I pointed a finger at him. "Stay out of this. That was your only warning." I turned to the bear that was still half-lying on the ground. "Have you had enough? Or do I need to beat some more sense into your thick skull?"

Do you want to spill his blood? Do you want to smell it? To taste it? Spill it and you can do whatever your heart desires with it, a velvety voice whispered in my mind.

"Who said that?" I rapidly turned around, looking for the source of the voice.

"You need to stop, Lucia," Anna said as she stood up, holding a rolled piece of paper. "What's gotten into you?"

"Shut up!" I bared my fangs at Anna, who flinched at the sight of them. I tried to focus on my ears, looking for who was telling me to kill. "We aren't alone."

Everyone started looking around, and the rest of my team drew their weapons. Daric stood up while another beastkin went to the aid of the wounded bearkin.

"Well, you're no fun," the voice spoke again, although this time it sounded more real.

Above me? I looked up and regretted it immediately.

A woman with unnaturally white, blemish-free skin hovered in the air, carried by two massive bat-like wings. Jet-black hair cascaded from her head and framed her beguiling face. A thin whip-like tail lazily wandered back and forth behind her. She didn't care about her lack of modesty as she floated in midair. It was as if she wanted everyone to look.

My instincts screamed at me to both run and kill her as my vision returned to normal.

"Oh no. She's hot!" Daric blurted out.

I rolled my eyes and stomped on his foot with everything I had.

"Ow. Why did you do that?"

"Shut up. We don't have time for your antics," I growled at Daric and pointed at the flying woman. "That's a demon."

"Oh," Daric said as he went back to staring.

The woman floated down lightly but stayed well out of reach of any melee weapons. She laughed as she focused on me. The sound wiped out all desire I had to butcher her. "Oh my, a beastkin who already knows what I am. Interesting." Her sultry voice trailed as she flapped her wings. "You had my curiosity before, but now you have my attention. I like you. I want you. I need you." Her voice dropped low, filled with unmistakable lust.

I extended my claws and took my combat stance. "Anna, now would be a good time for that angel of yours."

"I can't." Panic filled Anna's voice. "The blood anchor is blocking any attempt at magic I try."

The demon turned and started circling around me. "Of course not. If you just summon a demon, it would happily permit such magic. Summoning angels, yuck. A bunch of celibate buzz kills, if you ask me. No, you may not ask them to join our little meet-and-greet." The demon pouted her perfectly full lips as she crossed her arms under her large breasts. "But back to you, my future pet." She gave me a wicked grin that sent shivers down my spine. "Your bloodlust is intoxicating. I want to play a little game with you. Lose, and I add you to my collection. Win?" Her grin grew wider. "Well, nobody ever wins."

I couldn't reply. With my tail tucked firmly between my legs, I stood staring at the demon.

A stream of fire flew towards the demon. The demon rolled, barely dodging as she dropped a short distance before re-extending her wings.

"What are you all waiting for? Kill the sin of lust," Penny shouted as she held an orb of fire inches above her hand.

My instincts took over. I turned tail and ran. The demon's laugh, her grin, and the fire overwhelmed my logical faculties. One desire filled my mind as I ran. *I have to get out of here. Why me?*

"Why you little..." The sin of lust's screech filled the air. "Fine, you want to play too? So be it." As her voice trailed off, I turned back to look to see which way she was going. I watched her body shimmer, turn translucent, and then disappear.

My panic grew exponentially along with my eyes. *Invisibility? No, no, no, nonono.* I dropped to all fours and sprinted as fast as I could. As I ran, a familiar pair came into view, directly in front of me. *Lexia!* I sprinted for my sister, who froze as she turned away from her lover. To make sure I didn't hurt her, I slowed down a bit before I tackled her.

Lexia and I rolled together as I held my sister close. We came to a stop, and I clutched my sister close as I stood her up. "We have to go. There's a demon around and it just turned invisible and Penny is throwing fire and, and, and—" My mind sputtered, and I couldn't find any more words.

Lexia held my head in her hands. "Slow down. You said a demon?" I nodded. "What's a demon? Is it a threat?"

"Yes, and she could be anywhere. She's invisible and she wants me and she said she has a collection and Penny threw fire at her and Penny is holding a ball of fire—" More words poured from my mouth as I grabbed Lexia's hand and tried to pull her away from the village.

Lexia pulled her hand through mine. "No, we will stay and fight. I won't leave anyone behind."

"Why are you scared of fire?" Gifford jogged up to us.

"I just am. I always have been." My eyes darted around, looking for the sin. I also flicked my ears around, scanning for any sign that she had followed me.

"No, you haven't." Lexia approached me slowly. The concern on her face was obvious. "Stay with me. I'll protect you. Let's show this demon why you don't mess with my pack." She grinned as she grabbed my hand and pulled me back towards the village.

I easily kept up with my sister, even though I didn't want to follow her. There was no sign of the sin of lust as we approached the group of beastkin. The bear beastkin was still cradling his dislocated elbow as we stopped in front of them. He stared at the ground, avoiding eye contact with me. Daric and the others from my group all had their weapons drawn and were watching the sky for the demon. The other beastkin were on edge as their heads swiveled too.

I felt a pair of hands on my shoulders. "Got you," the sin of lust whispered in my ear.

I screamed and tried to leap forward. Even though I slipped from her hands easily, something caught my foot, and I tripped. I rolled over and saw a black-scaled tail wrapped around my ankle. The demoness laughed and flapped her wings.

I felt myself being pulled, so I dug my claws into the ground. Unfortunately for me, my claws shredded the soft earth, providing very little resistance. Since I couldn't hold her back, I growled and tried to slash at her tail. She lifted me off the ground and tugged at me. My attack missed horribly.

"Don't move!" Lexia shouted.

I leaned back as a horizontal blade of ice flew towards me and the sin of lust. A sudden pull tried to lift me to over the blade, but the blade flew right over me.

Suddenly, instead of hanging in the air, I was plummeting to the ground.

It wasn't a long fall, and I caught myself and rolled to my feet. The last third of the scaled tail hit the ground next to me.

"Why you—" the sin shouted. "This isn't over." Her body turned translucent and disappeared again. But the burning look in her eyes as she glared at me seemed to stay longer than the rest of her.

Lexia ran over to me. "Are you alright? You're not hurt, are you?"

I shook my head. "No, I'm fine. And..."—my cheeks burned—"thanks for saving me."

Lexia grinned. "You're my sister. Of course I'd save you. I won't lose you again. Never."

My heart beat faster. I could feel my inner wolf glaring at me. *Okay, maybe you're right.* My inner wolf had rarely been wrong before. *Having a sister could be nice. Especially since she's a really cool ice mage. I have a cool ice mage for a sister. I think I can get used to that.*

A smile spread across my lips as I followed Lexia and Gifford towards everyone else again.

14

DISTRACTIBLE SISTERS

"What happened to you, Victor?" Lexia asked as she raised an eyebrow.

The bear shuffled on his feet for a moment. "Your sister."

My sister pulled me close and hugged me with one arm. "Good girl." I wagged my tail. "So, what do we do about the demon?" She straightened up and released me from her hug.

"That was really a demon?" Victor looked at the other eleven beastkin flanking him. "I don't know. She was there one moment and not there the next. Like it was magic."

"Of course it was magic. Are you slow in the head?" Penny barked.

"Easy, Penny," Mark said. "Focus on the real danger."

Lexia shot Penny a glare. "Whatever Victor lacks in brains, he more than makes up for it in loyalty and strength." She turned her glare towards me. "Nice friends."

I turned to hear the members of my group running up to us. "There's two of her?" Daric asked as he stumbled mid-stride. He caught himself and stopped before he toppled to the ground. "She's..."

I growled at him as I flattened my ears and flexed my claws. *Don't you say it.*

Daric clamped his mouth shut. Silver shook his head as he stepped to the lead.

Anna let out a sigh and slumped her shoulders. "She's gone. It's safe."

"How did she run away?" Mark asked as he stood in the back. "How did she turn invisible?"

"Illusion magic." Penny walked up, still holding her ball of fire.

Alarms rang out in my head as I tried to turn and run. I ran right into Gifford, and we both tumbled to the ground in a heap of tangled limbs. A slight gust of wind blew past me towards my sister. I turned to look and watched Penny's ball of fire become encapsulated by a sphere of ice and snuffed out. My instincts calmed down, letting me work to untie myself from my sister's mate.

"Get rid of that," my sister said, her voice carrying with it a slight rumble of a growl. She glowed slightly. *Lexia's magic is so much more powerful than mine. I'm glad she can defend herself.* "I take it you're Penny. Don't scare my sister like that again."

"Who are you? You know my name, yet I don't know yours. Manners would dictate that you introduce yourself." Penny glared at Lexia. "You say you're her sister, but she didn't tell us she had a sister."

I lifted Gifford up and smoothed out my skirt. "Because I didn't know she was still alive. I thought she was dead, like everyone else from my village."

"Is this your village?" Golditress squeaked from behind Silver.

"Yes, it's where we were born," my sister answered. "And since I'm in charge here, you will tell me what you're doing with my sister." She crossed her arms as she glared at Penny.

"We're here to save the world," Daric chimed in while raising his hand.

I stepped in between my sister and Penny. "Lexia, please listen to me. I know what I'm about to say is strange, but we're simply doing our job. There are these things called blood anchors. They're somehow linked to the summoning of the demon king. I know only a few of the specifics, but that's why Anna here is researching them." I pointed towards Anna. "She's a conjuration magic specialist. And also someone who was at the same orphanage I was when the humans took me in."

Lexia relaxed as she listened to me. While I gauged what she was thinking, Silver cleared his throat. "How about we do proper introductions? My name is Silverlipankeltan. But you may call me Silver." He gave a deep bow, and he waved towards Dinar as I stepped to the side.

"My name is Dinar. Your fur is just as beautiful as your sister's." Dinar rubbed the back of her bald head as she deflected her gaze. "I wish my hair had been half as beautiful as yours." *What is she talking about? I guess I haven't seen her shave her head this entire time we have been together. But how did she lose all her hair and why doesn't it grow back?*

Daric snapped his hand back into the air. "I'm Daric and I'm a..." He looked at me as I glared at him. He had a terrified look on his face before he eventually came to his senses. "I'm the leader of this group." *Good, he's learning.* He pointed to Mark. "This is my best friend, Mark. That's Golditress, or Goldy for short. You know Penny. And finally, we have Anna, our independent specialist." Daric pointed to each person as he introduced them.

"My name is Lexia. I'm Lucia's sister. This is my mate, Gifford," Lexia said curtly. Daric deflated at the mention of Gifford being my sister's mate. "Who is this demon king you mentioned? And what does it mean that there was a demon here? I don't see this 'blood anchor.' Where is it?"

"It seems we have a lot to talk about," Anna said under her breath. "How about we set up some place to stay, and you join us just before nightfall so we can talk about the situation in a more professional way?" She smiled and put on a friendly face.

"Fine," my sister answered abruptly. "Find a suitable place on your own. Just don't get in our way."

"You don't by chance have any food you can spare, do you?" Dinar looked up at us with her pleading gray eyes.

Lexia turned around and grabbed Gifford's arm before starting to walk away. "Get your own."

I stepped in front of my sister. "Maybe you can share some. This area doesn't have much to spare. Don't be too harsh on them. That's why they hired me, to get food for them." Lexia's face never shifted as she glared at me.

I sighed as I lowered my volume so Mr. Goody-Two-Shoes didn't hear me. "It isn't like you earned yours all that fairly either. You took it from the humans. The least you can do is share it. I can help you get more after we leave and find a place with more wildlife."

The surprise on my sister's face was expected. "How did you know?" Her voice wasn't as quiet as mine.

"Shh." I put a finger to her lips. "When you gave me that heart. I take pride in my ability to know what I'm eating simply by the taste alone." I winked and smiled. "But seriously, we passed through the town you raided."

Gifford tensed up as he flexed his claws. *Are you seriously going to try that again?* Lexia placed a hand on his chest and pushed him back slightly. "Fine, but come with me. We need to explain the whole situation to you."

"That's fine." I sighed. "Just give them enough for today. They have some food left for tomorrow morning."

Lexia ordered the other beastkin that were standing there speechless to give them a single day's ration and to leave them alone. After Golditress handed me my pack, I followed my sister back to the house she claimed was our old home. Gifford excused himself to assist others with some tasks. After an uncomfortably long kiss, they parted, Gifford on his own and Lexia with me.

We walked through the house where I would be sleeping. I placed my stuff on the ground near the doorway. The room had two windows, one on each exterior wall. There weren't any shutters holding back the light from the setting sun. There was a broken dresser with moth-eaten clothes spread around the area. A pair of beds remained in the room, but only one was in a usable state. The other had collapsed and looked like something had torn apart the grass-filled mattress.

We spent a few moments cleaning the dust and ash from the bed before Lexia jumped onto it and sat down, her legs out to her side. She patted the space in front of her. "Come on, hop up. We can talk here." With a little less enthusiasm than her, I climbed onto the bed and sat like her. "Everything okay? You've been favoring your right hip this entire time."

I flattened my ears and curled my tail around my waist. "The guy whose arm I broke. Victor, I think you said his name was." My sister nodded. "He got a good hit on me. I think the bone may be a bit cracked. But it isn't anything to worry about. I'll be fine in the morning. My recovery will see to that."

"Your what?" Lexia's ears flicked forward as she sat straight up.

"My recovery aptitude..." I eyed my sister cautiously. "The oracle stone I used to learn my name told me I had it, along with my physical aptitude."

My sister's tail fell to the bed limply. "You forgot your name?"

I hugged my tail to my chest. "I forgot everything. It even took a couple of days to walk comfortably." *I know it's a half-lie, but I can't break her heart by telling her the whole truth.* "These last almost eleven years have been difficult, to say the least. Humans don't know much about beastkin. There was one person who had any idea about what I am. He pulled all my teeth out and then was murdered around the time a demon rampaged in the capital city."

Tears pooled in Lexia's eyes. "I'm so sorry that happened to you. At least your teething was handled correctly."

"Correctly?" Lexia flinched back from my volume. "Can you even conceive the pain I felt when they pulled all of my teeth out? That was the most excruciating moment of my life."

My sister flattened her ears. "They didn't use opopa oil?"

I twitched my ears. "What oil?"

"Opopa oil. You grind up and soak opopa stems, then boil off the water. It's a powerful, highly addictive oil that makes it so you can't feel any pain. We only use it in emergencies and when a primal beastkin's teeth come in."

My eyes twitched as my sister told me about this miracle painkiller.

My jaw hurt, and I noticed how much I was clenching it. "You knowingly give a highly addictive substance to children, a substance the rest of the world doesn't know about?"

Lexia tilted her head as she stared at me with wide eyes. "You aren't allowed to swallow it." *Because that makes it alright.* "It sometimes doesn't have any effect on a beastkin child, like it doesn't affect elves and dwarves. Any human who ingests it suffocates to death. If they put it on their skin, the area will swell up and tiny red bumps cover their body. It's incredibly painful for them. Only beastkin can smell it, and trust me, one whiff and you will never want to be near the stuff again." She made a show of shivering.

I blinked several times as we sat across from each other in silence. Once my brain caught up with the information my sister had told me, I shook my head. "So you're telling me there's a plant that contains an oil that makes it so some beastkin won't feel pain." My sister nodded. "It doesn't affect elves and dwarves, while humans are deathly allergic to it."

"I don't know what allergic means, but it sounds bad, so sure." Lexia shrugged. "It is one of our race's secrets."

I flattened my ears and bared my teeth. "Maybe you shouldn't keep that one to yourselves."

My sister flicked my nose. "Don't do that to your older sister." I rubbed my nose to get rid of the tickling sensation. "I'm not responsible for everything the entire beastkin race does. It's unfortunate that this secret caused you to suffer. But what would telling the rest of the world about it do? Nothing, so we keep it to ourselves. Elves and dwarves have their magic, orcs have their strength, goblins reproduce faster than rabbits, and humans have..." It looked like my sister's brain came to a crashing halt as she stared past me for a few moments. I waited patiently for her brain to reengage. "I don't know what humans have. What do humans have?"

I scratched my head as I thought about her question. "I guess nothing special. Some can cast magic, some of them are strong, some have more kids than sense, and they are rather fearful. But I see what you're saying. Each race has something over the others. We have our sharper senses and instincts."

"It's a bit more complicated than that, but yeah."

Her smile caused me to wag my tail. "But I saw you use magic. Is that not normal for a beastkin? Because I can use magic too."

Lexia squealed as she clapped her hands and rose to her knees. Her tail wagged vigorously behind her as she leaned forward. "My sister can use magic too? Let me see, let me see."

I couldn't watch my sister's display and not smile as I gathered up a small amount of magic into my hand. I coated my claws in ice and extended them slightly. My claws shimmered in the light coming from the window. Lexia's eyes glowed as she stared at my claws, breathless.

"Now that I've shown you mine, show me yours." I grinned as I dispersed the ice and released the magic.

"That's so cute."

Cute? That's literally an implement for killing. I crossed my arms and pouted at my sister's judgment.

"Don't be too hard on yourself. Just being able to use magic as a beastkin is a tremendous victory. Now watch this."

A fine fog escaped my lips as I exhaled. Even though the moisture in the air quickly condensed, I never felt even the slightest chill as my sister continued to drop the temperature in the room. Soon everything in the room was obscured by a thick fog that slowly descended to the floor, coating everything along the way in glimmering ice. Lexia sat with her eyes closed and her arms outstretched, glowing brightly from the magic she manipulated.

This is so not fair! She can use this level of magic. She's prettier than me, she has more powerful magic, and she's the leader of this group of people. Okay, maybe I don't care about that last one.

I continued to pout as I watched my sister flaunt her magical ability. She opened her eyes and curled the left side of her lip in a playful grin. She pulled her hands into fists, and I could hear the ice shift. The ice resting on the floor gathered together and formed into a large icy clawed hand. In a swift motion, Lexia clasped her hands together in front of her. The large hand pulled the ice in the surrounding area towards me and wrapped it around me.

"Gotcha." Lexia giggled as she held her magic.

Alright, two can play this game. "That's cute." I grinned and grabbed the thumb of the icy construct holding me. With a gentle shove, I broke the thumb off with a satisfying crack.

Lexia screamed in surprise and pain as she brought a hand to her forehead.

"Hurts, doesn't it?"

Lexia pouted and stared at me. "Cheater."

"I know. Mom made sure I was well aware of what it felt like when someone overpowered my magic." I looked down at the construct still holding me in place. *She's still holding it together. Impressive. I would have lost it if I could make anything even remotely this complex.* "While the cold doesn't bother me, do you mind?" I nodded to my restraints. *There isn't any need to hurt her anymore.*

The ice crumbled into a cloud of fine dust and settled around me. With a bit of magic, I pushed the ice off the bed.

"Who is this person you call Mom?" Lexia relaxed as she helped disperse the ice from the bed. "You know Mom is dead, right?"

I sighed. "I told you I was adopted. Similar to the people whom you said took care of you, a single woman decided that she cared enough about me that she saw me as her own child. It's a human thing." *Here I go, telling her my whole life's story.* "It all started when the orcs tied me up and put me in a cage..."

15

FIRE AND ICE

I stared at my still weeping sister. *She cried almost constantly throughout my story. How does she have any tears left?* She continued sobbing on my shoulder. I reached the end of my story at the part where I set off with the group of knights and Daric. *I still can't see him as a knight.*

Lexia leaned back, wiping her nose on her arm.

"It's alright, I think I turned out okay. For the most part. If you think about things generally." *Okay, maybe I have issues. Who doesn't?*

Lexia snorted as she giggled. "You have a strange sense of humor. Who would have thought we would turn out so different?"

I wrapped my arm around her shoulders and lifted her chin to stare into her eyes. "Those orcs attacking our village radically changed everything. There's no guarantee that we would have been similar if they hadn't. Because we both survived, by whatever miracle, we can have our chance at life." I shrugged. "Besides, just because I'm extremely violent, that doesn't mean I look for reasons to hurt people. I just enjoy every opportunity people give me."

The two of us stared at each other in silence for a moment before breaking out in laughter. Falling away from each other and rolling around, we continued laughing until it became difficult to breathe.

We ended up sprawled out on the bed, panting. I looked out the window. The sun had set some time ago, and the light from the three moons disrupted the darkness of the night.

"Uh, weren't we supposed to talk with the others?" I asked as I sat up halfway.

Lexia took a deep breath. She turned to lie on her side. "Yes, why?" I pointed to the window. Lexia turned and looked. "Oh, I guess we better get going then," she said as she shoved herself off the bed. I jumped off the bed and followed behind her.

We walked outside to look for Anna and the rest. It was easy to find them near the edge of town because they were the only ones that lit a campfire and huddled close to it in a half-burned-down single-story building. What little remained of the roof looked stable enough even with the fire damage.

"Who put out the fires? Shouldn't all the buildings have burned to the ground?" I asked absentmindedly.

"The others who found me helped bury the dead. The fires were already out when we got here. After the orcs were long gone," Lexia said softly. "When some of the bodies were unaccounted for, yours included, we thought that orcs took them to eat."

I shivered. *That's an unsettling thought. How long until they decided I was food, not breeding stock? But I don't remember them taking bodies.*

Our walk turned even quieter after such a morbid statement. Our silent steps led us to the campfire that my group had made. I stood outside the remnants of the collapsed wall.

Lexia noticed my hesitation, and I saw that she was about to snuff out their fire with her magic. "Don't. They need the fire to stay warm. I'm fine right here."

My sister frowned. "I meant to ask, but I got distracted. What happened? Why are you so scared of fire?"

"I don't actually know. Ever since I woke up without my memories, every time I've seen fire, I've felt this overwhelming fear. I can handle campfires to some degree so long as I can see them. But fire magic is the worst." I scratched my toe-claw through the dirt as I folded my hands in front of me. "It was really bad at first, and I just can't get a handle on it. I know it's a stupid thing to be afraid of."

Lexia stepped up and hugged me. "Don't worry about it. You want to sit out here while we talk?" she asked in a playfully soft tone.

I flattened my ears. "Don't treat me like a child. We're the same age."

"Yes, but I need to take care of my little sister." Lexia gave me a wink. "Besides, I can't stand the sight of bugs." I tried and failed to hold back my laughter. "Hey! You don't know what it's like waking up covered in biting ants." My sister released me and made a show of shivering.

I smiled. "I know what you're doing."

Lexia's ear perked up. "You do?"

"Yes, and I appreciate you trying to make me feel better." I wrapped my arm around my sister's shoulders. "Let's not keep our audience in suspense. They wanted to talk to us, after all." I waved to the onlookers, who stared at us, mouths agape.

The two of us giggled as we sat down on a section of the wall that made convenient seats for us. Dinar sat closest to the fire, shivering. *Is it that cold? I guess it's the middle of the ice season, we're a good distance north, and it's very late. I'm surprised they're all still up.*

Penny subtly glowed with magic as she held her hands towards the fire. "I see you two are getting along well."

"What, jealous?" I asked as I held my sister closer.

"No," Penny whispered as she averted her gaze. *You want me to believe that?*

"I guess since they're sisters, it's bound to happen. At least they aren't tearing each other's throats out." Dinar gave me a wink. "But you two are late. We thought you weren't coming."

I held up a hand to pause the conversation. *He'd better not bring up the whole reincarnated bit before I can talk to him about it in private.* "Before we continue, a rule needs to be instated." I glared at Daric and bared my fangs. "Daric, I don't want to hear a word out of you unless I ask you a question directly. And when I do, you answer that question only. No side thoughts, no ideas, nothing. The adults are talking. Is that clear?"

"But, but…" Daric's eyes went wide.

"Is that clear?" I growled as I stood up and flexed my claws.

Daric flinched and nodded sheepishly.

I sat back down. "Good. You need to remind me what we're talking about." I crossed my legs, leaned forward, and propped my head with my hands.

"We were going to talk about the blood anchor and the appearance of a sin of lust," Anna said, poking at the ground with a stick as she sat on a flat rock. It looked like she was drawing something, but I couldn't get a good look at it from my position.

Anna turned her head to look at Lexia. "First, I want to know: why did you believe me when the other beastkin didn't?"

Lexia smiled as she gave me a quick glance. "That's easy. My sister believes you, so I do too."

"So your sister tells you anything and you immediately believe her?" Penny pinched the bridge of her nose and groaned. "You are either stupid or naïve. Maybe both."

It was Lexia's turn to stand up and flex her claws. "Say that again and I will tear you apart. What do you know of my sister?"

Penny stood up and balled her hands into fists. "Not much, but still likely more than you would after having known her for less than a day." Penny's tone was getting on my nerves.

Lexia growled as I watched her start to channel magic into her hands. "You are an ignorant and selfish little elf. Did Mommy and Daddy not love you enough when you were little? Did you not meet their expectations for you?"

Penny's body exploded in flames that circled around her. Everyone jumped back from the conflagration. She let out a primal scream as she threw her arms out. Two streams of flames flew towards my sister and me. Panic overwhelmed me, and I leaned back and took cover behind a small section of the remnants of a half-burned-down wall. I poked my head out to see that my sister had never moved from her spot. Instead, a wall of ice had intercepted the fiery magic.

While the fire tried to melt a hole through the wall, Lexia took a step to the side and flicked her wrist. An ice spike the size of my arm materialized and headed straight for Penny.

Penny's eyes went wide as she tried to shift one of her flame beams to intercept the icy spear. My sister's projectile moved too fast for Penny to deal with. But instead of embedding itself in her chest, it protruded from Daric's left arm.

He willingly stepped in the way of my sister's attack?

I could see the pain in his eyes as he nodded towards me. "Deal with Lexia. I'll get Penny!" Daric shouted as he turned and hugged the flame-cloaked mage.

So he is capable of action. We need to put an end to this fighting. Once the streams of fire disappeared, I vaulted over my cover and grabbed my sister by the back of her neck. As gently as I could, I pulled her backwards. Lexia flailed her arms as she stumbled, about to trip over our improvised seats.

Instead of catching her, I ran to where she was going to land and cushioned her head as she fell.

My sister grunted as her back hit the ground while I safely cradled her head in my hands. "What are you doing?" Lexia asked as she stared up at me.

"I told you, it's my job to protect them. But I don't want you to get hurt, either," I said as I set her head on the ground. "I think it's time for a time-out."

"She started it." Lexia bared her teeth at me as she growled.

I placed my foot on her chest. "I know, and I don't care. Now stop acting like a child."

"But I'm your sister. You should be taking my side." My sister dug her claws into the ground at her sides.

I flattened my ears. "This isn't about who's right or wrong. This is about you two fighting. You need to stop it. Please don't make me choose between my job and promise or my sister."

Lexia deflated and flattened her ears as she turned to look away from me. She sat there for a moment. As she lay sulking, I could hear Penny complaining just as much as my sister did. The others were using the tactics of peer pressure and political ramifications to get her to at least act more civilized. I wasn't that concerned with their conversation as I stood over my sister.

117

I removed my foot from her chest and kneeled on the ground next to her.

"I'm sorry," Lexia whispered, still looking away from me. "I'll try to be more courteous to your friends."

I turned to look at the group behind me and saw that everyone except for Daric stood between Penny and my sister. With a slight grin, I turned back to my sister. "I wouldn't call them friends just yet." I grabbed my sister's hand. "But thanks anyway." *Maybe I should cheer her up.* "I could take you to meet my adoptive mother one day. Would you like that?"

Lexia turned to give me a weak smile. "Sure, maybe. Do you think she'll accept me as your sister?" She sat up and looked at me with shimmering eyes.

"Absolutely. Now let's get you off the ground and out of the dirt." *She really is easily distracted.* I stood up and pulled my sister to her feet. I helped brush off her back as she cleaned her tail using the same ice magic trick I used when a bath wasn't an option. *Great minds do think alike.* I grinned as I watched her.

My sister and I turned to watch Anna and Dinar walking towards us. "I think it's best for us to talk to you and leave Penny out of it. She needs some time to calm down. But unfortunately, this conversation can't wait." Anna quickly glanced back at Penny and then just as quickly returned her attention to us.

"You said that you're in charge here." Dinar walked to Lexia's side. "I suggest we find a quiet corner to talk away from your people too. This might be too much for them to handle."

"There's something else I want to talk to you about, but it concerns all of you," Lexia said as she looked down at the short elf girl. "It's about the coming war."

Dinar tensed up as she inhaled sharply. I stepped between them. "You three can talk about blood anchors and the demon over there." I pointed to a fallen tree near the edge of the surrounding forest. "I'll be back. Daric and I need to talk first." My sister gave me a concerned look. "Don't worry, I'll be back before you can finish talking about the blood anchors. Then we can talk about the favor you asked me for." I gave her my best smile.

My sister smiled back. "Okay," she said as she walked with Anna and Dinar to the place I'd pointed out. Anna didn't wait until they reached the spot before starting to talk.

I ignored them as I turned to see Penny storming off with Golditress and Daric staring at her with Mark and Silver behind him, a hand on each shoulder.

I sighed as I stepped towards the guys. *Why does my life have to be so complicated?*

16

PAST AND PRESENT DEMONS

"Is she going to calm down?" I asked as I stepped behind the three guys, standing as far away from the campfire as I could. *It'll make this mission much harder if I have to constantly watch my back for when she does something stupid.*

"Probably. She just needs some time alone." Silver was the first to turn around. "Whatever your sister said must have really gotten to her."

The other two turned to face me. Mark tied off a bandage around Daric's arm where my sister had stabbed with her ice. It was still bleeding, but a lot less than I would have guessed.

"I've never seen her act like that. Usually she's much more in control." Mark scratched the back of his head as he looked at the ground.

I raised an eyebrow at Mark. "And how long have you known her?"

"We've only just started working together this last season. But she frequently visited Midas and me," Daric said in a distracted tone. "She only talked to Midas, but never while I was around."

"So why is she here?" I crossed my arms and looked where I could hear her walking. *She's still walking away from us, so there isn't any chance of her barging in on our conversation.*

"She needs money," Silver said. Before I could thank him for stating the obvious, he held up his hand. "She has, as she put it, an 'insurmountable gambling debt.' That likely caused tension between her and her parents, based off what Lexia said. Also, if she doesn't make her payments on time, horrible people will come to do unspeakable things to her, by her words."

All of us stared at Silver, awestruck. "She told you this? When?" I asked.

Silver shrugged his shoulders. "She told Midas, and I just happened to be in the room at the same time. Why she got so violent over your sister's taunting about her family? I have no idea. Probably because it hit too close to home."

So we have a fire mage with parental issues and debt collectors that have her terrified. Why couldn't she be normal?

I nodded as I looked at the confusion on Daric's face. *So he wasn't in the room when that conversation happened.* "She must be desperate if she didn't care that you were in the room," I said. *But wait a moment. She's a powerful magic user.* "Who would have her that scared?" I asked absentmindedly.

"Don't know." Silver waved to the seats everyone was using before I arrived. "But it's rude to talk about a lady behind her back. She's more than able to explain her situation should she want to." Silver glared at Daric, who looked like he was about to say something. "Don't push her. Sensitive subjects should be treated as such." Daric deflated as he sat down.

"I'm going to keep standing back here, if you don't mind," I said as I eyed the campfire. "But there's something I need to talk to you about, Daric. It's about my sister."

"What is it?" Daric glanced up at me. "I take it you haven't told her you're reincarnated?"

"And I won't," I answered as I leaned up against a wall.

"Why?" Daric asked. Mark and Silver exchanged a look, then made themselves look busy with anything that could get them out of the conversation yet not require them to leave. "You aren't really her sister. You should tell her that. She deserves to know."

I sighed. "All that would do is destroy her. You didn't see the look in her eyes when she recognized me. She knew who I was the moment she saw me, even though we've been separated for over ten years."

"But you aren't really Lucia." Daric stood up and took a step towards me. "Just like I'm not really Daric. It's just easier to use that name in this world because that's what the oracle stone uses. My real name is—"

"Stop." I held up my hand. "I'm not like you. I didn't come to this world with all my memories intact. I told you that." My tail flicked back and forth as I stood up straight. "Whoever I was before doesn't matter anymore. That was probably The Voice's intent. Maybe it wanted to strip away most of my memories of myself so I could accept this life's identity. And I have. I am Lucia. Nobody else. I accepted that years ago, and if that means I have a sister who misses me, then I will be the sister she never got to have. Half of me missed her too. So don't tell her about it."

"I never thought of it like that," Daric whispered.

"And my sister has asked for my help." I threw my arms out wide. "She wants my help to depose the king of this kingdom. He's inciting the people here to attack our home for food. And I'm going to help her."

Daric's eyes went wide as he mumbled, "That means what we saw in Briarford will happen everywhere else too."

"Yes, Mr. Hero." My tail flicked back and forth even more sharply. "If that happens, that means there will be a war. I don't care what you think, but I don't want to go to war with my people. So if I can prevent it, I will."

"So what are you telling us?" Silver asked as he stared at the campfire.

I closed my eyes and took several deep breaths. Once my emotions were back under control, I opened my eyes and stared at Daric. "I need help. If you don't want to help, that's fine. I get it. But know that if I fail, you'll be fighting a war."

Mark stood up slowly. "And nobody wins if there's a war." His eyes looked distant.

Aren't you a little young to be sounding like you've lived through a war?

Daric punched his palm with his other hand. "We'll help you. Right, guys?" He nodded to the other two. Silver nodded his head while Mark gave me a thumbs-up. "This blood anchor isn't going anywhere. We can come back and study it afterwards. But if I can stop this war, then you better start recognizing me as a real hero." Daric's grin made me want to slam his face into the ground.

"Then you better deliver," I said as I moved to leave. *It still won't help your case, but thanks.* "Get some sleep. And I don't care if you can convince Penny to join us. She can stay here until we get back. Personally, I don't trust her not to burn me in the middle of a pitched battle."

I waved my hand at the boys as I went to see how the other girls were doing with my sister. But while I was walking, I could feel someone behind me watching me. I turned to see Daric staring at my butt again. *Will he ever learn?* I channeled my magic to create a ball of ice and crushed it with one hand.

As the shards of ice drifted to the ground, Daric quickly lowered his hands to his groin and turned away.

Good. He understood the message.

As I approached the second group, it looked like the girls were having a very civilized conversation. Once I got close enough, I was grateful as I listened in.

"Now do you understand what a demon is?" Anna asked with obvious exhaustion in her voice.

"I think so," Lexia said hesitantly. "And these blood anchors are required to create a summoning site for the demon king." She shook her head. "This is a lot to take in."

Anna placed a hand on Lexia's leg. "I know. I've been studying these for years. Expecting you to understand everything in just one conversation is a lot to ask."

"This is much easier to grasp after hearing my sister's story." Lexia put on a smile. "But how do you know there's one here?"

Anna waved her hand towards the buildings. "I've sort of attuned myself to feel their power. Don't worry about what that takes." She shuddered. "That means I just instinctively know which direction the nearest blood anchor is. But I'm wondering if it's the reason there's no wildlife around here."

Dinar scratched her chin. "It's not unreasonable. The air feels different here. Almost sickly."

Lexia's tail curled behind her. "What does all that mean?"

Dinar crossed her arms. "That's probably the cause of your lack of food. This blood anchor. What we don't know is how far its influence extends. Does it grow? How large is the Wild Kingdom in comparison?"

Anna nodded. "Yeah, you've made it sound like the entire kingdom is starving."

"I don't know how large the kingdom is." Lexia hung her head. "I've never seen a map. All I've been told is that this is the easternmost section of the kingdom and it stretches to the coast. Some said they believed it would take half a season to walk to the coast from the capital. But there's still some food found in the kingdom. It's just not enough. And each year, it's been getting worse."

"Are there any other places like this?" Anna asked.

"There's another place where nobody hunts anymore." My sister straightened up, her eyes going almost blank. "A hunter from a wandering pack said, 'South of the Heart of the Kingdom is completely lifeless.' That was two years ago." Her expression returned to normal. "But I still can't understand something. Why do these demons keep coming to our world? What are they hoping to accomplish? What do they want?"

Anna grimaced. "I wish I knew that. But that was something I was hoping to learn from these blood anchors. We know that they want to summon the demon king. But we don't know why."

"From my experience, all demons do is wreak havoc and don't have any long-term goals," I said as I got closer. "Although that sin of lust was different. She made me feel different. The other two sins I encountered didn't make me feel nearly as terrified."

"That's because wrath and gluttony are the baser sins." Anna turned her attention to me without skipping a beat. "If you're dealing with Greed, Lust, Envy, or Pride, you need to worry about any plans they've manufactured." Then Anna's face turned dark. "If you ever see the sin of sloth, there's only one thing you can do. Run."

I froze and curled my tail around my waist. "Why?"

"They're the deadliest of the sins. Not the most powerful, but definitely the deadliest. One book I read said that they're as deadly as a rider in certain situations." *That sounds pretty bad. Noted.* I nodded to Anna and relaxed as she finished her explanation. *Wait, what's a rider?*

"What do you plan to do about the sin of lust now that you know it's here?" Lexia asked. "Our people are struggling with starvation, and the king is sending people to attack your kingdom and raid your settlements for food."

Dinar and Anna went pale and slowly turned their heads towards my sister. "That was the thing I wanted to talk to you about," I interrupted. "I already talked with the guys, and they're alright with helping Lexia with her revolution. They want to prevent a war before it starts. I don't know what to do about the demon, though. But for some reason, she has her sights set on me." I paused as I saw the look in Lexia's eyes. "Yes, Lexia, I will help you."

"A war? Oh no. No, no, no, no." Anna grabbed her head and shook it. "I don't want to get involved in a war. But the news of another blood anchor sounds just as bad."

Dinar glanced at Anna as she broke down before she turned her attention to us. "And how do you plan on dealing with this king? Assassinate him?"

"If it comes to that," Lexia said with a nonchalant wave of her hand. "Originally I'd hoped we would remove him the way it's always done. Through an open challenge, one my sister would defeat him in. Any beastkin can walk up to him and challenge him."

"And what then?" Dinar glared at my sister. "What happens if she fails? What happens if she succeeds?"

Lexia raised an eyebrow as her tail jerked from side to side. "If she succeeds, she can name anyone to be the next king. I just don't know who that will be yet. And I don't want to think about what will happen if she loses."

"You better start thinking, kid," Dinar said as she crossed her arms. "And you better be prepared for whoever Lucia names to be challenged immediately, if I understand your traditions correctly. I'm guessing you aren't the first beastkin to consider taking him down. Yet he's still on his throne. Did you ever consider that?"

Lexia shook her head. Horror slowly crept into her expression. "I never thought about that."

"That doesn't surprise me," Dinar said under her breath. "And what about this assassination attempt? Do you know where he lives? Do you know the layout? What are all of your entrance and exit plans? How do you plan on killing him? And if that fails, what then?"

Where is all this coming from?

"What's wrong with you?" I stepped in between Lexia and Dinar. "She's just trying to make her home a better place to live. But to do that, the leadership of this land needs to change. The boys have already agreed to help." My tail whipped back and forth as my hands rested on my hips.

Dinar sighed. "There's nothing wrong with that." There was a brief pause as her expression slowly shifted to a light smile as she giggled. "I used to make a living from helping idealists like you with stuff like this."

"Wait, does that mean you were an assassin?" I blurted out as my arms and tail fell limp.

"That's one of the nicer things I've been called, but yes." Dinar wrapped her arms around her stomach as she curled up. "I'm asking these questions because all it takes is one mistake and everything you were working for crumbles down around you. Then you have to live the rest of your long life regretting letting down those who you failed and those who died because of your miscalculation. I was trying to leave that part of my life forgotten." Dinar curled up even tighter, and she wouldn't look at us anymore. "But now it looks like that's impossible."

Lexia and I stared, dumbfounded, as Anna wrapped an arm around Dinar.

"Where does this king of yours live?" Dinar's voice broke the silence.

Lexia grimaced. "The Heart of the Kingdom. Just north of your blood anchor."

17

CROSS-CULTURE CONVERSATIONS

Anna stood up with Dinar, her arms wrapped around the elf. "I think it's best we all get some sleep now. While I'm not part of a knight company, I'll help you with the demon. She won't leave you alone that readily. Dealing with her won't be easy, but we'll do it." Anna's eyes bored into me.

I slowly nodded my head. "And there's a blood anchor nearby. We can study that one after we're done helping my sister."

"If everything turns out well," Dinar whispered.

"Thank you so much," Lexia said as she bowed her head. Her tail wagged behind her as she stood up and turned to me. "You have some great friends."

Anna walked away with Dinar under her arms. Dinar kept breathing deeply, but I kept hearing her breath catch ever so slightly. *It sounds like she's trying to keep herself from crying. Everyone has their own demons.* I chuckled at that thought.

"I wouldn't call them all friends yet." I continued to watch the two girls return to their borrowed sleeping arrangements. "But they're getting close."

Lexia stepped in front of me, her eyebrows furled. "Those aren't your friends?" She crossed her arms and flicked her tail back and forth.

"They want to help you and don't ask for anything in return. That sounds like friends to me. Good friends even."

Guilt tugged at my heart as I stared at my sister. "It's just hard for me to let people get close to me." I wrapped my tail around my waist and grabbed it. "For most of my life that I can remember, I've pushed people away. I was afraid that if they got close to me, I would hurt them. I thought I was getting better at it, but I guess some habits are harder to break than others."

My sister's face softened as her tail slowed down to a calm sway. "That's going to make finding you a suitable mate much harder."

"Oh, please don't. I don't know if I'm ready for that." I released my tail and held up my hands defensively.

Lexia rolled her eyes. "Come on. You're fifteen, grow up. I can understand why you don't have one, being around humans like you have, but you're with your people again. It's time you found a mate. Gifford and I have been mates for almost two years now. Don't you want to be a mother?"

My face started heating up. "On some level, yeah. But now isn't really a good time. How can I possibly find love and raise a family when the world is in danger?" I stared at the ground as I lazily scraped a toe-claw through the dirt.

"Do you know that this demon king will arrive soon?" I shook my head. "So don't worry about him until he becomes a problem." Lexia wrapped her arm around my back and pulled me close. "Besides, you're too hard on yourself. Cheer up. I'm sure there's a man out there ready, willing, and able to handle you and all your quirkiness."

"I think we need to keep you away from the demon of lust. At least not before I know you won't let her control you." I smiled as I returned the one-armed hug. "You're probably pretty tired now, aren't you?"

"You're not?" Lexia asked as we started walking back to our old home together, side-by-side.

"It's a perk of the recovery aptitude. I don't need to sleep as much. Unless I nearly die. Then I sleep for a few days straight." I smiled despite the memories of when I had been nearly killed several times.

My sister's pout was adorable. "Why am I so jealous of my sister?"

she whispered. I couldn't hold back my laughter. It wasn't long before Lexia gave up on pouting and joined in laughing.

We got back to our childhood home and made ourselves ready for bed. Gifford was already in bed. According to Lexia, it was the one my parents had used. She joined him and left me to the bed we'd used earlier. I curled up and stared at the wall as I reflected on everything that had happened today.

I have a sister. A sister I've just agreed to help kill a king with. What's wrong with me? I mean, having a sister can be cool. She's nice, understands me, and is trying to get me pregnant. Okay, maybe not all great, but she has a certain social standard that she's known her entire life. I know I turned down the offer to return to the Wild Kingdom, but I've been somewhat happy since. I don't regret that decision. What if I take her back home with me after we help stop this war? Mom would definitely love to meet her. That would mean I'm asking her to abandon everything she knows in order to accompany me. But, at the same time, she'll probably ask me to do the same. What do I do? Do I have to choose between my sister and my mom? Can I make that choice?

My thoughts continued to spiral further out of control until I couldn't stay awake any longer.

I woke up to the sun's rays blinding me. With a heavy sigh, I sat up and stared at nothing. *I'm so glad I didn't have another nightmare. With how worked up I was last night, I wouldn't have been surprised if I had one.* I felt a tingling sensation in my arms and legs. After I slid out of the bed, I did my morning stretches.

It wasn't until my sister opened the door to my room that I realized anyone was awake. *She walks around as quietly as I do.*

"Morning!" My sister bounced into the room. Her tail wagged as she stared at me with eager eyes. "How are you? Did you sleep well?"

I blinked several times as I stared at her, too stunned to continue my morning exercises. With a quick shake of my head, I snapped out of my stupor. "No. I had a lot on my mind." I returned to stretching my back. *She's a lively one in the morning.*

Lexia's tail immediately stopped moving and drooped behind her. "What's wrong?" She inched towards me, holding a hand out towards my head.

I gave a rueful laugh. "Yesterday was quite a day. A day I would never have guessed I'd have."

Lexia tilted her head as she raised an eyebrow. "What do you mean? Yesterday was the best day ever." She paused as she looked to her left. "Okay, tied for the best day ever. Bonding with Gifford was an important day too."

I couldn't suppress a chuckle. "Your optimism is... something."

Now that I'd finished my stretches, I moved on to burning some of my excess energy. I walked up to the center of the room and placed my hands, shoulder-width apart, on the ground. Gracefully, I curled my legs up and extended my tail to help balance myself as I prepared to do some vertical push-ups.

"What are you doing?" Lexia asked as she took a few steps backwards and placed a hand on her heart.

I lowered myself carefully for my first push-up. "It's called exercising," I said as I lifted myself back to the starting position. "It helps burn off excess energy. It has also helped me get as strong as I am. What I'm doing right now isn't really going to make me stronger, though."

Lexia smiled as she crossed her arms and leaned against a wall. "What happens when you don't do this? And how are you burning anything like that?"

I continued my exercises. "It's a figure of speech. Have you ever felt an itch just to do something, anything?" Lexia nodded. "Well, I get that feeling a lot. It gets intense, and sometimes to the point where I've almost hurt people and destroyed a lot of property. This is a way to use up the pent-up energy for something useful. The stronger I get, the longer I can run, and the better I am at fighting—all things that help me be a knight and hunter."

Lexia hummed for a moment. "That makes sense. Is this because you're a primal?"

"Honestly, I don't know. It may have something to do with it, but I've always considered my recovery aptitude the main culprit." After I had warmed up slightly and found my balance, I started doing my vertical push-ups faster. "The beastkin ambassadors I met at the tournament said that it'll become more manageable as I get older. And it is getting easier."

"That's something I still can't understand. Why didn't you come back with Regimes? I know you said you didn't want to start over, but wouldn't everything be better when you're surrounded by your own kind?" My sister's voice caught in her throat.

My vision started getting fuzzy with all the blood rushing to my head. So that I wouldn't embarrass myself, I did one last push-up, but I added a little extra power to lift myself off the ground. While in midair, I twisted and turned to land on my feet with my arms out in front of me and my tail straight back.

Lexia's tail wagged after witnessing my performance.

"It's hard to explain." I looked at the ground, unable to face my sister. "Starting over completely is harder than you might imagine. Can you even consider what you would do if you lost every memory you have? Waking up and knowing nothing about yourself or anything around you?" I faced my sister and scratched the floor with my toe-claws.

Lexia slumped her shoulders as her arms fell to her sides. "I guess that's the hardest concept for me to understand. I don't think I'll ever understand. Every experience, every word, every event is locked in my mind forever. I don't know how to forget." She took a couple of steps towards me. "It hurts to know that I'll never understand what you've gone through. When you shared your story with me, I thought I caught a glimpse of what it was like. But now I know I will never truly understand." A tear slipped from the corner of her eye. "I promise to make things right from now on."

I chuckled as I leaned my back against the wall. "It's funny how similar we are sometimes. But just know that there's nothing to make right." I lowered myself while keeping my back against the wall until my legs were perpendicular to the ground. It looked like I was sitting in a chair, but there wasn't one. My legs were the only thing keeping me from sliding down farther. "So, what's the plan for today?"

My sister stared at me and tilted her head to the side again. "Is this another one of your exercises?" I nodded. Lexia wiped the tear from her eye and sat down on the edge of the bed in front of me. "Since we have you and your group, I think we should leave to figure out how to deal with the king. The questions Dinar asked last night told me how much I don't know and how unprepared for this I really am."

I arched an eyebrow. "So how did you become in charge of this group of potential regicides? And who are they even?"

"We're a bunch of people from a few of the wandering packs that disagree with the decision to go to war. We're a collection of a few hunters and gatherers. But nobody really knows how to fight." *Wait, you planned an insurrection with a bunch of peasants? You were doomed to fail. Dinar was right to question you.* "As for why I'm in charge, it's because I'm the strongest since I have my magic." She glowed and covered herself with ice. It was hard to see her as my sister, as her voice sounded colder than the ice she covered herself with.

"How much do you know about magic?" I asked as my legs tingled slightly as a low burn started in my thighs.

"Only what I've taught myself." Lexia waved her hand, and the ice flew off her body and out the window. Her fur seemed fluffier and had a brighter sheen to it. "Which isn't much."

"How many beastkin know about magic? How common is it?"

"I'm the only beastkin I know of other than you who knows magic." My sister lazily swayed her tail behind her as she leaned forward to rest her head in her hands. "Magic is rare in beastkin, and those who can use it usually can perform so little it isn't worth mentioning."

I grinned. "How would you like to learn about magic from one of the best mages in the world?"

"Really?" Lexia's eyes grew wide. "Who is that?"

"My mom. She's the one who taught me how to use what little magic I can." My sister's enthusiasm was infecting me. I held up my hands playfully. "If you ask really nicely, I can teach you a thing or two. Who knows how much better you could be?"

"You would?" Lexia jumped off the bed and hopped in front of me. Her tail wagged wildly, forcing her hips to sway with the motion. "Please, please, please. Teach me. Whatever you want, I'll get it for you. Do you want to take Victor as your mate? I can convince him for you."

Wasn't he the primal bear from yesterday? He was strong. I shook my head so violently that I almost fell over. "No. Get ahold of yourself, Lucia." I looked up at my sister, who had a wolfish grin, and I realized I'd said my thoughts out loud. I held up a finger to my sister's nose. "No. But I do have a question about him. Who would win in a fight, him or your mate, Gifford?"

Lexia never stopped grinning as she stood straight up. "That's easy, Victor. He's so much stronger. Are you sure you don't want him as your mate?" She winked at me.

I could feel my legs were almost to the point where the workout was finally reaching its important stage. "I'm sure." The tingling in the back of my mind wanted me to say something else. *For now. Stupid instincts.* "But strength isn't the only thing that determines who will win in a fight. Who has more practice at fighting? Who's faster? What about pain tolerances?" My sister's face slowly shifted from smug to worried. "If there's one thing that I learned about humans, it's that they know how to fight. And they taught me how to fight."

"So..." Lexia's voice trailed off.

"I think I can at least convince Silver to help me teach your little band to handle themselves if they need to." I answered her unasked question with a light smile. The look on my sister's face filled my heart with joy. *I'm such a helpful sister.*

After I finished some more exercises with Lexia watching me, we took turns brushing our respective fur. I let her borrow my brush since she said that she'd never had such a nice brush. Mine wasn't all that fancy, but it was quality, made from bristles from a small creature that I didn't remember the name of. Evalana had given it to me for my birthday last year and told me it was imported from Brentiveil, the dwarven kingdom.

Lexia walked with me as we grabbed a quick bite to eat. Gifford and I had pieces of lamb jerky for breakfast, while my sister ate some hard bread with her jerky. She and Gifford went to collect everyone else and get them set to leave. I walked towards my group's temporary housing. Everyone packed up, even Penny, and we set out for the capital city.

Hopefully the supplies we have will last long enough to find some more. This time, we'll procure them legally.

18

ANOTHER CAMPING SCENE

"Why am I following you again?" Penny complained as we trailed behind the lead group of beastkin.

We walked downwind of them since they said they didn't appreciate smelling the humans. *I don't blame them. They stink.* Many of the beastkin traveled through the forest much more easily than my group. And after almost two days of trekking through the woods, there was no end of the forest in sight.

"Because you didn't want us to leave you behind and you didn't know the way back home," Dinar answered for everyone.

"You promised I was going to be paid for this." Penny continued to drag her feet as we marched on. "All I'm saying is that this had better be worth it."

"The lives we save from stopping the war will be worth it," Daric said as he held up his arm, fist clenched.

"Other people's lives don't feed me. I'm not an animal," Penny grumbled under her breath.

I know that was a jab at some beastkin being able to eat humans. I growled at her. Penny flinched away from me. "If I hear you call a beastkin an animal one more time, I will eat you. I've had enough of your racist comments."

Penny didn't talk back to me as Dinar stepped up to her other side and shook her head. Penny glanced at me from the corner of her eye, but kept her mouth shut and rolled her shoulder to readjust her pack as she continued on.

I need to get away from her. The less I deal with her, the better. Daric can have her. I caught up with my sister and poked her side. She jumped.

I giggled. "Gotcha."

Lexia gave me a playful pout. "Oh, you're good."

"Hey, um, can you talk?" I asked as I looked around.

"Of course." The peppiness in her voice was a little annoying. "I've always got time to talk to you. What do you need?"

"I told you quite a bit about myself. But I don't know much about you." Lexia looked like she was going to pout, but I held up a hand before continuing. "Amnesia, remember?" My sister's ears flattened sideways as she looked away. *Is she blushing?* "How about you tell me how you learned magic? You said that magic is rare among beastkin. So who taught you?"

Lexia held out her hand and created a small ball of snow. "Nobody, at first. I figured it out because I could just feel something. It was hard to ignore."

"So can you see others channeling magic?" I asked as I saw her body light up with magic.

She nodded. "Although not very well. It scared me at first. But then I met Marot. He helped me understand what I was doing." She dropped the ball on the ground. "But he used earth magic, and not nearly as much as I could do with ice. He maybe could do about what you can do."

"You said 'was'—why?" I placed a hand on my sister's shoulder.

"He was already old when he taught me what he knew seven years ago. I was still traveling with a wandering pack at the time." A gentle smile touched her lips. "Believe it or not, by our standards you're a powerful mage."

I laughed. "Then my mother would blow you away. Compared to most humans, I'm well below average. Did that Marot tell you why an arc is measured the way it is?" Lexia shook her head. "It's the distance an average mage can use magic. My mom told me when I started learning magic."

"That means..." Lexia started, and I nodded, letting her know I already knew what she was going to say. "Can you teach me more? That thing you did with your claws was pretty cool."

I smirked and wagged my tail. "So now the big sister is asking for the little sister's help. Hm, maybe I shouldn't."

Lexia leaned on my shoulder and fluttered her lashes at me with the biggest pleading eyes she could. "Please."

I melted. "Fine." *Wow, I caved too quickly.* I glared at my inner wolf. *We can't spoil her like that.*

If my inner wolf could give me a smug smile, she did while she watched me from inside my soul, wagging her tail.

Lexia squealed as she jumped up and down, her tail wagging faster with each bounce. "Thank you, thank you, thank you. You're the best sister ever!"

I'm your only sister, I think. "Uh, we're it, right? No other family relatives I need to know about?"

Lexia shook her head. "Nope. Just us. But it would have been nice if we had some other younger siblings."

If I had other siblings, we wouldn't be orphans. I held the thought back. *There's no reason to rain on her parade.*

"You know how to make ice, so I can skip the basics." I created a ball of ice and held it out in front. "How much can you create? And how far can you manipulate ice?"

Lexia shrugged and pointed to a rock about three arcs away. "About that far away, and enough ice to weigh as much as Victor, maybe a little less."

"Okay." I held up the ball of snow and kept it hovering a couple of inches above my hand. "Now I want you to try to wrestle control of this away from me. Don't worry about the backlash."

Lexia tilted her head and flicked her ears. "Backlash?"

"You remember when I overpowered your magic by breaking it?" She nodded. "If your magic is strong enough, you can do the same thing while someone is channeling their magic, but you've got to be much stronger than them, magically speaking."

I felt a slight tug on the ice above my hand, but it wasn't much. My sister glowed as she channeled her magic.

"It looks like I can't." Lexia gave a slight pout.

I let the magic on the ball of ice go and let it hit the ground. "Don't feel bad. It takes a lot to overpower another person's magic. But I also have a feeling your magic isn't all that efficient."

My sister went into a full-on pout as she flattened her ears. "Now I know you're gloating."

Don't be like that. I pursed my lips. "No. When I first learned I could use magic, which was when I was ten, by the way, I magically fatigued myself almost instantly. I have to be efficient, otherwise I never get to use my magic much."

Lexia relaxed. "So how do I be efficient?"

"We'll start with a few exercises to find exactly how much energy you need to freeze water and not more than that. Anything colder is wasted energy." After I created another ball of ice, I handed it to her. "You want to aim for something like this. Your tongue will probably be the best way to feel its temperature." *Since you probably feel the cold as much as I do, which isn't much.*

Lexia and I worked on magic while making sure she didn't fatigue herself. I left her to practice as I moved around more to stretch my legs. Watching her was cute as she created little animal shapes of ice.

The sound of someone stumbling behind me caught my attention. I turned to see Anna holding on to the side of a tree. It looked like her foot had slipped off a root that she'd stepped on.

I sighed as I removed my pack and handed it to Silver, who took it and knew exactly what I was going to do.

Anna stared at me as she panted.

"You're getting better, but come on. Hop up," I said as I turned to give her a piggyback ride.

"No, I can keep going."

Anna's haggard breathing didn't convince me. "Hop on. You're going to slow us down. There's still some time before we stop for the night." I waved my hands to encourage her.

She slowly wrapped her arms around my shoulders and lifted her legs so I could hold them up with my arms. As I carried her, she buried her face in my shoulder. "I feel bad putting you in this situation," she whispered.

"Don't worry. I expect in another week or two you might be able to make the whole day of marching without any breaks or me carrying you," I whispered back. "You'll get there eventually. Just don't overdo it."

Anna gently squeezed her hands on my shoulders.

As I passed Penny, she grumbled something unintelligible under her breath. *You're lucky you can walk after attacking my sister and not apologizing for it.*

Dinar again pulled at Penny's sleeve. "Stop making her mad. She isn't stupid like you. One of the most important rules of hiring a guide is don't make them mad. They can lead you to the middle of nowhere and leave you to die."

Grim thought. A marvelous idea, though. I never thought about that. But also, that's frighteningly specific.

Lexia saw me carrying Anna and smirked before she slowed down until I was next to her. "Don't worry, the sun will set soon. We'll stop and rest for the night." My sister winked at Anna.

Anna eyed Lexia. "You want something."

She'd stated what I was thinking.

Lexia shrugged. "So? You have questions, I have questions, and I'm sure my sister has questions. You're free to ask me anything you want."

I could feel Anna tense up. "Why are you so infatuated with your sister? You've only just met her and know almost nothing about her."

Lexia's growl forced a growl out of me. She flattened her ears and looked away. "Fine. I'll try to explain it in a way you could understand. Not that I expect an elf like you would understand."

I could feel Anna about to interrupt her, likely to correct her about being a half-elf. Before she could get a word out, I bounced my next step, causing the woman to shriek as she tightened her grip on me. "Don't distract her," I whispered. *And please don't shriek in my ear like that again. I know that was my fault, but that still hurts.*

"As beastkin, we are naturally closer to each other because of our instincts." Lexia straightened up but didn't turn to face us as she kept walking. It was almost as if she was looking past everything instead of at nothing. "It's something that affects our choice of mate too." She held up her arm with the silver bracelet. "This bracelet marks that I've chosen a mate. That way, any male who's looking for a mate knows not to bother asking me."

I looked around at the other beastkin ahead of us and saw most of the beastkin had a band. Less than half of them were silver bracelets, and the majority were copper.

"What do the copper bands mean?" I asked.

Lexia's expression soured as her gaze seemed to return to normal, but she still kept looking away from us. "Those are the marks of someone who lost their mate. There are far more of them these days than ever before."

"Lost?" Anna leaned back slightly.

I flattened my ears. "Beastkin mate for life, right?" Lexia nodded. *Good, the books had that information right. But they never mentioned anything about the bands.* "Lost probably means dead."

We took several steps in near silence. Only Daric and the rest stomping through the forest made any sound.

"I... I'm sorry," Anna finally spoke up, her voice low and thick with regret. "You must truly be desperate if so many are suffering due to the lack of food."

"It's not just that." Lexia's voice was filled with anger. "More dires have appeared and made hunting more dangerous. It's all Daygon's fault. Things were fine before he became king."

Anna cleared her throat. "I find it hard to believe that he's at fault for everything that's troubling your kingdom. I don't know how a person could possibly cause more dire appearances. I don't know how they appear to begin with. Could he be responsible for that blood anchor? Maybe, but given how little you knew about demons, I imagine that's something the whole Wild Kingdom would struggle to know. So I doubt he's responsible for that too."

Lexia scoffed. "You doubt? What's there to doubt?"

"I doubt your certainty," Anna replied calmly. "And your ability to see beyond your anger and frustration. How old were you when the king took over? How long has he been in power?"

Lexia released a low growl. "He took over just after our village was raided by the orcs. And I'm not angry or frustrated." She stopped right in front of me and poked a finger at Anna. "The king is a weak, ineffective ruler who's allowed our kingdom to fall into ruin. That makes him part of the problem."

"Is he the only ruler? What about leaders? Your villages and cities must have some leadership." Anna's tone softened.

Lexia flexed her claws. "They're useless. They're doing nothing until the king tells them to do something."

"I don't know everything that's going on. And it sounds like you aren't willing to look at everything and keep a level head." Anna matched my sister's tone. "I'm just saying we need more information."

I put Anna down. "Alright you two." I extended a hand towards the two of them. "Calm down or I will make you."

Lexia sneered, completely ignoring me. "You think things change if you do nothing. We can't wait. People are dying."

"I'm not saying we shouldn't take action," Anna said. "I'm saying we should take the right action. And that means not blindly running at a problem."

"Enough!" My shout caused both women to jump and everyone else to stop and stare. "I've had enough and am putting an end to this right now."

Lexia stared at me with anger in her eyes. "You're not siding with her? I'm your sister."

I growled and bared my fangs. My sister cowered back. A slight pang in my heart registered as I saw the scared look on her face. *I needed her to calm down and listen.* "Your arguing is getting on my nerves."

"If I may?" Silver stepped up, surprising everyone. "I couldn't help but overhear your argument." He swiveled his head, and we looked around. Everyone was still looking at us. "Everyone heard that last bit. But it would be safe to say you both are right—"

Both women started shouting at Silver simultaneously.

"Stop!" I grabbed both of their shirts. *That silenced them quickly.* "I don't care who's right. All I care about is quiet. I expect this behavior from my sister. But you, Anna, you're old enough to act better."

"Lexia, we are going to do something," Dinar joined in. "But what you're asking is dangerous, and if something goes wrong, people die. You don't want that to happen, right?"

My sister relaxed in my grip. "You're right. I just got carried away."

"Anna, is it not natural for someone to want to change things for the better?" Silver asked. "Even if Lexia is wrong, it doesn't devalue her actions or her desire to pursue the one idea she has."

Anna placed her hand on mine and pushed. I released her, and she turned away. "It looks like I got caught up in her enthusiasm." She turned and held out a hand to Lexia, whom I released. "Be careful with your infectious enthusiasm. It can lead others into a dangerous situation if you don't know what's going on. I'm here to help. I really am. It's just that I think the demon has more to do with what's going on than we can identify right now."

My heart rate slowed down as Lexia walked away. "Lexia, I'm sorry for yelling at you like that," I said. "You're desperate. We're all here to help. Let us."

"It's been a long couple of days," Daric called from the back of his company. "Maybe we should just set up camp here and get some sleep. Things should look clearer in the morning."

I turned and tilted my head as I looked at him. *That's actually a reasonable suggestion.*

"Yes." Lexia's voice was almost as low as her head. "We can stop here for the day."

I went and placed a hand on my sister's shoulder. "I'll go hunting and see if I can find something. The extra time should let me look farther away."

Lexia didn't look at me. "I'll tell the others to go with you."

That's fair. But I hope we didn't just break my sister. I need to use this time to see if I can find some way of cheering her up.

19

HELP

We continued walking until we came to the edge of the tree line. Things had warmed up since we'd done nothing but travel south by southwest for almost two weeks. I let everyone set up camp while I went to talk with my sister. The beastkin dropped their litters that they carried their supplies with. The few that had backpacks placed them on the ground. A couple of beastkin pulled out some food and started dividing it among everyone.

"Hey, Lexia," I called towards my sister as she finished talking with the hunters. She faced me with a grim look on her face. "What is it?"

"We're out of food. They're distributing the last of it." She kept her voice low, despite knowing that every beastkin could still hear her. "I've been following the advice from Silver about how to ration. But it hasn't been enough."

"We've been trying to find food." I held my arm out towards the rest of the forest. "It isn't our fault that the only thing we've found has been rotting corpses."

"I know, and nobody is blaming you," Lexia said as she scurried to stand in front of me. "But it still doesn't change our situation. Hopefully we'll find some food once we hit the open plains."

"How long until we reach the capital city?" I placed my hand on my sister's shoulder and guided her away from everyone. "Also, have you figured out a complete plan for once we get there?"

Lexia's ears flattened as her shoulders drooped. "No, I've been more worried about just trying to keep everyone fed and healthy." *Being a leader must be hard.* "Our priority should just be getting food. My hope is Dinar and Anna are able to help more. They've been very helpful with their ideas so far. It just goes to show how bad of a leader I really am."

I smiled. "See, they want to help. You're letting them. And everyone is benefiting from it." Lexia relaxed a bit. "So, what kinds of animals can we expect to find in the plains?" I asked, still dragging my sister along.

She shrugged. "I don't know. I've never left the forest. None of us have."

I pinched the bridge of my nose and groaned. "You really haven't thought this through at all."

"I'm sorry. I didn't think about every detail. My only concern is removing a king who isn't trying to save his people but instead is trying to kill them," my sister shouted at me. "Dinar and Anna have already shown me how stupid I am."

"Then stop being so reckless!" I responded with a shout of my own. "If you fail, what then? If you're going to do something, do everything you can to succeed."

"Why are you being so mean? I don't want to fail. I want to save my people." Lexia's lips quivered as her voice lowered.

I relaxed. My heart hurt as I saw my sister getting upset. "Sorry. Not everyone can know how to plan an assassination like Dinar." I took a few steps back and turned away from her. "It's not your fault, and I shouldn't have yelled at you. I'm hungry, and I get easily agitated when I'm hungry."

"It's okay. We're all hungry." Lexia placed her hand on my shoulder. "I'm sorry for yelling first. I need help, more than I realized, from you and your friends."

Maybe everyone except Penny could be considered my friend. "I guess I should head out with the other hunters to look for food," I said as I glanced over my shoulder.

"Okay, just stay safe and good luck." Lexia gave me a toothy smile.

I left my sister to look for food, but more importantly, to cool my emotions. *Why did I snap at her? I just need to focus on something else. Hunting should distract me enough.*

The group of five other hunters stalked along the tree line towards the east. Following them wasn't effortless, but catching up to them was. The first one to notice me was the primal male cougar, Pren.

"How are you holding up?" Pren's jagged voice was the first to greet me.

"Can we just find some food this time?" I didn't even bother to look at him as I passed him.

I had no inclination to return empty-handed yet again. So I picked up my pace and left the other hunters to do what they wanted. *If they all want to follow me, that's fine by me. Although if they left me alone, that would be better.*

Shortly after my curt response to Pren, the others broke off into pairs, leaving one set of footsteps following me. I turned to see who the brave soul was.

A small—by beastkin standards—lynx girl followed me. Fina always followed me around when I spent any time away from the humans and elves. With a modest bust and hips, she looked like an adorable child, but I knew she was older than me. She loved to spy on me, thinking I didn't know she was there. The first few times I caught her watching me, she scurried away the moment I looked in her direction. While she wasn't a primal beastkin, her fuzzy cheeks of reddish-brown fur always put a smile on my face. Her fur made it look like she always had a white bow tie around her neck.

She kept her distance from me but didn't run the moment I turned to regard her.

I took a deep breath to calm myself before I did something stupid again, like taking my frustration out on someone who didn't deserve it. With more effort than I expected, I put on a smile for her. "Do you want to follow me? Or did you think that you have to follow me because everyone else has a hunting partner?" *I know she hasn't said a word to me yet, but I can always try.*

Fina took small steps as she sheepishly walked towards me. Her padded feet were completely silent. She stopped and curled her short tail around to her left. "Something's bothering you." Her voice was just as cute as her emerald eyes. "You need a hug?" she asked as she held out her arms.

I didn't know what possessed me, but I had to walk up to the short girl and pick her up and hug her. After I wrapped my arms around her, I lifted her up and held her close as I rubbed my cheek against her fuzzy face. Her toe-claws tapped my knees as she squeezed me back. I held back my strength so I didn't hurt her.

The longer I held her, the slower my heartbeat got, and my muscles relaxed. I didn't bother keeping track of how long I held her, but as long as she was okay with me holding her, I was going to.

Eventually, I held the lynx girl out and stared at her, this time with a genuine smile. "Thanks. How did you know what I needed?" I slowly set her down on the ground.

"You looked sad," Fina said as he folded her hands in front of her. "You don't want anyone to see it. Why?"

I stared at the girl as her tail swayed behind her and her feet didn't shift. "That's a good question. I wish I had the answer." My answer flew out of my mouth.

I didn't want to talk to Fina while looking down the entire time. A root that jutted out of the ground from a colossal tree made a convenient seat. I walked over and took a seat as Fina followed me. Her large, fluffy paws made as much noise as mine did—none.

"Most likely, I'm just tired of failing. Every time I went hunting with you guys, the only thing I found was a decaying corpse. We're out of food because I've failed so many times. I should've done better. I should've found something to eat by now. Yes, I know the ice season makes finding prey harder since many animals hibernate, but I've been able to find their dens in the past. So why can't I find them now?" I couldn't stop the torrent of words once they started.

Fina walked up and placed a hand on my shoulder. "You're the best hunter. You found more than us." *This is the strangest speech I've ever heard.* "You help us. You teach us. We did nothing for you. Let us help you."

I flicked my ears as I tilted my head. "Why? You know nothing about me. These are the first words you've said to me. I know you've been watching me, but why talk to me now?"

The lynx girl stood straight and smiled. "Those who help must be helped. I wanted to help, but couldn't. Now I can help."

I looked at her wrist and saw a copper band. *Lexia said that any beastkin who wears a silver band has a mate. But anyone with a copper band means they lost their mate.* "How long ago?" I asked as I nodded at her wrist.

Fina wrapped her hand around the band, and as she held it to her heart. "Fire season. No kittens."

It was my turn to hug her.

Fina quietly sobbed in my chest. *It was stupid of me to bring up something so painful. I never thought about how tough these people have it here. Things need to change. But to change things, we need to survive. To survive, we need food. Lexia and I can provide water for everyone, but there's nothing we can do for food.* I let the girl cry until her tears ceased. *It's only right since it's my fault.*

"Let's try to find something. Maybe we can change the circumstances of this kingdom, together," I said as I leaned back.

Fina nodded as she gave me one last hug before we set off to look for food. As we stalked the tree line looking for tracks, I turned to Fina as she stayed by my side. "I don't know why I opened up to you like that, but I'm glad I did."

Fina's ears turned towards me as her eyes grew wide. "I helped." Her smile warmed my heart.

"Yeah, you helped." My lips curled into a smile to match hers.

20

BAD NEWS

Even with Fina bolstering my spirits, our hunt ended just like all those before it—as a failure. However, this time I found a den of badgers. But while we investigated, something about the corpses bothered me. They had only just started to expand from bloating. There were no visible wounds on the animals. Until this point, I hadn't seen a corpse so recently deceased. I tentatively poked a hole in the flesh, and a black fluid oozed out of the incision.

After Fina and I were done gagging at the foul odor and I coated the claw with ice to cover the scent and wash it off, we carried one that I hadn't cut open back with us.

We carefully approached the camp carrying the badger corpse. All of my companions stared at the two of us with wide eyes.

"You know that's already decomposing, right?" Silver broke the silence first.

"Of course I do. I can smell the decay." I flattened my ears as I glared at the dragoon. "We brought it here to try to learn something. Another animal didn't kill it. There aren't any wounds on it. I was hoping one of you could help me figure out how it died," I said as I waved for Fina to place it on the ground.

"Who's your friend? She's cute." Daric watched my feline friend with far too much enthusiasm.

A short growl ripped his attention towards me. "This is Fina. She's helping me." I placed a hand on the top of her head and scratched gently. Fina closed her eyes as she leaned into my hand. *Is she purring? That's adorable. Now I want to keep her.* I shifted my attention back to Daric. "And do you remember what I told you about the bands?"

Daric stared at me, jealousy pouring from his eyes as he looked at Fina's wrist. His jaw clenched shut as he turned away and stormed off. "Not fair," Daric grumbled under his breath.

Fina hadn't stopped purring as she watched me with her beautiful, large green eyes. Her tail swayed back and forth as she clasped her hands close to her chest.

"Go get some food." I nodded towards the beastkin section of the camp. "Hopefully the others will return soon. Maybe they had better luck than us."

"You need help. I will help." Fina's voice rumbled slightly with her purring.

She's a person of few words but a lot of heart.

I watched Fina walk towards my sister. Lexia paced back and forth as she looked through the supplies. My sister turned to face the lynx just before she was assaulted with a fluffy hug. *There she goes again, helping.* I couldn't suppress a smile as I turned towards the group who were poking the dead badger with a stick.

"Well, it's definitely dead," Dinar said as she stayed out of arm's reach. She dropped to one knee as she studied it without touching it. "Are you sure it just didn't die of old age? I don't know much about animals."

"There were four of them huddled in a den together. All of them were dead and in the same condition." I took a few steps back and circled around to stand upwind. "When I cut one of them open, a strange black fluid oozed out."

Dinar and Anna both perked up at my sentence. "Dinar, can you hand me a knife?" Anna blurted out as she held out her hand.

Dinar held out her hand with a blade about four inches long. As

Anna reached for it, Dinar flicked her wrist and the short dagger somersaulted. When Dinar caught it, she held it so Anna could grab the handle. Anna carefully took it, and once she had a firm grip, she dragged the blade along the belly of the animal. The black fluid oozed out even slower than back at the badgers' den.

I took a few more steps back, not wanting to smell the wretched scent.

Anna held the knife up to her face as Golditress and Mark covered their mouths and walked away. I didn't blame them. "That's its blood." Anna's voice was barely more than a whisper.

"There is no way that's blood. It's too thick," I said as I waved my hand to dismiss the idea.

"And what do you know about blood?" Penny glared at me over her shoulder.

I growled at her. *I'm not going to answer that.*

She rolled her eyes as she walked away. "Whatever. Let me know if there's anything important after you finish playing with it. And clean yourself off after disposing of the body. I don't want to keep smelling it for the entire night."

As the nuisance left, Anna, Silver, Dinar, and I stared at the dead badger's extra-thick blood.

"So..." Silver broke the silence. "Any ideas on what could turn its blood black and make it so viscous?" He waved his hand towards the opening Anna had made.

Anna held the knife in front of her as she scratched the back of her head with her other hand. Dinar hummed to herself while I found a tree to lean against. *I don't have much knowledge of plants, outside of which ones are edible by human standards. Could a disease cause this? If that's the case, wouldn't we catch it? Also, it would affect the beastkin of this kingdom. I should ask Lexia if she knows of any recent events of people getting sick and dying.*

I stepped away to find my sister. She was snuggling up to Gifford while eating their meager rations. "Lexia, have beastkin been getting sick recently?" I asked as I approached.

"No?" Her voice trailed off as she looked confused. "What do you mean, get sick?"

"Things like unexplainable difficulty breathing or feeling hot no matter what you do. There can also be pain in your stomach and or head." I crossed my arms and lowered my head as I tried to think. "Also, lots of coughing or sneezing. Frequent dizziness can be a sign as well. Basically, anything that changes a person's behavior and causes them to feel unwell." *Nobody has ever asked me that. That's a much harder question to answer than most people would anticipate.*

Lexia crossed her arms. "I'm going to need to think for a bit."

"What about all the people who are afflicted with the frenzy?" Gifford asked as he looked at his mate.

"Yeah, your mother said there have been more occurrences of people falling prey to it over the years," Lexia said, still looking like she was lost in thought. "That's why she didn't want us leaving the pack."

"The frenzy?" I eyed Gifford skeptically.

"It's a condition that affects only beastkin. Whoever is afflicted will quickly get irritable and attack everyone, even those they call their mate. They run wild through the wilderness and usually die because a larger predator kills them. It's like no rational thought runs through their mind anymore. Like they are nothing more than a wild beast with the sole purpose of killing everything." Gifford's voice sounded like it wanted to catch in his throat. "There is a cure for it. Sometimes we can find them and restrain them to deliver it. The problem is that the cure is as likely to kill them as not." A tear sat in the corner of his eye.

I sighed. "The rest of the world calls it a beastkin going feral." *Or rabies in my last life.* I flattened my ears as I took a seat in front of the two. "I take it someone you know was afflicted with it? How does it spread?"

Lexia snapped out of her thoughts to grab Gifford and hold him close. "It's okay. I'll tell her. I know it hurts," she said as she stroked the back of Gifford's head. He was no longer holding back his tears as he softly sobbed on my sister's shoulder. "It was his brother, Ron. When they were eleven, they were out hunting and a wolverine attacked them. He and his brother fought until they killed the animal. But Ron was bitten pretty badly. When they made it home, it wasn't long before his brother attacked him and his parents before running off. Ron was found later, but when they gave him the cure, he didn't survive the treatment and died."

"I know this will hurt, but do you remember what that wolverine looked like, Gifford?" I asked the fox as he finished composing himself.

"How could I forget?" Gifford's eyes looked distant as his shoulders slumped. "It was constantly growling and snarling. My brother stepped in front of me as it charged me. Once it sank its teeth into my brother's leg, it wouldn't let go until we killed it. The whole time we were trying to kill it, it clawed his leg up even worse."

"That's enough." I held up my hand to stop him. I could clearly see the pain in his eyes as he recalled the memory. "You said there's a cure for the frenzy. What is it?"

"I don't know," the two responded simultaneously.

"Oh." I slumped my shoulders. "I'll leave you two alone. Sorry for bringing up such painful memories."

"Wait," Lexia said as I stood up. "About your first question, I've never seen a beastkin get sick as you describe it."

My ears perked up. "Thank you." I gave her a quick nod before walking away.

Beastkin can't get sick? I guess I haven't been sick even once in this life. But why? There has to be a reason why the frenzy, as they call it, still affects us. What would happen to a human if they contract the frenzy? Would they die? Can the cure work on them? Wait, what does this have to do with the badger I found? Stupid me. I got distracted again. Way to go, Gifford.

I poked the side of my head with a finger while I walked towards Silver and Dinar.

"So what did you talk about?" Dinar asked as she kneeled over the completely dissected badger. Organs were separated from the corpse and arranged in some strange formation around the body.

Well, would you look at that? It was a boy. And now he and the smell are everywhere.

"Nothing helpful to our current problem." I looked around and didn't see Anna. "Where did Anna go?"

"She left once Dinar opened it up and started pulling out the organs," Silver said as he glanced at the elf responsible. She simply shrugged before poking the organs with the knife.

"I wanted to see what the organs looked like." She poked a kidney with her knife. The kidney looked far too large for the animal. "I'm very familiar with human anatomy, but could you help me with badgers? Is there anything wrong that you see?" Dinar asked as she looked up at me.

"The kidneys are too big, the lungs are shriveled, and there's a lump that shouldn't be there next to the spine. Oh, and the heart shouldn't be that dark." I pointed to each anomaly as I mentioned it.

Two sets of eyes blinked simultaneously at me.

"That was quick." Silver's mouth moved despite his dazed look.

"What? Badger organs have more of a sour taste, but the muscles taste just as good as a deer's." I lowered my ears as they continued to give me a surprised look. "I don't judge you for eating your bread, fruits, and vegetables. Not only do I hunt, but I also take my prey apart and sell what I don't eat."

Dinar's eye twitched for a moment before she shook her head slightly. "Okay, if I ignore the lump you mentioned..." Dinar poked the kidney and more of the black blood flowed like thick honey from the organ. *What is she looking for?* "There's a poison I have only heard about that turns blood black and paralyzes the target. Once it paralyzes the lungs, it kills through suffocation."

"Is there a name for this poison?" Silver asked before I could.

"Strangling Devil," Dinar said without looking away from the corpse. "And before you ask, no, I don't know where it comes from. I heard about it from my..." Dinar hesitated as she looked at Silver. "My previous line of work. It's beyond rare, and turning its victim's blood black is the poison's marker."

"So why did you ask those questions if the color of the blood is all you needed to know?" I crossed my arms as I tapped my toe-claw in the dirt.

"Because I didn't want to believe it." Dinar's gray eyes shook as she stared at me. "If something has used such a rare and deadly poison on inconsequential animals, I don't want to see what it will do to us."

As I watched Dinar tremble in terror, fear crept into my mind.

Someone or something has been killing all the wildlife in an entire kingdom. Why?

Silver shuddered too. "I don't like this."

Dinar wiped the blade on the ground before making it disappear in her sleeve. "Too many coincidences? I agree." She wrung her hands together. "This feels like a trap."

"This kingdom is getting desperate, and the desperate are unpredictable yet controllable." Silver started pacing. "I heard rumors that a bunch of knight companies were being stationed around the borders of Rophmna. It's like someone is spreading our forces out."

"How's that possible?" I asked. "Knight companies are more or less independent outside of the king. King Ramos wouldn't be this reckless."

Dinar walked over and placed a hand on my shoulder. "But if each company receives falsified information to investigate possible attacks or missions, then there's nothing we can do. It'll look like business as usual to almost anyone."

"But who would do something like that?" *Didn't Captain Aenwyn say something about another company getting relocated or something?*

Dinar chuckled. "If anyone knew that, we wouldn't be in this situation to begin with. I almost believe that our mission is part of the larger plot."

I sighed. *Great, someone wants me away from the kingdom. There's no way I've made that many important enemies, is there? This is way above my pay grade. But the corruption in the kingdom will have to wait. We have more immediate concerns. Like a lack of food. I wish I knew what to do.*

SILVER TONGUE

I tossed and turned as I tried to sleep. *Yet another day unable to sleep. What is that now? Two days without food. I can't keep doing this.* My stomach continued to inform me of how upset it was at being so empty for so long. I stared at the ceiling of the tent I'd borrowed from Lexia and groaned.

"Listen, I'm not happy about the lack of food either. Now shut up. It's bad enough I can't concentrate on casting magic because of you." *And now I'm talking to my stomach.* I placed one hand on my stomach and the other on my head. "This headache is killing me. What I wouldn't give for a bite of anything at this moment." *I might as well get up. My stomach won't let me sleep any longer anyway.*

I crawled out of the tent after changing into another set of clothes. A gust of wind greeted me as I poked my head out into the moonlit night. With another groan, I stood to see who else was up. As I walked around silently, the wind continued to blow my fur around. My stomach constantly gave away my position.

"Windy day, isn't it?" I heard Daric's voice to my left. He spoke without his usual peppiness. I turned and saw him sitting on a rock, staring out towards the north.

"Are you really keeping watch? How can you see anything?" I

asked as I noticed that the campfire had burned down to smoldering embers. The rocks of the fire pit shielded them from the gusts.

"Do you think it's true?" Daric lowered his head to look at his lap and stared at his intertwined hands. As I stood next to him, he turned to face me. "Is there really something out there killing all the animals in this kingdom?"

"Are you still stuck on that?" *I guess he's been pretty distant for the past couple of days.* "After what Dinar said, I don't want to believe it, but yeah." My stomach growled to add to the conversation. "There hasn't been any food for the carnivores. I've never been so hungry in my life."

Daric returned to staring out ahead. "This isn't how I thought any of this would go. What do we even do?"

"They haven't killed every animal yet; it shouldn't be possible. But, at this point, I believe the damage they've caused is irreparable. This may mean that the Wild Kingdom is finished. Everyone will have to move to other kingdoms just to stay alive." I crossed my arms as I looked at the ground. "Someone wanted this kingdom to fall, and they've succeeded. I know, without a doubt, that Rophmna will slaughter the Wild Kingdom if a war breaks out."

"We can't let that happen."

"I know. Hopefully we can get the information Dinar needs to come up with a plan." My stomach growled once more. "I need food, badly," I said as I stepped away. *He doesn't sound like he'll be good company. But it does sound like the situation has finally hit him. Maybe the kid can grow up.*

Nobody else moved until the sun started rising. Everyone in both camps carried out their tasks in complete silence. Everyone packed up without a word or a bite to eat. Lexia and I knew that we needed to keep going. We needed to find a roaming pack, food, or reach the capital soon. Otherwise, things were going to go from bad to worse.

I couldn't walk straight. Lexia grabbed me as I almost tripped on a rock. "Lucia, are you okay?" She pulled me and sat me down on another nearby rock.

My vision was getting slightly blurry. "No. I'm *so* hungry." I knew my hunger needed to be satiated, and soon. "I can't get food."

Lexia ran her fingers through my hair. "You've tried. You've tried so much. This is all my fault. I pulled you into this war, my war, and now I can't help you." She sniffled. "We should have prepared more. Gotten more supplies. Something."

"If you think this is a war, you're very mistaken." Dinar's voice halted Lexia's sniffling. "You're a revolution, or more often seen as traitors and fools. It's things like this that make or break a cause."

"This cause was doomed from the start," a nearby beastkin said. Other beastkin gasped.

"Following Lexia was a mistake."

"We should have stayed with our packs."

The comments continued. All the beastkin following us were mumbling to themselves.

"Stop!" I nearly fell over as I shouted. Lexia almost didn't grab me before I fell to the ground. "Do any of you think you can do better?" I looked at them all, but I couldn't see any movements in my blurry vision. "Well? Do you?"

"Don't." Lexia's flat tone drew everyone's eyes. She wasn't looking up. "If anyone wants to leave, do so. Leave with my blessing." She stood up. *What's she doing?* "I'm not here to force anyone to follow me. This is my fight. I won't ask you to be a part of it if you're not willing. Have I done everything perfectly? No. And it hurts seeing everyone, even my own sister, suffering from my failure. I feel your pain too. But let's get to the capital together. We have to survive; that's more important right now."

For some reason, my vision straightened itself out, mostly. Lexia had dug her toe-claws into the dirt. The other beastkin exchanged looks as Dinar pinched the bridge of her nose. I saw Silver staring at my sister, almost nodding. *Right, we need to survive.*

As the other beastkin dispersed and continued traveling, Dinar walked closer. "Your sister can barely stand, let alone walk. This isn't a war. You shouldn't have ever treated it like one or called it one." Dinar waved for Silver to came closer. "Let Silver carry her. He's strong enough to do it."

"Why do you keep saying that?" Lexia asked.

Dinar turned and started walking away. "Because you, kid, need to grow up. Life isn't a fairy tale. It's unfair, cruel, and unforgiving. You need to expect things to go wrong. Then you stand a chance." Dinar walked past Silver. "Give her a hand, would you?"

Silver nodded as he wrapped my arm around his shoulders. As Silver and I walked together, I couldn't keep a smile off my face. *He's carrying me without complaining. I should try to stand up for Lexia, but I can't think of anything to say. All I'm good for is killing and looking tough. This whole leading thing isn't for me.*

It wasn't long before everyone had to stop and take a break. Silver panted as he set me down on a rock and sat next to me. Lexia was walking around, handing out waterskins she'd filled. Silver nearly emptied one on his own.

The dragoon let out a sigh as he handed me the waterskin. I could still hear water sloshing around inside it, so I took it. "How you feeling? Any better?"

I finished off the waterskin. "I haven't had anything to eat, so what do you think?" Silver flinched, and then he frowned. I slumped my shoulders. "Sorry. That wasn't nice. Especially since you've been helping me. There isn't a reason I should take anything out on you. It's just that I'm so hungry. I feel like my stomach is eating me from the inside."

Silver placed a hand on my shoulder. "We're all hungry. But you seem to be suffering more than everyone else. Why?"

I shook my head as I closed my eyes. "If I only knew. Mom would probably say it's because I eat so much already."

Silver placed his hands to his knees. "Yeah, you've eaten quite a lot since we've met. Which is odd, since all the other beastkin eat a fraction of what you eat."

I let out a pitiful laugh. "Lucky me."

"You're quite lucky. Two aptitudes—strong aptitudes too—a title, and a loving mother. Remember to count your blessings, and you'll find you're lacking far less than you thought." Silver's voice was somehow soothing.

I opened an eye and glared at him. "Aren't you a philosophical one. What do you do as a knight?"

I noticed that there was no sweat on Silver's brow as he continued to breathe heavily. *So dragoons don't sweat. That's interesting.*

Silver gripped the mace on his hip. "I'm an instructor. Companies hire me to teach new recruits the basics of marching and fighting in formation." Silver gave me an odd, almost mischievous smile. "I know it sounds weird, but I've found teaching to be quite rewarding. It lets me feel like I'm making a difference, even though I may never see it."

I gave him a chuckle. "No, that's your thing. And that's good that you know it. If you ask me, you should be leading, not Daric."

Silver straightened up, his breathing much more under control. "I feel that would be limiting. Tying myself to just one knight company would limit those that I can teach. But more importantly, I'm no leader—not like Lexia, or you for that matter."

I'm going to have to disagree with that last part. "Is that why you were watching my sister so closely? It looked like you agreed with what she did. Why?"

Silver curled his lips slightly. "So you saw that, did you? Sharp eyes." He shook his head. "Your sister's ability to manipulate the other beastkin to follow her like that, it takes some guts. She made them completely forget about her and focus on following her order. That's pretty skilled to distract them like that at that moment."

I shook my head. "No, she's not like that. She genuinely cares for them. She meant what she said. And I think they understand that. She wouldn't manipulate them like that. That's what made her take on this mission to kill the beast king. Because she cares about the people suffering and wants to change it."

Silver looked up to the sky; there was a wistful look in his eye. "That's even better."

I smiled "You know what's odd?" Silver turned his head to look at me. "I've always wondered why I've not seen many dragoons. Why is that? Do you know?"

Silver's face dropped and he turned to look at the ground. "Please, I don't want to."

I arched an eyebrow. "You don't want to what? Know, or talk about it?"

"Both."

A shiver ran down my spine and caused my tail to twitch. "Sorry." I stood up. "Listen, thank you for earlier. I'll walk so you don't have to work so hard."

I paused and snapped my head around. Something in the distance caught my attention. I immediately sprang to attention, ears forward, eyes wide, and my tail straight back.

22

HUNGRY

I looked harder until I saw, in the tall grass, a brown coat of fur. *A horse?* The horse trotted in the distance, ignorant of our existence. *I don't care. I'm so hungry I could eat the whole thing.* As if agreeing with my thought, my stomach growled. *Wait, horses usually run in herds, right? That means with one, there are more. But is it the lead or just plain lost?*

"What is it?" Lexia asked, running up to me.

"Food," I said as I licked my lips.

Without another moment wasted, I sprinted on all fours towards the horse. I didn't know where the energy came from, but I didn't stop to ask. There was some shouting behind me, but my thoughts revolved around the horse and how delicious it was going to taste. My vision quickly shifted to red as I focused on heading the creature off.

The horse must have seen me coming. Which wasn't that hard to believe since I stuck out rather obviously against the amber grass. Even though it changed course and attempted to flee, I easily gained ground. *Outrunning a horse isn't that hard for me. You were doomed the moment I saw you.* I released a growl as I pounced on its back.

The horse let out a shriek of pain as I dug all of my claws into its back and shoulders.

There was a snap below me, then the horse and I tilted towards the ground face-first. I pushed off and rolled as I landed, ending in a three-point stance. With my claws extended, I saw the horse flailing on the ground. Its front left leg was bent at a new angle, broken.

I pounced once again. This time, I dug my teeth into its spine at the base of the skull and easily severed its spinal cord as I crushed the vertebrae.

The horse fell limp and silent as my vision returned to normal.

Finally, some food. I didn't wait for anyone to catch up before I started peeling the hide off to get to the good stuff. I greedily tore into the shoulder meat as I heard the vague sounds of people running and talking from the direction I'd come from. As I gobbled up piece after piece of meat, my headache slowly became more tolerable. I didn't bother using my hands and just bit the meat right off the bone.

Bite after bite, I could feel energy filling me. I savagely tore the horse apart and stripped its meat from the bone, not wasting a piece. The front quarter was gone before I could control myself as my greedy stomach finally started digesting the meat en masse.

The blood tastes good, doesn't it?

It does, and so does the meat.

Would you like some more?

There's more, where? I looked up and whipped my head back and forth to see what the mysterious voice was talking about.

Those people over there running towards you, they look delicious, don't they?

Lexia, Victor, Fina, a few other beastkin with names I didn't remember, Daric, Silver, and Anna were all running towards me. *That's not food. Those are my friends.* I froze as I realized that something was talking to me mentally. I shook my head to get the voice out of my head.

Something placed its hands on my shoulders. "Don't lie to yourself. You know you want a bite. There is plenty of blood for you to spill," a husky voice purred in my ear. "Don't worry, I won't judge you."

I flattened my ears and growled. *I recognize that voice.* "You're right. I do want to tear someone apart."

"Oh, do you? Who is it?" The voice behind me rose an octave. "What's holding you back?"

I could feel her pressed up against my back. I grinned as I shifted my foot. "You!" Before the demon could slip away, I dug my claws into her wrists.

The sin of lust screamed in my ear, nearly forcing me to let go of her. She flapped her wings to lift into the air. "You little—"

I didn't let her finish as I pulled her forward in front of me and slammed her to the ground. The demon released a grunt as she collided with the dirt. She lifted her left leg and kicked off with her right. In a ludicrous display of flexibility, she folded herself in half to kick me in the face.

I stumbled backwards, clutching my nose. I forced my vision to turn red as I focused on the demon. A shimmer surrounded her as she slowly turned transparent.

You're not getting away again! I lunged and plunged the claws of my right hand into her gut, despite her attempt to lean away from me.

I curled my claws to grip her flesh and entrails as I focused on my magic. Slowly, the surrounding air cooled and a fine layer of frost covered everything within arm's reach of me. The succubus squirmed as she tried to pull my hand out of her. Her unintelligible cries of anguish continued now that my frost perfectly outlined her silhouette.

Blood poured from the wound in her stomach, soaking my fur. I slashed at her face with my other hand. My claws dug into the bone of her skull, no doubt leaving permanent grooves.

The sin dropped her invisibility and stared at me with fire in her eyes. She stabbed my right wrist with her claws in between the bones on my forearm.

Even though her claws didn't dig nearly as deep as mine would have, my fingers on my right hand went limp as the demon extracted my hand. We both released a growl and glared at each other.

Were her canines always that long? I kicked her front leg in the knee and heard something pop as her leg bent in the wrong direction.

She released my arm and flapped her wings to lift herself off the ground. I jumped up to grab the ankle of her good leg and pulled her back down, throwing her to the ground, face-first. She pushed herself up, but as she turned to face me, I pounced.

I attempted to bite her neck, but she shoved an arm in my face so that instead of chewing out her throat, my teeth sank into her fore-arm. As my teeth dug into the bones, I bit down harder, trying to crush them. The sin didn't scream in response; instead, she bit me in return on my shoulder.

My shoulder erupted in pain, forcing me to release her. As soon as I did, her tail wrapped around my waist and pulled me off of her. I landed, clutching at my shoulder, which continued to burn with pain. *What did she do? Why does it hurt so much?* I managed to scramble to my feet as a javelin of ice speared through the demon's right wing.

I turned and saw Lexia throwing another spear of ice as everyone sprinted towards me. The projectile flew through the air towards the demon, but she dodged it with a quick side-step. "Enjoy your victory for now, my pet." She flapped her wings and lifted off the ground, albeit just barely, as her one wing now had a hole in it the size of her head. "You will fall eventually. It is only a matter of time now." Her flight was slower than I could run, but the pain in my shoulder continued to grow.

I dropped to my knees and waited for everyone to catch up. My pain quickly flooded to unimaginable levels. My vision blurred slightly but continued to stay red. Everything burned as my muscles tightened and I curled into a ball. There was screaming, but I couldn't figure out where it was coming from.

"Lucia!" My sister slid next to me and wrapped an arm around me. "What's wrong?" Her voice sounded like she was yelling at me through a wall.

I tried to respond and tell her about the excruciating pain, but I finally learned where the screaming was coming from.

It was me, and my voice was disappearing.

So much pain. What's happening to me?

I heard voices around me, but they became impossible to under-stand. The only time I ever stopped screaming was to breathe, which became harder and harder with each breath. My red vision slowly turned darker and darker, but I wouldn't pass out.

Out of the corner of my vision, Dinar, Silver, and Daric pried my limbs apart. Dinar immediately started looking up and down at my body before moving to my shoulder. I watched her mouth move, but I couldn't hear any sound over the impossibly loud ringing. It looked like everyone was talking as they surrounded me.

As the edges of my vision closed in around me, I felt nothing from my body. I looked down at my hand, and the blood there didn't look right.

Everything went numb as I blacked out.

THE NEXT TIME I opened my eyes, I was staring at a roof.

Ugh.

My eyes reflexively squinted to hide from the bright light. Everything from the tips of my ears to my toes thrummed with a dull ache. Also, everything I saw continued to have a red tint to it. I took a few deep breaths to calm myself down and revert my vision back to normal.

Why isn't it working? I panicked as I sat up.

The stiffness of my body fought against me, but the adrenaline in my system made it a one-sided fight.

Someone had placed me in a large bed with a lumpy mattress. I wasn't in a room so much as a tiny hut. The building was round with almost nothing in the way of furnishings beyond the bed. Even calling it a building was a stretch. A table with my backpack and cloak sat on the far side of the room. A chair sat next to the table, occupied by a skunk beastkin.

The skunk jumped at my movement, and by the ear-piercing shriek and the general shape of the body, I knew the skunk was female.

She placed a hand on her chest as she calmed down. "Oh good. You're awake." Her melodic voice was much better when she wasn't screaming.

"Ha's gung un?" My words failed to come out the way I wanted them to as I continued to scramble out of bed. There was a tightness in my chest preventing me from taking deep breaths. I tried to stand up, but my legs buckled under me.

The woman shot up. "Oh my goodness." She scrambled over to me as I crumpled to the ground in an inglorious heap. "You need to stay in bed. You haven't fully recovered yet." She wrapped her arms around me and tried to lift me. "Oh my. You're heavier than you look."

"Im nul lat!" *What's wrong with my mouth? Why isn't it moving right?*

With a groan, the lady lifted me off the ground and roughly placed me back on the bed. "You're one big girl. Your mother must be proud of you," she said through labored breaths. The skunk sighed as she sat on the edge of the bed.

"Our mother is dead." Lexia's voice announced her arrival. She walked in through the curtain that served as the door to the shack. "But I imagine her adoptive mother has plenty to be proud of her for."

"You poor dear." I could see the sadness on her face from my position on the bed.

Lexia stepped next to the skunk. "Can you do me a favor, Charice?" The skunk hummed as she faced my sister. "There's an elf without any hair on her head. Please find her and bring her here. Tell her that Lucia has woken up."

With a quick nod, Charice stood up and left.

Lexia looked at me with a long face. "How are you feeling?"

"Ooin' isn'l urlin'." I slurred more words.

My sister chuckled at my attempt to talk. "Don't worry about talking, as funny as it is to hear you." She attempted to stifle another laugh but failed. "I'm glad you are awake. Your screams scared me almost as much as watching you lose consciousness."

I struggled to a seated position. "Air are le?"

Lexia sat on the bed next to me and assisted me by holding me up. "After you passed out and the demon fled, we hurried onward. On the way, we found the herd of horses that the horse you killed belonged to, and we took enough to feed everyone until we got here."

Okay, where's here? I looked around the room. My vision swayed as I moved my head slowly and flopped my arms up for a moment.

"We're at our destination, The Heart."

"'Has ha 'urs' nane erer." I slapped my face far harder than I would have liked. My sister laughed at my attempt to talk again. *My face hurts, the entirety of my body hurts, I can't talk, my body doesn't want to move correctly, and now my sister is laughing at me. Can today get any worse?* My stomach growled. *Oh, come on!*

Lexia fell backwards, laughing uncontrollably. As she rolled around, having the time of her life, I noticed there was a small pouch on her hip. I watched my sister laugh until she stopped breathing for a moment. Gasping, she sat back up and wiped the tears from her eyes. "I'm so sorry, but that was priceless." *Good. I'm so glad you're enjoying my suffering.* "You must be hungry. Here, I have something for you." She reached down, grabbed the pouch, and untied it from her belt loop.

As she opened it, drool streamed from my bottom lip as I stared at the raw meat. It was cut into small cubes. *Why didn't I smell that earlier? Now that I think about it, I can't smell anything at all. Whatever, I can worry about that with food in my stomach.*

"Now, you need—"

I didn't let her finish as I lunged for the food. Which was more of me falling on her and fumbling for it.

My sister extended her arm away from me as I drooled all over her. "Gross. Lucia, stop. You need to calm down." She tried to push me off with her other hand while still keeping the food out of my reach.

I overpowered her even in my debilitated state as I flailed my limbs around.

"Don't eat too fast, you could choke." Lexia's muffled voice came from underneath my torso.

I didn't bother with my hands. I just dove into the small bag, face-first. My teeth sank into the fleshy treat, but I found that I couldn't taste the meat like I usually did. *Even my taste is blunted?* Even though the meat had a fraction of the taste I was expecting, I was too hungry to turn it down. The next problem that plagued me was getting the meat from my teeth to go down my throat and into my stomach. I rolled over with some pieces still caught in my teeth, freeing my sister from her entrapment.

The meat rolled to the back of my mouth, just like I planned. But I couldn't swallow it. Several small pieces of meat sat in the back of my throat, not going where I wanted them to.

Lexia placed her hands on my shoulders and lifted me into a seated position again. The meat started falling down my esophagus, but one of the larger pieces got stuck. I turned to Lexia and placed a hand against my throat.

Lexia leaned me forward and struck me between the shoulder blades. After the third strike, the chunk flew out of my mouth and onto the bed. Lexia straightened me back up as I panted heavily.

"Better?" Lexia stared at me with a look of "I told you so." I nodded slowly. "I was going to help you, because your body is acting like a newborn's. Will you let me help you?" she asked as she grabbed the meat that I hadn't tried to eat. The look on her face filled me with guilt. So I nodded as I looked away. "Good girl." Lexia held up a piece to my mouth and made sure everything went where it was supposed to go.

One by one, I ate each piece with my sister's help.

23

NOW TIME FOR SOMETHING COMPLETELY DIFFERENT

Dinar thought it would have been rude to walk in on the two sisters sharing such a vulnerable moment. So the bald elf stood just outside the tiny hovel. She believed it best to stay on Lucia's good side. Maybe it was her paranoia from living as an assassin for more than eighty years, but something about Lucia told her that kid would, if given a reason, slaughter them all. And enjoy it too.

After all, Dinar believed nobody in their right mind would start a fight with a sin without backup.

"I wonder what's taking so long for your friend to get here?" the one sister asked.

After taking a few steps away from the curtain, Dinar dispelled the cushion of air under her feet. She walked into the hut to talk to the sisters. Lucia deserved to know what had happened to her.

"Have you finished getting her some food?" Dinar asked with a practiced smile.

"Yes, we just finished." Lexia turned to look at Dinar with a wide smile on her face. "You said that you wanted to talk to Lucia. But be warned, she can't speak very well right now. So try not to ask her questions, at least not until she's feeling better." The sisters shared a quick glance with each other. Lexia had a playful look in her eye while Lucia scowled as best she could.

The elf waved her hand dismissively as she shook her head. "No worries. Don't worry about talking, Lucia. I'll keep any questions to 'yes' or 'no' if I need to ask you anything. There's something I've learned that I want you to think about while you recover. I'll be busy, so I can't give it the thought that I would like to. And since you have a good head, maybe you'll think of something I don't."

Lucia's tail flopped back and forth behind her as her eyes widened.

Dinar walked over to the chair Charice had been sitting in when Lucia woke up. The two sisters kept their eyes trained on the elf. Lexia helped her sister turn her body so she was in a more comfortable position to watch Dinar.

"Thanks to you, I now know where Strangling Devil poison comes from. It isn't just a poison, it's a venom too. Yeah, a poisonous venom, apparently they can exist." Dinar saw the recognition on the younger sister's face. "That's right, it comes from the sins of lust. It's amazing that you're alive right now, let alone conscious. With the way the venom acted, the sin wanted you incapacitated yet alive. But after seeing your blood turn black from your injuries, I knew. So maybe it's weaker as a venom than as a poison. Or your recovery aptitude saved you." The elf pointed towards the bandages around Lucia's arm and shoulder. The wolf girl looked at her wrist and saw the five black dots Dinar was talking about.

"Are you saying that the sin of lust is solely responsible for the famine in our kingdom?" Lexia's voice rose as she stared at the bearer of bad news. "We need to kill her. Now!"

Lucia flung an arm into the frantic girl's gut. Dinar watched Lexia double over, clutching her stomach. Once Lexia looked at her sister, Lucia shook her head slowly. Dinar smiled at seeing one of the two sisters being reasonable this time, even if she was short-tempered at others. The elf reminded herself that she just needed to feed the girl compliments from time to time, to bolster her ego.

"It's hard to see you two as only fifteen years old. You both are far more grown-up than I was at your age. I mean, when I was fifteen, I was doing some really stupid stuff." Both sisters chuckled at the elf's comment. "But back to the serious part. Yes, that demon is responsible, somehow. But she now knows we're after her. And this whole situation feels too big to have her be the only one causing everything. So finding and killing her will require a trap that she won't see, and we have no idea what she's doing right now. She could be in this room right now for all we know."

"She could?" Lexia asked. The twins' eyes darted around the room.

Dinar waved her hand. "Relax. If she were here, I'm sure she would have made an appearance by now since we're talking about her. But that was a demonstration. Besides, I believe she's been following us since your home village. She can be anywhere, and any plan we make she could overhear and use against us."

The two girls on the bed slumped. Lucia barely stayed upright.

"One thing at a time. I'm going to do some scouting so we can deal with this king before a war starts."

"Why is that demon destroying so much?" Lexia asked nobody as she stared in disbelief at the bed.

"If I had that answer, I could save the world so much heartache," Dinar said as she stood up. "Just know that no matter what a demon says, they care only about themselves and will take advantage of you if you let them. If you give a demon an inch, they will take a kingdom. But as for you"—Dinar pointed to Lucia—"get some sleep. I know I said I wanted you to think about some things, but your recovery takes priority. This should help. Just think about dealing with the demon when you wake up." The elf focused her magic and slammed her sleep spell into the barely mobile beastkin.

Lucia curled into a ball just before falling asleep. "You can use sleep magic?" Lexia asked while she climbed out of the bed and tucked her sister in.

"Yeah, that's the only thing I'm good at. While my magic isn't nearly as universally useful as yours, I've found putting the right people to sleep can keep collateral damage to a minimum." An empty smile appeared on Dinar's face just as she turned to leave. "I should be back later today or tomorrow with a plan. Or at least enough details to start making one. Take care of your sister. She's the only one you've got. Treasure her."

"You don't have to tell me that," Lexia said as she ran her fingers through her sleeping sister's hair.

Dinar didn't stay to hear Lexia's comment. Instead, she hurried out and headed to the largest building in the center of the sad excuse of a city. There weren't many people here, given how many buildings there were. Dinar mused that many of them were abandoned. But the elf couldn't believe what she was in was really called a city.

She wondered how the beastkin could live in such squalor. Where were the statues, the gardens, the street vendors, or any sign of artistic display? Dinar accepted that her internal questions would remain unanswered. She'd seen slums look better than this capital city. The human cities, while undeniably bland, were still obviously cities. To Dinar, this was an oversized village in the middle of an underdeveloped kingdom.

The "city" was a disorganized mess of tiny ramshackle buildings built from multiple types of wood. Many of the buildings used three or four different-colored woods in their construction. Some of the small houses didn't have doors and used sheets as a barrier. Anyone who looked at the buildings closely would see several misaligned boards and planks cut at off angles. Dinar wondered who taught these people how to build. Many of the structures looked like they would fall down if a powerful storm blew through.

The streets were barely fit to be called that since they weren't arrayed in nice neat lines, but instead circled around each building. The only reason Dinar could identify them as roads was because they looked like the most packed sections of dirt.

As the elf walked, she peered through a window or two. While the outsides of the buildings looked barely put together, the furniture inside showed her that every building she looked into was someone's home. And whoever lived there stored only the barest of essentials inside.

The more the elf walked through the capital of the Wild Kingdom, the more she was left wondering how these people had lived like this for so long.

Dinar continued to walk down the streets, lifting her hood to cover her face. The few beastkin that were out were staring at her. The elf knew that lifting her hood wouldn't make the stares go away, but it made them easier to ignore. A bald elf was a rare sight, and for good reason. After all, no elf naturally went bald. Her most defining feature was a constant reminder of her greatest failure and the reason she could never return home. Dinar knew the beastkin didn't know what her bald head meant, and she was determined to keep it that way. The fewer people who knew about it, the better.

It didn't take her long to arrive at her destination. Several beastkin walked in the front door, including two children. Her mind was flooded with questions. *Wasn't this the palace? Why are they taking their children to see the king? Shouldn't he have better things to do than deal with brats?* More thoughts stewed in Dinar's mind as she followed the people in.

The elf stopped and stared at the sight that greeted her. No throne room, no holding room for visitors, and no walls other than the ones supporting the roof.

It wasn't a palace, it was a warehouse.

Dinar was in the wrong place. She recognized that as she watched beastkin families walk through and just grab food, clothes, a basket, or any other daily supplies they wanted. She couldn't believe what she was seeing.

Off to the side, a wolf beastkin with brown fur sorted through baskets of apples. The man removed anything that looked damaged or spoiled. Dinar approached him, but he continued to work, ignoring her, until she cleared her throat. The wolf looked around for a moment, not seeing her at first since she was at least twenty inches shorter than him.

"Oh, hello there. Are you looking for someone to help you find something?" His voice shook, not out of nervousness, but from tiredness. Now that Dinar was closer, she could see the fur around his mouth had partially turned gray.

"Yes, but I have some questions first." Dinar opted for a more innocent tone. She thought he might think of her as a child, given her youthful appearance and size. "What is this?" The elf waved her arms at the display all around her.

Confusion spread across the beastkin's face. "This is where everyone comes to get what they need. And if they have anything they don't need or anything extra, they give it to a caretaker such as myself." He placed his hand on his chest and gave a slight bow. "My name is Bando. May I have yours, child?"

Dinar held back her amusement at the elderly beastkin's predictability. She was far older than him. At two hundred and three years old, she humored the old man. "Dinar. Just Dinar." She put on her most professional smile. "So, you're saying anyone can just come in here and take whatever they want? And not pay?"

Bando closed his eyes as he took a deep breath. "Another foreigner who knows nothing, of course. What are they teaching kids these days?" He opened his eyes and looked at her with pity. "We don't take what we want, but what we need. Also, everyone is expected to give back when they can."

No matter how hard she tried, she couldn't understand how such a system could work for long. Every scenario she thought of ended with someone killing another or taking advantage of the system. Shaking her head, Dinar sighed. "Sure, whatever. Do you at least know where the palace is?"

The wolf beastkin growled. "Your parents need to teach you some manners." He dug his claws into the table that held the baskets of apples. "And what is a palace?"

Dinar pinched the bridge of her nose. "Do you know where the king lives?" She'd had enough of this game.

"The longhouse at the head of the town." Dinar raised an eyebrow, bidding Bando to continue. "North." He raised his arm to point.

"Thank you," Dinar forced herself to say. As she turned to leave, she lifted the side of her hood and flashed the wolf a glimpse of her ear. "I can guarantee you, I'm far older than you and my parents died before you were born."

Dinar left the old wolf to grumble something unpleasant about elves. She'd heard it all before. Now she had her heading and her mission. It was time to go to work.

Dinar's stride quickened as she cushioned her footfalls with a small pocket of air on the bottoms of her boots. It was one of her favorite uses of magic and incredibly useful for any infiltration missions. Her current mission of protecting Daric wasn't her usual job. Midas kept her busy enough, especially recently, with the rise of a demonic cult causing problems for the last dozen years.

Midas never used her talents as a former assassin. In fact, he ordered her not to kill anyone unless it was in self-defense. She was simply his messenger. For that, she was thankful. But with how things were, even she couldn't ignore Lucia and Lexia's request.

As she found what she believed to be the building the beastkin had told her about, one thought ran through her mind.

One more time, then never again.

24

SEEING RED

Dinar's first order of business was to check for all entrances and exits, whether they were a door, window, chimney, or, like one time, a waste drain.

Dinar wished that memory could be forgotten with the other uncountable memories she'd left behind over the years.

As she circled around the building, a curious sight in one of the windows caught her attention. A lion beastkin was leaning out one of the windows with a forlorn look.

While Dinar watched, the beastkin sighed before turning back into the building. The bald elf froze, hoping he wouldn't notice her. It looked like he was talking to someone.

Dinar moved to see who he was talking to. Her heart nearly stopped when she saw the sin of lust who'd bitten Lucia stabbing a finger into the lion beastkin's chest. The demon's wing was mostly healed, and she pushed the large man back with nothing more than a finger and an angry face.

There was too much distance, so Dinar couldn't hear what the demon was telling the beastkin, but she stopped in the middle of her berating to turn her head and look directly at Dinar.

Dinar's heart skipped a beat, and it leaped as a pair of hands touched her shoulders. Instinctively she grabbed one of the daggers she kept hidden in her sleeves and turned to slash whoever touched her.

It was the sin of lust hovering in the air and laughing as she easily floated away from the attack.

Dinar didn't hold any desire to prove her bravery and turned to run as fast as she could. She even channeled a little wind magic to speed her up.

She needed to warn the others, and she didn't bother putting the blade away as she sprinted through the streets.

MY EYES FLUTTERED open as my consciousness drifted in and out. A stiffness plagued my body, like I had slept in one spot for an entire day. Yawning, I stretched out in the bed. *This bed isn't comfortable. I want my bed back at home. Whose bed is this?* I sat up straight.

A skunk sat in a chair with some of my clothes on the table and one of my shirts in her hands. She was slowly and carefully threading a needle around a small tear in my shirt. *Oh, now I remember. I fought the sin of lust and she injected me with her venom, which paralyzed me.* As my emotions came down from their panic, I noticed something was still wrong. *Why is my vision still red? I need to ask Lexia if she knows anything about this. Mom didn't.*

The skunk's ears twitched as I moved out from under the sheet. She lifted her face and thankfully didn't shriek this time. "Good evening. Did you sleep well?" Her voice was softer than I remembered, but the way she smiled irritated me, though I didn't know why.

I flattened my ears. "What are you doing to my clothes?" *Oh hey, I can talk again.*

She held up the shirt and pointed at the series of holes she closed up. "Just patching the holes. What bit you?" she asked as she lowered her handiwork.

"I didn't say you could touch my stuff." I growled and flexed my claws as I stood up.

The woman curled her tail around her waist as she placed the shirt down gently. "I'm sorry. Your sister asked me to fix it for you. If you want to do it yourself, I understand. I was just trying to help." She held her hands up in surrender.

Then why are you making me so angry? My stomach growled. As I took a few deep breaths, I closed my eyes and tried to relax. "I'm sorry. I didn't mean it." The lady slowly lowered her arms, but still gave me a worried look. "I guess I'm hungry."

"Ah, my oldest brother's mate is a primal wolf, and she gets a bit snap-happy before breakfast too." The skunk beastkin relaxed completely. She stood up and flashed me a smile. "Would you like me to show you where to get food?" she said as she extended a hand towards me.

I frowned. "I'm sorry, but I don't remember your name. Mine is Lucia."

"Charice," she said with a giggle.

I extended my arm and held Charice's hand. "I would be very grateful if you could show me where to get some food." As we reached the doorway, I let go of Charice's hand and held up a finger before she could ask a question. I trotted over to the table and picked up my magic cloak. Charice stood at the door patiently waiting for me to tie the strings. "Sorry, this cloak is special to me."

"It looks good on you. It really compliments your eyes." She extended her hand again, and I took it. "I'm surprised you haven't been bonded yet. Still looking for someone special?" She gave me a wink.

I whirled my head away from the woman. "Well, kinda." *Is it warm today or is it just me?* "I just don't think I'm ready for that yet. Also, I've spent all my memorable life around humans and elves. Most of the time they don't really pique my interest, if you know what I mean. And those that do are strong but dumber than a pile of stones."

I turned to see if she wore a band and saw the copper band on her wrist. "Ah, a girl with high standards," Charice said as she looked at the sky. "I'm sure you will find the man you deserve somewhere. Just don't give up too quickly, alright?" She peered at me from the corner of her eye.

"I'll try." I lowered my head and slumped my shoulders as I

continued to walk. "What I don't get is why everyone is obsessed with me not having a mate yet. First, it was my sister. Now it's a stranger I just met." I flicked my ears and pursed my lips as soon as I realized my thoughts had just flown out of my mouth. I slowly turned to see the frown on Charice's face. "You're a nice stranger." I put on an innocent smile.

My sheepish attempt at complimenting her didn't undo the damage I had caused. But after a few moments of walking through the nearly deserted streets, she started up a conversation, asking how I'd come to spend most of my life around humans. I gave her the very condensed version and didn't go into many of the details of what my life had been like. She warmed up to me after I finished talking. Charice talked about her family and her six kids, who were all adults with their own mates, and her three grandchildren, with hopefully more on the way. The sun setting made it uncomfortable to look in the direction we were walking because we stared right at it.

I walked with the skunk beastkin to the center of the town to a large warehouse-looking building. Charice told me that it was called The Heart and if I ever needed anything, I should just walk in and grab it. She made sure to drill into my head that I needed to give back if I could. I walked in with Charice and she gave me a tour of possible options, all of which were noticeably underwhelming.

A wolf beastkin who was sorting some apples looked a bit disgruntled and kept mumbling something about arrogant elves. *I think I should stay away from him. Penny likely said something stupid again. It isn't my job to clean up after her mess. Besides, I don't do apples.*

Charice took me straight towards the meat distribution while talking about everything along the way. *It's so nice not to have to explain to people that I can only eat meat. This lady even asked which meats I like more. And if I like certain organs or not. These people understand what it's like for me. Here, I'm not unique. There are plenty of others just like me.* While I thought about my lack of exclusivity, I heard two pairs of familiar footsteps. An obnoxiously familiar voice accompanied the footsteps.

"And you guys don't use any money at all?" Daric asked a thin hare beastkin who was almost as tall as me if you didn't include his long oval ears.

"Yes. If you are going to take something, please consider giving something in return," the man responded in a low yet stern voice.

Daric waved his hand and shook his head. "We're with the group who brought all that horse meat yesterday."

I tried to ignore Daric as I looked for food. *This is new. I haven't had a rattlesnake before. I wonder if it tastes different from a python.* The growl of my stomach overshadowed my thoughts. Not wanting to prolong my suffering, I picked up the meat and waved goodbye to Charice as I carried my whole, yet-to-be skinned, rattlesnake. As I moved to stand behind Daric, I sliced the belly of the snake, starting from the tail, giving myself a quick bite.

"And what did you do to help with catching the horses?" I made sure my voice carried a slight rumble to it as I whispered just above his head.

Daric jumped and nearly hit me with the top of his head as he spun around. "What? What do you..." Daric placed his hand on his chest as he took a few deep breaths. "Oh, it's you. I helped carry the extra meat." He flexed his biceps as he puffed out his chest.

I glared at Golditress. She shook her head. "He just ate some and put some in his pack for later."

My glare returned to Daric, and I flattened my ears.

Daric laughed nervously. "Goldy, why do you keep selling me out like that?"

"Because someone has to keep you honest," I growled.

"What did you do to earn that..." Daric pointed to my breakfast. "Is that a snake?"

I held it up and smiled as I pulled out the long intestines. "Yes, specifically a rattlesnake. I'm curious if it tastes different from the pythons I've had back home." The hare beastkin shook his head as he returned to whatever he was doing, leaving me with the two humans. "Where are the others?"

Daric shrugged. "Dinar started dishing out orders. Mark, Penny, and Silver are patrolling around. They're supposed to be looking for signs of the sin of lust. Anna wanted to talk to her angel to see if he could help us against the demon while she checked out the blood anchor. Apparently it's just outside of town."

Don't those take a lot of people dying in one place to create? And on top of that, who created two in this kingdom? I grabbed my head with one hand. *Ah, why does my head have to hurt from all this mystery? But there's something wrong with me. I can't focus, and I have no idea what else is happening.*

I eyed the pair closely. "And what are you supposed to be doing? Where did the other beastkin go?"

"I don't know." Daric rolled his eyes. Golditress flinched at Daric's tone. "Dinar told us to make sure we had something other than horse meat to eat. So, here we are. What are you doing? Should you be up and walking already?"

"Yes, the venom Dinar said you were suffering from sounded quite dangerous." Golditress folded her hands and gave me an expectant look. "Maybe you should rest some more."

"Um, where are you staying? Does it have a place where we can sit and talk?" I asked. "I kinda want to talk someplace a little more private."

I took a chunk of meat off the tail, bones and all. Golditress winced as I chewed the meat and separated the bones. *It tastes the same. How disappointing.*

"Yeah. They gave us a small place to stay while we visited. These beastkin have been very hospitable. Almost too much so." Daric looked from side to side.

I waved my hand to direct them to lead the way. I followed the two humans, eating as I did. They quietly led me through the town to the outer edges of the northeastern side. They led me into a small home, and once inside, it looked like it was large enough for maybe four people, if you were okay with sharing beds. I saw just Daric and Golditress's packs sitting next to the two beds.

Daric waved towards the table and pulled out a chair for Golditress to sit in. I sat down across from them, finishing my meal. I spat out the last of the bones before I tossed them out the window.

"Isn't that littering?" Daric gave me a confused look as he sat down.

I shrugged. "They're bones. I think of it as fertilizing."

"Isn't that against some kind of law?" Daric started tapping his fingers on the table. "I get the feeling that the laws of this kingdom are pretty lax, but shouldn't we get to know them before we do something to get in trouble?"

I waved my hand and shook my head. "It doesn't matter what the laws are. If I wasn't a knight, I probably wouldn't know half as many laws as I do know, and I only know the major ones."

Golditress looked concerned. "Why? Didn't your captain drill them into you for weeks until you memorized them?"

I laughed. "She tried. Oh boy, did she try." I straightened up. "But no. Laws shouldn't make someone a decent person. And I find the absoluteness of laws far too stifling."

"But if there were no laws, it would be chaos." Daric threw his arms up. "Laws tell people how to act."

"I'm not stupid." An exaggerated sigh slipped from my lips. "Some people need those laws. The only thing I care about is what punishment I'll need to serve after I inevitably break the law."

"Why would you intentionally break the law?" Golditress asked.

I glared at the woman. "Because there are times when the laws don't serve me and the right thing is to do something deemed as wrong." Daric opened his mouth, and I growled at him. "I don't go looking for trouble; trouble finds me. I just end the trouble as quickly as possible."

"But..." Daric's voice barely escaped his lips.

I dug my claws into the table. "I'm done talking about this. Besides, I need to come up with ideas for dealing with the sin of lust. Do you want to help with that?"

"Do you know what happened?" Golditress asked in a quiet voice. *It almost sounds like she didn't want to ask.*

I tried to put on a cheerful smile. "Don't worry, no lasting damage. Dinar explained it to me. Although, first thing this morning, I was a mess. I couldn't even talk correctly." I shivered. "Lexia kept laughing at me whenever I said anything."

Daric looked down at the table. "Dinar talked to you already?" His voice was more somber than I'd ever heard from him before.

"Yeah, she did." I tried to sound cheery. "What she said makes me believe that the demon has been tormenting this entire kingdom, but I can't figure out why. Why would she go through all the trouble of killing this country so slowly? Doesn't she need large bloody sacrifices made in a short time to create a blood anchor?"

"That's what Anna said," Golditress said as she fiddled with the tips of her hair.

"And a war between two kingdoms will give plenty of battlefields for them to create all the blood anchors they need." I absentmindedly started carving grooves into the table.

Daric slammed his hand on the table. "We have to stop them. We can't let any more blood anchors be created. If we can prevent them from summoning the demon king, it'll be even better than defeating him."

Golditress turned her head towards Daric. "Unless Anna can figure out a way to lift the blood anchors, it'll be a war of attrition with these demons. They have time and resources on their side." She propped her head on her hand as she leaned on the table. "These demons sound even more dangerous each time I hear about them."

I failed to hold back a laugh. "You're telling me. I've even fought three of them."

"That sin of lust looked like it wasn't a danger to you until it bit you," Daric said as he looked at my shoulder.

My shoulder twitched at the memory of the fight. I reflexively grabbed it and rubbed it.

"Yeah, that venom was something else. It's really messed me up. My vision still hasn't corrected itself." Both humans jerked to sit straight up and stare at me. "You want me to explain, don't you?" I asked as I tried to make myself smaller. They nodded. I took a deep breath. "Well, ever since I can remember, whenever I get angry enough, my vision always turns to a reddish hue. And when I got older, I learned to control it, somewhat. Now I'm in full control of it. I use it because it helps me focus on everything and block out pain. It's much harder to control my emotions in that state, which is why I use it for fighting and hunting."

"So you're some kind of berserker?" Daric asked without holding back a laugh. I glared at him. He didn't stop laughing until I growled louder than he laughed. "It was a joke. Don't be so serious all the time." He took a few deep breaths to slow his breathing.

I continued to growl as I narrowed my eyes even farther. Daric leaned back when he noticed I didn't stop. "The last human I ate tasted like dirt. And that snake wasn't enough to fill me up. I wonder if you taste like dirt." A tingling in the back of my mind slowly grew as I found myself standing up.

He smells like he would taste better than dirt. Good, my sense of smell has returned.

Hold on a moment, did I just think that? Why? Yeah, it was a terrible joke, and I hated it. But it isn't something I want to kill over. And why did I say I wanted to eat him? I don't eat people if I can help it.

A ringing in my head drowned out my other thoughts as my visions turned a darker shade of red. Everything I could see looked like it was covered in blood, except for Daric. Every detail of him popped out in excruciatingly vivid detail. From all the minor damage on his clothes to how he stood with more weight on his left foot, I saw everything.

One absolute feeling ran through my body, one I couldn't fight.

I needed to kill my prey, and my prey was Daric.

My body moved without my consent. For the second time in my life, I lost all control.

25

FRENZIED MOMENTS

While Lucia bared her fangs at the two humans, Daric stood and lowered himself into a defensive stance, his shoulders squared with the snarling wolf.

"Lucia, this isn't funny." The fear in the man's voice only encouraged the beast woman.

She picked the table up and threw it against a wall. The two humans looked towards Daric's sword, propped up against a bed in its sheath.

The moment Daric looked away, the out-of-control wolfkin pounced. By the time Daric realized that Lucia had moved, she was only inches away from him. He attempted to catch her, but her momentum knocked him off his feet.

Snarling, the wolf beastkin landed on him and didn't waste any time digging her claws into his chest. Daric's skin held back most of Lucia's claws, but line after line of blood appeared on his chest, soaking his shirt.

Daric frantically attempted to shove Lucia's claws away. Unfortunately for him, Lucia's strength made it impossible to do anything to stop her. He tried to roll her over so he could get out from under her, but the only thing he succeeded at was getting his left shoulder stabbed inside the ball joint. The attack forced a cry from him as he felt Lucia's claws scraping against his bone.

Drool dripped from the wolfkin's mouth as she opened it wide.

Daric struck out at Lucia's face with a punch. The hit connected, and there was a brief moment of shock on her face. Complete and unparalleled panic overruled any rational thought Daric could have had as Lucia released a heart-stopping snarl and lifted her claws, ready to slash at his face.

As the claws raced for Daric's face, he brought his good arm up to block and closed his eyes.

The attack didn't connect.

Instead, the sound of a wooden chair shattering filled the small hovel. Golditress stood over Daric, holding a portion of the back of the chair he had sat in.

Lucia hit the ground in a heap.

"Thanks." Daric extended a hand to Golditress.

Lucia bolted up. For the first time, the two humans looked into the unhinged wolf's eyes. There was no white in the sclera. Her eyes were so bloodshot that red surrounded the sapphire-blue irises. Something was wrong, and they both knew it. But they both also understood that they didn't have the time to analyze the problem.

Another bloodlust-fueled snarl came from Lucia as she locked her eyes on Golditress before lunging for the girl. Daric leaped to intercept the girl, trying to save his friend.

A feral grunt escaped Lucia as she and Daric tumbled through the upturned table. The shabby construct crumbled under their weight. The boy tried to pin her to give him any advantage to strike back. He didn't succeed in holding her down for any length of time as Lucia slashed her claws across his face. A single line of blood poured from his eyebrow while three more lines gouged his cheek just below the eye.

Daric threw another punch with his uninjured arm. This time, he aimed for her temple to knock her out as quickly as possible. The punch landed short, and he instead hit her in the corner of her eye, the blow deflecting off her face.

Lucia responded by biting his hand as it passed into her view.

Daric howled in pain as his bones lost the battle against her jaw muscles and sharp teeth shredded his flesh. The tactic of punching a dog in the nose ran through his mind as he desperately wanted her to release his hand.

Daric acted on his idea and punched with his free arm. The punch was pathetic compared to his earlier ones. Even though he didn't put as much strength behind it as he wanted, when Daric's punch connected with Lucia's nose, she flinched back and released him. Daric cradled his mangled hand as blood poured from it.

Lucia slammed her hand into Daric's throat and pinned him to the ground in one fluid motion while he was distracted. Suffocating, Daric frantically grabbed at her arm.

Golditress rushed to dislodge Lucia. Bringing her knee up, she struck the side of Lucia's head.

Lucia fell to the side, releasing Daric and falling defenseless to the ground. Golditress charged her again when the wolfkin stirred. The human girl lifted her leg to kick Lucia one more time, hoping that would be the blow that would bring her down.

If Lucia hadn't moved, it would have been a perfect kick and likely knocked their feral companion unconscious. But Lucia didn't stay still.

She lunged towards the charging girl. Golditress's leg wasn't fully extended and her balance was slightly off as her attack struck much too early. The mitigated force put Golditress in an awkward position as her foot got caught in the bend of Lucia's armpit.

With a snarl, Lucia slammed a hand into Golditress's sternum, claws puncturing her flesh easily. The sound of bones cracking accompanied Golditress as she flew away from Lucia into the opposite wall.

As Golditress bounced off the wall, she collapsed to the ground in a heap, completely unconscious. A small spot of blood stained her hair on the back of her head.

In shock, Daric watched in horror as his friend crumbled to the ground.

THE DOOR to the home opened, and with a dagger drawn, Dinar gasped at the sight before her. Daric lay on the ground holding his neck, Lucia panted as blood dripped from her claws and stained the fur around her lips, and Golditress lay in an obviously unconscious pile.

Lucia turned to face the newcomer. Instead of charging, she lowered her ears and sniffed the air. Dinar instantly saw the blood-red eyes Lucia stared at her with. No, she didn't stare at the elf, but past her. It was like something else had her attention.

Before Dinar could get a word out, Lucia ran on all fours towards her. After many years of honing her instinctive reactions, Dinar jumped backwards the moment she saw Lucia move. She wanted to keep as much distance between her and the wolf beastkin throughout the fight as possible.

Dinar froze when Lucia didn't chase her. Instead, Lucia turned and sprinted in the direction she'd come from. The direction of the longhouse where the king lived.

"Where's Lucia going?" Lexia called from down the dirt street.

Dinar turned to see Lexia running towards her. "Towards the northwest, where the king lives." She turned to see the horrible condition her friends were in. "What I want to know is what possessed her to do this." She pointed to Daric and Golditress. "And why were her eyes so red?"

Lexia grabbed Dinar's shoulders and turned her to face her. "Red eyes? Are you sure?"

"Without a doubt," Dinar replied.

Lexia's eyes grew wide as she released the bald elf. "No." Her voice was barely more than a whisper as she stumbled back a few steps.

"What? What is it?" Dinar put her dagger away in the sheath she had concealed on the small of her back. "Do you know what happened?"

"The frenzy." Lexia turned to face the northwest and ran to follow her sister. Dropping to all fours, she sprinted as fast as she could.

Dinar looked at her companions. Regret filled her heart as she moved to help the humans. No amount of chastisement was going to fix this mess, and Dinar knew it. Seeing that Daric was heavily wounded and Golditress wasn't conscious, Dinar didn't need to think about who needed the more immediate aid.

WHILE DINAR ASSISTED HER FRIENDS, Lexia chased after her sister. Lucia had the worst possible affliction for a beastkin.

Tears streamed from her eyes as she dashed through the town, ignoring everyone. The other beastkin who saw her running must have seen Lucia and decided something was wrong and joined in behind her. Soon, a small crowd followed the silver-furred wolf beastkin as she ran closer to the head of the town.

Limbs burned and muscles ached as Lexia sprinted faster than she had in her entire life. It was a race against time, one she knew she had no right to win, regardless of how much she desired to. Lexia neared the northernmost buildings and saw the longhouse. Two figures stood facing each other. One stood on two legs, while the other was on all four.

A muscular male primal lion beastkin hunched forward slightly as he bared his teeth. His adversary, an attractively athletic female primal wolf beastkin, released a snarl as she charged at him. Her cool blue cloak was a stark contrast to everything around her.

Lexia froze as she watched her sister attack Daygon, the beast king. The small crowd of beastkin following her also halted to watch the spectacle. Lexia knew that the crowd didn't know that Lucia was under the influence of the frenzy and that they would think this was just another attempt for the right to rule, and if she said Lucia had the frenzy, she didn't know what would happen. This might be the only chance Lucia got to kill the king.

Lexia continued staring, unable to decide what to do as her sister charged the king.

DAYGON WAITED PATIENTLY for the wolf girl to make the first move. She pushed off the ground and reached out with her claws for

Daygon's throat. The king sidestepped the obvious attack effortlessly. The wolf landed and dug her front claws into the ground, turning on them to face him.

Daygon lowered his right arm and performed an uppercut slash of his claws. The wolfkin twisted her body and leaned to her left, making the attack miss as she charged again.

The wolf struck out with her claws at the lion's torso as she stood up to face him on two legs. The king leaned backwards to keep himself just out of reach. The woman's claws passed by harmlessly, but the king had to backpedal to keep his balance. She continued to pursue him as she slashed at him with her left hand and stepped towards him. Daygon turned his body and braced himself on his left leg, then grabbed her wrist with his left hand, halting her attack before it could reach him.

With a snarl, the wolf girl struck out with her right hand, aiming for Daygon's face. Daygon grabbed her wrist again, leaving him with his arms crossed. He was confident now that he had the girl in his grasp that she was no longer a threat to him, so he moved to uncross his arms so she would be in the unbalanced position. He tugged, but her arms continued to push toward him.

During the moment his concentration lapsed, the wolf's claws nearly reached their target. Surprise flared on Daygon's face as the wolf snarled and leaned forward, jaws snapping. The lion positioned his crossed arms under her chin to hold her back.

The wild woman continued to snarl and snap her jaws as she reached for Daygon. Seeing the spit flying from her mouth and the red of her eyes, the king's heart dropped. He lamented as he recognized another child lost to the frenzy. He dug his toe-claws into the ground, but he could feel the dirt giving way to the girl's pushing. Before today, Daygon's strength had never been contested. Yes, there were those who thought he should no longer rule and fought him one-on-one. But none of them were close to his level of strength. This girl, while still not as strong as him, was dangerously close.

Regret ran rampant in his heart and showed in his eyes as he held back the tears.

"I am sorry, child. I have failed you," Daygon whispered, but the silver-furred beastkin didn't react. She simply snapped her jaws and reached her claws towards him.

Daygon pushed back and lowered his shoulder. The move forced him to release her claws, and one buried itself in his back, just above the shoulder blade. The king lunged forward, ignoring the pain, and raised his shoulder into the wolfkin's bottom jaw. A click sounded as the blow knocked her upwards and backwards for a step.

With a growl, the wolf snapped her head back down to stare at the lionkin. Daygon charged the woman with his claws outstretched.

The frenzied wolf didn't bother to deflect his attack. Instead, she took one claw to the torso and the other to her right bicep. Her claws opened up his torso in return. One set of claw marks dug into his rib cage, with one claw slipping in between the bones and nicking his lung. The other claw slashed at his collarbone and got stuck as she pulled at the bone.

Daygon slapped at the claw stuck on his collarbone, eliciting even more pain that he had to ignore, then kicked the woman in the gut, drawing four red lines just above her waist.

Sliding to a stop thanks to her toe-claws, the wolfkin growled before she charged again. Daygon realized that the frenzied girl no longer cared about her own safety. He resigned himself to one more attack and threw his arms out wide. She dug her claws into Daygon's chest and gut. He made sure that the wolf would not strike any vital areas before allowing the attack to land.

The wolf girl leaned forward once her claws were embedded in the lionkin's flesh. Before she could sink her teeth in, Daygon slammed his hand into the side of her head. The wolfkin flew to the ground and landed on her hands and knees, her cheek decorated with four red lines and her jaw dangling slightly ajar. Daygon's flesh was ripped open where her claws had dug in.

With a growl, Daygon brought his hand to the woman's head again, this time sending her sprawling to the ground. The wolf beastkin moved only slightly as Daygon panted, and he strode over to her.

"I know you may not hear me, but I wish you could have killed me," Daygon whispered as he raised his hand one more time before bringing it down towards her skull.

A CYLINDER of ice struck his wrist, forcing his blow to miss Lucia's head by inches. Daygon turned his head towards Lexia as she frantically ran towards him. "Stop!" Lexia shouted once Daygon looked at her. "Stop, Lucia's my sister." Tears streamed from her eyes.

Daygon stood up while watching Lucia's chest slowly rise and fall, but the rest of her body didn't move.

Lexia needed to keep her sister still. She summoned her magic and willed it to cover Lucia. Thick ice encased the immobile wolf girl's wrists and ankles.

"She has the frenzy," the king said as he looked at his opponent's twin. "Do you wish for her to be subjected to the cure? She may not survive or be left in a worse state. Will you make that decision for her?" The king remembered every time he had seen someone fail to survive the cure, including those that were driven mad by it and took their own lives.

Lexia slid and cradled her sister's head, tears streaming unimpeded. "Yes. She'll survive. I know she will," the girl answered without looking away from her unconscious sister.

"Very well." Daygon turned to the building and cupped his hands around his mouth. "Grant! Bring the cure to the front!" Daygon bellowed loud enough to cause Lexia to flinch. Daygon turned to face her and opened his mouth, but no words came out.

"How touching. One sister caring for the other." The sultry voice drew the two beastkins' attention above them. Naked and wounded, the sin of lust flapped her wings as she stared at the two. Lexia noticed that the wing she'd punched a hole in had sealed slightly, and the wounds her sister inflicted had healed some. "However, after what she did to me and now that her mind is gone, I want you to dispose of her."

Lexia stood up, her claws extended. "You did this to my sister." Her voice carried the rumble of a growl. "I'll kill you." Ice magic formed in Lexia's hand as a spear manifested. With a flick of her arm, the spear flew towards the demon.

The demon drifted to the side as the icy projectile sailed past her. "Deal with her." Her voice carried, felt heavier as she glared at the conscious sister.

As Lexia created a larger spear, Daygon grabbed her shoulder and threw her to the ground.

A fire burned behind the wolfkin's eyes as she stared at her king. "That's a demon! What are you doing?"

The king's eyes were nearly closed. "I know." His voice sounded tired.

Lexia climbed to her feet. "Then why are you helping it?" She prepared to create another spear of ice.

"Because I have no choice." Daygon couldn't look at the girl as he answered her.

"That's right, pet." The sin floated down and hovered behind the lion king. Placing her hands on his shoulders, she grinned at Lexia. "He has been so gracious to serve me, but alas, I'm growing bored with having only one toy. I want more, and your sister seemed like she would have been fun. And with your magic, I can see that you could be just as much fun. So, what do you say? Want to be my pet?"

Lexia couldn't control her magic and released it as she stared in disbelief. She knew that the king didn't deserve to rule, but to serve a demon willingly was something she couldn't begin to believe, not after everything Anna and Lucia told her about demons. Even seeing all the facts in front of her made her question if she'd heard everything correctly.

Lexia shook her head frantically. "I will never serve you, demon. I will kill you for what you did to my sister!" she screamed as the temperature dropped around her by the second.

"I wouldn't do that if I were you." The sin of lust wagged her finger back and forth as she flapped her wings to hover over Lucia's exposed head.

Lexia took a few steps forward so that the ice covering Lucia was in her area of control and flung her arm up. The ice covering Lucia shifted to a point, grew, and pierced the demon before she could move. Instead of screaming in pain from being impaled, the demon just smiled. Lexia stood staring, flabbergasted, as the image of the sin slowly vanished into nothing.

"I told you not to do that."

Lexia heard the sultry voice behind her this time. She spun around to see the demon hovering right behind her.

Why couldn't Lexia hear the flapping of the wings behind her? She didn't have the faintest idea. She didn't have time to ask as a tail covered in black scales slapped her in the face. The wolf tumbled, head over heels, before landing on her back. Lexia couldn't tell what caused her head to spin more: the blow from the demon or the tumble she took. In the end, it didn't matter as she stared at the sky in pain, disoriented.

The demon touched the ground ever so softly as she laughed. "Oh, how I love that look." She strutted towards the downed sister. "You beastkin are always so stubborn, but everyone has a price." The sin of lust placed her foot on Lexia's cheek and tilted her head so she could see Lucia. "One word from me and she dies. Now be a good girl and surrender to me. Become my pet and I will spare her life this time."

Daygon stood next to Lucia with his foot next to her head.

Lexia couldn't focus on her magic as her head throbbed from the pain. She lay still for a few moments as she cried. "Leave her." The whisper was barely audible.

"What was that?" The sin leaned forward slightly as she turned her ear towards the beastkin.

"Leave my sister alone and I will submit." Lexia couldn't believe the words she was saying, but she wanted to save her sister.

The sin's grin grew impossibly wide. "See, I told you. Everyone has a price." The demon looked up and pointed to Daygon, who stood silently the entire time. "Go, lead your people to attack the humans. No more delays. Leave the girl."

Daygon glanced at Lucia one last time before he turned to face the crowd that had followed Lexia. He walked over to them to give them instructions to leave for war.

Lexia didn't have the luxury of paying attention to him. She had a demon grinning above her. The beastkin felt a tug at the very core of her being and didn't fight it. A deal was a deal, and she wasn't in a position or state to fight.

MARK STOOD in the shadow of a building as he witnessed the mobilization of the beastkin and the demon-controlled king from afar. He watched as Lexia stood and followed the sin of lust, tears streaming from her eyes. Mark couldn't imagine a worse scenario as he waited for everyone to leave, a deer beastkin stood with a bottle in his hands at the front of the building.

Slowly, they both walked towards the restrained wolf beastkin.

INTERLUDE: THERE'S MORE
THAN ONE HELL

The years of the two souls played out before the two multidimensional beings in moments. The Voice, manifested as a small violet sphere, watched them in earnest, hoping that its deal with The Broker wouldn't have to be utilized. The clouds gathered together to serve as a viewing portal pulsed as The Voice noticed The Judge willed them to slow down.

"Your two souls' predecessor has forced them to work together." The Judge's voice echoed throughout the small pocket dimension of white marble. "He's done some of your work for you."

The Voice pulsed gently brighter. "Thankfully. Those two stand a much better chance together than alone."

Seeing the man engineer all his plans to coax the wolf beastkin girl was interesting. Some of the plans were crude, simple but effective in the short term. Others were unnecessarily complicated to a level The Voice couldn't follow and suspected that The Judge didn't understand either.

The boy grew up and matured more physically than mentally. That worried The Voice. Seeing the beastkin girl and her temperament left it wondering whether or not they could have a lasting relationship.

The two continued to watch more closely as the two souls on Centari worked together and met up with the original beastkin soul's sister. Watching them interact left The Voice calmer. It was glad to see the beastkin sisters getting along and growing closer with each interaction. After the girl was adopted by the elf, she grew and matured and found her reason for fighting. The sister looked like she would be someone who would be a critical asset for her in the future.

Unfortunately, the demons' work had been far too thorough. Traveling through a kingdom that was slowly being starved and coaxed into attacking the neighboring kingdom was taking its toll on the two souls and their traveling companions.

"That demoness is dangerous." The Voice floated closer to the clouds. "Something about her isn't right."

"She is more powerful than a usual sin." The Judge's beam of orange light pulsed. It almost felt like the powerful, multidimensional being was exclusively thinking about the demoness. "If there weren't four riders, she would be the next candidate for a rider in that hell. She is feeding off the bloodlust and animalistic desire for reproduction of the beastkin. The beast king's own bloodlust towards her only feeds her strength. She's found a way to tap into and feed all desires, not just carnal desires."

The Voice hummed. "The sin of pride serving her is an achievement in itself. I didn't know the sins of pride from that hell could work under another demon that wasn't the ruler of that hell."

Another nine clumps of clouds coalesced into nine viewing portals. Each portal led to a different plane full of differing levels and types of pain and excess. One showed a burning plane full of warring demons and devils of every shape and size slaughtering each other endlessly. Another showed an endless labyrinth of iron where souls wandered aimlessly in vain hopes of escaping. A third showed a desolate cityscape, ruined with acidic rain pouring down on the buildings and people, causing them unimaginable pain but never letting them die.

One portal stood out from the others. A mountain surrounded by red thunderclouds above a sprawling intact city was topped with a miasma of darkness. In that miasma two purple dots focused in the direction of the portal, and The Voice felt the loathing and burning desire for its complete and utter annihilation pour from there.

The Voice couldn't stand such an overwhelming feeling and slowly backed away until it couldn't anymore. The Judge had restricted The Voice's movements from the dimension they shared. It knew the demon king was there and that they were watching him. And from what The Voice felt, it seemed the demon king no longer believed killing The Voice was enough.

"All nine hells are as unique as the denizens that inhabit them. In this case, the succubus has only limited and tentative control over the fallen angel. One mistake on her part, and he will turn on her." The Judge's statement closed the viewing portals to the hells.

The Voice relaxed now that its first major infraction could no longer see it. Things calmed down again as they resumed watching the two souls. The Voice still couldn't shake the feeling left from the demon king from the eighth hell.

All its hope still lay with the beastkin. She was strong, not stupid, and had decent connections. Everything The Voice hoped would help deal with the demon king when he invaded was lining up for her. It was almost like a storybook with how much she struggled and overcame her challenges. But the challenge in front of her threatened to ruin everything. One demon and one bite were destroying all the beastkin woman's sanity and leaving her a mindless animal.

"But it looks like your original plan is failing." The Voice knew that was what The Judge was going to say. "The boy won't be enough as he is. If she dies, so does your freedom."

The Voice watched as the wolf girl got bitten by the demoness. It saw the infection building until it overtook her senses. If it had a heart, it would have skipped a beat when the king knocked the girl out. Watching the cure being administered to the wolf girl was torturous. It wanted to help but couldn't. It needed that soul to live. Everything hinged on her life.

But a portal opening behind it tore The Voice's attention from the soul it was watching. It wasn't a viewing portal, but one for traveling.

Panic again filled The Voice as The Broker walked through the portal just before it closed.

Standing as a humanoid shape, the being was far from human. A black-and-white checkered suit danced at the whims of a lanky, near-formless being of darkness. Where one would think to see skin there was nothing more than a light-consuming darkness surrounded by an otherworldly outline that was impossible to describe. The more you looked at it, the harder it was to see.

In his "hand" was an ornate cane that clicked on the marble and sounded like shattering glass as it echoed through the minor plane. A solid gold serpent with ruby eyes swallowing its own tail formed the handle and cradled a round, brilliant cut diamond. The slender shaft was a glistening silver etched with meticulous engravings of unimaginable creatures while clutching onto the base of the diamond.

The Broker's voice was smooth, almost hypnotic as he sauntered towards The Judge. "Well, isn't this a surprise?" He lifted his cane and twirled it in front of him with one hand and stopped it to point at The Voice. "A very nice surprise indeed. It looks like someone's been a bad soul-manipulating guide of the trials."

"You are here to uphold your end of the bargain you struck with the accused," The Judge said.

"Yes!" The Broker lifted his arms up and raised his cane in both hands. He laughed maniacally. His laughter grew as he grew larger.

Every laugh sent a wave of dread through The Voice.

The orange pillar of light flashed and The Broker returned to his previous size. "Only when I say so."

The Broker shrugged as he crooked his cane in his armpit. "Huh, okay." He wrung his hands together as he turned his shoulders towards The Voice. "I've got big plans for your twelve labors."

Suddenly, death didn't sound like a bad option to The Voice.

26

INNER STRUGGLE

The events of my frenzied state played before me like a scene I couldn't look away from. From the moment I'd attacked Daric to throwing Golditress against a wall, I'd screamed at myself to stop. But I couldn't. A part of my mind couldn't comprehend the concept of stopping. Everyone was an enemy, a threat I needed to eliminate. It wasn't until I saw Dinar that a scent filled my nose other than blood. It was the scent of the sin of lust. If I couldn't stop myself, the least I could do was direct myself to kill her.

It didn't take much convincing to redirect my fury to hunt down the scent, and when I did, I wasn't sure if the bloodlust was from rabies or genuinely mine. In the end, I didn't find her, but I found someone who reeked of her scent. Whoever he was, he was stronger than me. There was no technique in my fighting. The only thing I could feel was the absolute desire to rip him to shreds. I wasn't all that surprised that he baited me in, and I was glad his blow knocked me out.

In the blissful darkness, my mind was more or less my own again. There was a nagging in the back of my mind, making it harder to think. *Now that I have the frenzy, what do I do? I'm not dead; I'm not in nearly enough pain for that. So how do I get control of myself again?*

*Can Lexia or any other beastkin get me the cure? Will my recovery apti-
tude help me survive? I really don't want to see The Voice right now. It
kinda sucks that my life is so out of my hands.*

My mind felt like it fell further down into a pit, a pit that I could
see. As I slowly drifted to the ground, my body manifested the closer I
got to landing. Once my feet touched the rocky ground, I could
control my body. I looked around the pit I stood in the center of. At
least eight arcs in diameter, a circular area stretched out with no way
in or out, except up. Above me loomed the darkness that I'd fallen
from.

*Alright, I'm alone in a rocky pit with nowhere to go. Is this a dream?
If so, what's the point?*

Behind me, I heard a growl. A deep, feral growl. A wolf stood,
baring its fangs. It was twice as tall as me and covered in silver fur.

I extended a clawed hand out to pet her. My tail almost wagged
with relief at seeing her. "Ah, it's you again. The frenzy really did a
number on you, didn't it?"

As if to answer my question, the wolf pounced at me. I recoiled
my arm and jumped to the side, well out of reach of her massive claws.
My inner wolf ran towards me, snarling as she snapped her jaws at me.

"Someone needs a time-out."

I backpedaled and created a cage of ice around the wolf. My magic
in the real world would never allow me to create something so large at
such a distance or even that fast. But this was my mind, and I was
going to be in control.

Ignorant of the icicle bars, the wolf ran through them effortlessly.

Alright, new plan. Just stop her. This time, I created a solid wall of
ice between the two of us and made it as thick as possible. Ultimately,
it was more like a giant block of ice than a wall. She didn't break
through it as effortlessly as she did the cage. No, instead she rammed it
and shoved it into me.

Unprepared and shocked that she could move it, the wall of ice
shoved me into the dirt wall. The curvature of the wall kept me from
being utterly crushed. But I was still pinned.

Panic really set in as the colossal wolf climbed on top of the block,
never taking her eyes off me. I willed the block to grow taller and never

stop growing. It did. The block went upwards towards the darkness, carrying with it my out-of-control inner wolf.

As the darkness swallowed up the wolf, I released the breath I didn't know I was holding. The moment my shoulders slumped as much as they could, I heard a growl at my side.

I turned to see the massive wolf on the ground, staring at me with blood-red eyes. *Oh no.*

The wolf raised a paw and slashed at the block of ice. Chunks of dirt and ice exploded from the place her paw struck. The block of ice released me as it glided across the ground away from me. Four huge gouges in the dirt wall caught my attention just before I focused on the threat before me.

"If I die, you die, remember? Just so you know, I'm not ready to die again." I punctuated my point by spreading my feet apart and crouching slightly, ready to move out of the way of her next attack.

My inner wolf didn't disappoint me. As she lunged at me, jaws open wide, I ducked and dashed under her. She tried to follow me, but she didn't defy her physical limitations. Instead, she tried to swipe at me with a paw, but I moved to the outside of the leg she put her weight on. I jumped up onto her back and grabbed handfuls of hair.

The wolf didn't like that. She told me how much she didn't like that as she spun around and turned her head back to snap at me. No matter how fast she turned, she couldn't reach me as I held on between her shoulder blades. I was, unfortunately, getting dizzy, so I lowered my head and focused on the fur I was holding on to. *I really wish you weren't so big. Then this might be more of a fair fight.*

On and on she spun with me on her back. If I'd counted the revolutions, I would have certainly gotten sick.

Eventually, the wolf didn't reach as far back as she snapped at me. Her spinning slowed down. I could feel her heart racing in her chest and her lungs failing to keep up with the need for oxygen. Without a doubt, I knew she was getting tired. I looked down and saw that my hands were losing their grip on the fur.

I quickly realized that I wasn't losing my grip, there was simply less to grip. My inner wolf was shrinking. Panting heavily, the wolf stopped moving and continued to shrink until she was my size.

I hopped off her back to watch her, but I stumbled as I stepped on the ground. My body felt weak, like I had spent an entire day working out.

She fell to the ground on her side. Her panting continued as puffs of dust flew away from her mouth.

I walked over and looked down at her. Her once-red eyes were back to normal. "Did you get that out of your system?" I leaned closer and put my hands on my knees as I panted. "Good, because it looks like neither one of us wants to do that again."

A whimper came from the wolf as she shifted her head as if to respond. I could feel fear coming from her, fear of retribution and of death.

I shook my head as I sat next to her. I lifted her head and placed it in my lap. "It's okay. Don't worry. I'm not angry. None of this is your fault. You have nothing to fear from me, remember?" Our scenery changed as I stroked her fur and gently scratched behind her ear. The memory of when we first met unfolded in front of us like a play.

As the memory faded, darkness surrounded us, but we remained as we were. The wolf in my lap lifted her head and nuzzled my stomach.

"I meant what I said back then. We're in this together. That means I'll protect you, just as you've protected me." I hugged the wolf's head and cuddled her close.

As we sat together for what felt like forever, I could feel my inner wolf's body warming up. I opened my eyes to see her body glowing. Before I could react any further, her body burst into flames, as did everything around me.

My pyrophobia took over as I attempted to scramble away from anything on fire, an impossible task since everything was on fire, including me. Pain wracked my body as it felt like my blood burned, my skin burned, everything inside and out *burned*.

I screamed in pain and unparalleled fear. Everything in my mind disappeared.

First, I heard my screams, then I opened my eyes to see a wooden roof over my head. My body hadn't stopped feeling like it was on fire, and the vivid images of being surrounded by fire were still fresh in my memory. I tried to sit up and roll around to put the fire out, but I felt resistance as my left arm pulled on something. Still panicking, I pulled even harder until I heard something snap. My arm flew into view as I tried to roll around again. I saw a piece of rope tied around my wrist and a section of broken rope extending for a few inches from it. I looked down to see both of my legs were tied to the corner posts of the bed with ropes that wrapped around my knees. With a quick look at my right hand, I saw that it was also tied to one of the bed's corner posts.

I effortlessly severed the rope that held my arm. With both my arms free, I sat up and cut my legs free. My body still burned, and moving made the pain even worse. I took a deep breath as I pulled my arms and legs in as I screamed and rolled around.

While I rolled around, I noticed a wooden basin in a corner of the room. It looked like a barrel larger than some bathtubs that had been cut in half and filled with water.

Water! That will help, right?

I locked my eyes on it and fought through the pain as I stumbled towards the bathtub. The water looked and smelled fine, but even if it didn't, I would have still jumped in.

As my body plunged into the liquid, relief hit me after a sharp spike in pain. I could feel my body cooling down, but it was still far too hot to be normal. I submerged as much of my body as I could, leaving the bare minimum of my face exposed.

As I lounged in the tub, a strange sound headed towards me. It almost sounded like clopping, but the water in my ears distorted the sound too much for me to be certain. The sound of a door opening was unmistakable, and I lifted my head high enough to look around the room.

A deer beastkin walked in. He was sickeningly thin. Small antlers that barely came to three points adorned his head. The clothes he wore were tattered and had several small holes. A copper band hugged his wrist. His big brown eyes were half covered by his eyelids like he hadn't slept in days.

He turned to look at me, and his eyes opened a little more, but not much. "You got yourself to the washtub, I see. That's good." His voice sounded more tired than his eyes looked. Each step he took towards me was slow, and I could see a slight shake in his knees as he put his weight on them. "I can see the boy was not exaggerating when he said you had the recovery aptitude."

"Who are you? And can you tell me why my body feels like it's on fire?" I took a moment to investigate my appearance. Since I'd jumped in the tub without looking at myself, I didn't notice if I had any clothes on. I confirmed my suspicions: I was naked. "Please tell me everything you know about what happened to me. I seem to be missing a few details." I moved towards the edge of the tub to hide more of my nakedness.

The deer closed his eyes and slowly leaned his head forward. "My apologies. My name is Grant. I am the king's personal advisor." As Grant lifted his head, he hobbled over to the bed and sat on the corner closest to me.

"Nice to meet you, Grant." I watched his mouth as he talked; his teeth exposed him as a primal beastkin. His face also looked frozen in a permanent frown. "But could you start by telling me what happened to me? I know what I saw, and that I had the frenzy, but why am I not a murderous monster anymore?"

"That is because I gave you the cure." Grant's casual tone caused me to raise an eyebrow at him. "It's also the reason you feel, as you put it, 'like your body is on fire.' The most common side effect of the cure is a terrible fever. One that burns the entire body—"

"Any other side effects I need to know about?" Again, my mouth blurted out without waiting for the man to finish.

Somehow, the deer's frown deepened after my interruption. I sheepishly ducked into the water more and flattened my ears. "Kids, especially meat eaters, don't have any patience these days." He shook his head, and I submerged my mouth to keep it from running off again. "There have been times when those who receive the cure don't survive and never wake up. Also, there are those who have awakened who were so distraught that they took their own lives before anyone could stop them. One time, a poor boy was left unable to do anything more than flail about. He couldn't eat or do anything on his own for the remainder of his short life."

Every possible outcome that he gave me dropped my heart further and further down. *So I'm one of the lucky ones, aren't I?* I looked down at the water and at my overheating body. I started shaking as I lost the ability to think.

"Child, don't be afraid."

I lifted my head on hearing the deer's voice. My vision blurred from the tears forming in my eyes.

Grant stood up from the bed and walked over to me. "I know that hearing those potential outcomes is terrifying. However, you are alive and, from what I can tell, well along in your recovery. Do not fear what could have been. You are young. You still have most of your life left to live. Don't squander it by moping about what you had no control over and fearing what didn't happen."

"Where's the guy who knocked me out? What happened to him?" I wiped my eyes with the back of my hand.

"Sadly, the demons led the king away. They want him to start the war they ordered." *Did this guy just say that demons, as in more than one, ordered a war?* "Maybe I should get that human. Mark, I think his name was."

"That would be a good start." I barely held back a growl. "And bring me my clothes, too."

27

PREMEDITATION

While Grant left me to soak in the water, my body didn't seem to cool down much. The water helped keep things from getting unbearably painful, but it didn't mitigate the problem. I even stood up to see if things would change, and they did. The heat and pain grew in intensity again until I dropped back into the water. I tried to use my magic to reduce the temperature, but it felt like I was magically fatigued already. Not wanting to do any more damage to myself, I just stewed in the water.

Okay, I'm officially going to go stir-crazy if I have to sit in this tub for any longer than today. I stared up at the ceiling until I could hear a total of three sets of footsteps, two humanoid and Grant's hoofed feet. *I thought he was only grabbing Mark. Who else is with him?*

Mark, Silver, and Grant walked into the room. Silver stood tall while the other two hunched forward slightly. While Grant's excuse was his age, I was suspicious of Mark, whose eyes darted around the room. *Why is he trying so hard to avoid looking at me?*

"How are you feeling?" Silver spoke first with a soft and caring demeanor.

I wrapped my arms around my legs as I brought them up to my

chest. "Other than feeling like my blood is literally boiling in my veins right now? I'm extremely confused."

Grant retook a seat on the bed. Some of his joints popped as he settled. "You changed the moment I mentioned demons. I thought it was best to bring the strangers who knew you and cared about your safety. How come so many humans and elves follow you?"

"Because I'm their guide." From the frown on Grant's face, I could see he didn't like my answer. "I grew up in the human kingdom and I'm a knight there. We were on a mission to investigate the blood anchors when we ran into my sister..." I paused and looked around. *She would have been here begging to be one of the first people to see me wake up.* "Where's Lexia?"

Both Silver and Grant turned to look at Mark, who was holding his hands together and staring at them. Mark shifted his weight from one foot to the other. "She's gone."

I flattened my ears as I glared at the boy. "What do you mean?" I injected a growl into my voice. "You better start talking!"

Mark didn't lift his feet as he backed away from me. "The sin of lust took her. She traded her freedom for your life."

"If you know, that means you were there. Which means you watched her do that. That means you stood by and did nothing!" I dug my claws into the side of the basin of water as I leaned closer towards Mark. "Why would you do that? I thought you were a knight. You should have done something."

Silver stood in front of me, blocking my vision of Mark. "Water-falls. There's a good explanation."

"I watched the lion beastkin knock you out like it was nothing. I stood no chance against him, and when the sin showed up, there was nothing I could do. Your sister just ran in there without thinking. I know my limits. There is no way in this world I stood a chance of fighting a sin after it defeated both you and your sister. And if that lion served her, all I could do was watch." Mark stepped out from behind Silver. "If you think I don't deserve to be called a knight, I believe you. I never earned that right. My relationship with Daric is the only reason I have the chance to be one. But this..." Mark lifted his arms up and waved them around. "This is more than I can handle.

There is no training for this. I was never ready for this, and I never will be."

"Then what are you still doing here?" My vision shifted to red as I bared my fangs at him.

"Because I want to make it right." A single tear formed in the corner of his eye before falling down his cheek. "Yes, I am weak. But I'm not useless. I want to do the right thing, but I'm not you. You have the strength and power to influence people, to challenge the strong, to do the right thing. I don't have that." More tears joined the first in a slow cascade. "I'm not foolish enough to think that ideals change the world; power and money do. Neither of which I have. But ideals shouldn't be ignored either."

"You're right. Ideals won't save my sister. I will. Now get out of my face before I rip you apart." I turned my back to everyone and stared at the wall. Mark's footsteps and sniffling grew distant as he left. Silver and Grant, however, hadn't moved. "What do you two want?"

"Is there a chance she's still infected with the frenzy?" Silver's voice didn't sound directed towards me.

"No. This, I'm afraid, is the temperament for one such as her. Even if it's a bit extreme." Grant's voice sounded even more tired than before. "Even with the circumstances as they are, that was incredibly rude of you, child. He wanted to help. You should have given him the chance."

"He can help by getting out of my way." *He should never have come.* I lowered myself back into the water and crossed my arms. "How long am I supposed to stay here, anyway? How long do these side effects last?"

"That's a good question." Grant hummed to himself for a moment. "I've never seen someone recover so quickly. Maybe two days at the earliest. Maybe longer. It's hard to tell with you. Hopefully by then you can rein in your anger and start thinking with a clear and open mind."

"My sister doesn't have two days." I continued to sulk.

"This is extreme, even for you," Silver said as he walked towards the door. "I believe it best to leave you behind, along with Golditress. Neither one of you are in any shape to travel."

My ears shot up as I jerked myself around to face Silver. "What did I do? How bad is she?"

Silver stopped mid-stride and turned to face me. "So you can feel remorse for the havoc you cause." He crossed his arms and glared at me. "She's unconscious but still breathing."

"What about her eyes? Are they dilating in the light? Do they get smaller as you hold her eyelids open? What about her head? What does the wound look like?" I couldn't ask my questions fast enough. To keep myself from asking more, I held my breath as I waited for Silver's response.

"Everything's fine. We've all had basic medical training. Her breathing is shallow but consistent. Not everyone heals as fast as you. She hasn't been out for an entire day yet." Silver lowered his arms to his sides. "But that doesn't change your situation. Unless there's someone else who can use healing magic in this place, you'll have to sit out."

I released my breath. "Good." *But she was the only one in our group who could use healing magic to speed up my recovery. No, I don't need her. I can't believe these words are about to come out of my mouth.* "I have an idea. There's another option." I closed my eyes. "Please bring Penny. I need her help."

I opened my eyes to Silver's bewildered expression. "You want to talk to Penny? I don't think that's such a good idea. Maybe that fever is affecting your mind. When was the last time you ate?"

I flattened my ears. "So what if I'm hungry? I'm not crazy. How much do you know about magic?" I crossed my arms as I leaned farther under the water.

"Not as much as I should, it seems. How can Penny's fire magic help you?" Silver turned his head towards Grant. "Do you have any idea what she's planning?"

Grant shook his head. "I do not. My belief is that your assumption of her mental state is more correct than she is willing to admit. I'll fetch her some food. It'll help with the recovery. Although I don't know if there's much left after everyone left to follow the king." The old deerkin stood up and strolled towards the door on his bony legs.

I rolled my eyes. "Right now, I can't use magic. It feels like I'm magically fatigued. If I wasn't, I would do this myself. But I'm about to let you in on a secret. One that I would very much want you to keep to yourself." Silver's right eyebrow rose at that. "There's a thing called unfocused magic. All magic users can manipulate it, but it doesn't do anything. Not until we focus it on manipulating the elements or conjuring something. If I focus my magic, it becomes ice or water manipulation magic. The part I want you to keep secret is this: When learning to focus our magic, especially at the beginning, we don't always use everything. Sometimes we absorb extra unfocused magic. It affects everyone differently. Some people sneeze uncontrollably. Others lose the ability to see." Grant stepped out of the room. *Even if I whisper this, Grant is still going to hear me.* "Me? I act like I'm drunk."

"I thought you said that you can't drink alcohol. So how would you know what being drunk is like?" Silver scratched the back of his head.

"I've seen enough people get drunk to know what will happen." I waved my hand dismissively. "Besides, that's what it was described as to me by my mother and best friend. So after Penny forces as much unfocused magic into me as she can, I need you to keep me from drowning in this water. I'll probably say strange things and act quite foolishly before falling asleep. After I wake up, I should be good to go."

"But how does this help you?" Silver shook his head slightly as he held up his palm, as if to reach for the answer.

"My best friend's mom figured out that, with my help, if you infuse someone with unfocused magic, you can bolster their aptitude. Or one of their aptitudes if, like me, they have two."

"Does this work for everyone?" Silver almost sounded desperate.

I shrugged. "It isn't as good of an idea as you think it is. One, only those who can use magic can even absorb the unfocused magic. Two, there is always a reaction, and they never leave you in a state to be able to take advantage of the boost."

"I don't want to ask about how you were able to learn all this, do I?"

I shook my head.

Silver hung his head. "I thought so. Alright, I'll do as you ask. You seemed to have calmed down. All I ask is that you be nicer and more forgiving in the future." Silver stared at me from the corner of his eye as he turned to leave.

I shrugged. "I can try. But I won't promise anything." *Maybe I was a little harsh with Mark. But I'm temperamental, get used to it. At least until we finish our mission. You won't have to deal with me again after that.*

While I waited for Grant or Silver to return, I replayed my memories of the fight with the beast king.

So now I know why he smelled like the sin of lust. He's working for her. But what were those things he said to me? He sounded remorseful about my state. Why would someone willing to serve demons be so sad? His fighting style was very rudimentary, almost like he'd never had a challenge fighting anyone. Simyn sparred with me many times to make sure I knew how to fight someone who was on equal footing with me.

I looked down at my wrist where the sin of lust had punctured my skin. The five dots of black blood were gone, along with any sign that I had even been injured. *She's going to pay for what she did to me and my sister. But she wanted me. Why did she take my sister instead? What are that demon's plans? Anna told us that the sins of lust are the most conniving of the sins, seconded only by greed. When I see her again, I won't let her get a word out before I rip her throat out.*

I flexed my claws and visualized them covered in red as the sin clutched at her torn neck, failing to keep her blood from spilling out. *Yeah, that will be just perfect. I'll show that sin a new meaning of wrath.* My smile grew wider the longer I let my imagination run wild.

A strange scent snapped me out of my imagination, and Grant's steps caused me to turn and face the doorway. He walked in carrying a yellow sphere with black spots half the size of his torso.

"What's that? I thought you were getting me food." I lifted my arm out of the water for a moment to point at the object the old man carried.

Grant continued to walk towards me. "It is called a lionant. I don't know how you feel about eating insects, but this is what was available. Apparently, one of the hunters said there's a hive of them to the east. He managed to bring a few of them back." He carefully set the sphere on the ground next to my tub.

"I've never eaten a bug before. Then again, I haven't seen a bug large enough to eat. Some of the largest bugs were the size of my palm, but nothing came close to this large." I stared at it.

It smelled off. *It doesn't smell like any insect I know.* I poked it with a claw, and it started spinning. As it did, I saw two holes on opposite sides. Each hole revealed a pale white flesh with two tube-like things running through it, one reddish-pink and the other a yellowish-white color. While I had reservations about eating it, my inner wolf didn't. *If you say so.*

I picked it up off the ground and held it. The chitin was expectedly tough, but when I stuck my claw inside the meat, there was no resistance. I scooped out a small bite with a spin of my claw. My stomach growled as I hesitated once more. I took a deep breath, closed my eyes, and plopped the meat into my mouth.

Nothing? "It tastes like eggs." I looked back and forth between the lionant and Grant.

"Is that a good thing?" Grant raised his eyebrows and gestured with his hand for me to elaborate.

"No. There's no taste at all. I can smell it, but there isn't much to smell. And the taste just doesn't exist. I hated eating eggs when I was a kid." I slumped my shoulders as I looked at the food provided to me.

"Well, beggars can't be choosers. Now eat." Grant crossed his arms after he pointed to the center section of the insect.

My ears drooped as I stared at the flavorless meat. *Now I want nothing more than to go home.* I chuckled. *Who would have guessed? I'm spoiled. I want actual food again. This is going to be awful.* I cringed as I slowly cut section after section of meat out and ate it. The texture was fine. My teeth didn't feel any resistance as I chewed, and I only chewed as minimally as possible. I wanted this experience to end as quickly as possible. Each bite I took cut away at my appetite faster than my hunger. By the end, I was holding back my gag reflex with each bite. After I had eaten most of it, I couldn't take it anymore.

I placed the remnants back on the ground and shivered as I turned away from them. "I'm done."

"See, that wasn't so bad." Grant's voice was the liveliest it had been yet.

That's easy for you to say. You weren't the one eating it. "Go eat a pinecone," I grumbled, just barely above a whisper.

"What's a pinecone?" Grant asked as he walked over.

I sighed and shook my head. "Never mind."

Penny and Silver finally showed up. *Took them long enough.* Penny stomped her feet as she approached me. I turned to see the elf's face twisted in anger. "If I do this, you will take me home right away." Her voice didn't hide her seething anger.

"Deal." *Before she can ask for anything else.*

Penny stumbled as her angry face turned to confusion. "Really?"

I looked to my left, then my right, and back to Penny. "Yeah."

She narrowed her eyes as she stared at me. "That was too easy. I thought you loved it here. What's your game?"

I rolled my eyes and held up a finger. "One, I never said I liked it here. I've enjoyed meeting and getting to know my sister, but my home is still back in Aquittemia." I lifted a second finger. "Two, we can leave as soon as I'm able. Which should be sometime later today." I lifted a third finger. "And three, we are going to make a quick stop along the way. There's a king and a demon that I need to kill."

Penny blinked several times, her face emotionless.

"How do you know where they're going?" Silver walked around to Penny's side as he spoke.

"Grant said that the demon wanted to start the war. They're going to Rophmna. We'll catch up with them and, hopefully, deal with them before they run into any other knights or villages."

28

DRUNK AND DISORDERLY

"Why do I get the feeling that you planned this?" Penny glared at me.

I shook my head. "Believe me, nothing about this was planned. You just made it too easy for me to take advantage of you." I slammed my eyes shut. *I didn't want to say that last part.*

"Take advantage of me?" It was obvious Penny was angry. I could hear her stomp her feet until she was right behind me. "Let's see you take advantage of this."

What started out as a tingling sensation quickly grew into a buzzing throughout my body and finally developed to the point where it felt like my entire body was vibrating. *Don't focus the magic, just let it absorb.* Fighting all the training Mom had drilled into me when I was first learning to use magic, I did the hardest thing for me to do this entire life: nothing.

My mind slowed down, and every thought was quickly lost in a syrupy fog. I opened my eyes and saw the grin on Penny's face. "Listen..." I felt like I wanted to say something, but whatever I wanted to say was no longer important. "Do you have a boyfriend?"

Penny's grin fled and was replaced by a look of abhorrent terror. "Why are you asking that? I used too much, didn't I?"

I swayed my head back and forth. "You're a grumpy person. Others call me an angry person. They all want me to have a mate so I feel better. Maybe you need one too."

"Grumpy? Mate?" The elf's cheeks pulsed a bright pink as she looked around the room for anything to look at that wasn't me.

Silver's eyes bulged. He looked like he was holding his breath.

"Hey, don't hold your breath. Breathing is better. I like you. You're big and strong."

Penny whirled around to face Silver. "Are you laughing?" Her voice rose to an uncomfortably high pitch. "This isn't funny."

"You're right. It isn't funny," Silver said through his clenched jaw. "It's hilarious." The dragoon's usually stoic and serious demeanor broke down into boisterous laughter.

"Stop laughing!" Penny stomped her feet with her arms firmly pressed to her sides.

"So the big lizard man does laugh. It's kinda weird." *There's a sound I can't quite narrow down to what it is.* "Do you breathe underwater, Silver? It sounds like you're laughing but coughing up water at the same time."

Silver slowed his laughter. Penny swiveled her head back and forth between Silver and me. With a deep breath, the dragoon calmed down. "I'm surprised you can figure that out by my laughter. Your ears must be something special. But yes, I can breathe underwater."

I started bouncing up and down while clapping my hands. "Oh, oh, can we go fishing together? I want to go fishing. I was supposed to go fishing, but you guys had to come along to ruin my fishing trip with Mom, and now I'm here in a puddle of water with no fish." A deep longing filled my heart and stomach as I looked down at the tub of water. "Who wouldn't I kill for some fish right now?"

"You told me to expect you to act drunk, but this is something I wouldn't have expected to see from you. Honestly, I was half expecting you to turn extremely violent. But this side of you is almost cute." The way Silver's smile touched his eyes made them look beautiful.

But what was that about being almost cute? "I'm cute." I crossed my arms and pouted.

"What are you, a child?" Penny shook her head before turning towards Silver again. "Wait, she told you what was going to happen? And you didn't warn me?"

Silver shrugged. "She said that all magic users experience something different and that she would be embarrassed if anyone else knew about it. I figured that as a fellow magic user, you would respect that."

"I plan on exploiting it." Penny gave me an evil grin.

"Hey, I showed you mine. Now you need to show me yours." I lifted my soaked arm out of the water and pointed at the elf.

She crossed her arms and shook her head. "Not on your life."

"You could at least tell her what would happen," Silver said as he took a few steps towards us.

"That's not fair." I leaned forward and grabbed the edge of the tub. "I'll make you show me."

Penny took a step away from me, but it wasn't enough. My leap for her was effortless, and I landed right on the defiant little woman. Water splashed everywhere, and even more poured out from my fur onto her. I pushed some unfocused magic into Penny as she squirmed, trying to keep the water out of her face.

"What are you doing? Get off of me, you animal." Penny tried to push me off, but I lowered my head so that my wonderfully sharp fangs were inches from her nose.

"I'm not an animal. I'm a beastkin." *Is it me or is it getting warm in here?*

Penny's squirming grew. "What did you do to me? You didn't, did you?" Her writhing paused for a moment as she looked at me with realization in her eyes.

I grinned.

"Get off me!" Her voice cracked and rose in pitch. "No! It's too late!"

I felt a pair of hands grab me by the waist. "Alright, back in the water with you." Silver picked me up.

I lowered my feet and stood up on my own. "Okay, if you say so. It's hot out here." My legs buckled as I went to take a step.

Silver caught me before my face planted itself firmly on the ground. "Easy there." He wrapped his arms around me and dragged me to the tub. "Okay, you're heavy. Where is all this weight coming from?"

"I. Am. Not. Fat!" I shoved Silver and fell into the tub of water with another glorious splash.

Silver reached in and pulled my head out of the water. "Are you alright?"

I spat out some of the water. "No, you just called me fat."

"I said you were heavy, not fat. There's a difference. There is nothing fat about you," Silver said as he pulled me towards the edge of the tub.

The sound of hooves walking caught my attention. Grant's eyes bulged to the edges of their sockets. He stood up, and in a trance-like state, walked out. Then the sounds of fabric tearing drew my attention towards Penny as she ripped at her clothes and discarded them.

She screeched as she flailed on the floor, trying to get out of her clothes for some reason. Her voice pierced my eardrums. The shrill sound of her voice made me cover my ears to block out the pain. Eventually, Penny stopped flailing around and stood up. She was completely naked, and her eyes burned as she stared at me.

"Happy now?" she asked as she displayed her naked body to Silver and me. But the sound of her voice was painful. Every syllable was like a nail driven into my ear. "Of course you can't hear me. Why am I even bothering?"

"Why does your voice hurt so much?" I covered my ears and tried to duck my head under the cover of the tub.

"Wait, you can hear her voice?" Silver asked. His voice wasn't a painfully wicked screech.

"You can hear me?" Penny mimicked Silver's confusion. Her voice continued to be at an impossibly high pitch.

"Yes. Please stop that shrieking. It hurts." Tears escaped my eyes as I slammed them shut.

"Why can you hear her but I can't? What's she saying?" Silver held me by my shoulders.

"I don't care what she's saying. Her talking hurts. Just go." I waved my hand in the direction I thought the door was.

"You caused all my clothes to feel painfully itchy and now you tell me to leave? Did you just tell me to walk around naked?" I screamed with each word Penny said. "I don't think so."

The clopping sound returned. "Is that you, miss?" Grant's voice called out. "I'm going to ask you to please refrain from talking. That is..." There was a brief pause. "Uncomfortable to hear. I understand from what Lucia said earlier that this is a temporary condition. Is that correct?" There was another pause. "Good. You may stay here until it has passed. Feel free to use the bed. Lucia will need to stay in the water until I'm sure she is well."

The slapping of bare feet on the ground told me Penny was walking around, and when I opened my eyes and looked up, I saw that she was crawling into the bed. It was at that same time that I yawned and looked at Silver. *He looks cuddly.*

I wrapped my arms around one of his and pulled it close. Now that his shoulder was at a better angle, I rested my head on it. "Oh, this is nice. You're nice and soft, Silver." I nuzzled his shoulder while my mind drifted to sleep.

29

HUNG OVER

'm hungry. Why is the first thing I always think about every morning my stomach? I opened my eyes to see that I was still holding Silver's arm in a death grip. *His arm has suffered enough, I think.* The sun hadn't crested the horizon yet, but it still stubbornly illuminated everything in a dull light through the windows.

As I released Silver's arm, he groaned. "Finally," he exhaled in a relieved tone. The dragoon pulled his arm back and cradled it gingerly. He looked up at me with a grimace. "Did you sleep well?" he whispered.

Everything felt normal, and my vision was normal. I rotated my limbs, and they felt good. "Yeah, I think so." I stood up to see if my body was still going to overheat. "And it looks like I'm ready to go."

Silver turned his head. "Maybe you should dry off and put on some clothes first," he continued to whisper as he stood up. "I'll leave you two ladies alone so you have some privacy. If Penny needs her clothes, please knock on the door and I'll go get her stuff for her."

Penny? What is she still doing here? I looked around and saw that Penny was sleeping in the bed. The woman slept on top of the covers in the nude. Her breathing was erratic, like she was in the middle of a dream. *So that's why he's whispering.*

Water still cascaded from my fur like hundreds of little waterfalls. With a frown, I began squeezing as much of the water out of my fur as possible. When I was no longer flooded with liquid, I stepped out of the wooden tub and used my magic to freeze what was still in my fur. The chill of the ice felt relaxing, so I basked in the sensation for a few moments. *I can't do this all day. My sister needs my help, and the longer I wait, the longer she suffers.*

I focused on the ice I created and pulled it all down. The sounds of the shattering ice crystals woke up Penny. She shot up with a shout.

"Good morning." I tried to put on a smile for her. She panted as she flicked her head from side to side. "Get ready. We're leaving as soon as possible."

"What?" Penny looked at me, her eyes glossed over in a milky-white film.

"Do you want to go home?" I asked as I pushed the last of the ice to the ground.

Penny shook her head. "I do. But it's so early." She placed a hand at the base of her throat. "Good, my voice is back." *Did you lose it somewhere?* The elf shot me a glare. "What happened last night stays between us, got it?"

I flattened my ears as I leveled my gaze at her. *You can't tell me what to do, pipsqueak. But what are you talking about? What happened last night?* "I won't talk about it if you don't." *An empty threat, but I'll just ask Silver since he witnessed the whole thing. In private, of course.*

"Good, now get some clothes on."

"Pot calling the kettle black." I pointed at the elf's exposed breasts. Penny looked down and hurriedly lifted the bedding to cover herself. Her face and ears brightened to a soft pink.

We both turned away from one another in a silent agreement to end this moment as soon as possible. I threw the pile of clothes I saw on the floor, which I suspected were Penny's, onto the bed with their owner. The two of us quickly dressed in silence.

I finished first. Once I no longer heard Penny shuffling around with her clothes, I turned around to see some of her clothes loosely hanging off her body, damaged. *Did I do that last night? How messed up was I?* But as I looked at her clothes more closely, I could see that the tears were jagged. *Okay, now I'm more confused. Who tore up her clothes? It wasn't me; my claws leave much cleaner cuts.*

"I hope you're happy." The venom in Penny's voice wasn't subtle at all. She stomped towards the door and threw it open.

Silver jumped at the sudden opening.

"Move."

Silver stood to the side and let the disgruntled elf march away. He turned to me with a look of confusion. "That could have gone worse."

I flexed my claws and stretched. "So, how bad was it last night?"

Silver continued to stare at me. "You don't remember what happened last night?"

"Things are a little hazy after she asked if I had planned everything." I shrugged before returning to my morning stretches. "Do you mind filling in the details for me?"

"Wouldn't it be better if I just didn't get involved?" Silver grumbled to himself as he sat on the edge of the bed. While Silver recounted last night's shenanigans, I thoroughly stretched every muscle out.

After Silver finished with how little sleep he got, I blinked a few times. "I'm surprised she didn't use any magic. But as for Penny losing her voice, it was never gone." Silver tilted his head. "My hearing is far superior to yours and hers. That means I can hear things you normally can't. Like things that are really quiet, but also things that are really high-pitched. Loud noises are uncomfortable, and high-pitched sounds are painful."

"You really like gloating, don't you?"

"Where does the line between gloating and stating facts sit?" I scratched the back of my head.

Silver stood up. "In your choice of words."

I looked up at the ceiling as I tried to think about what I'd just said to him. "Oh, I guess I can see how that comes across as gloating. Anyway, let's get going. Since I'm completely recovered, the sooner we leave, the better."

"Are you certain everything's fine?" Silver's tone shifted lower. "I can see why you're in such a rush. But if we don't think this through, we could make things worse."

"What is there to think about?" I growled as my tail lashed back and forth. "I'm going to kill that demon for what she did to me and my sister. She won't run away this time. I know all of her little tricks; she doesn't stand a chance."

"Remember, this time you don't have to be alone." Silver walked over and placed a hand on my shoulder. "We said we'd help you. Let us."

I took a deep breath and closed my eyes. "You're right. It's just that I've been so focused on doing things myself for so long, I can't remember what it's like to have others help me." I opened my eyes and reached for Silver's hand on my shoulder. "Thanks. I mean it." *I guess I'll need to apologize to Mark now.*

"It is a pleasure." Silver's eyes softened, and a smile graced his lips. When my stomach growled, Silver looked at it. "I guess breakfast is the first order of business."

I chuckled. "Yeah, but if I have to eat another ant, I will kill someone."

"Please tell me that's a joke." His voice was laced with concern.

I wrapped my arm around Silver's shoulder and led him out of the room. "That all depends on what my breakfast is. But don't worry, it won't be you. I like you too much."

Silver chuckled nervously.

I let the dragoon change his clothes and inform the others to meet at The Heart. As I walked through the building, there wasn't much sound until I heard Grant's familiar footsteps. *What's he doing this early in the morning?*

Eventually, I found him standing next to a bed with a female lion beastkin. The woman's features were strikingly fierce yet alluring. She lay on the bed, motionless. Her eyes were a dull yellow and devoid of any motion. If I hadn't seen her chest slowly rising and falling, I would have guessed she was dead.

"Who is she?" I whispered as I stood behind Grant while he looked down at the woman.

"Avice. She's the king's mate." The sorrow in his voice tugged at my heart. "Ever since the demons came and tortured the poor girl, she hasn't moved unless ordered by the female demon. The things they did to her while they made the king watch would leave anyone a husk of their usual selves. Before all of this, she was so lively and incredibly friendly." Grant turned and faced me, tears running down his cheeks. "This is what we have had to live with. We aren't strong enough to defy them, and the king can't fight them. Please, if you have any love for your kingdom, kill them and save us."

A tear escaped from the corner of my eye. "This isn't my kingdom, but I promise you, those demons will answer for everything they've done. I will be their executioner."

"There's a second demon." Grant wiped the tears from his eyes. "Although he didn't torment us like the sin of lust, as those people called it. If anyone didn't do what he said or stay out of his way..." Grant paused and looked around. "He would crush their skull."

"What does he look like? Maybe Anna can tell me more about him."

Grant rubbed the back of his head. "He looks like a human, but also not. He almost glows, and he has a large pair of raven wings coming from his back."

"The only thing I know for certain is that he sounds like another sin." I crossed my arms and stroked my jaw.

"Just, please, do what you can. I know it's unreasonable for me to ask so much from someone so young, but something about you makes me want to believe you're the one who will save us." Grant's eyes shimmered, and I could see the admiration in them.

"Just take care of her. I will..." I shook my head. "No, *we* will do what we can."

I left Grant to take care of Avice. *Hopefully when I kill the sin of lust, she'll recover. Or at least pass away peacefully. It sounds like the king is as much a prisoner here as everyone else, perhaps more so in some ways. But I made my promise to kill him for my sister. If Avice can recover, I hope one day she will forgive me for it.*

The sun peeked over the horizon as I walked through the desolate streets. As I walked, everything was eerily silent. *Where is everyone?* I made it to The Heart and walked inside. Two other beastkin walked around. I followed my nose to the section with food that I could eat, and my heart dropped at the sight in front of me. *You have got to be kidding me.*

Only two types of meat were available: the lionant meat from yesterday or whole field mice. I looked around some more, only to find nothing else. When I asked a caretaker, they confirmed that was the only meat they had and expressed their condolences. Begrudgingly, I scooped up a dozen mice and waited for the rest of my group to join me. I was not a fan of tasting fur and my claws were too clumsy to remove the hide on something that small, so I coated each mouse in ice and swallowed them whole. The ice helped them slide down the back of my throat.

I nearly finished the last mouse when I saw everyone in the group walking towards me. I expected them, but I didn't expect to see three beastkin walking with them. Fina, Victor, and Gifford walked towards me. All nine of us stood in a circle and sized each other up in silence. *Gifford makes sense. Fina, I can see because of her desire to help. Victor, I've got nothing.*

"What are you still doing here?" I pointed towards Victor.

"You're strong and loyal." The big bear averted his gaze. "And I think you're pretty. Also, I see that you haven't bonded with anyone yet. So..."

Everything around me cracked as I tried to comprehend what he'd just said. The only sound that followed was the collection of jaws hitting the ground in spectacular fashion. *Is he crushing on me? Someone is actually crushing on me? And he thought to ask right after I recovered from a near-death experience? Not cool, dude!*

"Uh, no." Victor nearly crumpled at my response. *Don't tell me the only reason he stayed was because he wanted to be my boyfriend.* I sighed. "Listen, I just recovered from the frenzy and learned that the demon took my sister. Now isn't the time to ask if I want a mate." I took a deep breath and held it for a moment. "If you ask me after I save my sister and prevent this war, I might, and I mean might, think about it."

"Wait, are you really going to..." Daric started.

I bared my fangs and released a vicious growl at Daric. His mouth clamped shut as he took a step backwards.

I glanced at Penny before turning back to stare at everyone. "I made a promise that we would leave today after I finished recovering. So that's what we're going to do. But there are some things we need to discuss first." Everyone found an excuse to look at the ground. "Who stays behind with Golditress? Any takers?" Nobody broke the silence. "Listen, Mark, I'm sorry for what I said earlier. I was upset, but I nominate you to stay."

"No." Daric immediately spoke up. "He stays with us."

Anna raised her hand. "I can stay."

"You're the last person I want to stay behind," I said as I turned to Anna.

"She'll only slow us down," Dinar said. "If you're in a hurry to catch the king and the demon, we need to move quickly."

I flinched. *She's right. Even if I carry her, we won't move as fast as I'd like.* "But we're very likely fighting two demons. We need her angel." I waved my hand at Anna.

"Lucia's right." Everyone turned to look at Mark. "If we're fighting demons, I'll be nothing more than a liability."

Daric grabbed his friend's shoulders. "You don't believe that. You're a great fighter. We need you."

Mark shook his head. "I don't believe that. Nobody here believes that." Mark's expression turned despondent. "I have nothing to contribute to the fight like Anna or Penny. Dinar and Lucia are the most skilled fighters we have. These three beastkin won't know the way to go to bring her back."

"It looks like she can make that decision for herself." Dinar pointed behind me.

I turned and saw Golditress limping as she trudged towards us. My heart twisted in my chest, tears poured from my eyes, and my breathing turned ragged. "I'm so sorry."

The words were barely coherent, but Golditress locked her eyes with mine. Her lips curled into a smile. "I know."

30

ONE STEP AT A TIME

ina ran up and wrapped her arms around me. "No, you didn't hurt her." If my ears weren't as good as they were, I probably wouldn't have been able to hear her whisper. My emotions quickly quieted down as I stood in Fina's arms.

I tapped Fina's elbow. She released me from her hug. "But I did hurt her. I know it wasn't my fault. It was that sin's fault. Somehow she infected me with the frenzy and caused me to attack my friend." There was the sound of Daric grunting, as if someone had punched his gut. *Thank you, whoever did that. I'm glad I'm not the only one who isn't interested in his antics.* I nodded toward Golditress. "But are you sure you should be walking around right now? I know you can't use your healing magic on yourself."

"Why doesn't it work like that?" Silver asked.

That's a good question. I don't actually know why. Mom just said that it doesn't work.

"Can you sate your thirst by drinking your own pee?" *That's disgusting! Why did you say it like that?* Golditress lowered her head as she tapped her chin with a finger. "That may not have been the best way to describe it. It's impossible to describe. Mostly, it feels, I don't know, wrong. It doesn't work regardless."

"Can we do the same thing that Lucia did with Penny?"

Silver, please stop talking. I rolled my eyes. "No. She doesn't have the recovery aptitude. Don't suggest that again." I turned my head and glared at him.

Silver leaned back and raised his hands defensively. "I was just trying to help."

"I think I can travel." Golditress straightened her back. "Although probably not at the pace you want to."

"I have an idea." Dinar's words pulled everyone's attention to her. "What if we were separated into three groups?" She pointed to Gifford and the other beastkin. "What are your aptitudes?"

"Fishing," Gifford answered.

I've got to take him with me when I go fishing now. It can be a whole family event. Mom and Lexia would love it.

Dinar's finger moved to Victor.

"Recovery."

Bonus points for the bear. I had to swallow my drool before it escaped. *No, not the time, and I haven't committed to any relationship yet.*

Finally, the elf's finger led to Fina.

"Running."

I should have noticed her having an aptitude like that. I wonder who's faster, me or her?

"Yeah, this could definitely work." Dinar smiled as she lowered her arm. "The three groups are the beastkin, Golditress and Mark, then everyone else."

"Why three groups?" Penny crossed her arms as she tapped her foot.

Dinar turned her head and glared at Penny. "Because the beastkin can run faster than us. Golditress will slow us down, but I don't feel comfortable with her being alone like she is. Mark can take care of her."

"Do you want us to lead the way so we can scout out the situation?" I asked.

Dinar's face lit up. "Yes. You can also hunt for food once we get to places that have some. Just don't engage without us. Also, we need to talk about you guys leaving a trail for us to follow if you see that they've changed direction."

"Among the things we need to talk about..." I turned to Anna. "Grant said there was a second demon. He told me it looked like a human with black-feathered wings. It also had a slight glow to it. Any ideas?"

Anna lifted her eyes to stare up at the ceiling. "Definitely a sin." Her face contorted into a grimace. "Only one comes to mind. And that's a bad sign. Unfortunately, it sounds like a fallen angel."

"Fallen angel?" Victor looked uncomfortable saying those words.

Anna took a deep breath. "All sins have two names. One is the sin that they are, and the other is a simpler way to refer to them. Even if it's much less used." She held out her hand and started counting on her fingers. "The sin of pride's a fallen angel. Lust, succubus. Wrath, chimera. Greed, dijin. Sloth, specter. Gluttony, cyclops. And Envy, medusa."

Those names sound familiar.

"Those are the names of mythical creatures from my world." Daric's jaw dropped as he blurted out the words.

Dinar waved her hand to dismiss Daric's pointless statement. "Anything we need to know about trying to kill them?"

Way to have your priorities straight, Dinar.

Anna looked uncomfortable as everyone stared at her. "Well, lust is an illusion magic user, but it looks like she also has a venom that carries the frenzy. Pride demons are very powerful magic users. They specialize in manipulating lightning."

"Don't forget that both of them can fly," Silver groaned.

I scowled at the dragoon. "Way to be a ray of sunshine."

"He's right. We need options to attack them if they take to the skies. Mostly Penny with her magic." Dinar took a step towards me. "How much can you do with your ice magic?"

I shrugged. "The best I can do to a flying opponent is make a spiked ball and throw it at them. I know it isn't a lot, but I can only manipulate anything within my arm's reach."

"How much can you do?" Penny's tone grated on my ears. "Are you quick at making these spiked balls? Can you even throw them?"

Fine, a demonstration then. I channeled my magic and froze the water in the air before pulling it into a sphere in the palm of my hand. Just as Penny's eyes went wide as she recognized my channeling, I gently tossed the projectile towards her. "Catch."

Penny let out a squeak as she cradled her hands to catch it. As soon as it hit her fingers, she let out yet another squeak. "Ow!" She immediately dropped the icy ball. Penny stared at her palms as the ice landed on the ground without bouncing much. "Why did you make it sharp?" She wiped her palms on the sides of her legs.

"To prove a point." *That's a good one. I like that one.* I heard Daric snickering off to the side. "No, it isn't as flashy as your fire, but it will cause some damage if it hits. I don't know how agile the pride demon is, but the lust demon is very agile."

Penny scowled. "Does that mean you want me to kill the succubus?"

"No, I want to kill her." I grinned, exposing all of my sharp teeth. "This is personal." Everyone except Gifford exchanged worried looks. Gifford's expression never changed. I looked him in the eye. "We'll get her back, I promise." *I've made a lot of promises lately, but they all hinge on me killing that demon. So I have no problem making them.* "I can't wait until I rip her to shreds."

"You're doing that thing again," Anna mumbled. I turned to look at her, confused. "You're speaking your thoughts."

"Oops." I grinned. "She's going to die. So what if I enjoy killing her?"

"I remember a little wolf girl who broke down in tears after she killed two people who kidnapped her." Anna looked at me with concern in her eyes. "I know you don't shy away from violence, but this, this is another level."

"That little girl grew up killing hundreds of animals. And I enjoyed it." I narrowed my eyes at Anna. "If everything is so keen on killing me, it's only fair that I return the sentiment." I relaxed. "Besides, it's a demon. Don't tell me you feel sorry for it?"

"No, I'm just worried that the frenzy changed you." Anna relaxed slightly but still kept an eye focused on me.

"Don't worry about me." I waved my hand. "Let's just get ready to leave." I pointed at Gifford. "See if you can find out where that lionant colony is at, please." *I can't believe the words that are about to come out of my mouth.* "We're going to need to eat, and that's a source of food we know about."

"What happened to killing someone if you had to eat that again?" Silver's voice shuddered.

"I have two someones in mind. So long as this doesn't take more than three days, I'll be fine." I turned and walked over to the field mice and grabbed several handfuls. *This should be enough for now. Fina will probably love these things.*

"Aren't you forgetting something?" I heard Dinar call behind me.

I looked down at my hands before turning around. "No?"

Dinar shook her head. "We still need to talk about how you're going to direct us."

I flattened my ears. "Okay, you got me. I forgot."

Dinar smirked as she walked up to me. "And that's why I'm in charge of the planning." She waved at me to follow her outside.

It didn't take much for us to work something out while the others collected what supplies they could. We agreed to gather at the eastern edge of town. *I should say goodbye to Grant and Charice.*

I walked through the streets, again noticing there weren't many people talking, and it didn't smell like there were many people either.

Grant was walking up to the front door of the longhouse when I arrived.

As I followed him in, he turned to face me. His face looked more tired than when I last saw him. "Hello, Grant," I said as I closed the door behind me.

"Good morning, Lucia. Have you decided what you're going to do?" Grant turned to walk farther into the building.

"Yeah. We're leaving today." I followed behind the deer beastkin. "I came here to pick up my things." Grant stopped walking and turned around as I paused for a moment. "And to say thank you one more time."

Grant lifted his hand. "You don't need to thank me, child. It is my responsibility to care for those who have suffered from the frenzy."

Wait, if the demon gave me the frenzy, it could give it to my sister just to get to me. I need that cure. I flattened my ears. "Is there any chance you can tell me how you make the cure? Is it hard?"

"Hard? No." Grant opened the door. "It's just difficult to get the ingredients."

"Sorry, but is there a way I could get a batch of the cure for my sister, just in case? I'm going to save her from the demon. And the demon can inflict her with the frenzy."

Grant's ears lowered to stick straight out. "Oh. That's understandable." He shuddered. "And a lot to take in. But, follow me."

I followed the deer into an unlit room that reeked. Several unfamiliar and terrible smells assaulted my nose. It took a lot of willpower to walk in. Once I was in the room, my eyes watered.

"You get used to the smell," Grant said as he pulled away a curtain to let light in.

I blinked several times as my eyes adjusted. It looked like I was in a makeshift kitchen. But this kitchen's walls weren't lined with pots, pans, or utensils. They were lined with dried plants, including three kinds of mushrooms I had never seen before. It also didn't help that I couldn't recognize any of the dried herbs. In a corner of the room, there was a small stone basin with metal grates over it and a small iron pot on them. There were several dents and even a bit of rust on the pot. *That's definitely not sanitary.* A barrel sat next to it, filled only a third of the way up with water. There was a small stack of broken branches in another corner.

He walked over to a basket sitting next to the firewood. He leaned over and pulled out a clay jar. "There is still one ingredient missing and one last step." I watched the jar as the old man handed it to me. "It needs the blood of a survivor of the frenzy. A few drops will do, but you must only add it just before forcing the afflicted to swallow it."

"You made me swallow this?" I opened the jar and raised an eyebrow as I stared at the thick brown liquid. "And I didn't throw it back up?" I flinched as I sniffed the brew and covered it again. *It smells awful. Or is that because this room stinks?*

"We gave you the tonic in small doses. Primals are the hardest to administer to."

"Whose blood did you use for my cure?"

Grant's face turned into a sorrowful smile. "Mine. That advice I gave you was through experience."

Now I feel guilty. I placed my hand on his shoulder. "Thanks for everything." I turned to walk away. "And goodbye."

After taking a couple of steps, I could feel the bottle getting heavier. The weight of everything around me felt oppressive. The room I'd woken up in after receiving the cure was nearby. I walked in and sealed the door shut with ice. After I was sure I would be alone, I walked to the bed, fell to my knees, and let all of my tears flow freely.

I'm not a hero. This weight, this responsibility, is so heavy. Can I really do this, save everyone, stop a war and kill two demons? Am I allowing everyone to follow me to death? What hurts the most is that we don't have time to get Mom or the rest of The Maidens. We have to do this now. I know I felt confident about killing the sin of lust. But every time I've had an encounter with a demon, I was left barely alive. Someone was always there to save me. With everything going on, will they be there for me this time? I want to stand alone, but I don't think I'm strong enough. I'm stronger than everyone else, and I'm the best fighter in The Maidens. But that doesn't mean I can't die.

The weight of all my responsibility continued to crush me and threatened to bury me.

Dying terrifies me. I've died once. It was awful, and I've had so many close calls with death that I'm beginning to question if The Voice hasn't been throwing problem after problem at me. But I can't just let Daric do the job alone. He won't be able to. I took this job without truly understanding the scope of the responsibility. Unlike Daric, I woke up. I can see the enormity of the task at hand. Save the world—it's never that simple. Even though I was released from my duty, this world has become my home. And I will defend my home. I will defend my family.

The weight felt less oppressive as I visualized the faces of my family and friends. The weight never went away, but it felt like I could carry it again.

If the demon king is more powerful than these sins, I won't be able to stand against him alone. Especially since he has an entire race of demons under his rule. Nobody knows how many demons there are. Are my actions really affecting this greater war that is being waged? I guess I can only take everything one step at a time. There's no way to know how many steps there are on this journey, or where it will end. But I know my next step. And that step is saving my sister. Then I will take the next one, and the next.

The tears ended, and I stood up. After I collected my things, I wiped my face before I dissolved the ice and left. My soundless steps were heavy as I strode towards my confrontation with the demons to save my sister.

One step at a time.

MATE VS. MARRIAGE

The sun sat at its peak as Fina, Gifford, Victor, and I ran ahead of the others. I had one last job before I left. I made sure everyone's waterskins were full. Also, to say thank you for all the food, I filled some barrels in town with ice, as much ice as I could create before I became magically fatigued.

The four of us ran on all fours as we started out at a blistering pace for a human. Fina and I made sure to keep things slow enough for Victor to keep up. His size didn't make him a fast runner, but he was still faster than a human. Our two limitations were Victor's speed and Gifford's stamina.

We stopped periodically to make sure everyone stayed hydrated. Once the sun was about to set, we rolled out the bedrolls. By the end of the day, even Fina was feeling the strain of running for as long as we did. We ate field mice and lionant meat before settling in for the night. Victor and I took turns watching for any trouble while the others slept. There was a period where the other two weren't awake yet but the two of us were done sleeping.

I lay down looking at the stars. Victor walked over and sat nearby.

"Is there anything I can do for you?" Victor's voice was quiet as the other two kept sleeping.

I sat up to look the bearkin in the eye. "Why are you asking?"

The bear started rubbing his hands together. "It's just that I maybe wanted to talk with you for a bit."

I lay back down and looked up to the sky. "Then if you want to talk, you can start by telling me why you're here."

"I, uh, just told you." I could hear Victor shuffle his feet as he responded.

I closed my eyes and took a deep breath. "No, why are you helping me on this selfish, impossible suicide mission?" I opened my eyes to look at Victor.

He started scratching at his head. "Well, since Lexia went with the one you called a demon, and you said demons were bad, I've got nowhere else to go. I don't know what to do. Following you just felt right, since you're Lexia's sister and all. Besides, I think you look beautiful."

I sat back up and rested my hands on my knees. "Right, that."

"Do you not think you're beautiful?"

"No," I sighed. "It's just that you wanted to ask me to be your mate, yet you don't know much about me. And I don't know much about you either. Since we've met, we've barely exchanged more than a few words. This is the most I've talked you, ever. You're almost as bad as Daric."

Victor lowered his eyes as his round ears shifted lower. "Sorry. I didn't mean to make you angry."

"I said almost." I gave the bear a smirk, and he brightened up. *The first thing we did was fight. You didn't ask me to be your mate as your first words to me. That puts you ahead of the rest of the competition.* "You aren't the first guy who's asked me to marry them."

"Marry?" Victor tilted his head.

"It's the humans' way of saying bonding." I pinched the bridge of my nose. "Right. I'm not originally from the Wild Kingdom. Well actually I am, but not really. It's sort of confusing."

Victor leaned forward with an expectant look in his eyes. "Lexia told me you lived with humans. What's that like?"

I rolled my eyes. *Where do I begin?* "They're loud, they stink, and they're completely ignorant to how weak they really are. Well, usually." I folded my legs to my side. "There are exceptions, of course. I was adopted by an elf. She taught me how to use magic, and she's been my mother the whole time I've been living in Aquittemia."

"But you've said that other men have asked to be your mate. Did humans ask you?" Victor asked, his voice rising.

"Shh." I placed a finger to my lips. "Fina and Gifford are still sleeping. They'll need every bit they can get. But yes, humans and elves have asked me, and not just Daric either. But they always try to show off how strong they are or something equally stupid. But when I say no, they don't like that answer. And after I literally throw them away, they tend to get aggressive. Human males don't like it when I'm stronger than them."

"I don't understand," Victor said. "Shouldn't they want a strong female? That's how you get stronger cubs."

I laughed. "Humans don't think like you." Victor flinched at my comment. I shook my head. "While humans don't belittle women, they're still a male-dominated society. I work for the sole female-only knight company in the entire kingdom. And there's only one other company that has a woman as its leader."

"Oh." Victor slumped.

He doesn't really know what that means, but he's trying to be sympathetic.

"I've talked a little with my sister, but tell me about you." I extended a hand towards the bearkin. "Why haven't you bonded? How old are you?"

Victor straightened up and placed a fist on his chest. "Ah, um, right. I'm sixteen. And I haven't bonded yet because no woman has caught my attention. Not like you."

I narrowed my eyes. "Not caught your attention? Or have they already bonded and you were just late to the party?" Victor looked at me, confused. "Sorry. I guess I'm asking if you haven't bonded yet because there was nobody left to bond with?"

Realization hit Victor's face, and he turned his head. *If he could blush under all that fur, I imagine he's blushing pretty hard right now.* "Uh, actually, it's..." The bear beastkin slumped his shoulders and drooped his head. "I've always wanted to mate a woman stronger than me."

My tail went stiff behind me. I opened and closed my mouth but didn't say anything. A warmness spread across my cheeks as I turned away. "How about we wake the others and get moving for the day, and we talk about this later?"

"Okay." Victor didn't move. Instead, his head and shoulders dropped even lower.

Ugh. I don't know how to handle what he just said. Is he only attracted to me because I beat him up when we first met? Great, now things are going to be awkward between us.

We woke up the others, and after I filled the waterskins again, we took off at a slightly slower pace. Gifford whined about his soreness from our running. I tried to comfort him by saying that this would only take a few days.

We continued running until all of us felt something was off. *I recognize this feeling. There's a dire nearby.* The multitude of tracks we were following led straight through the dire's territory. I looked up and saw that the sun was beginning its descent.

"Do we go around?" I turned to inspect the condition of the others.

Victor was panting, but I could see him recovering with each breath. Fina's breathing was as hard as mine, which meant she was taking a deep breath every once in a while. She could keep going without much difficulty. Gifford had his hands on his knees as he gasped for air.

"How about a break?" Victor asked, as he looked at Gifford.

"Yeah. Please," Gifford wheezed.

I'm surprised he can talk, gasping like that. "We can eat some food and rest. But we need to decide what to do with the dire's territory." I motioned for everyone to sit.

Gifford dropped to the ground without any resistance. Victor opened his pack and took out more of that despicable lionant meat. I groaned as he handed me a piece wrapped in some leaves. Fina accepted it without a complaint, while Gifford guzzled water.

I shook my head as I watched Gifford. "Just be glad I can make more."

"Are we getting close to catching up to my mate?" Gifford asked as he flopped the rest of the way to the ground with his arms spread out.

"All of their tracks are easy to follow, but they're hard to understand." I scrutinized the footprints below me. "It's impossible to tell how many there are or how long they've been here. Maybe the closer we get, the easier it will be. But there's still the dire between us and them."

"The dire? What is it?" Fina asked as she finished chewing on some lionant meat.

"Hopefully it isn't a dire lionant queen." Victor swiveled his head as he scanned the direction we were traveling.

"It's possible that a lionant queen is causing us to believe there's a dire nearby." I grimaced as I took a bite of my food. "The queen won't attack us directly, but she'll send all of her warriors. Ant queens don't leave the nests. Lionants should be no different." I shrugged. "At least that's what I learned."

"There is a dire." Fina flattened her ears as she curled her tail.

"But the question remains, do we go around or through?" I looked at everyone's faces.

Victor didn't have much of a reaction. Gifford was still hard to read, since he was still exhausted. Fina looked towards the ground as her tail curled around her waist.

Why is she scared?

"The longer we take to catch up to them, the longer my mate suffers," Gifford said as he sat up. His breathing had slowed somewhat. "We don't know how large its territory is."

"The others following us?" Fina looked towards me, her ears still flat.

"Can we kill a dire?" I looked at the three.

For a moment, we all exchanged glances in silence.

"Yes." Victor broke the silence. "You're strong, and we can help you."

After I finished another tasteless bite, I forced myself to swallow it.

Maybe we can eat the dire. Anything will be better than this bug. "Have any of you ever seen a dire before?"

Victor and Gifford shook their heads.

Fina wrapped her hand around the copper bracelet on her wrist. "One killed my mate, Darmin. A spider."

The three of us held our words back as Fina mourned the loss of her mate. *She knows how dangerous this is. A dire spider? That sounds awful and terrifying. I do not want to see that.*

I moved to sit next to Fina and wrapped my arm around her. She leaned into me as she sobbed silently. "Dires are seriously dangerous. Not only do we not know what we're up against, but we may not be enough. A dire boar attacked me when I was ten, and that was a frightening experience." I continued rubbing Fina's arm as I watched Gifford look more and more worried. "Do we wait for the others? With everyone, we can do it, but we'll lose a lot of time."

"Could the demons have killed it for us?" Victor resumed eating, finishing the last of his lionant. "If they did, we have nothing to worry about. Though the scent is still around. How long does it take before it goes away?"

I held up one finger on my free hand. "It takes one week." Victor and Gifford looked at me with skepticism. Even Fina looked up as she stopped sobbing. "A couple of years ago, a dire wolverine invaded my territory, and I asked the knights of the company I joined to help kill it. I stayed back and watched after leading a dozen knights to it. It took a week after it died to get the smell out."

Fina sat back up and wiped the tears from her eyes. "Thanks."

I smiled. "I helped?"

Fina smiled back. "You helped." She gave me a hug. "We go through. Your sister needs help."

"We go through. Any objections?" Victor and Gifford shook their heads. "Alright, let's get ready to go if you're feeling better, Gifford."

DINNER IS SERVED

Gifford needed a little longer to recover enough to go again. We slowed down slightly, just so we weren't too tired if the dire animal was still alive and around. Victor still left deliberate claw marks in the ground as we traveled; his were the largest, and the ones that Dinar could follow.

All four of us were constantly on edge as we followed the tracks that started drifting southwards. We continued traveling for most of the day. As the sun was getting close to touching the horizon, a sound caught our attention. A heavy pounding to the south drew my eyes towards the origin.

Running straight for us was a colossal grayish, almost-white rhinoceros. *So much for the demons killing it.*

"Spread out." I waved my arm to the side as I extended the distance between me and Fina. My instincts screamed at me to run. *If my instincts are screaming, what are the others hearing?* "Don't run, it will catch you and kill you. We need to fight."

"You know how to hunt one?" Victor asked as he moved farther away. "Have you hunted one before?"

As the dire continued its approach, I fought the urge to run. "I haven't. But based on physical appearances, it should be similar to a boar."

"And what do you mean by that?" Gifford's voice was noticeably less masculine.

"The only really dangerous spots are the front and underneath it." I turned to face Gifford. The fear in his eyes was obvious. "Get ahold of yourself. Every book I've read about dires says they're almost intelligent. We need you and your claws. Its hide is going to be tough. We'll have to bleed it, slowly. If we spread out, it can only target one of us. Once it charges through, the others will run up its sides and jump on and try to cut it open as much as they can."

The dire rhinoceros didn't stop or slow down. But as it got closer, I could see more details. It had three horns. Starting from the tip of its nose and moving up, each one was half the size of the one below it. The largest horn went from the end of its face to the top of its head. Its four round legs held up the massive girth of its body that undulated with each step. Wrinkles and scars covered its body. A long whip-like tail poked around from behind the animal.

It was staring right at me.

Why is it always me? What did I do to deserve this? Fine, you wanna dance? Let's dance. You're big, slow, and cumbersome. You can't catch me. "Everyone, get ready to jump on it."

I darted to cross everyone, and the rhino followed my movements. *That's right, follow the pretty wolf.*

The others lined up so that Victor would jump on the rhino's left side while the other two would jump on the right.

The rhinoceros charged towards me with no regard for the other three. It was getting close far too quickly for my liking. It was also taller than me, and I wasn't short. *Most reports say that rhinos are only as tall as a human. Why do dires have to be so big?*

I picked up the pace as the beast got closer. The ground shook with each thunderous step. After I ran past the others, I could hear the dire's breathing right behind me. I dug all of my claws into the ground to halt my momentum. My fingers and toes cried out in pain as I pulled myself directly ninety degrees away from the rhino.

A breeze pushed on my back as I heard the fumbling steps of the lumbering creature.

I turned my dive into a roll and caught myself as I turned to face the rhino. As we had planned, Gifford and Fina were clawing into the animal's side. Victor was kneeling on the ground. Several red lines decorated the dire's left side. *It looks like Victor can't climb on, but at least he left a mark.*

The rhino stumbled for a few steps before it stopped and turned to face me. *Is it really ignoring those two like that?* I took the chance to dash for the side that Victor had clawed up. Victor had just stood up and began his charge anew. I continued to sprint for the side as the rhino turned to keep its dangerously large horn between us, and it kept up with me as I tried to run a circle around it. *How are you keeping up with me? Aren't you supposed to be slow?* As we continued to spin, Fina and Gifford stopped slashing at it.

Gifford flew off the rhinoceros just as I ran faster. I was slowly gaining ground and could see its vulnerable side.

The rhino dropped its horn, stepped forward, and attempted to gore me.

Dodging was unnecessary because I was running so fast that I was already well past where the dire animal struck. With such an opportunity presented to me, I couldn't help but take advantage of it.

My vision shifted to red as I pounced on the side Victor had clawed. I latched on with the claws on my hands before I curled my legs up and dug them into the belly of the rhino. A bellow from the dire hammered my ears as it turned to reach me. I flattened my ears and gritted my teeth as I attempted to withstand the auditory assault.

As I raked my claws with my left hand through the rough hide, I could see how thick its skin really was. *I didn't cut through its hide?* I looked at the cuts Victor had made. The hide was three inches thick. My claws, as sharp as they are, extended to the same three inches. *Gifford's claws are the same length as mine, but Fina's are a little shorter. She isn't doing anything to it. Victor's four-inch claws will be our key to killing it.*

I heard Fina let out a shriek of pain. *We need to bring this thing down quickly.* I continued to slash at its ridiculously thick skin, aiming for the cuts Victor had made, trying to slash at the same spots repeatedly to dig my way through.

Pain exploded from the middle of my back as I was pressed closer to the rhino. *That felt like someone just broke a wooden training staff over my back.*

Fina shrieked again.

I turned and saw the rhino's tail swinging towards me. When the tail whipped across my back, I growled to suppress the pain.

Fina climbed on top of the dire animal's back and dug her claws in. Seeing her up there with the look of absolute determination felt odd. I suddenly felt even closer to her, like she was my sister.

A deafening roar from Victor interrupted my admiration of the lynx. He leaned forward as he displayed his challenge to the rhino.

Our prey answered by charging towards him.

I continued my assault, finally drawing some blood as I made it through the hide.

The rhino's tail came to strike me again. I braced for an impact that never came. Gifford pounced on the tail and bit down on it. He wrapped his arms around the appendage and dragged his toe-claws through the ground, halting the strike. *Thanks.* My respect for Gifford grew as he growled and tried to dig his fangs into the tail.

Fina halted her crawl towards the rhino's head as it charged towards Victor. The lumbering motion of it running also caused me to halt my attacks and just hang on. I saw the dire animal lower its horn as it neared Victor. Victor crouched low. As the rhino attempted to gore him, Victor wrapped one arm around the horn and slapped at the face of the rhino with the other.

Even though Victor had essentially caught the charge, he didn't halt it. He impressed me as he kept his legs behind him and straight. His toe-claws dug into the dirt as the rhino pushed him forward. Victor slowed the dire animal enough so that Fina and I could resume our strategies. As Fina climbed towards its face, I dug for its internal organs. Gifford continued to jerk side to side with the movements of the rhino's tail.

The rhinoceros bellowed again as it tried to shake the bear off its horn. Victor moved with the head, keeping his grip on the face as he clawed at it. Fina made it to her destination and slashed at the animal's eye. The screech of pain was the only momentary warning we received before the dire animal flailed.

I dug my hand into the deepest cut and hooked my claws in for the best possible handhold. *Is that a bone that I feel? Yes, I made it to its ribs. A little more and I can pop its lung.*

Gifford lost his grip on the tail as it threw him off. Victor was thrown off too.

The dire twisted and turned in every direction it could. Fina grabbed the beast's ears as she barely held on. I lost the grip on the hand that wasn't buried in the animal's hide. But I twisted my body so I could regain my hold before it jumped again.

It continued bellowing even as it slowed down. As soon as Fina's footing returned, she resumed her attack on the rhino's eyes. Before she could cause it to buck around wildly again, I desperately scraped my claws towards its lung. I forced my way between two ribs until it felt like I had stuck my hand into a pocket.

Got it! Time to get off this crazy ride.

I hooked my claws as I dragged them out, freeing my blood-soaked arm.

Before I could push off, Fina shoved her arm into its eye socket.

The rhinoceros bucked and sent Fina airborne. There was a spectacular spray of blood as Fina's arm exited the opening she'd made. The lynx twisted her body in midair and landed gracefully on her feet, her arm dripping with blood. I couldn't hold on any longer and flew off, but I didn't land nearly as gracefully as the feline. I tumbled away from the wild animal.

"Stay back!" I held out my hand to Victor, who looked like he was going to go back in again. "I punctured its lung. It's going to die slowly."

Blood poured from the wounds Fina and I had made. The rhinoceros continued flailing, blinded after Fina took its second eye. We watched it throw its weight around from a safe distance. Moment after moment, the dire animal jumped and twisted its body. We didn't move. We only watched as its precious blood left its body.

Its movements suddenly became labored and slowed down drastically.

Victor took another step forward.

"Wait," I said as I ran over, grabbed his arm, and pulled him back. "We don't need to go in just yet."

The bear gave me an annoyed look. "It's dying. There's no need to let it suffer like this."

I scowled at him as I held up a finger. "And we don't need to risk our lives to do so. When it lays down, then we can move in for the kill. But not before."

Victor scowled back but didn't move. My vision returned to normal. *I approve of your sense of morals, but a certain level of practicality will keep you alive much longer. If you wanted to win me over, you're doing an excellent job. But again, not the time. You're making it tough for me to say no when the time comes. While my instincts are already eager to accept you, my rational mind isn't. Not with everything that's going on and will go on. It would be really irresponsible if the demon king arrived and I couldn't join the fight because I was pregnant.*

I shook my head to clear it of the distracting thoughts just in time to see the dire rhinoceros's front two legs give out. It collapsed to its knees before falling to its side. Its breathing was shallow, and I could hear a wheezing sound as it inhaled.

The rhino hit the ground with a thud and let out a strange sound. It started off as a high-pitched squeal that lowered into a rumble. *Victor was right. I almost feel bad about this. Almost. I'm getting hungry just looking at it.*

Victor placed a hand on my back and gave me a shove. "Finish it."

I caught myself as I approached the wounded animal. *Never assume an animal is dead until you kill it.* The memory of Zane's first lessons five years ago brought a smile to my face. I kept my distance away from its face and horns as I walked up to its back. *I don't think my claws are long enough to reach the arteries in its neck. This is going to be gruesome.* I stood behind its head as I looked into its bloody eye sockets.

I was right. The beast tried to resist me as I dug my clawed hand through its eye socket and into its brain. It spasmed in its last moments as I tore its brain apart. When I pulled my arm out, it was finally dead.

I looked at the others and smiled. "Who's hungry?"

The guys licked their lips while Fina was busy licking the blood from her arm.

33

CRUDE YET BEAUTIFUL

Victor used his longer claws to cut through the rhino's hide. After that, we worked together and peeled the skin back to get to the good part. For science, I tasted a piece of the skin: it was terribly bland while easily being the chewiest thing I'd eaten in two lifetimes. We exchanged all the lionant meat for rhino meat. *I'm so glad I'm not the only one who finds the taste, or lack thereof, repulsive.* Gifford piled the discarded meat a safe distance away from the rhino.

Gifford suggested we sleep here for the night. Of course, he waited until we were all burying our faces in chunks of the rhino. I was in a blissful haze as I savored the wonderful flavors. Rhino meat tasted like a cross between fish, horse, and boar, all wrapped up in a special blend. Nobody held back, as we all ate far more than we should have. It was cute to see Fina attack the chunk of intestine she asked for.

Even though Fina wasn't a primal beastkin, she had a strong preference for meat. Nothing could stop Gifford and me, being the carnivorous primal beastkin that we were, as we took bite after bite. Victor even had a smile on his face as blood dripped from his lips.

After we stuffed our stomachs to the brim, I coated the remains in ice. *The others can break it down and get some food too. Hopefully the ice will keep it fresh enough until they get here. And we have breakfast ready for us in the morning.* I encased the remains in a solid layer of ice before I magically fatigued myself. Since we were going to sleep and I would wake up refreshed, I wasn't worried. *Besides, I use my magic more defensively anyway. And with the dire rhino dead, there's unlikely anything here to threaten us.*

We slept through the night with our normal watches between Victor and me.

Again the two of us were up before everyone else. This time, I was glad to see Victor wanted to talk to me. We put a little more distance between us and the other two, but I wanted to make sure we could still see them. I sat with my back against the frozen rhino.

Victor sat down next to me. "So Lucia, I couldn't help but see how much you were enjoying that meat earlier." I gave him a toothy smile. "And watching you do that thing with your ice magic was also pretty cool. How does magic work?"

I glanced over my shoulder at the encapsulated carcass. "Anything was better than that ant meat." We both laughed quietly. "But it's kinda hard to explain. There's this feeling that I can will water and ice to move how I want it to."

Victor's eyes went wide as he gave me an expectant look. "Do you think I could use magic just like you and Lexia?"

I grimaced. "Honestly, I couldn't tell you." I scratched the back of my head. "What my mom said was that you have to be born with it. But if you don't know how to use it, you could go through your whole life without knowing it. But once I learned I could use it, I can't not think about it."

Victor's eyes never shifted. "So can I? Will you teach me?"

I let out a cross between a groan and a sigh. "I'm sorry, but I can't help you. Mom never told me how to teach anyone. If you already knew how to use magic, I might've been able to give you a pointer or two." I looked straight ahead towards the two sleeping. "Maybe my mom could tell you, and she could teach you. I know Lexia wants to learn from her. But to do that, you would have to leave the Wild Kingdom and follow me back to Rophmna."

"I see," Victor said with a slightly deflated tone. "That's a big decision."

I looked at him from the corner of my eye and saw he'd lowered his head. "So was asking me to be your mate."

The bear flinched. "You're right." He started drawing in the dirt with a claw. "I forgot that you're not from here. But maybe, if we can make things right after we save Lexia, I won't need to stay here. I could go with you."

I raised an eyebrow. "You would do that? Are you sure? Don't you have family here?"

Victor kept drawing in the dirt. "No, there's nobody waiting for me. I have no attachments here other than my promise to help Lexia and now you."

I leaned forward and curled my tail around my waist. "What about a family? Do you have any siblings?"

He shook his head. "None living. My mother died giving birth to me. I was lucky there was another woman who gave birth just before I was born so I could be nursed." There was almost a dreamy look in his eye. "Her daughter, Cirra, was my closest friend growing up. We were inseparable."

"What happened to her? Why didn't you bond with her?" *He obviously cares for her.*

"I would have." Victor stopped drawing for a moment. "If she was still alive."

I shut my eyes. *And there I go again.* "I'm sorry. I didn't know."

"It's fine." He looked up at me, and a single tear sat in the corner of his eye. Then he lowered his head and pointed to his drawing. "This was something she drew whenever she felt lonely."

A large circle with three upward-curving lines spread out from it. The three lines eventually ended at the same point. On the bottom line on each side was a row of semi-circles. On the bottom of the large circle were three triangles with all three tips touching the circle and the sides touching each other. The top of the circle was adorned with an oval with a circular indent near the top on the section that was still over the large circle.

It's a bird. He drew a bird?

"She always admired birds. There was never a more free-spirited foxkin." He gave a slight laugh. "She told me she drew this because this was as close to flying with the birds she could get. She was always jealous of them. 'They can fly around the world and see everything, and if something is interesting to them, they can swoop down and check it out for themselves. There's nothing holding them back.' It's what she always said when she finished drawing it."

I couldn't look away. I couldn't think of anything to say. The crude yet beautiful drawing left me speechless.

"I draw it to remember her." I could feel Victor looking at me, so I looked at him. His face was stiff, but his voice shook a little. "Every time I'm scared to do something or am worried about trying something new, I draw it knowing that Cirra would have jumped at the chance to try something new. She never saw the world like she wanted to. So even if it's just a little bit, I will see it for her."

I could feel myself getting choked up. To calm down, I started petting my tail. "I've hurt my friends. All my life, I've hurt those closest to me. Danger follows me everywhere." I looked up at Victor. "Are you sure you want to be associated with me? I'm an attractor of unpredictable and often deadly forces. One of my closest friends lost her arm and three years of her life because she was close by when a demon attacked."

Victor lifted his hand. "I—"

"No." I silenced him. "I don't want to hear an answer today. Think about what you really want. And I mean it, really think about it. Don't tell me your answer until after we save my sister. Then, and only then, if you still want to bond with me, I'll give you my answer."

Victor lowered his hand and looked back down at the drawing.

I stood up. "Please don't think I'm trying to be mean and not thinking about your feelings. It's just that I need to think about it myself. So please, give me some time to think." I placed a hand on his shoulder as I left him to his thoughts.

As I kept walking, a small pang of remorse grew in the back of my mind. *I know you want him to be our mate.* My inner wolf wasn't happy with my decision, but this was something both of us needed to

252

agree on. *If I can only have one, it better be the right one. It's not that I've said no yet. It's just I can't say yes yet. So please, I need you to give me more time too.*

I could feel her giving my soul a hug. It was warm, but my heart felt a little heavier with each step I took away from Victor.

34

REGICIDE

W hile the others slept and Victor thought about what I'd said, I took some time to locate the tracks of the king and those following him. As the sun poked itself over the horizon, I woke the other two. Gifford required a lot of prodding to get moving. *I'm going to whip you into shape. If you're going to be my sister's mate, you're going to need a certain level of combat readiness.*

My ice hadn't melted, even when Fina and Gifford were ready for breakfast. I shifted the ice around so that we could eat more of that deliciously savory dire rhino. *Now I need to eat a regular rhino to see if there's a difference between the flavors.*

After breakfast, I resupplied our water and coated the rhino with more ice to make it last as long as possible.

We resumed our mission as we followed the tracks. The uneasiness we felt didn't go away, but since we'd killed the dire responsible, it was much more manageable. Our journey took us until nightfall of another day. I tried to pay attention to the tracks more closely and could tell we were catching up. The ground was softer, and the footprints we followed were more defined the longer we traveled.

We went through our routine and rested. Familiar rolling hills lay in our path when we woke up the next day. Victor left another drawing of his bird. *It's hard not to see him do that now. I wonder how many times he's done that since I've met him.* Gifford dragged his feet even more. I had to remind him that his mate's life was at stake. *If we haven't already crossed it, we should be close to the kingdom's border by now. Hopefully we aren't too late.*

We caught up with the king and the beastkin following him. Despite all our planning, we failed to predict one scenario.

A small town was being sacked.

From our vantage point, we could see the bodies of beastkin, men, women, and children lying scattered between the buildings.

"We're too late." My voice shook as I stared at the carnage with my three friends.

"What do we do now?" Victor's question was what we were all asking ourselves.

We stood in silence as the beastkin attacked the town. From what I could guess, there were well over a hundred beastkin attacking the village. *What can the four of us do?* I shook my head. *I came here to kill the king to prevent this.*

"Gifford." The fox beastkin turned to look at me. "If the king were to die, could we get all the beastkin to leave?"

"If you kill the king, you will be the queen and can tell them to do whatever you want." Gifford stared at me, his face expressionless.

I turned back to look at the town. "So, I guess I commit regicide. Like we originally planned. We can't wait for the others to catch up."

"What do the rest of us do?" Fina asked.

"Find my sister." I stepped forward and turned to face the three. "Just don't give in to the demons while I deal with the king. If either demon presents a deal, don't take it. No matter the terms." I looked Gifford in the eyes. "You especially." He nodded slightly. "Keep them busy, but don't put yourself in danger. Please."

Fina walked up and gave me a hug. "Stay safe," she whispered into my shoulder.

I returned the hug and looked at Victor. "No heroics from you, either. If you die, then you won't be able to be my mate, got it?" Victor smiled as he nodded. *I really hope I don't break his heart by stringing him along like this.* "The sin of lust won't be easy to find, but at least get my sister out of there. She'll be much easier to find." *If she's there.*

I turned to look for King Daygon. My heart sank when I found the primal lion beastkin standing next to a human with large black wings. *Can things get any worse?* My heart pounded in my chest as I marched towards the king.

Daygon's tail flicked back and forth as he shifted his feet almost unnoticeably. He was watching the raid, but it looked more like he was a chained pet, unable to leave his master.

I could hear my instincts screaming to avoid them, but I'd made a promise. It was a promise I intended to keep.

There are things more important than survival. If this war begins, I'll be seen as nothing more than a savage beastkin. Nobody will treat me as anything more than someone who could attack them at any moment. I've worked hard to get people to accept me and treat me as an equal. Yes, I've been a bit abrasive. But I always had a good reason. This war can undo all the work I've done. Mom will still accept me, but will we have to leave? Will she suffer for adopting me? I can't let that happen.

With each thought, my instincts relented, and by the end, they followed me.

The sin of pride noticed my presence first. I saw his lips move as he gave me one look before he looked back at the town.

The beast king turned to face me. He walked towards me. "I remember you, little one." Daygon's voice rumbled, even though he sounded heartbroken. "You survived."

"Yes, and I'm here to fulfill a promise to my sister." I extended my claws.

"And what promise is that?" Daygon stopped and stood tall.

"To remove you from your throne." I waved my arm towards the town. "This needs to stop. You need to stand up to the demons. And if you can't, then you need to be dealt with."

"If I'd known that this is what would become of my kingdom when I took that deal, I would've let them kill me. They ordered me to attack the humans, but they wouldn't tell me why. It sickens me to know my people have been used so callously." The king's eyes looked empty. "But since I was born without an aptitude, I grasped at any chance to change my life. Unfortunately, some deals are too good to be true. And for that, I am beyond forgiveness."

"Will you fight now?" *I'll give him this one chance.*

"I can't." He spread his legs apart. "I can't resist them. You need to kill me. Then you must stop them and save our people. I only hope that this time, you succeed." The lion closed his eyes and took a deep breath before opening them again. "They ordered me to deal with you. It's an order I can't refuse, and I'll not ask you to join. So resist with everything you have."

I shifted my vision until it was completely red. "Then there's nothing left to say."

We bared our fangs at each other. Daygon roared as I let loose a deep howl. All of my senses focused on him. I sprinted forward, and Daygon matched my movements. While everything around me slowed down, the lion beastkin didn't. *He's fast. But I'm faster.* I created a small blade of ice around each of my claws and coated my forearms in a layer of ice. Daygon stumbled at my use of magic. That was all the opening I needed.

I lunged for my opponent's torso with my right arm extended and my left arm hung low. Daygon slid to a stop and dodged to his right. He turned and swung his left hand, claws extended, towards my face.

I halted my charge. *I was right. He doesn't know how to fight.* From my opponent's blind spot below, I raised my other arm up and leaned back. His claws passed in front of me harmlessly while my attack shredded through his thigh. The lion flinched and pulled his leg back as he favored his wound.

I stepped forward and stabbed at his face with my left hand. He leaned to the side and reached for my arm. As soon as his hands wrapped around the ice covering my arm, I grabbed his elbow and slashed it open. Daygon's left arm went limp. With a quick pull, I extracted my left arm effortlessly and slashed the lion's face at the same time.

Blood poured from the four red lines I opened on the king's face as he growled and charged me. I sidestepped. He stumbled past me and I slashed my claws across his gut. Daygon collapsed to his knees, clutching his stomach. I casually walked to stand behind him.

"Who are you?" Daygon's voice had lost its rumble.

"My name is Lucia Silverbreeze, knight of the kingdom of Rophmna." I buried my claws in the space between his neck and collarbone. "For attacking the kingdom, I sentence you to death."

"I've heard of you. The Stray." He gurgled and spat out a glob of blood. "Lead them..." His words gurgled in his throat as I removed my claws.

I watched the king collapse to the ground, dead. "Sorry, but I won't be the queen. I just want this war to end." I flicked the bloody ice from my claws.

Your reliance on your strength to win all your fights was your mistake. The beastkin in this kingdom must really not know how to fight.

I turned and saw that the black-feathered demon stood still, watching me. *He didn't move. Why? He just let me kill their puppet. Did he not care?*

"My, my." I clenched my jaw at the sound of Lust's voice. I turned and saw her floating in the air above my sister. "That was a spectacular performance."

Where are the other three? They were supposed to find and distract her or get my sister out. I looked into my sister's eyes. The normally bright blue shine was gone. My sister wasn't looking at me; she wasn't herself.

I extended my claws as I leaned forward. "What did you do to her?" I growled.

The succubus leaned forward and slid a finger down Lexia's cheek. "She kept fighting against me, so I had to rein her in. Also, with this, I helped her see her true potential. Do you have any idea how powerful she is?"

The demon raised her tail and pointed. I looked to see where she was pointing. My heart nearly exploded as I saw Fina, Victor, and Gifford encased in ice near one of the village's buildings.

"You will release them and my sister."

The sin of lust smiled wickedly. "Or what?"

"I will kill you in the most painful way I can think of." I focused on my magic and re-coated my claws with ice.

"And if I comply?" The way she drew out her words taunted my inner wolf.

I bared my fangs. "I'll kill you much quicker."

"You have gone and destroyed one of my toys." The sin of lust tapped her chin with a finger. "Apparently, the frenzy dulled your fighting prowess when you fought him the first time. He never stood a chance against you now that you've recovered. Even after all the strength we gave him." The demoness shrugged her shoulders. "While that's interesting information, I have a new puppet to play with. A better puppet." She pointed to Lexia. "How about you play with her? This will be so much more fun to watch. Oh, and don't worry, she's completely conscious but unable to act on her own. She does whatever I want, whenever I want." Her voice dropped as she purred each word. "However I want."

My inner wolf threatened to push me aside and take over. I reined her in as I looked at Lexia's blank eyes as I returned my vision to normal. "Lexia, I'm sorry. This is going to hurt, but I promise she will pay for every moment she made you suffer."

A lonely tear formed in the corner of her eye. *Is she crying? I doubt the sin is that manipulative to force her to do that. That's Lexia's honest emotion. Maybe she can break through the demon's control. But if it was easy, she would have done it by now. I guess it's my job to wake her up.*

I spread my arms as I leaned forward. Lexia's body glowed with the telltale sign that she was channeling magic. Around me, the ground glowed with magic. I bolted towards Fina, Victor, and Gifford. A pillar of ice formed in the spot where I had been standing.

I need to get them out, but they need to stay out of this fight. It's time to use everything Mom taught me about magic against my sister.

35

THE PRIDE OF LUST

I could hear the whistling of a spear of ice flying towards me. When I turned my head, I saw three spears headed my way, and Lexia was making a fourth. *She's controlling my sister's ice magic by controlling her. Does this demon really understand what my sister can do? She's acting like she doesn't. My sister can control magic at a range of three and a half arcs. It's a wonder that Lexia doesn't have the ice manipulation aptitude.*

I stopped and caught the first icy spear, using my magic to give me a better grip. The sin of lust pouted. "Did you really think it was going to be that easy?" I asked as I flipped the spear around in my hand. I didn't let the demon respond before I hurled the projectile towards her.

The spear split the air as it flew towards the demon. She shrieked as she waved her arms in front of her. While I caught the second spear Lexia threw towards me, my sister shattered the spear just before it reached the demon. I couldn't suppress a toothy grin. My sister's half-created spear broke apart as it hit the ground.

I spared a moment to peek at the other demon. He was standing still with his arms crossed, looking almost bored.

So she really is flying right there. That's the real sin of lust. The demon must know that most beings can only manipulate one source of magic at a time. Some elements get around it slightly. The sin knows that my sister doesn't need to concentrate on the spears once she launches them because of their momentum. But it looks like she's under similar restrictions, and she's controlling my sister through magic. That means she can't use her tricks to turn invisible and create illusions of herself.

I waited for the third spear and caught it just as easily as the first two. The sin of lust's eyes bulged at the sight of me throwing another spear at her, followed shortly by the second. A wall of ice flew up and blocked both weapons. *That might give me the time I need to take care of the others.*

I dashed over to the others, channeling my magic to collect any ice I touched on my arms. The first of my friends that I reached was Fina, and I placed my right hand on her face. My magic worked just as I wanted it to, and all the ice covering her face covered the back of my hand and forearm. Once my forearm held all the ice, I let go of the magic that moved it. Fina's head slumped forward, completely limp. I listened for her breath; she was alive.

I moved on to Victor and collected the ice on my left arm. Once his head was free, I listened for his breathing while I used the ice around Gifford's face to connect the two large chunks of ice around my forearms with a ribbon of ice around my back. After I made sure Gifford was breathing, I turned back towards my sister and the sin of lust just in time to see a massive icy claymore threatening to cleave me in half from above.

I raised my arms and caught the blade in between the ice bracers I made for myself. As the blade contacted my bracers, I threw the sword to the side, away from Gifford. The sword bit several inches into the ground before stopping and exploding into countless sharp projectiles. I raised an arm to protect my face, but a lot of the shards cut or embedded themselves in me.

When I turned to look at the demon, she was grinning.

The demon is learning. I could feel the magic as I focused on my armbands, draining me. *I won't have a lot of time. Lexia isn't powerful enough to expropriate any ice I control with magic, but I can't do the same to her. There's too much ice on my arms now that if I don't main-*

tain control, she'll use it against me. She can't use magic for long, because she's always been inefficient with it, and I think I have a larger reserve. But it looks like the demon doesn't have that problem.

While I sprinted towards my sister, I dropped the temperature of the ice around my arms and compressed it. It shifted from a transparent substance into a bluish-green color and became completely opaque. The effort was draining, but I knew the ice was incredibly hard now. I spared another quick look at the sin of pride standing on the sidelines. He hadn't moved an inch.

Maybe if the demon thinks I'll attack my sister, she'll let her guard down. Hopefully my attacks earlier didn't make her too paranoid. The sin used my sister's magic to create a giant icy war hammer. I continued running straight for my sister, knowing another attack was coming.

Lexia swept her arm from left to right, and the hammer swept horizontally, following the same path.

I jumped and easily cleared the strike aimed at my hip. But as the weapon flew under me, I turned my body and slashed my claws into the weapon's head, leaving four deep gouges.

As my sister recoiled from the backlash, the hammer dropped to the ground. *You aren't going to use that trick twice.* Once I landed on the ground in a three-point stance, I sprinted on all fours towards Lexia.

The sin of lust flapped her wings and casually flew backwards while lifting herself higher into the air. *Good. Stay nice and relaxed.*

Lexia lifted her hand, and I could see the ice forming on the ground in front of her.

A field of stalagmites formed and grew out to half an arc away from her. *I guess the only way to reach her now is to go over.* When I jumped, I kept my arms under me just in case the demon wanted to try something.

The demon didn't disappoint. A stalagmite grew to intercept me.

I moved my forearm to block the attack with my bracer. The stalagmite shattered as it crashed against my denser ice.

Lexia stumbled back as I continued to sail over the failed attack. Because my sister took a few steps backwards, my landing was less than ideal. Instead of jumping over her head, I collided with her chest. Our bodies tangled up as we tumbled to the ground. As soon as my vision righted itself, I heard the demoness laughing.

My sister's eyes opened.

"Sorry, Lexia, this is going to hurt." I slapped my hands on the sides of her neck and squeezed to put her in an unorthodox sleeper hold. Lexia's eyelids fluttered and her body went limp. As soon as she stopped moving, I let go.

The demon wasn't laughing anymore; instead, she shrieked in pain. I turned and saw her holding a hand to the side of her head. "You have been annoying for too long!" She pointed at me with the other hand.

That was not what I was expecting. Then again, I don't know how she uses magic to manipulate a person. Maybe I should ask Mom after this is over. I manipulated some of the ice from my forearm and created a spiked ball before disconnecting it from my icy armband. After carefully catching it, I waited until the demon's wing moved back up before I hurled it at the bone in her wing.

The sin of lust's eyes opened wide, and she tried to avoid my projectile, but she couldn't move fast enough to dodge. My spiked ball slammed into the bone on the top part of her left wing. There was a satisfying crack as I heard it break.

The demon plummeted to the ground, screaming in both pain and fear as she fell.

I didn't wait for her to hit the ground before I charged. As she hit the ground gracelessly, I pounced on her back.

"Get off of me, you mutt," the sin of lust screamed as she tried to roll and throw me off.

"You're grounded!" I grabbed her good wing with one hand and slashed at it with my claws. In two swipes, I severed it. *I'm going to rip you apart, limb by limb.*

Her scream was wonderful. I threw her wing away and buried my claws into her back. The demon wrapped her tail around my waist and threw me off her. I tucked my limbs in and rolled into a four-point stance. Blood poured from the wounds my claws left, but that was nothing compared to the blood squirting from the stump of her missing wing.

That demon of pride can't still be just standing there, can he? I looked, and he was.

"No more games!" The sin of lust turned to face me. Her eyes were filled with a look I could only imagine I'd had when I attacked Daric and Golditress. "Pride, kill her!"

I turned to look at the fallen angel that had been standing by, watching without moving or showing any interest. His face was still just as disinterested. "Are you telling me what to do?"

The succubus's look of rage melted into one of fear.

A flash of light blinded me. The ear-piercing explosion that followed deafened me. It was a sound I was all too familiar with. I lifted an arm to cover my eyes as I reflexively reached a hand to the base of my neck.

That's right, it's gone.

The memories of all the times I'd activated the amulet dissipated one by one. Memories of a small piece of jewelry that, every time I got angry, would flash with light to blind me and everyone around while also deafening everyone with a thunderclap. I'd tried to bury those memories, but every time a thunderstorm passed overhead, they resurfaced. *And now it looks like that'll happen every time someone uses lightning magic too.*

When the last memory faded, my vision and hearing returned while my anxiety abated. I straightened up and looked around. The sin of lust was lying on the ground. Burns covered half of her body as she convulsed in agony. The smell of burned flesh filled the air as I let go of the magic around my bracers, the ribbon shattering behind me.

Did he kill her? He had to have. No mercy. No hesitation. I slowly turned to face the sin of pride. *I'm fast, but I'm not the-speed-of-light fast. How do you fight someone so powerful?*

The sin of pride strolled towards me. "So, are you going to tell me why three of my brethren have marked you?"

"Marked? Me?" My voice quivered as my instincts screamed at me to run.

The fallen angel scowled. "Yes. Now tell me why both Gluttony and Wrath marked you as interesting. You can skip Lust. She is a slave to her whims."

I tucked my tail around my leg. *Do I keep talking? If he's talking, he isn't zapping me with lightning, right?* "I don't know. I met them both when I was younger. What do you mean, they marked me?"

The demon crossed his arms. "Whenever a sin sees someone who has the potential to become a sin like them, they mark them. If they can make them fall far enough, they will take their soul to the demon realm to be transformed into a demon."

They wanted to turn me into a demon? "Why?" My question flew out of my mouth.

"Because one of the ways a demon can get stronger is by creating other demons. When a soul is corrupted, part of its power is transferred to the closest demon." The sin dropped his arms to his sides. "But you still haven't answered my question. If you ask one more question, I will kill you," he said with an emotionless expression.

No, no, nonono. "I have a short temper and I eat a lot of meat and I enjoy hunting and fighting," I blurted as I flinched.

"I don't see anything special. All I see is a quivering, frightened dog." The demon sounded more bored than before.

"Wolf." I stomped my foot. "I'm a wolf."

A smile crept on his face. "So you have some pride after all." *Oh, no. I've caught his attention too.* "Someone like you was never in her plans, but I don't much care for her plans. I started her war like she wanted, but now I'm free to do what I want."

"Stay away from my sister." Lexia's voice was hoarse. The demon and I both turned to watch her stand up. She started glowing with magic.

I raised my arm as I ran towards her. "Lexia, no!"

3 6

QUEEN ME

Lexia raised an arm, and the ground around the fallen angel froze. A layer of ice wrapped around his legs and anchored him to the ground. The demon looked down as he tried to take a step, but couldn't. The glow of magic slowly grew around the sin of pride as I ran towards my sister.

"You think you can hold me back?" All traces of the demon's boredom were gone. He lifted an arm and pointed his palm towards my sister. "Die!" His glow flashed brightly before a bolt of lightning blinded me for a moment. The thunder assaulted my ears.

I stopped running and rubbed my eyes to ease the pain. When I opened them again, I looked at where my sister had been standing.

She wasn't standing anymore. She was lying on the ground, arms and legs spread wide. I could see some wisps of smoke rising from a darker patch of fur on her stomach. All the feelings of fear I'd felt up to that point evaporated and turned to rage. My vision shifted to red and then to black, leaving only one person visible, the sin of pride.

You hurt my sister, now you'll pay with your life!

I dropped to all fours and sprinted towards the demon. With a little more effort, he lifted his legs out of the ice, which shattered as it failed to hold him back.

I let out a growl just before I pounced.

While only slightly turning his head, the sin of pride looked at me and caught me with his right hand around my neck. His fingers wrapped around my throat and squeezed.

I raised my claws and gouged his wrists on both the inside and outside of his forearm. He dropped me instantly as he recoiled his bloodied arm.

As soon as I touched the ground, I reached out with my right hand to slash at his gut. Everything slowed down, including the demon's movements as my claws pierced his robe, flesh, and muscles. But when I tried to rake my claws through his bowels, he grabbed my wrist just past the ice on my forearm. He instantly dislocated it as I swiped at him with my other claws.

He didn't let go as my claws opened up four deep lines of crimson. Instead, the demon brought his bloody arm in and slapped me with his limp hand. My shoulder exploded with pain as it popped.

The blow sent me tumbling to the ground.

When I came to a stop, my shoulder and wrist burned. I suppressed the pain throbbing in my face as I looked at the demon. I grabbed my dislocated shoulder and put it back with a growl, then I did the same for my wrist, before I gave each of them a short, quick check to see if they still had their full range of motion. They hurt a lot, but the demon strutting towards me wouldn't let me heal.

The sin of pride began glowing with magic. *I won't make it in time. We're too far apart.* I focused on the ice around my forearms and pulled a spiked ball off again. The demon's glow grew, and he lifted his left arm.

Before he could discharge his lightning, I hurled my projectile, aiming for his raised arm. The spiked ball embedded itself in the demon's palm. Just as the demon flinched, there was a flash and what sounded like an explosion, reigniting the ringing in my ears.

It didn't sound like thunder alone. Almost like there was a secondary explosion, one that was accompanied by thousands of tiny little whistles. There was a prick in my shoulder. As I shook my head to reorient myself, I noticed a small stream of blood running down my arm from where a tiny piece of ice stuck out.

The demon was in much worse condition. When I looked at him, he was cradling his wrist, his hand missing and blood gushing out of the stump. He lifted his head, and his face was full of unbridled hatred.

Okay, what just happened? Did my ice explode when his lightning touched it?

I sprinted towards him as he moved towards me. *It doesn't matter. He's weak. Now's the time to get him.*

Just before we collided, I ducked low and dove for his leading leg. When my foot collided with his kneecap, I heard a crack, and his leg bowed backwards. The demon turned so his leg would roll around me as he fell to the ground.

I caught myself with my hands and pulled myself towards the fallen angel. My pounce landed me on his chest, so I aimed my claws at his throat.

He leaned forward so my claws slashed his cheek instead, then slammed his remaining hand into my side. He followed through with his hit and forced me to the ground next to him.

The demon lifted his arm again and swung it down towards my head. I kicked at his non-busted leg with my toe-claws extended, shredding his thigh. The kick also pushed me away from him enough so his arm landed a few inches from my face. Before he could regroup, I lunged forward and bit into his forearm. He pulled back reflexively, carrying me along with it.

While my fangs dug into his awful-tasting flesh, I stabbed at his chest with my claws. His ribs deflected several of my claws, but some of them still dug in. The demon threw his arm out wide with me still hanging on by my teeth.

I hit the ground, but I wouldn't let go of his arm as I felt my teeth latching onto the bones in his arm. I growled as I locked my jaw and bit down harder.

I turned my body until I was on my hands and knees. Then I pulled the fallen angel by his arm while I walked on all fours backwards. He struggled to find enough traction to stop me. He lifted his other arm, and I could see the bones of his forearm sticking out slightly. Before I could guess at what he was planning, he threw his stump like a punch towards my eyes.

I lifted one arm and blocked the attack with the ice on my forearm. As his attack collided with me, it pushed my arm into my face and smashed my nose.

My eyes watered as my nose throbbed, but I refused to let go. The demon tried to draw his arm towards himself, but I dug all of my claws into the ground and refused to budge. He tugged his arm back again, and there was a slight pause as I saw his feet moving under him.

I pulled at his arm again, this time spinning to my right and yanking down as much as I could. The demon landed face-first as I dragged him to the ground. I continued pulling his arm until he was completely flat.

Once his beautifully vulnerable back was exposed, I stabbed my right claws into his forearm and let go of it with my teeth. I jumped on his right wing, folding it back over the left one. As I pulled his arm with me, I could hear two things pop. The demon didn't scream in pain but growled as he tried to push himself up with his stump of an arm. Before he could, I shoved his face back to the ground and wrapped my jaws around the back of his neck.

After my teeth sank into his flesh, I whipped my head back and forth. I got off his back and throttled his body around until his head flew off in one direction and his body fell to the ground at my feet.

He tasted like ash, so I spat out the chunk of his neck toward his body. "Am I special enough for you now?"

Blood poured out of the body in response.

I took a deep breath and closed my eyes to calm down.

Lexia!

I sprinted towards my sister, who hadn't moved. When I slid to her side, my body reminded me of every injury I'd received, namely the dislocated joints. I used the last of my magic to transform ice on my forearms into braces for my shoulder and wrist. When I turned to inspect my sister, I could see her chest moving. *That's a good sign.*

Her shirt was completely ruined. The fur on her chest was fine, but the fur on her stomach was blackened. When I parted some of the singed fur, I could see the sign of a bad burn the size of my hand print.

Her breathing was slow, but I couldn't hear anything abnormal. I carefully checked her back and found that her hips were both dislocated, and I felt what I thought was a fracture. But her tail was fine, and her head and neck felt fine too.

She should live, but it will be a long road to recovery. Sadly, I still don't know about anything else the lightning did to her nerves. Golditress is coming, but should I let her use healing magic on her? She'll grow older. And there might be someone else who needs her magic more.

The sounds of yelling and screaming pulled my attention away from my sister. "Right. There are still beastkin fighting against the kingdom," I reminded myself. *How am I going to get all the beastkins' attention?* I looked at the king's body.

An idea popped into my head. "Me and my bloody ideas."

I walked over and severed the king's head from the body, then took it to one of the shorter buildings. I needed to take a few steps back and get a running start to jump onto the flat roof. Once I jumped high enough, walking on it wasn't difficult. I stood on the edge and looked out over the streets.

Some humans and elves held blades while others held makeshift weapons to fend off snarling beastkin.

I held up the head of the dead beastkin king. "Everyone, stop!" I shouted at the top of my lungs. Thankfully, most everyone did. *Okay, that worked.* My heart pounded in my chest. I looked around at everyone who was looking at me. *Say something.* I opened my mouth, but no words came out. *Anything!*

A crisp, commanding voice broke the silence. "She killed the beast king. She is your queen now."

I turned to see who'd spoken.

A woman walked into the street from under the house I was standing in. She was elderly with gray, almost white, hair. She stood mostly straight and only leaned forward at the shoulder blades. She raised her arm and pointed to me as she turned her head. Her gray eyes looked at me from a gaunt face.

"Uh, right." I couldn't take my eyes off the old woman. Something about her itched at my instincts. *One problem at a time.* "I want all of you to leave. Grab the wounded and take them away from here."

The woman pointed towards the rest of the townsfolk. "All of you need to stop fighting too."

The menagerie of beastkin didn't protest as they helped each other retreat and took anyone wounded with them. It looked like some of them even took the dead, too. The townspeople didn't attack after the lady told them not to, although they didn't lower any of their weapons or back off.

The old lady still watched me with a smile. It sent a shiver down my spine. I gave another glance to the people of the town and saw the fear and confusion in their eyes.

I don't know how to fix this. It's probably for the best if I just get everyone out of here.

I jumped down from the roof next to the old woman. "Thanks."

"It was no trouble at all," she said while still grinning.

Once I was standing next to her, everything about her felt wrong. Her voice, her smell, her skin, none of it added up. Such a clean voice didn't belong to an old woman, and it sounded a little deep for a woman's voice, too. Her scent was hard to pick out from the blood and sweat, but there was a hint of perfume about her.

I watched the woman closely. "How did you know I killed the beastkin king and that it also made me queen?"

"I watched through the window of my home." She pointed to the building I was just standing on top of. I turned to look at it. "Also, I know more about the beastkin and their culture than these backwater idiots."

You know you're living in the same town as those backwater idiots, right? I arched an eyebrow at the lady. "Look, just keep people here from getting too upset about what happened. It looks like these people will listen to you."

"They always do."

The woman's statement sent more shivers down my spine. I backed away slowly from the creepily wrong woman. My instincts couldn't decide what to make of her. Throughout the conversation, they kept changing their opinions about her. One moment they wanted me to run from her, the next they wanted me to kill her, only then to want her to be my friend. I shook my head as I left to get away from everything.

Victor, Fina, and Gifford had woken up, but they were still frozen from the neck down. *Right, what do I do about them?* Also, as I looked around, I saw two beastkin carrying Lexia. *And where is the body of the sin of lust?* The sin of pride's headless corpse was right where I left it.

That little... A growl escaped my lips as I clenched my jaw. *She survived! I can't spare the time to hunt her down either. She better not get near my sister again.*

37

THE WEIGHT OF RESPONSIBILITY

"Did you get her?" Gifford's question snapped me back to the situation at hand. "Did you save Lexia?"

"Mostly." I clenched my jaw. *How am I going to explain to him that she was struck by lightning magic and is severely injured?* "She's alive, and she should live for now." It was hard not to choke on those words.

All three of my friends were awake, but none of them were strong enough to break the ice from within. "Can you use your magic to get us out?" Victor's ears were low.

I shook my head. "No, I'm fatigued." I looked around and saw the war hammer made of ice. "But there might be a way to get you out of there." Without looking back, I walked towards the icy weapon.

I doubt my sister has ever seen a war hammer, so that means that this is what the sin of lust thought was a good way to make this weapon. It's terrible. If anyone were to swing this, it would likely fly out of their hand, and not because it's made of ice. And if they somehow held on to it, the handle would just snap from the impact. I shook my head as I dropped the hammer. *The old-fashioned way, then.*

I walked up to Victor first. "Sorry, but this might hurt a bit."

Victor clenched his jaw and closed his eyes. "I'm ready whenever you are."

Victor's left arm reached out in front of him. *If I break his arm free, he should get the rest of himself out. It would be the easier arm to free.* I dragged my claws across the ice around his shoulder before I grabbed his elbow. Then I pushed down on his arm, and the ice shattered around his shoulder but left the rest of his arm covered.

I pouted as I looked at the results. "That didn't work like I hoped it would."

Victor opened his eyes. "If you free my elbow, I should be able to free my hand on my own."

I grabbed his forearm. "Hold your shoulder as still as possible."

He nodded. I brought his arm up, and the ice at his elbow cracked and broke apart. Victor moved his arm to test its range of motion. He nodded towards me. "Thank you."

I returned the nod, then walked to Gifford. *Lexia loves him, but he hasn't done much for her. It's time to change that.* I took my claws and scored the ice all over Gifford.

He watched me as best he could. "What are you doing?"

I waited until I finished scoring all the ice before I stood in front of him. "I'm disappointed in you." Gifford's ears went flat and his eyes went wide. I kicked him in the stomach. The ice shattered as he flew backwards and landed on his back, clutching his gut.

"Why?" The fox rolled on the ground and looked up at me.

I glared at him. "That was for all your complaining on the way here. My sister loves you, but I don't think you're enough to keep her safe." Gifford wrapped his tail around his waist as he curled up into the fetal position. "That will change." I pointed my finger at him. "Once we get home, you're going to train like a knight until I'm satisfied."

He meekly nodded. *Good boy.* I turned and walked towards Fina. My tail whipped back and forth as I saw the worried look in Fina's eyes. *Now I know how Aurtour feels about Evalana.* I took a deep breath and relaxed before I broke Fina out of her imprisonment. I scored her ice just like I had done for Gifford. Instead of violently kicking the poor lynx, I started squeezing the ice around her arms and legs.

While I worked, Victor finished up, breaking himself out to the point he could walk around. "Why didn't you do that with me?"

"Because you're big." I turned my head and looked at the bear beastkin. "Your arms are too big for me to do this," I said as I turned back to free Fina's second arm. "Besides, I knew you just needed to get started and could take care of the rest."

Fina placed her hand on my ice-covered shoulder. "You're hurt. Rest."

I shook my head. "I don't have time to rest. We need to get these people back home and away from here as fast as possible. The knights of this kingdom are likely on high alert after what you did to that village before we met you." I turned to look at the town. "If there's a company nearby and someone jumped on a horse, they're likely on their way now. And trust me when I say that, depending on who it is, we might not get any chance to explain before we're slaughtered."

Gifford stood up but kept holding his stomach. "What do you mean?"

I couldn't hold back a heavy sigh. "There are some knight companies that take combat a little too seriously and enjoy it far more than what's healthy. One such company, the Crimson Tide, has been banned from Aquittemia, the city I live in. All because several of their members tried to attack me."

It's problematic that they're usually one of the first companies to volunteer to deal with border disputes. It's like someone wants a war to start when they send them.

Fina covered her mouth as she gasped.

I held up my hand. "Don't worry, they didn't stand a chance. There were only four of them, and they were drunk. I could taste the alcohol in their blood when I bit off a hand." I laughed. The three just stared at me. *Oh, come on. That was funny.* I crossed my arms and pouted. "Either way, I got into a lot of trouble over it. But since I wasn't completely at fault, I only had to pay a heavy fine. They got banned because they promised to get me back later. I have never seen Captain Aenwyn so angry."

"Why did you get in trouble? Were you not defending yourself?" Victor asked as he scratched his head.

I shrugged. "Humans have different rules. Something about excessive force, disrupting the peace, and the consumption of human flesh. But I didn't consume it. I spat it back out." I shook my head. "But I need to stop getting distracted. We need to leave now." I pointed towards where all the beastkin were gathering.

As we finished getting all the ice off the three, we turned to leave. I took one last look at the town to make sure there were no angry mobs chasing us. But when I looked at the building that I'd jumped off, I didn't see any windows. *That woman said she watched me through the window, but there aren't any. And how did she know that he was the beast king? Nobody said that, right? Another reason to leave. Something is really not right here.*

A growl escaped my throat. *I don't have time for this!* I stomped my feet as I followed my three friends.

When I arrived at the location where the beastkin were nursing their wounded, everyone stopped what they were doing to stare at me. Those that could walk stood in front of me. The look in their eyes told me they wanted me to say something. I looked at Gifford and nodded my head towards the crowd.

Gifford bowed slightly. "They are waiting for your command."

I flattened my ears. *Right, I'm the queen now. I wish someone knew what to do. Now I wish I hadn't skipped out on so many squad leadership training sessions. I don't want this. I could never be a good ruler. If I'm queen, then I have to leave Mom, have too much responsibility, and I'll never be able to do what I want. Someone will always want something from me. Maybe I can give the job to someone else. But until then, these people need leadership and to make their way back home. Let's start with the immediate problems.*

I took a deep breath. "Who knows how to treat the wounded? Raise your hands." Several beastkin raised their hands. "Get everyone that's wounded to that side of the camp and treat them. Start with those who are the most severely injured." I pointed to the far side of the camp.

Everyone turned and took a few steps away from me. "Wait." I held up my hand. All the beastkin stopped and turned to face me. "You four, I have a different job for you." I pointed to four of the largest beastkin—a bearkin, a rhinokin, and two boarkin. "The rest of you take care of the wounded."

All but those I'd pointed to proceeded to follow my command.

The rhinokin stepped closer to me. His horn grew from his forehead, not his nose. "What do you want from us, Beast Queen?" His voice was deep and clear.

I shuddered at being called such a strange title. "You four need to collect the dead and place them over there." I pointed to the other side of the gathering of beastkin. *I know that's important. But what do I do with the dead? Do I order them to burn the bodies?*

The pain in their eyes was obvious, but the four silently nodded and went to complete their task. My heart pounded in my chest. I lowered my head and stared at the ground.

"You want help?" Fina asked as she placed a hand on my shoulder.

"Help, answers, anything you can give, I'll take it." My voice sounded distant, even to me. "I don't know what to do right now."

Victor stepped up and placed his hand on my other shoulder. "Do what you think is right. You're the queen now. We'll follow you because you've proven your strength. I don't know what happened, but you stood up to the two you called demons. Everyone can see you care for your people."

"But they aren't my people. I'm not from the Wild Kingdom. My home is Rophmna." My voice sounded choked up and tears threatened to burst from my eyes. "I'm not a queen. I don't know the first thing about leading a country, let alone a country full of people who have a culture different from my own. I don't deserve to be queen. Someone somewhere is better suited to be the ruler than me. And there has to be a way for someone else to be king or queen without me fighting to the death." The tears that threatened to fall fell.

"Don't underestimate yourself." Gifford's statement caused me to turn to look at him. "Seeing you this concerned about doing the right thing is admirable." Gifford's tail swayed back and forth as he gave me a hard stare. "I thought you simply disapproved of me as Lexia's mate, but those things you said were out of love. Just like you saying that you can't be the queen because you believe the Wild Kingdom deserves better than you."

The foxkin walked up and wiped the tears from my eyes. "You really are an extraordinary beastkin, aren't you?" *Buddy, you have no idea.* "You can simply name the next king or queen. That was Lexia's plan, after all."

My heart started slowing down. "But who did she plan on naming?"

"She didn't have that part figured out. She kept saying that she would figure it out when the time came." Gifford averted his eyes as he scratched the back of his head. "So pick whoever you think would be best."

I brushed off Victor and Fina's hands from my shoulders. "I'll think about it. But I have a question that I wish I never needed to ask." Gifford looked at me, very confused. I could imagine Fina and Victor having the same look. "How do you guys deal with your dead?"

"We bury them," Gifford said without changing his facial expression. "What did you think we do?"

I shrugged. "The humans burn their dead. Something about the fear of necromancy. But they have the decency to allow relatives to burn the bodies whenever they can." I looked at the pile of the dead. *Nine. I expect there will be more before nightfall.* "Make sure they're taken care of, and see to it that all those who don't make it are taken care of quickly." I couldn't look at Gifford as I placed my hand on his shoulder.

"Why?" Fina asked.

I turned my head to look at the woman. "Because the bodies can bring diseases. That's a problem we can't afford to deal with."

I walked through the wounded, looking for my sister. It took a little while, but I found her. The cheetah beastkin caring for her looked at me with confusion when I told him to leave her with me. I sat down and inspected her injuries and found that they hadn't become worse when she'd been moved. I watched her chest rise and fall, but I couldn't do anything for her. As I sat and thought about who should rule, I blocked out the rest of the world.

It was impossible to ignore what was going on around me when most of the beastkin near me stood up and started walking in the direction we came from. I looked up and saw Daric and his group walking towards us. *Maybe one of them can help me solve some of my problems.*

3 8

PASS THE BUCK

Reluctantly, I stood up and left Lexia's side to greet Daric and the others. I took a quick glance to see that the sun was nearly touching the horizon. *Have I been sitting here for that long?* The group gave me a curious look as I stepped past all the beastkin, making a wall to block the way to the wounded.

"What's happening?" Dinar was the first to run up and ask a question. "What happened to the plan?"

I pointed to the town. "It was a little hard to wait while they were attacking the town. So I improvised."

"Good. Does that mean we can leave?" Penny asked, without hiding her displeasure.

"Unfortunately, not yet." I couldn't look the elven woman in the eye. "Things happened, and I'm kinda the beast queen now. So, yeah, I need to deal with all this."

The shock on all of their faces was expected. *I think they're taking it pretty well. I'm not.*

"So what now?" Daric's eyes shifted back and forth between me and the other beastkin behind me.

"I need your help." I poked at the ground with my claws. "There's too much going on for me to understand everything by myself. I have no idea what to do. The people of the town let the beastkin go without a fight. It was kind of surprising, but something doesn't feel right."

"Before you go too far with your story, let's just get your new subjects calmed down." Silver pointed behind me.

New subjects? This is getting worse and worse. I'm not cut out for any leadership thing, let alone royalty.

I turned and saw several of the beastkin looking antsy. I lifted my arm as I turned and walked towards all the beastkin. "Don't panic, they're allies. Go back to doing what you were doing. Take care of the wounded."

Thankfully, the crowd dispersed.

People are doing what I say. This is weird.

Silver stepped up next to me. "I know my knowledge of medicine isn't as good as yours, but I'll help where I can." He didn't give me a chance to say anything before he followed the beastkin.

"Daric, go help him." Dinar gave the man a shove towards Silver. "I doubt Lucia wants your opinion on what to do." *Does she know me that well? Am I really that predictable?* Dinar turned to Penny. "Go brood somewhere else."

Penny huffed before she sauntered away from everyone else.

Dinar and Anna stood and stared at me. "I probably should help with the wounded." Anna lowered her head as she took her first steps towards the wounded.

I held up my hand and stopped her. "You're the last person I want out of this conversation." She lifted her head and cocked it to the side. "The demons were acting weird. And I have a few questions about the possibility of a new blood anchor."

"You know?" Anna's eyes bulged.

I flinched at her screech. "What?"

Dinar stepped in front of Anna. "Maybe you should tell us what happened."

"You're going to want to sit down for this one. Follow me." I waved them to follow me back to my sister.

Dinar and Anna followed me and sat on the ground next to Lexia. I told them the entire story after I answered their questions about the dire rhinoceros. They sat and listened with a frightening devotion.

I took a deep breath after I finished retelling the events. More tears spilled from my eyes, and my heart threatened to burst from my chest.

"Are you okay?" Dinar's question threw me off guard.

"It's just so much, so quickly," I whispered.

Anna moved to sit right next to me. "It's okay. We're here to help you now."

I turned to look at her. "But I don't know where to start."

"So let's start at the beginning." Anna's smile calmed my emotions a little. "What are all your problems? We'll sort through them one by one."

I dragged my claw through the ground to draw a line in the dirt. "I need to find someone to replace me as king or queen. My sister is severely injured. There was that strange woman in the town. The demons were up to something. Some knights could be on their way here. These beastkin need to go home, but their home is suffering from a terrible famine and a lack of wildlife. A new blood anchor may have been made. And war could still happen regardless of what I just did." With each problem, I wrote a number in the dirt.

"To start with, your sister isn't the only one hurt. But if you say she'll be fine, that's one problem that we can put off for later." Dinar kicked her foot to wipe away the last number I wrote in the dirt. I opened my mouth to complain, but Dinar lifted a finger. "We'll take care of it, just not right now." I flattened my ears. *She's been reasonable so far. That shouldn't change, right?* "If other knights are on their way, we'll just explain the situation."

"Don't panic, but yes, there's a new blood anchor. I can feel it," Anna said with a frown, and wiped two numbers out. "Yes, that makes four that we know of, but all the research I have says they need eight. But with how the demons are acting..." She shook her head. "I couldn't tell you what they're planning. But they *are* planning something."

I flattened my ears. "Yeah. If they wanted to make blood anchors, they could have just made them in the Wild Kingdom. Why here? Why now? What was the point of this whole war?"

Dinar groaned. "I don't like it either. But you killed the demons, so their plan's ruined, right?"

"I wish," I sighed. "The way they were talking, it sounded like there was someone else who was really the mastermind. This wasn't the sin of pride's plan. He seemed bored, more like someone assigned him to be here."

"We can't do anything then." Anna kicked another number I'd written down as she crossed her arms. "It terrifies me that we don't know enough of what's going on. But at this moment, we can't do anything. So let's move on but keep it in the back of our minds."

"And then there's the beastkin here. What about the lack of food for the Wild Kingdom? Or the fact that I'm the queen now?" I waved my hand to the beastkin, using whatever cloth they could get their hands on to apply rudimentary bandages.

Dinar glared at me. "If I remember correctly, the original plan was to have you kill the king. You did that. So what was your sister's plan for getting you out of this role you don't want? Or did she plan on leaving you on the throne?"

I shook my head. "No, Gifford told me I just have to name someone. Once I do, I'm off the hook. The problem is, I don't know who would be good for the job."

"Just pick someone, anyone." Dinar waved her arms out wide. "They can't possibly be worse than a king who let two demons control him. And if the people don't like who you pick, they'll sort it out themselves. They determine leadership through duels, so let them fight it out. Whoever wins becomes the next monarch. At least that's how I understand it, based on everything I've learned recently."

That's probably correct. "But I don't know if I can just do it." I slumped my shoulders.

Dinar let out an exasperated groan as she stood up. "Look, I'll make it easy for you." She walked over to the nearest beastkin. "Hi, my name is Dinar. What's yours?" Dinar asked in a polite tone as she held out her hand to a male ferret beastkin.

The ferret beastkin turned and gave Dinar a look of confusion. His black fur lightened up closer to his hands and feet until it was gray. He stood up, and he looked about the same height as Mark.

"Why do you want to know, elf?" When he opened his mouth to talk, I saw his sharp canines and other needle-like teeth.

Dinar dropped her hand and slapped her thigh. "I was trying to be polite. I just need the name of a beastkin. Are you going to tell me your name, or am I going to find someone else?"

"Stop it, Dinar," Anna said.

"Belcot," the ferret beastkin said. "My name is Belcot. Why do you need a beastkin's name?"

Dinar pointed to me. "Because that is Lucia, your queen. She doesn't want to be queen. So you are as good of a replacement as anyone else. You're just convenient." The elf turned to face me and pointed at Belcot. "Here you go. Just name Belclot the new king and problem solved."

The ferret bared his fangs at Dinar. "It's Belcot."

"Whatever." Dinar waved a hand to dismiss him.

I looked the beastkin up and down. "Can you lead? Do you know how to be a king? Do you even want to be king?"

"Enough already," Dinar groaned. "Just give him the job. You don't need to interview him."

I glared at the elf. "I can't do that. That's irresponsible. It should be someone who knows what the job is. Someone who knows what it's like to be the king. I don't—"

Hold on. It can't be that simple, can it? I stood up, not bothering to look at anyone in particular.

"Hey! Where are you going?" Dinar called after me as I walked towards the tallest hill nearby.

I walked halfway up the hill and turned around.

"Are you going to name someone else or not?" Dinar shouted even louder.

I looked down at Dinar. "I am, but not Belcot." I cleared my throat as I looked at the rest of the beastkin. There were some beastkin moving people from the injured group to the deceased group.

I'm sorry I couldn't do more. And I'm sorry for what I'm about to do. But I can't be the queen. Please forgive me, Grant. I hope you use this opportunity as best as you can.

"Listen to me!" Everyone stopped and turned to face me, making my mouth dry and my tail curl around my leg. My heart started beating in my chest at a steadily increasing rate. *No, this isn't the time for that. This is important.* I closed my eyes and visualized waterfalls. I could feel my heart slowing down. *Just focus on the waterfalls, not their stares.* I opened my eyes again. "Do any of you know the way back home?"

"I do," I heard someone answer, but I didn't catch who said it. But when I saw Belcot walking towards me, I hoped he was the one who said it. "I know the way," Belcot reiterated.

I guess I need him after all. Ironic. I took a deep breath and concentrated on the waterfalls in my mind. *Here's yet another reason why I can't be queen. Public speaking is too much for me.* "I want all of you to bury the dead. After you're done, take the wounded and follow Belcot here." I pointed to the ferret beastkin to make sure everyone knew who to follow. "He will lead you back, and once you get there, you will tell Grant, the old deer who is caring for the previous king's mate, that he is now your king."

The collection of beastkin looked amongst themselves and mumbled to each other. There were too many people talking to distinguish what anyone said, but based on their tone, they sounded confused.

"Why him? There are plenty of others who are stronger than him." I heard the voice from the crowd, but I couldn't figure out who said it. It didn't matter since several others started nodding their heads in agreement.

They were all thinking about it, but only one of them had the courage to ask.

I relaxed my body. "Honestly, I don't want to be the queen. I'm not really ready or cut out for it." I relaxed my tone, trying to sound more casual with them. "Not every—"

"But you were stronger than Daygon. You have to be queen."

My head snapped to the wolf beastkin who'd interrupted me. With a growl and a flash of my fangs, he backed away and tried to make himself smaller. "I'm talking. Don't interrupt me!" The wolfkin nodded. I returned to looking at the crowd and regained my focus on my waterfalls. "As I was saying, not everything has to be about strength. Daygon was actually stronger than me. But I defeated him easily because I'm a trained fighter. I was smarter than he was. Lots of people trained me in the proper way to think, strike, and move in a fight. Maybe it's time someone smarter led you."

There was more grumbling from the crowd. I turned to look at Anna and Dinar. *Help me, please.* I hoped my face could relay my unspoken request.

Anna turned to Dinar and waved her hands towards me. Dinar pinched the bridge of her nose as she groaned something about not learning her lesson. The elf walked over to me with a near-expressionless face and stood next to me.

"You are really going to owe me for this," she whispered to me.

"Anything you want. Just make them agree," I whispered back as I turned to face the crowd of skeptics.

Dinar cupped her hands around her mouth. "Shut up!" Every beastkin recoiled from the shout, especially me. Dinar lowered her arms and stood up as tall as her small stature would allow. "Alright, now that I have your attention. Do what Lucia says. If you're worried about Grant being a terrible king, don't be. He's old, but he has an idea of what to do. You have nothing to lose if you just follow him for a few years. Things can't possibly get any worse for you than they already are."

I saw some of the beastkin nod in agreement, while others looked even more confused. *Why are they being so difficult? They left the town without arguing or fighting. What changed? Did they not really want to fight humans? That's a good thing.*

"Who are you?" A different beastkin stepped forward. A female boar beastkin stared at the elf. "Why are you telling us what to do? You're just an elf."

I turned to see Dinar's bottom left eyelid twitch erratically. "This elf was born before your great-great-grandparents were. Actually, even before that." Any and all sense of composure was gone as Dinar glared at the boarkin who'd belittled her.

I jumped in front of her and placed my hand on her chest. "Stand down." Dinar brought her gaze to meet mine. There was a fire in her eyes. A fire I knew all too well. "I said, stand down." I punctuated my command with a subtle growl.

The fire in Dinar's eyes died down. She gave one last glare at the boar beastkin before she stomped back towards Anna. "I said this was a bad idea. This is the thanks I get for being helpful. Why didn't I listen to myself? Stay out of politics. You do all the dirty work so all the important people can keep their hands clean. All that so at the first sign of something going wrong, they drop everything on you and you become a pariah."

She knows I can hear her, right?

I shook my head. *I can worry about her past later. Although she makes it sound like she's old. How old is she really? Didn't she tell me she was an assassin? What do assassins have to do with politics?*

My mind went blank as I looked back towards the town.

A line of horsemen was riding in our direction.

"Dinar." The elf halted her tantrum to look at me. I pointed towards the oncoming squad. "We have a problem." Dinar turned to look and went pale.

A banner flew in the wind behind the horseman. Most knight companies didn't bother with carrying their banner around unless they had a specific reputation. The banner held a symbol I'd wished I would never have to see again.

Emblazoned on the banner was a blood-red gauntleted fist with three drops of blood falling off it.

The Crimson Tide. Why, of all the knight companies in Rophmna, did it have to be them?

OLD WOUNDS

I ran up next to Dinar, who stood frozen in shock. "Dinar, gather Daric and the others to meet me over where they're piling the dead." Dinar jumped when I pushed towards where Daric was working. "Go!"

"Why do I have the feeling this mission was cursed from the start?" Dinar asked under her breath.

I'm sorry. This is probably my fault. Ever since I started this life, nothing has been simple or peaceful. Why do I have to face so many life-threatening situations? I'm only fifteen.

The beastkin who were standing and watching me started looking towards the oncoming knights.

"Everyone, you need to leave. Now." My shouting got everyone's attention. "Everyone who can walk, start heading home. If you can carry someone, carry someone who can't walk. Don't bother bandaging anything that isn't serious." I watched everyone's faces fill with fear. "You're out of time."

"But we can fight." Belcot looked to be the only one who wasn't scared.

I grabbed him by the throat and pulled him close. A deep growl escaped me. "They will slaughter you. I saw how you were having difficulties fighting townspeople, who were wielding whatever weapons they could find. These are knights. Humans who are trained and equipped with high-quality weapons and armor." I could smell the ferret's fear. It smelled a lot like urine.

I shoved him towards the way back to the Wild Kingdom. "Your job isn't to fight. Your job is to make sure everyone makes it back home safely." I pointed behind the ferret. "Now do your job."

Belcot stumbled to a stop. "Where are you going?" he turned and asked me.

"To buy you time so that you all have a chance." *And hopefully not to my death.*

Belcot responded with a look of determination and a nod before he walked over to help a beastkin whose leg was wrapped in a blood-soaked bandage. *Not a bad guy. Hopefully he's enough to get them home.* I turned and saw Daric staring at me with his mouth wide open.

"What are you looking at?" I growled. Daric sputtered something completely incomprehensible. After growling and rolling my eyes, I turned the man around and shoved him. "Now isn't the time to lose your head. Go, I'll catch up."

Victor, Fina, and Gifford ran up to me through the slowly migrating crowds. The rhinokin that I'd ordered to deal with the dead accompanied them.

"What about those who didn't make it?" the rhinokin asked.

"Leave them." My heart ached slightly as I answered. I could see the pain on his face. "Don't worry, I'll make sure they're taken care of with the respect they deserve."

He nodded.

I took a deep breath as he walked away. *I'm the wrong person for this. How is it that I keep taking charge of the situation? Why doesn't anyone else step up?*

"You look tired."

Fina's comment snapped me out of my mental rabbit hole.

I gave the lynx a wry smile. "It's been a long day. Each crisis has been followed up by another. I just hope this doesn't go as badly as I think it will."

"What do you want us to do?" Victor's voice was quieter than usual.

"You're going to leave with everyone else."

Gifford, Fina, and Victor all gave me the same look of worry.

"Take my sister and leave."

Gifford shook his head. "That's not what she would want." Gifford's spine straightened. "That's not what I want. You want me to grow strong enough to defend her. If I run now, that will never happen."

"I still haven't heard your answer," Victor said as he stood next to Gifford.

Fina stepped to also stand next to Gifford. She didn't say anything. She didn't need to—I knew by the look in her eye that she wasn't leaving either.

"Then..." *They won't go. Alright then.* I looked at Lexia. "Then take care of her. Make sure she's safe. I don't want to lose her, not again."

"I don't want to lose you either," my sister interrupted in a hoarse voice.

Gifford and I dropped to her side. Gifford started crying as I hugged her. "You're alright," I whispered.

Lexia chuckled, which sent her into a coughing fit. "I'm glad you're safe. But what's happening?"

Gifford grabbed Lexia's hand. "Don't worry about it. You've done more than enough. Rest. It's my turn to protect you."

I looked at the foxkin. *Well, would you look at that? Maybe there is hope for him after all.* I stood up, and when Gifford looked at me, I nodded. "Keep her safe."

Lexia reached out a hand towards me. "Where are you going?"

"To deal with yet another problem." I couldn't give my sister a smile before I left her in the care of my three friends. *No, they aren't my friends. They're closer than that.* My instincts flashed an emotion through my mind. *Yeah, that's a good phrase: pack mates.*

Daric and the others were looking back and forth between the Crimson Tide and me. When I finally joined up with them, Daric stepped up to me, sweat pouring down his face.

"Do you know who that is?" Daric rubbed his hands together as he avoided looking at me for longer than a moment. "Have you heard the rumors?"

I looked at everyone's faces. I could see the fear in their eyes. "The rumors make them look worse than they are." Everyone froze as they stared at me with confusion. "I may have had a hand in why they were banned from Aquittemia, but there are some rational people in the company."

"Then why did you send the beastkin away?" Dinar asked while visibly shaking.

"Because I'm not taking any chances. I'm offering myself up as bait to keep them preoccupied." I looked at the company headed our way. "We don't have much time left. Just—just let me do the talking."

Daric simply nodded as he stepped back with his group. I stood half an arc forward of them while I waited for the knights to reach us. We didn't have to wait long, but as I prepared for them to do something stupid, they showed some restraint. All sixteen of the knights on horseback stopped in formation. The knight at the head of the line urged his horse to move a few steps forward before he dismounted.

He leaned the spear that was in his hands against the saddle. "This isn't how or where I imagined seeing you again." The knight removed his helmet, revealing shoulder-length straight black hair. His dark-brown eyes could easily be mistaken for black. As he tucked his helmet under his armpit, he touched the scar on his face. Starting from just under his left eyebrow, it traveled in a straight line, missing his eye and passing over his fat lips. It was a scar I'd given him. "I haven't forgotten you."

And now a fight is inevitable.

The man stood in full plate armor. He favored his longsword that sat on his left hip. I also knew he detested shields.

"I've tried to forget you, Barney," I said as I crossed my arms. The knight's eye twitched. "What are you doing here?"

Barney tightened his fist around his sword. I could hear the leather of the hilt groan in his grasp. "We were told Alelry was going to be attacked. It's so unfortunate that we arrived late and didn't catch you in the act. So now we're here to avenge the deaths of everyone in Alelry."

So that's the name of the town. Good to know.

I raised an eyebrow. "Everyone? There were people still alive when I ordered all the beastkin to leave."

Barney grinned. "So you're the one responsible for the attack on Alelry?" He laughed. "I knew one day you would turn on Rophmna. I'm so glad that I get to be the one to cut you down. Fate has decreed my vengeance just."

I extended my claws as I took a more battle-ready stance. "I'm the reason the people of Alelry didn't suffer more losses. The beast king ordered the people to attack. Not me. And who told you Alelry was going to get attacked?"

"It doesn't matter who told us. She was right, that's all that matters. Where is this 'beast king?' If he's responsible, you should be able to provide some proof. How do I know you aren't making that up?" Barney's smugness permeated his voice. "What's the matter, don't got any?"

"I killed him for attacking the kingdom. Just like I killed the demons that were controlling him." I bared my fangs. "I'm doing everything I can to prevent a war."

But it seems like someone has gone out of their way to start one. Bringing the one knight company that hates beastkin the most to find beastkin attacking a village. They didn't need to do much other than point them in this direction and let their prejudices take them the rest of the way. Them being here is not a coincidence.

"You didn't get them all. Besides, what could demons possibly want with animals? There's no way demons are this active. They were dealt with five years ago." Barney drew his sword. "You summoned them here."

"Animals?" My vision started shifting to red.

"Stop!" Anna cried out as she ran to stand in front of me. "She's telling the truth. Nobody summoned any demons."

That's not a good place to stand, Anna. Her last sentence finally registered in my brain. *What are they talking about?*

Barney dropped his helmet as he pointed his sword towards Anna.

"Who are you? And who are they?" *How didn't he notice the group standing behind me? Talk about a one-track mind.*

"We're the knight company Omega Gamma, and we enlisted the aid of Lucia and Anna," Dinar said. She turned to Daric. "I said that right, right?"

"Yeah," Daric whispered. His eyes were bulging; he wouldn't look away from Barney. "I-I'm Daric, son-son of Jacomus, King Ramos's brother."

"Grow a backbone," I snapped at Daric. "I thought you wanted to be the hero. Now's the time to step up."

Daric flinched but didn't say anything.

Barney glared at Daric without lowering his sword. "So you are the king's favorite nephew? Pathetic," the knight spat at Daric. "King Ramos would be heartbroken if he learned that his favorite nephew was to aid a traitor to the kingdom."

I growled. "The only traitor here is you."

Barney shrugged and pointed at Daric. "If you were to, I don't know, apprehend or execute the traitor, I might be able to look the other way. Just this once."

I looked up at his men, who were still mounted. They hadn't moved an inch.

"What are we waiting for? Grab her." Penny pointed at me. We all turned to face her. "I'm not going to pay for her stupidity. She—"

Don't you dare! My growl shut her up. "I've said it once. I will not say it again. I did *not* kill those people. There were still people alive when I left."

"Every man, woman, and child lay slain." The venom in Barney's voice poured out. "That town is flooded with the blood of the innocent. The blood you spilled."

Who killed an entire town? When? Wait, the blood anchor!

"We were told the beastkin brought demons with them and that a silver-furred beastkin led them. And would you look at that, you have silver fur. We saw those beastkin leaving as we approached. I imagine you ordered them to retreat to attack another town later."

Penny threw her arms up. "I don't want to be here anyway. I just want to go home and get paid so I can free myself from this idiocy."

Barney pointed his sword at Penny. "You're either with us or you're against us."

"It was a demon that killed them!" I shouted. "That's possible, right, Anna?"

Anna took a moment to think. "Yeah, since a new blood anchor was created..."

Barney lowered his voice, sounding as menacing as possible. "You summoned the demons. You don't deserve a trial. The only thing you deserve is a slow and painful death. You brought the demons, and now I'll make you take responsibility."

Penny took a few steps towards the Crimson Tide.

Silver's voice halted Penny's movements. "You do that and you'll forfeit your pay."

Penny looked to the ground, and everyone watched the turmoil in her mind manifest in her facial expressions. A few moments later, she screamed as she grabbed her head. "I'm not doing this for your benefit." She stared at me. "I just really need that money."

"If it's money you're after, I'll pay you double if you aid us." Barney's voice sounded impossibly sweet.

Penny didn't hesitate as she strode to stand next to Barney.

Barney grinned as he glanced at her. "Wise decision."

"Let's see if you say that after you see the bill," Penny replied, not hiding her disdain for the man.

"You're going to die first," I snarled at Penny.

Penny's face was emotionless. "You won't even touch me. I know you're afraid of fire."

That won't stop me. The edges of my vision started blacking out as Penny became the sole focus of my rage. A tingling sensation slapped me in the back before I was consumed with the need to kill her.

Dinar was a beacon of magic. She smiled. "Don't waste this."

What—

I couldn't finish my thought before Dinar's magic exploded, washing over everyone. It felt like there was a cloud forming in my mind, demanding I stop everything. I growled as I fought it. Eventually, I recognized the intended effect as my eyes slid closed.

Dinar was trying to put me to sleep.

I tried to shrug off the magic that flooded the area, but it held on. It continued to pull at my mind and I could feel my thoughts growing sluggish.

No!

My inner wolf pushed me from behind, and my mired thoughts quickly returned to normal. I could feel her still behind me, her anger spilling over into me. My vision was still red when I opened my eyes.

What was that for? You were trying to put me to sleep. Why? I looked around and saw that everyone was lying on the ground—everyone except Dinar, Barney, and me. *You were giving me the chance to defend myself.*

Dinar fell to her knees. "See, I knew you could do it." She collapsed to the ground. She didn't fall asleep like everyone else but passed out.

I already respected her, but now she deserved so much more. A familiar feeling filled my heart. One that matched the feelings I had for Victor, Gifford, and Fina.

I turned to see that the knights on horseback had fallen to the ground, and their horses had curled up and fallen asleep. *I thought horses sleep standing up. Maybe that magic was so powerful it made them sleep lying down. If it was that powerful, then how is Barney still awake?*

Barney's eyes were bloodshot, and his face turned a dark red. "What did you do to my men, witch?" *Is he the one human who can match my temper?* "I'll kill you all!"

The knight lifted his sword as he charged Dinar.

I stepped in front, flexing my claws.

40

KILLER

I snarled as I charged Barney. He lifted his sword up and brought it down. I sidestepped and slashed my claws at his face, but he leaned back, my claws missing by inches.

The berserk knight lifted his sword in a one-handed swing towards my arm. I recoiled just in time and stepped to my left to get behind his swing. Barney wasn't as out of control as I had hoped. He returned his second hand to his blade and swung it back towards me.

I had to step back or risk getting eviscerated. As Barney's sword passed in front of me, I tried the same tactic of going behind the swing and grabbing for his arm.

I need to get within his reach.

Again, Barney's sword didn't allow me to get close. He pulled back his blade in a draw cut, causing me to recoil one more time.

I growled as he lined his blade up for a thrust.

There's something off about how he's able to keep up with me. Maybe...

Barney thrust his sword towards my gut. I easily sidestepped to my left. He twisted his wrist and swung his blade at me. I threw my ice-covered wrist into the blade. There was a satisfying clang as the steel caught on the dense ice.

There was a hesitation in Barney's movements, and I took advantage of it. I wrapped my hand around his metal-covered wrist. He pulled against me as he extracted his sword with his free hand, but I pulled his arm towards me when I saw him lift his blade.

Even though both of us were pulling against each other, I had the overwhelming advantage with my physical aptitude enhancing my strength. Barney's attack floundered as I turned and forced him to attack through himself. He stumbled, failing to keep up. I kicked his leading leg and released his wrist.

Barney hit the ground in a noisy heap.

Now I have you exactly where I want you.

I stomped on Barney's wrist, pinning his weapon to the ground. The knight howled as he tried to roll into my leg. My foot slipped off the metal as his shoulder rammed into my knee. I dropped to the ground, but I grabbed Barney's shoulders as I went down.

We rolled for a couple of spins. We continued until I hoisted the knight up with my hands and feet, Barney flailing as I did.

Then I pushed him up as hard as I could. His sword fell from his hand as he ascended.

I rolled out from under Barney before he plummeted to the ground. Coming to a stop in a four-point stance, I threw Barney's sword away from where we were fighting. Barney screamed as he hit the ground, right arm first. There was a strange grinding sound when he did.

I didn't let him stand up before I pounced on him. He tried to throw me off, but I pinned him to the ground.

"You are nothing more than a wild animal that needs to be put down," Barney said in a threatening tone. I saw the hate in his eyes.

I leaned in close and bared my sharp fangs. "You're worse than a rabid animal. People like you need to be exterminated. All my life, I've done the best I could not to hurt people first. But there are limits to my patience. And when people like you call me nothing more than a wild animal, I feel inclined to show you the beast you fear so much." I grabbed the back of his head and lifted it off the ground. "I didn't create this side of me. You did."

I slammed his face into the ground. There was a satisfying crunch that came from his face. When I lifted his face again, blood was pouring from his unmistakably broken nose.

"Lucia, don't!" Daric yelled.

I turned to growl at the coward.

Daric held his arm out as he ran towards me.

"No!" My shout caused Daric's steps to falter. "He was going to kill me and all the beastkin. He threatened all of you. Why are you protecting him?"

Daric looked at me with an unusually determined face. "He needs to stand trial." He took another step towards me.

I felt Barney squirming in my grip, so I slammed his face into the ground again. "We don't have time for that. I don't know if you listened to what he was saying, but he said something killed an entire town. There are other demons. I don't know if I have it in me to fight another sin. It'll be impossible if we have to watch him. What's stopping him from trying to kill us during the fighting?"

"But you can't kill him in cold blood," Daric whimpered.

Barney wasn't moving, so I left him and stood up. I stomped towards Daric. "Cold blood? There's nothing innocent about that man. He wasn't going to give me the same courtesy of a trial. He was even going to use Penny to kill us."

Daric backpedaled a few steps before he tripped and fell. "But we can't stoop to his level. We're heroes."

"No, you're a self-proclaimed hero. Me? I'm a hunter. And hunters kill."

There was a sound of metal moving behind me. When I turned around, I saw Barney moving again. With a growl, I pounced on him again. *This time I won't be so nice.* I pulled him back with one hand and bit down on his throat. In one quick movement, I pulled a huge chunk of his neck out.

Blood squirted out of the wound, and nothing Barney did stopped the flow.

I released him and let him die from the blood loss. When I turned back to Daric, I spat the flesh out, even though it tasted good. *Mom would be upset if I ate a piece of him.*

Daric stared at me, all the color drained from his face.

"What's the matter? Too much blood for the hero?" I taunted.

"You—you killed him." Daric's eyes quivered as he couldn't look away.

"You act like this is the first person you've seen die."

"It is," Daric whispered.

I rolled my eyes. "What kind of knight are you?"

Daric pointed a finger at me. "How could you kill a human like that?"

"Human?" I snapped. "For your information, just because he was a human, that doesn't make him worthy to live. What about me as a beastkin? I'm not human. Does that make me less than him?"

Daric shook his head as his eyes grew wide. "No, I—"

"I don't care!" I screamed. "Ever since I came to this world, someone has always tried to kill me. I had to kill two humans when I was five because they kidnapped me and were about to sacrifice me to summon a demon." My toe-claws dug into the ground with each step I took towards Daric. "I don't have such a cushy life where I'm privileged to have such morals. No, I kill for a living, and I enjoy it. What separates me from them is I don't start it, I end it." I finished my tirade with a claw poking into Daric's chest.

"But—"

"Dinar saved all of us. Do you think he wouldn't have sent his soldiers to attack us too? Could you have killed them?" I grabbed Daric by the chest and hoisted him up. He stared at me silently. "They wouldn't have had a problem killing you, trust me. I made a promise to bring you all back. And because of that, I'll let you deal with Penny." I dropped him.

I turned away from the ignorant human. *You can sit there and quiver for all I care. Now, what am I going to do with all those other knights? Actually, I'm going to wake everyone else up.*

I made my way to wake up Silver and check on Dinar. A few light slaps later, Silver shot up with a panicked look.

"Easy, it's okay." I placed a hand on the dragoon's shoulder.

Silver rubbed his face with one hand. "What happened? The last thing I remember was that knight and you were arguing. Then Penny agreed to help him attack you."

I shrugged. "All true. Dinar used a powerful sleeping magic." I looked at the unconscious elf. "How did she affect so many people at once?"

"How did you stay awake? And what happened over there?" Silver pointed towards Barney's corpse.

"I killed him," I replied flatly. "How did I stay awake? Let's just say I was too angry to sleep." *Daric and Golditress didn't really know how to handle my red vision. So I'm just going to keep that to myself from now on.*

Silver glared at me. "Did you really have to kill him?"

"Believe it or not, he didn't go to sleep either. So he didn't give me much of a choice." I stood up. "He deserved it. Do you want to help me get the others up? Daric's already awake."

Silver sighed as he stood up. I gave a quick glance towards Daric and saw him sitting and holding his knees to his chest. I shook my head as I headed for Dinar.

Her breathing was weak, and I also noticed she didn't have the natural magic glow elves always had. *How much magic did she use? She isn't just magically fatigued, she's magically exhausted. I can't do anything if I'm fatigued. How did she push herself that far?*

I picked her up and carried her towards my sister. After I set Dinar on the ground next to Lexia, who I was glad to see sleeping, I woke up Victor, then Fina and Gifford. I stopped Gifford from waking Lexia. She needed the rest, and if she was already sleeping, I wasn't going to let anyone interrupt her. I gave them a quick summary of the events that had happened.

"What do we do now?" Gifford asked.

I sat down next to my sister. "Good question. I don't know."

Fina looked to where the other beastkin had fled to. "The others?"

"You can go if you want." I could feel fatigue setting in. "I would be sad to see you go. You've been a great friend. I wish we could've spent more time together."

Fina gave me a curious look. "No. We stay."

"This is my home. And I want Lexia to come with me and meet my mom." I looked at my sister's peacefully sleeping face. I couldn't suppress a smile. "As hard as it would be, if she didn't want to go, I would let her go to her home."

Victor placed a hand on my shoulder. "She'll go with you. Twins like you two are always much closer than other sibling pairs."

"How common are beastkin twins?" I asked absentmindedly.

"Almost as rare as the physical aptitude," Gifford said in a light-hearted tone.

I chuckled. "How about we rest here for the remainder of the day? I can't keep going after everything I've done today. Even I have a limit." *Hopefully Silver can deal with the remaining knights. I don't think I have it in me to deal with people anymore.* "Let's just worry about recovering and we'll see what we have to do in the morning."

"What about the blood anchor you were talking about earlier?"

Victor's question caught me off guard. Not because he heard me, but because he bothered paying attention. "What's done is done." I slumped my shoulders. "We're in no condition to fight a demon. I don't have the energy. My sister and Dinar are out of commission. Daric is useless. You three don't stand a chance. Sorry."

The three nodded, understanding that it wasn't meant as an insult.

"That leaves Anna, Silver, and Penny," I said. "And right now, I don't trust Penny. Silver is competent, but I don't think he'll be able to handle a demon alone either. Anna's angel is our only hope. And I don't know how powerful her angel is compared to the sins I've fought."

"Do you want us to continue with burying the dead?" Victor pointed to the pile of bodies that remained.

"Yeah." *I promised, didn't I?* "Can you give me some of the rhino meat? I can help set up the tents. I'm out of magic, so no ice tent for me."

Fina fetched me some food, and we shared some with the others too. My sister eventually woke up on her own and asked for some food too. Dinar never moved even when we placed her in a tent.

Victor and Gifford buried the dead beastkin after they ate. We could hear Anna and Silver arguing with the knights of the Crimson Tide. Eventually, they took their dead captain and headed south.

Daric didn't move even when the others were setting up their tents and getting ready to camp.

Even though everyone asked me what I'd said to him, I never told them. It was something Daric needed to get straight on his own, and I didn't want them to influence him.

I watched the clouds roll in as the sun fell behind the horizon. Victor took the first watch, since I needed the rest to recover my magic. I didn't talk to Lexia about coming with me as we settled into the tent together. *She can keep sleeping. It's something that can wait for the morning.*

41

NOT SO DUMB

My sleep was fitful at best. I couldn't shake the feeling that something was wrong. My fears were solidified as Victor pulled open my tent. When we locked eyes, I could see something had scared him.

"There's something wrong with the sky," the bear whispered.

That's probably the worst thing to hear first thing in the morning. But since I don't see any light behind him...

I scowled. "Does this have something to do with the lack of light outside?"

Victor shook his head as he waved for me to follow. Before I moved, I checked to see if my magic had recovered. It had, but Victor's face left me feeling anxious. I pressed my ears flat as I crawled out of the tent.

The sky still held a single moon while the other two were gone, signaling the start of the next season. *It's the start of the water season now.* But the red tint of the night sky left an ominous feeling in my gut.

I stared at the little spots of stars still hanging in the night. "Yeah, that's not good."

"What does it mean?" Victor continued to whisper.

I shook my head. "No idea. But I think we should wake everyone up. Has Daric gone to bed yet?"

"The human?" Victor pointed towards Daric as he sat still, holding his legs to his chest. "No, he hasn't moved an inch."

I really broke him, didn't I?

"Go and get Fina." I turned to duck back into the tent with Lexia. I gently gave her a nudge until she woke up. Her eyes fluttered open. "Hey there, sleepyhead. How are you feeling?"

"Everything hurts," Lexia groggily replied. She relaxed and stared at the top of the tent. She placed her hands on her chest. "What's going on? I'm still tired."

I grimaced as I stared at her. "I understand, but there's something wrong. Something might happen, and I would feel better if you were awake."

"Okay." She rubbed her eyes. "Do I have time to borrow some of your extra clothes?"

I smiled. "Yeah you could. But just so you know, they might feel a little tight around the chest."

"You're the cute one. I'm the sexy one. But I'll endure it. Just because I love you so much."

We giggled together as I fished out a spare shirt from her pack for her to wear.

I helped my sister sit up. "Don't worry, we grabbed your stuff before we followed you. You can get one of your shirts. Victor carried it with all of his stuff."

She gave me a mischievous smile. "He really is a good man for you. I'm sure if you asked him, he would say yes."

He's already asked. My cheeks burned as I couldn't look my sister in the eye. "I'm still not ready..." I fiddled with my tail.

"Leave me alone!" Penny's scream ruined the moment. "Let me sleep!"

I flattened my ears. "Of course she would cause a scene." *And ruin the moment.* I gave my sister a smile before I crawled out of the tent. "Don't push yourself. Take your time."

"Go be a hero, sis." Lexia gave me a wink.

Please don't call me a hero.

Anna, Silver, Victor, and Fina were standing in a semi-circle facing Penny.

Anna pointed to the sky. "Penny, look up. This is an emergency."

Penny scowled but followed Anna's instruction. "What—what is this?" She lowered her head and looked right at me. "What did you do?"

I reflexively extended my claws and growled. "Do you really think I did this?"

Penny didn't say a word, but she continued to stare at me out of some misplaced challenge. A challenge my instincts wanted to answer.

"I let you live because of the promise I made. I allowed Daric to determine your fate. But if you keep this up, there will be no more mercy."

"Is that a threat?" Penny asked in a low, strained tone.

I bared my fangs. "It's a prophecy."

Silver stepped between the two of us. "Both of you, stop!" He glared at me before he turned and gave Penny the same glare. "You said it yourself. There might be another demon. Being at each other's throats will only make the demon's job easier. Anna, is there a demon that you know of that can cause the sky to turn red?"

Anna scratched her head as she stared at the ground. "I don't know." She sounded surprised at her own answer. "No sin is that powerful. But if it's more powerful than a sin..." She lifted her head, and the horror in her eyes sent my instincts into overdrive. "A rider."

The two whispered words echoed throughout the group.

My tail curled around my leg.

"That's bad?" Fina's question broke the silence.

"Lucia can stand against a sin alone. But the sins are to the riders as the fallen demons are to the sins." Anna's dilated eyes continued to stare into the distance. "If a rider is here, we need to run."

"Why can't we fight a rider? If Lucia can take on a sin on her own, why can't all of us defeat it?" Victor stepped up to stand behind me.

Silver's face turned sour. "If we had spent a couple of seasons, if not a year or two together, learning each other's fighting styles and improving our coordination, that's a possibility. Right now, we would do nothing more than get in each other's way."

"So we leave?" Fina walked to stand in between Silver and me. "Where?"

"I want to go home." Penny pursed her lips as she stomped her foot.

A voice barely louder than a whisper joined the conversation. "We need to stop it."

We all turned to the source. Daric sat huddled on the ground where I'd left him before I went to sleep. Slowly, he turned his head to look at us. "We need to stop it." There was more conviction in his voice as he repeated himself.

"And why do we need to?" I raised an eyebrow. "And I better not hear the word 'hero.' We had that conversation once." I pointed my finger at him. "There are plenty of better-trained companies already mobilized for war if the Crimson Tide was already nearby. We need a trained company, not a bunch of nobodies."

Daric stood up and brushed the dirt from his pants. "This is about doing what we know is right. We can do it. I have faith that we can."

"Dinar and Lucia's sister are both in no condition to fight, and Mark and Golditress still haven't arrived. We're all that we have." Silver waved his arm towards the tents that held Lexia and Dinar.

"We can still do it." Daric didn't flinch, nor did his voice grow weaker.

He's gaining more confidence with each obstacle we put up. "Do you want to die again?" I asked the idiot.

Daric shook his head. "I intend to live through this. I think I can come up with a plan if I know more about the rider." He turned to look at Anna. "What can you tell us about the riders?"

Anna lazily kicked a small stone. "Not as much as I would like. It's not that I never wanted to learn about them, it's just that my teacher has struggled to find information about them. What I know is that there are always four of them. They each have a moniker: Ruin, Death, Fear, and Pain."

"They sound like a pleasant bunch." I cringed at my horrible comment.

Anna glanced at me, and I thought I saw the corner of her lips curl. "Everything says that they are powerful magic wielders while also being exceptionally strong. And that killing them is incredibly difficult, even to the point where one book says you can't."

"And you want us to face one?" Penny gave Daric a sidelong glare. "I really should just leave you to die."

I glared at the elf. "Why haven't you left? You talk so much about wanting to leave, yet you're still here. Go already."

Penny stared at me as she clenched her jaw tightly. *I think I can hear her teeth groaning.* "You know I can't find my way home from here."

I pointed to the northwest. "Aquittemia is that way. Leave."

"I'll starve before I reach it," Penny continued to grumble.

"You can survive a little more than a week without food before things get too difficult. So long as you pace yourself properly." I crossed my arms.

"That's a death sentence and you know it." Penny turned her head towards Daric. "If I return empty-handed, I'm as good as dead."

"If you help us, I'll reinstate your pay." Daric's voice was emotionless.

"I don't think you should do that," Silver said. "She betrayed us once. What's stopping her from doing it again?"

"What's going on?" Victor whispered behind me.

I rolled my eyes as I turned to face the bearkin. "The elf backstabbed us for the sake of money." Victor didn't look like he was getting it. I sighed. "Money is something humans use to trade for goods and services. They aren't like beastkin. Helping the community is nothing more than a side effect of their selfish goals."

"I don't understand," Fina joined in.

Describing a culture that I've been living in for the last ten years, which isn't too different from where I came from, shows me that humans really are stupid. The beastkin aren't much better. They have too little desire for self-improvement. People really are flawed creatures, aren't they?

"Are you okay?" Victor's question interrupted my introspection.

I shook my head. "Yeah, I just got lost in thought for a moment. Although Penny hasn't directly told me the details, there's a story behind why she needs money to live. I don't know how or who, but she owes a lot of money to some people who won't like it if she doesn't pay them back."

Victor looked at Penny. "If she's having trouble getting the money, shouldn't the people be understanding and give her more time? So long as she honors her side of the agreement, what's the problem if it takes a little more time?"

I waved my hand. "Don't bother understanding it. There are some mean and evil people. The demons should have been enough of an example for you."

Fina curled her tail around her waist. "People are demons?"

"No, no," I quickly answered. Fina relaxed enough to let her tail sway behind her. "They're not demons, but they can commit evils just as horrible as demons."

"Why?" Fina stared at me with a longing look in her eyes.

I chuckled. "That's a great question. One I don't have an answer for."

I turned back towards Daric and his group to see Penny sniffling as she packed up her tent. Silver and Anna were working on the rest of the camp.

Daric slowly walked towards me. "We'll need your help." Daric stopped a little out of arm's reach and extended his hand. "Will you help us?"

"Why do you think you need to be the one to do this? I still can't understand that," I said as I pinched the bridge of my nose.

"If I run this time and others are hurt, I won't be able to live with myself. You were right: I can't be the hero of the stories I remember. Maybe I'm naïve in thinking what I do matters, but I believe not doing anything is worse." Daric's stare never relented. "This isn't about guilt or innocence. This is about not permitting evil to continue. If we don't stop it, we might as well be the ones who released it."

I growled at Daric.

"I thought you were brave. But if this rider scares you, you can run with your tail between your legs." Daric lowered his hand. "You really aren't the 'Big Bad Wolf.' You're a spineless pup."

I lunged at Daric. He didn't move as my hand slammed into his chest. I pushed him into the ground as hard as I could. I could hear a few ribs cracking as he gasped for air.

I bared my fangs inches from his face as I glared at him. "You really are stupid." I stood up and walked towards the other three packing up. "Don't pack up just yet. You can go back to sleep for a little longer." Anna, Silver, and Penny gave me confused looks as they shifted their gazes between me and Daric.

I walked by Daric and glared at him as he tried to get his breathing back under control. "We leave when Mark and Golditress arrive."

After Daric nodded, I left him to writhe on the ground.

Victor and Fina stepped up to walk beside me as I went back to my sister's tent. "You should help," Fina suggested with a quiet voice.

"I am." I took a deep breath to keep myself from snapping anymore. "Go back to bed and get some sleep."

Victor and Fina didn't say a word as they turned to the tent they shared.

I crawled into my sister's tent and saw a wide smile on her face. *You were listening to the whole thing, weren't you?*

"What made you change your mind?" Lexia asked as soon as I sat down next to Dinar.

I watched the elf's rhythmic breathing. "He called me a coward. I'm not a coward."

I could feel my sister's smile widening. "And who is this big, bad wolf?"

"That would be me." I gave my sister a toothy grin.

As I sat in the tent watching over my sister and Dinar, Anna walked over to help Daric up. "You know, you shouldn't antagonize her like that." Anna sounded like she was scolding a child.

"Yeah, but it worked, didn't it?" Daric wheezed.

He played me like a fiddle! He's going to pay for that. Later.

4 2

CONTROL VS. PAIN

After Lexia went back to sleep, I snuck out of the tent so I could keep watch. The night was eerily quiet. Usually I could hear something, but the only noise was Anna's sleep-talking. And based on what she was saying, it must be a wild dream.

I don't know how she does it. Knowing that something far more powerful than a sin is out there right now would keep me awake. But we need her angel tomorrow. We should be far enough from the blood anchor that it won't interfere with her summoning.

My nerves made it impossible to sit still, so I resorted to pacing around the tents. I tried not to think of what we could face. *The names of the demons were terrifyingly vague. Now that I've seen more than one sin and Anna told me their informal names, I can guess what the ones that I haven't seen are like and what they can do. But these riders are a complete mystery.*

The sun started poking up over the horizon. I looked at the sky and still saw that it still held its red color. But it wasn't as simple as everything in sight being red. No, there was a large area, but I could see the edges of it. By my best estimate, the center was over the town that had been attacked.

310

When I looked at the town, something caught my eye.

Something was headed our way.

"Wake up!" I shouted and started kicking tents. "Something is headed towards us. Get up!"

Nobody wasted any time. My companions and Penny flew out of the tents, weapons in hand. Dinar didn't come out, but my sister did. Her movements were sluggish and pained. Their eyes were wide as their heads swiveled back and forth. One by one, everyone focused on the thing heading towards us.

"What is that?" Anna asked, squinting.

"I don't know." I stood next to her. "It looks like someone riding a horse, but it also looks wrong. They're completely red, even the horse."

Daric turned his head towards us. "Is that significant?"

Anna drooped her shoulders. "I already told you, I don't know as much as I like." She took a few steps behind us and grabbed several pieces of paper. "Maybe the spirit of control can give us some information to use."

"Why have you been so reluctant to summon this angel?" Silver asked as we all watched Anna place the pile of paper on the ground.

Anna closed her eyes and glowed with magic. "Because I can only summon him two more times."

"Until..." Daric started talking.

One glare from me shut him up. "She's concentrating." *She summoned it quickly the one time at the village.* I turned to watch Anna work.

There was a smile on Anna's face as she stood over the papers with weird markings—*a glyph, if I remember correctly.* The paper glowed and started floating in the air until a beacon of light engulfed the paper. When the light died down, instead of a stack of floating papers, the familiar sight of a large angel stood.

Anna bowed to the spirit. "Thank you for coming. I'm sorry to call you like this, but I believe there's a rider loose in the world."

"Do not fear, young one." The angel turned to face all of us. "Do not fear, any of you. If you fear, the demon will win."

I stepped closer. "Does that mean it's a rider?" The angel nodded. I pointed towards the figure walking towards us. "Is that him over there?"

There was a moment of silence from the spirit of control. "Yes." His voice sounded regretful.

"Guys..." Daric interrupted us. "It's moving faster. It's running now."

The angel strolled past us and stood as the vanguard against the oncoming demon. "That is the Rider of Pain. He knows I am here."

"But this rider"—Victor scratched his head—"what's his purpose, and why is him being here a reason for alarm?"

"Because demons, riders especially, have an unequivocal hatred towards all angelic beings." The angel sounded like he was sighing. "I cannot hope to face him alone. And whatever his other reason for being here is, I don't know, but it can't be for good. He must be stopped here and now. Will you aid me?"

"He was heading towards us before Anna summoned you," I said. "I have a feeling he might have something against us. Does he have any weaknesses? Anything we should avoid?"

I could feel everyone eagerly waiting for the answer to my question.

A glow surrounded the angel's hands and materialized into interlocking chains. "Despite his title, he cannot feel pain. So, if you wish to inflict a wound, aim to deal as much damage as possible. He will accept a wound if that means he can inflict a greater wound on you. And stay away from the horse mouth."

"Don't you mean the horse's mouth?" Penny didn't hide her fear.

"No, the mount and rider are one and the same." At the angel's response, we all snapped our attention towards the demon.

The Rider of Pain was one of the most disgusting yet appetizing things I had ever seen.

A large war horse galloped towards us. The horse's skull was completely exposed, and its teeth looked too sharp to belong to a normal horse. Starting from the jaw and the back of the head, sinuous exposed muscles held the skull in place. As I continued to look down the rest of the body, there wasn't a shred of skin to be seen. The hooves were black, and pus lined the connection between the muscles and keratin. A gaunt humanoid sat atop its back. But the angel was correct: there was no separation between the rider and steed. Instead of arms, two spear-like appendages that looked like a bone protruding out of the muscles of his forearm nearly touched the ground. Like his mount, the rider didn't have any hair or skin.

The sight of so much red meat looked delicious, but the pus and yellow veins started putting me off my appetite. And the closer it got, the more my instincts agreed with me.

Lexia leaned on me. "Is that...? That's disgusting."

I wrapped my arm around my sister to help hold her up. "Stay out of this. You haven't recovered enough. I don't think I can fight properly if I have to keep an eye on you."

Lexia let out a quick growl. "Why do you always do the fighting? Why do I have to stay back while you risk your life? I don't want to sit back and worry about my little sister."

I removed the arm I was supporting her with and gave her a slight shove. She landed on her butt. "If you think our enemy will only give you a light shove like that, you're in for far worse. There's something else you can do. Take care of Dinar, keep her safe." I looked at Fina and Gifford. "Make sure she stays put."

Fina nodded and moved to help my sister up. Gifford wrapped my sister's arm over his shoulder as he held her.

"Why are you treating me like this?" Lexia whined.

I turned away. "Because you're my sister. I want you to come home with me." I could hear my sister's gasp while I refused to look back as Fina and Gifford took her to the tents.

"If you want to get out of this alive, you had best cooperate, Penny." Silver tightened the straps of his shield as he stood next to the elf.

I took the lead. "We need to keep him away from Dinar and Lexia. Let's go."

There was a gust of wind behind me, and when I turned to look, I saw the angel gliding over my head and towards the Rider of Pain. We all followed him. I went slow enough to stay with everyone. My instincts screamed at me to turn away with each step.

The angel didn't wait for us.

Maybe watching the angel fight can give me some insight into what the rider can do.

Once the angel got close to the demon, the glowing chains reached out and wrapped around the horse's head. The horse head pulled against the still-gliding angel and threw him to the ground. The spirit folded his wings and rolled to his feet before he pulled at the chain again. This time, the rider stumbled forward for a few steps and swiped at the chain with a spear-arm.

The chain shattered, causing both parties to stop and regain their footing. The spirit of control struck again with a chain aimed for the horse's front legs. With a quick hop, the attack was dodged, and the horseman galloped towards the angel. He aimed his spear-arm at his opponent like he was jousting.

The angel took a couple of steps back and to the side, but the rider adjusted his movements. At the last moment, the angel turned his body, causing the rider's attack to slip past him. The angel grabbed the grotesque limb and turned with the horseman's movement. A glowing chain wrapped around the muscles and extended to the ground.

The demon stabbed at his opponent.

The angel released the demon and hopped backwards to dodge. The attack fell short, and the rider had to turn because his arm, wrapped in chains, was anchored to the ground. After lowering his arm, the demon stomped a hoof onto the chain and destroyed it utterly.

"Not bad, little birdy." The demon's voice sounded like a man who was trying to talk with a mouthful of water. "But it will never be enough."

"Who summoned you?" the angel asked.

The horseman's hooves alternated pawing at the ground. Each time a hoof touched the ground, a small puddle of water appeared. "It doesn't matter what summoned me. Just know that we are coming for you and your precious Seraph."

"That is impossible." The angel summoned another chain and started swinging it in a circle at his side.

The horseman chuckled, the sound like a drowning man laughing. It sent shivers down my spine. "That's not for you to decide."

The horseman charged, puddles of water expanding with each step he took. The angel flung the chain like a slingshot towards the demon's humanoid face. Even though the horseman lifted his arms to block, the chain still flew in between and struck the demon's face.

There was a bright light, forcing all of us to shield our eyes and stop running. I had to blink a few times to get the last of the spots out of my vision. When I looked at the demon, his human head was turned one hundred and eighty degrees.

That looks like it hurts. He doesn't look that tough.

Laughing halted my thoughts. The demon was laughing, even though his neck was clearly broken.

Not only is his head not on straight, but he has a few screws loose too.

With a sickening crunch, the demon's head righted itself. The demon rolled his head from side to side. "Thanks for that. I've had that kink in my neck for years."

Every fiber in my body wanted to run, but my body wouldn't move.

The angel threw another chain at the demon's horse head. A spear-arm intercepted the projectile. As the glowing chain wrapped around the monster's arm, the spirit crouched down and braced himself. It looked like it didn't help much. When the demon pulled the chain, the ground gave way to the angel even though his stance held strong.

"I cannot face it alone. Assist me," the angel cried out in a strained voice.

Right, we're supposed to help. But my instincts don't want to. I don't want to.

Daric charged first, sword drawn. Silver followed shortly after, but both men were overtaken by a giant ball of fire.

Victor didn't leave my side and stayed with me, Penny, and Anna. Sweat dripped from Anna's brow.

I don't have to fight in the middle of the two guys. I can stay back and use ice spikes to attack from a distance. So far the only thing I need to fear is those arms, right?

I created a pair of icy bracers and focused on making them as dense as I could in a short time. With my forearms covered in opaque blue ice, I pulled a small amount of it off and turned it into a spiked ball.

The demon pulled on the chain with a grunt, and the angel lost his footing and stumbled forward a few steps. In a swift motion, the spear-arm reached out for the angel. The spirit of control turned his body, but the spear pierced through his left wing right at the bone.

The demon reared up and attempted to stomp on the angel with his hooves, but Penny's fireball hit first. A plume of smoke grew from the point of impact. I held my projectile tightly and waited for the demon to show itself.

As the black smoke billowed off, the demon's body slowly came into view. He was staring at Penny. His eyes were no longer humanoid —they were two holes of darkness. His body didn't show any signs of damage from the magic except that his torso seemed to look a little duller compared to the rest of his body.

I moved to put some distance between me and Penny. I moved left while Anna moved right. Aiming for his face, I threw my projectile as hard as I could. *He may not feel pain, but can we still debilitate him? We just watched him recover from a broken neck like it was nothing.*

The ice spike embedded itself in its intended target. I even saw the demon's head rock backwards from the impact. Daric stabbed his sword into the front of the demon's shoulder. Silver used his mace to strike at the spear-arm that was piercing the angel's wing, and his attack dislodged the appendage, freeing the angel.

"Are these yours, little bird?" The demon didn't flinch as he backpedaled a few steps.

The angel stood up; his wing hung limp at his side. "They are here to stand against you and the evil you represent."

"So much for enjoying myself." I could hear the disappointment in the demon's voice.

With a heavy stomp of his hooves, a colossal geyser of water engulfed the demon. The surrounding area slowly filled with water until we were standing in three inches of it. Once the geyser stopped flowing, revealing the demon once again, something felt off. My instincts screamed louder than ever before.

"You're all going to beg for death when I'm through with you."

I froze at the demon's statement.

43

DON'T FEAR THE PAIN

There was an odd moment where nobody moved. Blood dripped from the demon's eye that still held my ice spike. The wound Daric had inflicted also bled, although it looked like it wasn't deep enough to hinder his movements.

My nose picked up a scent that wasn't around before. *Salt? Is this salt water?*

The demon wiped the spike from his eye with an exaggerated swipe of his spear-arm. To my surprise, there wasn't an eye, just a bleeding socket.

I didn't have time to question it any further as the rider charged Silver and Daric.

Silver raised his shield to intercept the spear aimed for him. The shield held even though the blow knocked him backwards.

Daric didn't move as quickly, and when he tried to leap away, the rider's spear-arm cut through his gambeson and into his side.

The angel created another chain and swung it around to hit the horse head. The chain wrapped around the demon's neck. This time, there was a stream of steam coming from where the chain made contact with the demon.

The angel ran past the demon and pulled as hard as he could.

Penny threw another ball of flame.

I stumbled backwards and saw that Victor was just as petrified as me. *I need to move!* I tried to focus and turn my vision red. But I couldn't. My fear overwhelmed my rage. *I can't fight like this.*

Anna trudged through the water to help me up. "What's wrong? Why aren't you helping?"

"I can't." My voice was barely a whisper.

The angel pulled the demon to turn his back towards us. But the demon kicked a hind leg, and a small geyser intercepted Penny's magic, turning it into a harmless puff of steam.

"You have to," Anna pleaded.

I stared at her, wide-eyed. "I can't get angry. I'm too scared."

Anna's face scrunched in a pained and sorrowful expression. "Forgive me."

Oh, no. Not again.

Anna reached and pinched my ear. Despite my previous constant complaints, she pulled my ear right to her face. "Are you a whiny puppy or a ferocious monster? Fight, you coward!"

I clapped my hand on my ear as I cried in pain. Even though over the years I had been getting better at handling loud noises, this hurt far more than Nora's amulet. Anna hadn't released my ear from her grip. I growled and reached for her wrist. My vision flooded with red as I squeezed.

Anna squeaked as she tried to pull her arm back.

I bared my fangs. "I am not a monster!"

Anna smiled. "Go get him," she whispered.

Yeah, yeah. Congratulations! You made me angry. You didn't have to yell in my ear.

I released Anna's arm as I stood up. I flexed my claws and felt that the cries of my instincts were easier to push back. As I made another spiked ice ball, Daric lifted his sword and dropped it on the rider's flank as the mist cleared. His attack barely grazed the demon's flesh. Silver rammed his shield into the rider's side, trying to tip him over. The rider didn't fall or move.

The demon destroyed the chain holding him and kicked his hind legs towards Daric, striking his right arm and making him stumble backwards. The angel wrapped another chain around a spear-arm.

I lengthened the ice spikes before I launched my projectile, aiming for the back of the demon's head. The rider's head lurched forward as my attack landed and stuck.

Penny threw another fireball that met the same end as the last.

Victor stood frozen in fear despite Anna trying to push him like she'd pushed me.

We performed the same routine of dancing around and inflicting superficial wounds while the angel kept the demon from turning away from him and focusing on us several more times. Every time the rider would charge at the angel, we aimed to trip up his movements. After Penny's magic struck the demon the first time, it never got close again. No matter what form her magic took, a pillar of water always intercepted it. Victor had backed up and neared the edge of the pool of water.

I can't make anyone fight. Honestly, he's the smart one here.

No matter what damage we inflicted, the demon never flinched and never slowed down. We could move him with the force of our attacks, and several of my spiked ice projectiles littered his head and shoulders, but he kept attacking us in a growing frenzy. We weren't winning the battle of attrition, and I knew it. The problem was that I didn't know how to break the stalemate. I could focus and suppress my instinctual fears, but I couldn't come up with a plan.

The demon made another attempt to stab the angel. The angel held the chain wrapped around the human torso with both hands. Silver tried to perform his staple attack of ramming his shield into the front leg the moment it lifted off the ground. But before his blow connected, the demon dropped his foot back to the ground instantly, and Silver failed to trip the demon.

There was a sickening crack, and the horse neck folded in half and looked right at Silver as he stood next to the shoulder. Everything slowed down as the demon's horse mouth opened and a thick grayish-brown cloud spewed from the maw.

Silver tripped as he tried to get away. But as he landed with a splash, the smog engulfed the dragoon. I froze as an eerie silence blocked everything out.

Silver's coughing ended the silence. Slowly, he crawled out of the smog, which slowly thinned out and dissipated. His mace wasn't in his hand, and he used his shield to pull himself forward through the water. His coughing fits worsened until he retched and spewed blood.

Daric ran to scoop Silver up and dragged him towards Anna. That gave the demon all the opening he needed. His horse neck snapped itself back into place as both spear-arms reached out and pierced the angel's torso. Anna fell to her knees, screaming and holding her head. The rider stabbed the angel again as he pinned him to the ground. Each stab caused Anna's screams to increase in intensity.

Penny didn't throw another fireball. This time, she shot out a jet of fire. I jumped as the eruption of flame left Penny's overlapping hands. The desire to run threatened to overwhelm my rational mind.

As predicted, a geyser of water blocked the flames. A steaming cloud grew from the confrontation of elements and quickly swallowed up the demon as he brutalized the angel on the ground. Anna never stopped screaming.

Penny didn't stop channeling her magic. It looked like she was pouring more magic into her flames.

She's fighting her element's opposite. She's acting like she hasn't met her match like this before. Now she's desperate and trying to brute force it.

Penny let out a primal scream as she trudged towards the pillar of water obstructing her magic. Steam continued to create a barrier, hiding the angel's demise. Sweat poured down Penny's face as she pushed on. Anna stopped wailing and stared at the cloud as Daric pulled Silver past her. Silver continued to vomit blood, but in between episodes, he moaned in pain.

As Anna quieted down, so did Penny. The rage on Penny's face disappeared as fear quickly replaced it. She didn't halt her attack, but I could see it getting weaker. Once the beam of fire was half as wide as it was at its peak, the water pushed back and swallowed her flames before it washed the elf away.

When the water settled, Penny was sitting on the ground. She coughed up water, dazed. The steam lifted to the sky to reveal the Rider of Pain, untouched by the flames. But when I looked closer, his entire body wasn't as shiny as it was before, like everything was dry. His wounds were still bleeding, and all of my ice spikes were gone. In their place, a trickle of blood oozed out. But the water around the demon was red from the angel's perforated corpse.

Daric lowered Silver to the ground as he turned back to see the dead divine being. His sword fell into the water as his grip failed.

The demon grinned as he strode towards Penny. He lifted a spear-arm, and a geyser erupted where Penny was sitting. I watched as she flailed. She was at least two arcs off the ground when the geyser stopped.

Penny screamed as she fell. She landed feet-first, and as she hit, everyone heard and saw her leg bones shatter. Splinters of bone protruded through her clothes as she crumpled to the ground. My ears burned from the piercing screech she let out.

He's picking us off one by one. We need to do something. My heart raced as I looked around. I watched Victor as he ran away. *Go, live, warn the world if you can. At least warn the others to get out of here while they can.* I turned to face the demon. *It doesn't look like we'll survive this.*

The rider also turned to see Victor running and stepped towards him.

You won't touch him! I snarled as I sprinted towards the demon.

Daric joined me in my charge.

The demon turned towards us and lifted his arm in a slashing motion. A blade of water rose up and headed right for us. I pushed Daric to the left, and I went to the right of the blade. Daric stumbled a few steps, but regained his footing before continuing his charge.

Okay, that's new.

I channeled more magic to freeze the water around me and pull it towards me to make armor out of ice. It took more effort than usual to freeze the water and even more effort to manipulate it. Eventually, I focused on making just a breastplate out of ice. *Why was that so hard? Was it because it's salt water?*

My vision turned a darker shade of red as I flexed my claws.

The demon stood and leveled his arms at the two of us with a smile on his face.

44

PAIN TOLERANCE

The demon charged towards Daric while keeping a spear-arm aimed at me. Daric planted himself in a defensive stance with his sword held in a low guard. There was something different in his eyes as he took a deep breath. I went wide and prepared to attack from behind. Even though the water slowed me down, I thought I could outrun the demon.

I heard splashing and turned to see Anna running away. *Please, go. We'll buy time for you to get to safety. Hopefully.*

The demon stabbed towards Daric. Daric rotated his sword as he stooped to take a step forward and to the side. He lifted his sword to deflect the demon's attack over his shoulder. Without disrupting his momentum, he continued to rotate the sword so that when the rider ran past him, his blade would drag across the demon's entire side.

I heard the weapon slide across several bones.

While the demon continued running without showing any sign of receiving the wound, I stayed out of his reach until he went past, then followed behind. I pounced and dug my claws into the demon's flank. My claws shredded the exposed muscles as I failed to latch on.

It turned around, and blood poured from the new wounds we'd inflicted. But I noticed none of his wounds had healed.

I stepped next to Daric. "He isn't regenerating. Maybe we can do this."

"Are you telling me demons regenerate?" Daric tightened the grip on his sword.

I flexed my claws. "The sin of gluttony did. I thought since he was supposed to be more powerful, he could do it too."

As the demon galloped towards us again, the two of us lowered ourselves into defensive stances. The demon dropped both arms into the water then swung them upward, unleashing two water blades towards us.

Daric went to dodge to the side, but I pulled him towards me and lined us up so we would stand in between the two blades as they went by.

"Go for the horse head," I whispered in Daric's ear as I moved him to stand in front of me.

He nodded.

We waited for the demon to level both arms and attempt to pierce us. I took a step back before jumping onto Daric's shoulder and pushing off him, causing Daric to drop to a knee.

The rider raised both arms to follow my trajectory and released his gaseous breath towards Daric.

I grabbed the spear-arms as they lunged towards me, and with a flick of my wrists, I pulled myself towards the demon's human parts. All of my claws dug into the demon's flesh.

Daric didn't flinch as the fumes flowed towards him. He rolled forward under the cloud that had singlehandedly incapacitated Silver and drove his sword into the base of the horse neck. More of the noxious cloud poured from around Daric's sword, forcing Daric to retreat. But when Daric jumped to his left, his sword slipped from his grasp, and he left it behind.

My right hand dug into the demon's shoulder. The demon attempted to headbutt me, but I jumped and somersaulted myself onto his back. I tried mauling the human portion in front of me again, aiming for the neck and head as much as I could. When my claws hooked into the back of the demon's neck, he twisted his torso where the hips would be until there was another crack, and his arm knocked me from his back.

I brought my arm up to block his. There was a sizzling sound as his arm struck my icy bracer. I had to twist to catch myself and land in a four-point stance.

The two of us had inflicted more damage on the demon in the last two exchanges than we had when the angel held his attention. The human head lolled limply forward, and the horse head would have done the same if Daric's sword wasn't holding it up. Copious amounts of blood poured from dozens of wounds, but they showed no signs of slowing him down. And more of the grayish-brown gas continued to leak from around the sword, but there was less of it compared to before.

What does it take to kill this guy?

Daric ran towards me. "Lucia, can you use your magic ice powers to make me a sword?"

I wanted to roll my eyes. *If you didn't just leave your weapon in any old place, you wouldn't have this problem.* "Yes." My tone didn't hide my disappointment.

I focused on channeling my magic. Remembering how difficult it was to make ice from the salt water earlier, I tried to make the weapon from moisture in the air, but it was just as difficult to manipulate as the salt water. *Does salt make things more difficult for me? I need to ask Mom later.*

I looked at my two bracers. *They'll have to do.* Pulling them off, I increased their density as much as I could and created a sword that was similar to the one he was using before. But I placed extra attention on the handle, making it just long enough for Daric to hold it with both hands and forming the pommel so it wouldn't allow his hand to slip. I even added extra texture so his leather gloves had more grip.

When I finished making the weapon, I could feel myself losing my connection with my magic.

I passed the sword to Daric.

"That's so cool," he said as he marveled at my creation.

"It's the only one you can have. I can't make another or use any more magic." I turned to face the demon. "Don't lose it. And if you do, you had best get your old sword back."

Daric took a few practice swings. "The balance is weird, but it grips better than I thought it would. How often do you do this?"

"Now isn't the time. Focus, you idiot," I growled.

The demon didn't charge again. He instead sent out two more of his water blades towards Daric. I shoved Daric out of the way and watched as the water blades collided with each other.

Is he focusing on Daric now? Why?

I ran out to the side. "Circle around to the other side," I instructed Daric.

"Okay," Daric replied uncertainly.

Just as I thought, the demon is definitely following Daric's movements now. What changed? The sword?

I sprinted towards the rider's back and jumped on again. He started bucking, so I dug my claws into his back and horse butt. My toe-claws shredded the demon's body, but my hands dug in and hooked around his ribs.

I was relieved to see Daric charge the moment I had the demon's attention. The rider's arms flailed as he kicked and turned, trying to dislodge me. Daric sidestepped a wild kick from the front legs and brought his new sword down on the horse neck, just below where his other sword was stuck.

A hot knife through butter would not compare to how easily the weapon cut the head off. As the demon reared backwards, his horse head flew off and spun through the air, sword included. Wisps of steam floated off the stump as it plopped on the ground.

I was not prepared for the demon to continue leaning backwards. I tried to push off, but the demon's human section landed on my leg and tail.

Growling, I kicked at the demon, but instead of freeing myself, all I did was shred more of his face and even ripped off his bottom jaw.

More of the grayish-brown gas poured out from the stump of the neck and spread towards me.

I turned and dug my claws into the muddy ground and pulled. I struggled frantically to get away from the fumes. The demon tossed and turned to stand up, giving me the chance to get away just before the gas reached my legs.

After scrambling to my feet, I turned to see the heavily injured demon backing away from Daric. The stump where his horse head had been looked like something had cauterized it. There wasn't any more of that gray-brown gas pouring from the stump, and the bit that had been around was dissipating.

Why is my ice doing this now and not earlier? Why? Does fresh water hurt him? Did it have something to do with how he doesn't have a shiny appearance? Did he cover himself in salt water?

I couldn't answer my questions while the demon sent another pair of water blades towards Daric, forcing him to jump backwards. The demon backpedaled more, and I ran up and kicked his hind leg before he could set it down. The demon created another water blade and sent it towards Daric before his legs crossed and he sat down.

The demon turned his human torso to strike at me with his arm. I ducked under the attack and jumped to slash at his remaining eye. He tilted his head so my claw went into the eye socket of the one I had already destroyed.

Daric's splashing steps behind me told me he was getting closer.

The demon stood up, and even though I clung to his face and reached for his eye with my other hand, he stomped his front leg on the ground.

Everything around me exploded in water and launched me flying backwards.

I hit the ground hard with a splash. My entire body was much heavier from soaking up as much water as it could in such a short time, and I could feel it when I tried to sit up and see what had happened.

Daric was also on the ground, but he was closer to the demon than I was. The demon reared up and threatened to drop his hooves on Daric, but the human tucked his legs in and rolled to his feet. When the demon's hooves splashed where Daric had been, they created a shock wave of water that pushed me back down.

Daric stumbled backwards but stayed upright. He charged the

rider, who didn't move as the ice sword cut into one of its front legs, just above the knee. The severed leg fell away from its host.

Good, now his mobility is ruined. I stood up and felt the salt water pouring from my fur.

The demon lost his balance and tilted towards his left, directly into Daric's swing.

Daric swung the sword at the demon's human torso, but as the blade entered, a bony spear-arm halted his weapon from cutting through him. It looked like Daric flinched and tried to pull his sword back out, but the rider shoved his other spear-arm into Daric's belly.

I lost focus on everything as I watched Daric grab the bone piercing his stomach. When the demon lifted him off the ground, the ice sword got unstuck, and by some miracle, it was still in Daric's hand.

Daric raised the weapon and shoved it into the elbow of the arm holding him up. The blade sliced through, and the last of the tissue ripped as Daric carried the spear-arm to the ground.

My body felt like it moved in slow motion as I sprinted on all fours towards the rider. The demon turned only his head and sent a blade of water towards me. Even weighed down, it wasn't hard to dodge the magic. Dashing to my right, I closed in on the demon. His movements seemed the slowest they had been yet.

He lifted his arm up just as I pounced, and I noticed he had placed the geyser in my path.

The rushing water swallowed me up, but I felt like I was falling. It was a feeling that was justified as I hit the ground on my stomach. I looked up at the demon, who couldn't reach me with his one good arm without moving. But he likely couldn't move without falling because, instead of a spear-arm, another torrent of water battered into me.

The water poured on me and pinned me to the ground. I couldn't push myself up and out of the water. Water continued to flow and push me to the ground in a reverse geyser. Holding my breath, I fought futilely against the current. It didn't stop or ease up, and eventually, my lungs burned with the need to breathe.

I clenched my jaw as I pulled myself forward, hoping to get out of the magic before I passed out and drowned.

45

A SOUR VICTORY

I pulled myself forward and fought the overwhelming onslaught pouring down on me. Despite the progress I made, I never made it out from under the torrent of water.

Is this how I die, by drowning?

My limbs went numb and failed to move. I couldn't hold back anymore. My mouth opened, and I inhaled. Water flooded into my lungs as I felt my consciousness fading.

The insurmountable pressure ceased, but I was too weak to push myself out of the water. *I don't want to die.* I clung to any shred of consciousness I found. Moments after the water stopped, I heard someone splashing towards me. They turned me over.

Blinding light and the sudden rush of air shocked my senses. With a gasp and a painful coughing fit, I expelled the water. Each expulsion of salt water left a burning sensation in my lungs. I blinked several times as my eyes adjusted to the light. All my limbs still felt numb, and my ears were ringing from the abuse they received. After more coughing, someone turned me over and slapped me on the back. More water flew out of my mouth.

Finally, I inhaled fresh air. I never knew I could miss it so much.

I turned to see who had saved me, but the sight of the demon impaled by an icy spear caught my attention first. The spear was massive. It simultaneously pinned the rider and held it off the ground. More steam wafted from the human torso where the weapon penetrated.

Who did that?

"Mom?" I asked in a raspy voice. It was the only person I had seen create such a massive ice construct.

"Who?" Fina's voice sounded more lovely than ever before.

I turned to see the lynxkin holding me up with Dinar's help. "Dinar?" My voice was still barely audible.

"Take it easy. It's over," Dinar whispered. The two of them helped get me into a seated position. Dinar grunted as she made sure I could sit on my own. "Wow, you're heavy when you're wet."

I glared at the elf. "My fur can soak up a lot of water."

Dinar smiled. "You're going to be just fine." She looked behind me. "I wish I could say the same for the rest of them."

The water level around us lowered and eventually disappeared. Fina and Dinar joined me in a look of disbelief.

"What happened?" Fina asked as she continued to look around.

We lost.

I wanted to say those two little words, but they never left my throat. My fur was still soaked, just like the ground. Fina and Dinar's clothes also dripped with water, and the smell of salt was still heavy in the air.

By now, my breathing had mostly returned to normal, and my limbs were gradually regaining their strength. "Go... others..." It was still hard to breathe. I put a hand on Dinar's arm. "I'll be fine... eventually."

Dinar nodded as she cautiously stood up, never taking her eyes off me. "Fina, go help Daric. Whatever you do, don't remove the thing impaling him. Just carefully take him to Lexia."

Lexia's here? Where?

Fina gave me a quick, sorrowful look. I gave her a nod, and she stood up and headed towards Daric, who was still lying on the ground clutching the spear-arm that was impaling him.

Hopefully he can pull through.

I put my hands on the ground and pushed myself up. My legs wobbled as I tried to keep from falling over.

Silver, Penny, and Daric were all motionless. I saw, at the edge of the water, that Lexia was on her knees panting while Victor stared at me, horror in his eyes. *So she was the one to make that. Wow, I didn't know she had it in her. He didn't run to save his life, he went to get help. I should thank him for that.*

I took a step and lost my balance, collapsing to my knees. *But for now, I need to rest some more.* I waved at Victor to come to me.

Instead of walking towards me, he took a step back.

I continued to wave him over.

He wouldn't move. His mouth moved, but I couldn't hear what he said from this distance.

Lexia turned her head towards Victor. "Take me to her." Her voice was much louder and I could hear her. Victor shook his head. "Just do it. I guarantee she won't be mad at you."

I flattened my ears. *So that's what he's worried about. He thinks I'll think less of him for running. No, I needed help to overcome my fear. If we're praising anyone, it should be Daric and Silver. Those two faced the demon without hesitating. But they don't have the instincts we have. Since he ran and went to get my sister, I should reward the teddy bear with a hug. I'm surprised that Dinar's moving. She's likely pushing herself since she's magically exhausted.*

I waved Victor over one more time. His shoulders slumped as he helped my sister stand and supported her as they walked towards me.

When the two of them stopped in front of me, Lexia pushed off the bearkin and tackled me. Tears flowed from her eyes as she squeezed me. "I'm so glad you're alive."

I hugged her. "I'll be fine." Victor looked like he was holding his breath. "Thank you, Victor."

Victor's pupils grew as wide as they could. "But, but—"

I smiled. "I understand what you were going through; I needed help myself. Anna knew how to push me into action. Even if you hadn't returned with my sister, I wouldn't have blamed you. Honestly, I was glad you got away safely." I looked down at my sister's head. "And I can't thank you enough for bringing my sister when I needed her most."

Victor just hung his head wordlessly.

"Even though you said you didn't want me to help?" Lexia gave me the puppy-dog eyes.

I rested my head against hers. "I was wrong."

After recovering some more and being doted on by my sister, we looked to see that the demon's body had never moved. *Finally, he's dead. That took a lot. And there are three others just like him. Mom isn't going to believe this. Neither will my captain.*

Dinar stepped towards me with a tear rolling down her face.

"What's wrong?" I asked.

She sniffled. "Silver's dead."

"How? Why? When?" Questions flew from my mouth before I knew I wanted to ask them.

Dinar wiped the tears on her face with her sleeve. "He had a lot of blood around his mouth and face. And there was more in his throat. I think he drowned in his own blood."

My knees gave out, and my sister gently placed me on the ground. "He's dead." I looked up at Dinar. "Daric? The demon stabbed him and he stopped moving. Please tell me he isn't dead too. Please!"

Dinar looked even sadder. "He's... still hanging in there." She turned towards Daric. "I don't think he has long. He needs help right now, but none of us can do that. Golditress still isn't here yet."

My head snapped towards Victor, who had been silently following us. "Go get her. You know which way we came, right?" Victor nodded his head slowly. "Then go get her and carry her back here as fast as you can."

There was a look of absolute determination in the bear beastkin's eyes before he sprinted off as fast as he could on all fours.

"Where's Anna?" I looked around but couldn't find her. "I know she ran as soon as the angel died, but she didn't come back with you guys."

"No, she didn't run to us. Not like Victor." Dinar rubbed the top of her head. "Where did she go?"

I stood up and gave my sister a slight push away. "I'll have to track her."

Lexia stepped in front of me. "I'm going with you."

I shook my head. "You know I have the recovery aptitude. I'm fine."

"I don't care," my sister said as she stomped her foot. "You're not leaving me again."

"I'll come back." I forced a smile.

Lexia growled and flattened her ears.

"Fine, let's go."

It was easy to find Anna's footprints in the muddy ground at the edge of the water. Somehow, we'd fought the demon in a shallow bowl where the water perfectly pooled. *Is that a coincidence? Nah. I've got other things to worry about.*

We followed the footprints back to the town. *Why did she run this way? She can feel the anchors, and she said that there was a new one here.*

Lexia was moving, but still far slower than me.

"You alright? Do you need to take a break?" I stopped for her.

She leaned forward and placed her hands on her knees. "No. There's just something wrong."

My heart leaped. "What? What's wrong? Are you hurt?"

"No, it's my magic." She stood up, still panting. "It's never felt like this before."

I raised an eyebrow. "How much do you know about magic fatigue?"

"Only that the weird emptiness is called that. But I've felt that before." She raised a hand and stared at it. "When I get to that point, I can still feel the magic. It's just much harder to. Almost like I have to put in an amount of effort that's not worth it."

I feel a "but" coming.

"But this isn't like that. There's no magic. And it hurts. Like there's a pain in my bones that just won't go away." Lexia turned and looked at me. Her eyes shimmered as she held back the tears.

"How long have you felt like that?" I asked in a forced, calm tone. *Hopefully if I'm calm she will be too.*

335

"Ever since I created that giant spear of ice. I didn't know I could make something so large." Lexia's tail wrapped around her leg as she hugged herself. "It happened so fast. I saw you in the water, and I just got so, so angry. The only thing on my mind was killing that monster."

I wrapped my arms around my sister. "Shh. It's okay. I've got you." She returned the hug. "I understand how that feels. But do you know what magic exhaustion is?"

"Magic exhaustion?" Lexia looked at me longingly.

"Magic exhaustion—it's something not all magic users can even reach." *This'll be something Mom'll need to talk to her about.* "There are only three things that I know about it. One, it's bad but not usually life-threatening. Two, it comes only when you push yourself too far."

"And the third thing?"

I closed my eyes. "I can't reach it. My magic isn't nearly as strong as yours. My reach is pathetic by most magic user standards, so I'll never be able to channel enough magic to reach that point. And once I'm magically fatigued, I can't feel the magic. It's gone."

"Oh." Lexia lowered her head.

"Don't worry. Mom'll help you out. She'll teach you everything you need to know about magic and then some." I squeezed my sister gently and smiled.

"But you don't know about it." I could hear the defeat in my sister's voice. "She didn't teach you?"

I chuckled. "That's because I was never the best student. I couldn't sit still for very long."

Lexia giggled. "I can see that."

"Feel better?" I lifted my sister's chin to look her in the eye.

She smiled. "Yeah. Thanks."

"No problem." I turned to look at the town in front of us. "Now let's see what that knight meant when he said that someone killed everyone in town. And hopefully find Anna somewhere safe."

"Is this the town that the beast king attacked?" Lexia stiffened.

Great. How do I make it so she doesn't feel guilty while not lying to her? "That's not important. There were people alive here when I left it. So something happened after that." *That should do it. Deflecting always works.*

"Something doesn't feel right." Lexia turned her head towards me. "Are you sure she went in there?"

I don't feel anything weird. It must not be something important or dangerous to me.

"If you don't think you can do it, that's fine. Just wait here until I get back." I tried to sound as upbeat as I could. "I promise I won't be long. Go in, get out. Quick."

"No," Lexia said flatly. "We go together."

I waved for her to walk forward. She took a step. While I saw the hesitation in her second step, she took it anyway. Then the third.

I smiled as I stepped up next to her. *Way to go, sis.*

4 6

DISTRACTING

L exia and I walked into the city, and a grisly sight greeted us. Bodies of humans, elves, and beastkin remained scattered around untouched.

Lexia and I kept quiet as we prowled through the streets looking for Anna. On our way, there was a large puddle of blood, supplied by the dozen or so bodies lying in the middle of it, with numerous papers soaking in it. I picked up one paper on the edge. Summoning glyphs decorated it. I looked at the other sheets; they all had the same glyphs inscribed on them. One caught my attention more than the others. It was glowing with magic.

I took it as I resumed my search for Anna.

There was a rustling sound in one of the nearby buildings.

Someone's alive?

Lexia and I dashed to a window of the building where we heard the sound coming from. Instead of seeing a living person, we saw something much worse. A humanoid creature with deathly pale skin sat hunched over a crate. It looked like it was rummaging through the contents.

Lexia gasped at the sight. I pulled her down as I ducked under the windowsill when the demon turned its head. I put a finger to my lips, urging my sister to be quiet.

She nodded as she swallowed and curled her tail around her waist.

I pointed a finger back to where we'd come from and nodded my head in that direction, and Lexia followed behind me as I turned to lead her to safety. My tail flicked behind me and brushed up against something as I walked on all fours.

"Achoo!"

Lexia's sneeze caused me to jump.

I glared at her. She returned my glare and pointed to my tail. *Did you just accuse my tail of making you sneeze? That's rude. My tail is perfect and would do nothing like that.*

The fallen demon's faceless head swiveled around to peer out the window. There weren't any eyes, nose, ears, or mouth on the creature's head. *Didn't they have a mouth the last time I saw them?*

As soon as its head turned towards us, it stopped and pushed itself out of the window.

I grabbed my sister's shirt and pulled her behind me. She screamed as she tumbled to the ground.

The demon's limbs also didn't look the same as I remembered. They weren't long and gangly, at least once you got past the elbow and knees. The forearms and hands were huge and full of rippling muscles. Its feet were similarly muscular, and they looked to be the size of my head.

I didn't have time to admire its grotesque, disproportionate body. It cocked its arm back to throw a punch while it ran towards me. I rolled to my feet and prepared to catch the punch and throw it over my shoulder.

My plan mostly worked. I caught just behind the creature's wrist and ducked to toss it over my shoulder. The creature's arm snapped in half, but its feet never left the ground. The bone protruded from its forearm and sprayed a bit of its milky-white blood in my face.

Not what I was expecting.

While the sight of the broken bones distracted me, a fist landed in my side, and I went flying into a wall. My vision flashed white for a moment as my head hit the structure.

I shook myself to regain my focus. I heard the demon running towards me again. It lifted its massive foot and prepared to stomp it on my head.

With a push, I slid backwards and avoided becoming toe-jam.

I rose to a four-point stance. I growled as I charged the demon. It swung its good fist downwards. If I wasn't so angry, I would have rolled my eyes at such a pathetically telegraphed attack. I sidestepped to the right of the demon's shoulder.

It turned and attempted to backhand me at the same time. I stayed below the attack, and when I stood up, I uppercut my claws into his skull and didn't stop until I'd buried my entire hand in its head.

The demon went limp. I pulled my hand out and watched the body collapse into a heap. After seeing my blood-drenched hand, I shook it in a fruitless attempt to get the liquid off. The sulfuric smell it gave off repulsed every bit of me.

Gross.

"Are you okay?" Lexia appeared out of nowhere and started inspecting every inch of me. "What was that?"

I pushed my sister away. "I'm fine. That was a fallen demon—the weakest type." There was a slight throbbing at the back of my head.

I put my hand on the place that hurt and checked for blood.

"You're bleeding." Lexia grabbed my hand as she panicked. "Oh, no. You hit your head again. Please tell me you remember me."

I flicked Lexia's nose. "Stop. From what I remember of the fallen, they're dangerous in large numbers. If there's one, there are likely more. We don't have time for this." Lexia snapped her jaw shut as she nodded. "Good. Listen to me and follow my instructions and we'll be fine." I made to lead the way but stopped, turned my head, and glared at my sister. "And keep my tail out of your nose."

"You stuck *your* tail in *my* face," Lexia grumbled.

Didn't the knights of the Crimson Tide see these demons? Or did they think that we were responsible for summoning them? They weren't here before, so who summoned them? And how did they summon so many? Do each of those papers summon one? That's a question for Anna when I find her.

Eventually, we made our way to the center of the town. All along the way, bodies of men, women, children, and demons littered the streets.

The town center had a large well, and around the well was the most disturbing sight I could conceive of. Something had pressed the bodies of the fallen demons into thin lines for what I had to guess was another summoning glyph.

While holding back the nausea growing in my stomach, I could hear someone crying. Lexia nodded when I pointed in the direction the sound was coming from. We walked into one of the smaller houses to find Anna huddled in a corner, clutching her knees to her chest.

"Keep an eye out," I whispered to Lexia. She nodded and turned to keep watch.

I walked over and sat down next to Anna, wrapping an arm around her shoulders.

She continued to cry. We just sat there without saying a word. Slowly, Anna leaned more and more on me.

"You want to talk about it?" I asked after Anna stopped sniffling for more than a breath.

Anna relaxed enough to let her legs go. "Want? No."

"Are you okay at least?" I kept my tone and volume soft.

"No."

"Can I help?"

Anna sighed. "I don't know."

I slumped my shoulders. "Do you know what helps me?"

"What?" Anna turned and looked at me with a hopeful expression.

"A distraction." I gave her a wide, toothy smile.

Anna gave me a sour look. "You were always easy to distract."

"So is my sister." I turned and winked at my sister.

"I am not!" Lexia screeched.

"Are too." I gave her a wide smile and another wink. *Play with me here, sis.*

My sister puffed out her cheeks and then gave me a knowing smile before returning to her pouting face. "Well, you're worse than me."

"Am not." I pouted. "We're the same."

"Are not." Lexia stomped towards me.

"Are too."

"Are not."

"What are you, children?" Anna interrupted us.

I playfully swayed my head from side to side. "We're fifteen. So, by human standards, yes."

Anna giggled and then broke down into laughter. Lexia and I joined her.

"You really are someone special," Anna said as she wiped the tears from her face. "Thank you. I needed that."

"See, being easily distracted isn't a bad thing." I gave Lexia a smirk. She smiled back. "Would you like another distraction?"

Anna looked surprised. "Don't you want to know why I ran away?"

I shook my head. "Whenever you're ready, I'll listen. But I don't think it's a good idea for you to think about it right now. So, I prescribe more distractions." I held the paper I'd picked up earlier in front of Anna. "Can you tell me more about this?"

Wait, wasn't it still infused with magic earlier? Does that mean it became useless when I killed the demon?

Anna took one look at it and buried her head in my shoulder. I threw the paper away and hugged the poor girl. Lexia sat down on Anna's other side and hugged her too.

"Sorry, I didn't know," I whispered.

Anna didn't say anything for a few moments. Meekly, she turned to look at the paper I'd thrown away. "You're fine. It's just... It hurts to look at that glyph now. After the rider killed the spirit of control, anything related to conjuration magic is painful. You understand magic whiplash?"

I nodded. "When someone overpowers your magic, it hurts." My eyes went wide. "Is it like that?"

Anna gave a wry smile. "Yeah, only much worse. Summoning takes a greater magic than most other magic. So the whiplash is proportionally worse."

"I... I don't know what to say." My voice quivered.

Anna gave me a knowing look. "Don't worry about me. I'll just take some time to recover. In about a week or two, it'll be like it never happened." She then looked down at the ground, dispirited. "That glyph was used to summon a fallen demon. Then something—I'm guessing another sin—used the bodies of the fallen outside to create a summoning glyph to bring the rider to our world."

"Was using the bodies of the demons important? And what other sin is there?" Lexia asked with strange enthusiasm.

"Well, I didn't kill the sin of lust. She got away. But I doubt she was in any state to pull that off." I flattened my ears and curled my tail around my waist. *How many sins are in this world?*

"Based on the disturbed ground around the glyph and the mutations of the fallen, my guess is the sin of greed did that. Did they require the bodies of the demons to make the glyph? I couldn't tell you the answer." Anna's comment sent a shiver down my spine. "Dijins are capable of powerful earth manipulation on top of creating illusions. But their illusions aren't as good as a sin of lust's."

"Can a demon summon another demon?" Lexia curled her tail around her waist.

Lexia and I are so much alike. But I shouldn't let her see me scared like this.

Anna shook her head. "No, that's impossible. A person from this world has to summon them."

"So where did all those papers come from? And would each one summon a fallen?" I asked as I turned and looked at the glyph. "And does their being in a pool of blood and bodies matter?"

"Yes. Blood is the catalyst for summoning demons. Their glyphs won't do anything unless blood is spilled on them." Anna raised her hands to her temples. "Angels are different. They constantly drain the summoner's magic the longer they're here. Any idiot can summon a demon if someone gives them a working glyph."

We're getting serious again. Time for another distraction.

"Even a little girl who was kidnapped and killed her kidnappers?" I watched to see if Anna's face changed, hoping she would remember.

"Yeah, that could happen." The horror that spread across Anna's face was priceless. "Wait, I didn't mean that." I giggled while she panicked. After I giggled for a bit, she scrunched up her face and gave me a light punch on my shoulder. "You did that on purpose."

I wagged my tail and smiled. "Distraction tactics."

The other two smiled at me. "You're too good at that," Lexia said as she pouted. "How many times have you done that to me?" She looked like she was counting in her head.

"It works, doesn't it?" I couldn't suppress my smile. "Mom got really good at it too. Especially during the times when I was in heat."

"You talk about her a lot. Is she really that special to you?" Lexia softened her tone.

I leaned back and stared at nothing. "Yeah. Sure, things were rocky and difficult at times. We had our differences, but I've learned that she really loves me. And I've learned to love her back. Actually, right now I miss her constant nagging when I get into trouble in town. Or the times I come home dripping with water from the rain. Even the times I walked in the door with blood in my fur from hunting while she was teaching a student magic and I scared them senseless." A tear rolled down my cheek.

"Let's get you home then," Anna said as she stood up. She offered me her hand.

"Huh?"

"You're homesick. I can see that now. You've helped me. Honestly, you've done more than the rest of us. But what have we done for you?" Anna looked at me guiltily.

I shrugged. "Indirectly, you introduced me to my sister."

Anna slumped her shoulders. "We didn't do that. That was nothing more than pure chance. I'm guessing since you're here and in such a calm mood that you killed the rider. Am I right?"

"Yeah." I flattened my ears and stared at my motionless tail. "Silver didn't make it." Anna gasped. "And Daric might not make it either. He needs Golditress's healing magic if he has any chance of surviving."

"Let's go." Anna helped Lexia to her feet. "It's time I stop being selfish and hiding like a child." The flatness of her voice was disheartening.

Anna tried to pull me to my feet, but I stood on my own. Even though we were just laughing and distracting ourselves, none of us could change the gloomy atmosphere. When we walked outside, I looked at the glyph made of crushed, fallen demon bodies. I noticed several other bodies—eight after I counted them—lying around the large glyph. They were all human, and they wore heavy black cloaks over their clothes.

One body seemed out of place. He was larger than everyone else, and his clothes were colorful. I recognized the face even though it was twisted in agony. *Decklin? What? He summoned the rider? Then the rider killed him. Why? How has he been free for all these years since he ordered my kidnappers to kill me when I was a kid? I have to tell Mom and Aenwyn about this.*

The memory of the old woman popped up in my mind. On our way out, I looked for her body but didn't find it. *Anna said that a sin of greed could use illusion magic. But I don't smell the perfume anywhere. So either the demon has a special interest in smelling good, or someone else is responsible.*

We returned to the others and saw Golditress kneeling next to Daric. Gifford and Mark were standing and staring at the rider's corpse. After Golditress finished healing Daric, he looked a bit older. It was hard to tell. His beard grew from barely visible to a proper scruff. His clothes and gambeson looked like they were a bit too small for him now. Through the entire experience, he never moved.

We took Silver's corpse to the other beastkin and buried them together. Mark carried Penny. Her legs were completely deformed and useless. She woke up screaming in pain just before we settled in for the night. Golditress examined her legs, and after asking me a few questions, she told Penny that everything below her knees was too far damaged to save even if she could use her healing magic. The screams that followed left me feeling sorry for her.

I hated her, but after hearing that she would likely never walk again, even I couldn't blame her for her reaction. That wasn't a fate I could live with. Evalana created a prosthetic arm with her earth magic. Theoretically, Lexia and I could do the same with ice magic. Penny couldn't do that with her fire magic, and I imagined creating a leg would be much harder, let alone two.

I stared at the sky as everyone but Penny tried to sleep. She never stopped weeping, and she wouldn't accept anyone's sympathy. The elf just crawled to her tent and cried the entire day.

The red tint in the sky had gone.

Six of us faced the Rider of Pain. He killed Silver and the angel. Nearly killed Daric and me. Crippled Penny. And mentally scarred Anna. We won, but at what cost?

I couldn't sleep. My mind wouldn't let me. So I stayed up the entire night, even when Victor urged me to go to sleep. And when the sun rose over the horizon, we packed everything up in an eerie silence. Penny sat off to the side and watched us.

Daric woke up in the morning and, after a few quiet words, didn't say anything else. He just walked over to the spot where we'd buried Silver and said, "Sorry."

When we headed out, Penny wouldn't allow anyone to carry her except for Mark. Mark was probably the worst choice, but she wouldn't let any of us beastkin near her. Not that we wanted to be after she screamed at Daric that everything was his fault. He didn't deny or defend himself. He hung his head as he accepted her accusations.

Nobody wanted to talk, but everyone knew where we were headed. We walked past the desolate town, doing our best to put the entire experience behind us. The terrain quickly turned into rolling hills. Mark needed frequent stops to rest while carrying Penny. When we stopped once again for lunch, Fina pointed out someone was coming.

I turned to see who it could be. It looked like another company of knights, all on horseback. They had no banner, but they didn't need one. I recognized their armor.

With a sigh of relief, I informed everyone who was coming. "Captain Allen and the Brilliant Crusade will help us."

Finally, a friendly face. If he's here, then we're closer to the capital than I thought. I'm almost home.

47

HOME, SWEET HOME

We continued to sit and rest while we waited for the Brilliant Crusade to arrive. The horses galloped in neat rows until they got close, then slowed to a trot and spread out into a more casual riding formation. A knight with the largest plume on their helmet ordered everyone to stop with a single raised fist.

I stood up and strode over to greet the man who saved my life when I first arrived in this world.

Captain Allen took his helmet off and smiled at me. His hard face had started showing his age. *At least this time he didn't have to save me from orcs like he did ten years ago when we first met.*

He hooked his helmet on the saddle and spread his arms out. "Lucia, it's so good to see you. My, you've grown up... a lot."

I giggled as I leaned forward to hug the human. "You won't believe how happy I am to see you."

Allen broke from the hug first. "You look awful. Who are the others? Who are the other beastkin?"

I turned to look at my companions. "They're friendly. One of them is my sister, believe it or not. But it's a long story. We're tired, beaten, injured, and broken. Can you help us get back to Aquittemia?"

The captain gave me a panicked look before turning it into a sad one. "I would love to help. But there is the possibility of a war with the Wild Kingdom. I need to be ready to deploy to defend any towns."

"You won't have to worry about that." I forced a smile at Allen's shock. "Again, it's a long story. I can tell you some of it while we travel back. How far are we away? I'm kind of lost right now."

I could see the smoke building in Allen's mind as he tried to come to terms with everything I'd just told him. His mouth opened for a moment, but no words came out.

"That's hard to believe." He finally broke the silence. "I want to believe you."

"Then believe me," I begged. "I don't have a reputation for lying, do I?"

Allen turned to look at the ground. "You don't. But what if you're wrong?"

"I was the beast queen for a short while, so trust me when I say that it's been settled and there is no war." I flattened my ears and flicked my tail. *I really didn't want to tell him that. But I don't know what else will convince him.*

"You what?" he shouted.

I flinched. I heard a few of the others behind me moving and saw some of the knights reaching for weapons. "Easy. No shouting, please. It hurts."

"Sorry. Were you really the queen?" The knight eyed me suspiciously while lowering his voice to a more civil level.

"For a short time. I relinquished that responsibility to someone more appropriate." *I hope.*

Allen rubbed the back of his head and shifted his feet. "I guess we can escort you to the capital. Someone is going to want to hear that."

"Yeah. I can already hear the lecture Mom's going to give me when I get home."

Allen laughed. "I don't envy you. Her lectures still scare me to this day. But I'll let you handle that when you get home." He motioned for me to lead the way to the people behind me. "Introduce me to your friends, and we'll see what we can do for you."

I led Allen to everyone. "Everyone, this is Allen, Captain of the Brilliant Crusade. Allen, this is everyone."

Dinar stood up and gave him a salute. "Sir, my name is Dinar, just Dinar."

"Nice to meet you, Dinar." Allen gave a slight bow of his head.

Mark stood up and mimicked Dinar. "My name is Mark, sir."

"Golditress, Captain." Golditress performed a textbook salute.

Allen held up his hand. "You all can drop the formalities. Rank means little in the wilds."

"Penny," the elf said with an unnecessary level of hostility.

"My name is Anna, and I'm an independent conjuration specialist," Anna said while she waved. "I am—was—studying blood anchors."

"And you four?" Allen pointed towards the beastkin, who eyed the knight.

I pointed to Lexia and moved my finger along as I introduced each of my friends. "That's my sister, Lexia. Then we have her mate, Gifford. Then there's Fina. And last but not least, Victor."

Daric didn't move and continued to stare at the ground as everyone introduced themselves to Allen. "We're the knights of the Omega Gamma. I'm the captain, Daric."

What happened to him? He has to be taking Silver's death hard.

Allen crossed his arms. "So you're the one we were all told to look out for."

Daric lifted his head towards Allen, but I grabbed Allen's shoulder and turned him to face me. "What do you mean you were told to look for him? The knights from the Crimson Tide didn't mention anything like that. They even labeled us traitors and attempted to kill me."

"Yeah, King Ramos is stepping down from the throne. But then there were reports of raids from the Wild Kingdom, so he postponed." Allen gave me a look of concern but didn't resist me. "Because of that, your father is asking for your return, Daric."

"What?" everyone from Rophmna asked simultaneously.

Allen panned his head to look at all of us. "How long have you been away?"

"I don't know," I said unconsciously.

"We met twenty-seven days ago," Lexia answered in a flat tone.

I gave my sister an annoyed look. *Oh, right, memorization. It must be nice to be able to remember everything at the drop of a hat.*

"That puts us at about five weeks, I think," Dinar added. "Wow, we weren't gone as long as we thought we would be."

"Silver's gone forever." Daric slumped his shoulders and poked at the ground with his foot.

Allen extended his hand towards Daric. "Come with me, son. We need to talk, and you need to hear this." I cocked my head to one side. Allen gave me a soft smile as he helped Daric to his feet. "You aren't the first captain to lose a man on a mission, nor will you be the last. And the first one is always the hardest." He turned his attention towards Daric as he led him away from us. "Listen, it's alright to feel what you're feeling. It means you're human. If you didn't feel this bad, I would have worried for the rest of your people."

"But it was my decision that got him killed. We shouldn't have fought the demon." Daric walked with Allen but didn't look at him.

Allen let out a heavy sigh before he turned to face his men. "Drue, come and help the others get ready to travel. Give them anything they need." He continued to lead Daric away. "Let's talk more in private."

I turned and watched a knight dismount and remove his helmet. A familiar scarred face smiled as he walked towards us. There were a few wrinkles forming on his brow and around his cheeks. He spread his arms out wide. "I knew you would grow into a beautiful woman one day."

I crossed my arms and flicked my tail from side to side. "Thank you, but don't even think about it." *He can try to hide it all he wants, but I can see him staring at my breasts. If he's so interested in mine, I'd have to try to keep him away from Lexia.*

"Ouch." Drue placed his hands over his heart. "Why would you think so little of me? My children are almost as old as you."

"And yet you keep staring," I said with a growl in my voice.

Lexia stepped in front of me and took an aggressive stance.

Drue blinked several times as his eyes bounced between Lexia and me. "Uh, how are there two of you? And why is one more lovely than the other?" Drue's voice matched the confusion on his face.

Victor and Gifford jumped in front of us, both growling at the man. I rolled my eyes and grabbed them both by the scruff of their necks. Both men dropped to their knees as they turned their growls into whimpers.

"Down, boys," I said while suppressing a giggle. Drue eased the grip on his sword. "He will look, but so long as he doesn't touch, there won't be any problems. He won't touch, right?" I glared at Drue and bared my fangs at him.

The color drained from Drue's face. He raised his hands in surrender. "Yes, ma'am."

"Good. If you didn't, I would have to break your arms." I released the two men. They stood up and rubbed the back of their necks. "But it's nice to see you, Drue. This is my twin sister, Lexia."

"You never said you had a sister. I thought you said everyone from your village was dead." Drue gave me a skeptical look.

I scowled. "I had amnesia, remember? I forgot that I had a sister." Drue's cheeks flushed as the realization hit him. "But can we get some food and a few horses? We have one person who can't walk and a couple who are too tired to walk."

Drue's attention turned to Penny and her bandaged legs. "Yeah. Hopefully we can escort you back to Aquittemia. You all look like you've had it rough."

"We're going too," Lexia snapped.

Drue took a step back. "Okay. I never said that you couldn't." Again, Drue lifted his arms in surrender. "You're a grown woman and can make your own decisions." Drue turned away from her and faced the other knights behind him. "I can see how she's related to Lucia, temper and all," he muttered under his breath before continuing on his way.

Lexia's tail danced behind her as she watched Drue walk away. "I remember you said he was friendly in your story, but I couldn't stand how he looked at us."

I poked Lexia's chest. "These are going to attract a lot of attention. Humans have some kind of obsession with them." Lexia's eyes went wide and her body stiffened. "Lexia—what's wrong?"

"It's gone," she whispered. I flicked my ears towards my sister. She relaxed slightly, but her eyes were still wide. "I can't feel the demon anymore."

I grabbed my sister's shoulders. "You could still feel her? Where is she? What's she telling you to do?"

She shook her head. "No, she's gone. I didn't know that was her until her presence left."

I turned to Anna. "Care to elaborate?"

Anna shrugged. "I don't know. Maybe whatever mark the sin left on her is gone. Maybe she finally found a dark hole and died from her wounds. Take it as a good sign. Your sister is now truly free."

Lexia broke out of my grip and hugged me tightly. "You hear that? I'm free of her awful orders."

I blinked a few times before I returned my sister's hug. *Something doesn't feel right. Maybe I'm overthinking it. If that demon didn't die in a hole, the next time I see her I'll make her wish she had.*

Drue returned before Allen and Daric with several horses. They were "happily" donated by several of the knights who watched us closely. We set out towards Aquittemia, which, by Allen's estimate, was a week away.

During the trip, I tried to fill Lexia, Victor, Fina, and Gifford in on the basics of human society. I mostly focused on laws and currency. The whole idea of money took almost an entire day to get through.

Daric kept his distance and moped along, but he never fell behind. Anna, Mark, and Dinar rode on horses for the rest of the day. Penny was a fountain of seething hatred anytime someone looked at her where she lay on a litter carried by two knights.

After the first day, we set up camp. It was refreshing to have someone else worry about how it should be set up. Allen ran the entire show like the professional he was. I sat back and let him. Lexia still needed me to sort of guide her when dealing with the other humans. *She's still too overprotective of me. Maybe we're overprotective of each other.*

Day after day, we continued without anything going wrong. I even took Fina out hunting several times. Victor kept looking my way, but he kept his distance. Although I frequently saw him scratching at a silver bracelet with his claws.

By the end of our journey home, the other knights were badgering us to go hunting for them. They started behaving the moment I threatened not to share with them.

Allen's estimation was correct. One week later, late in the evening, we stood staring at Aquittemia's stone walls and heavy gates. *Home, sweet, putrid-scented home. Who do I see first? Mom? Captain Aenwyn? Great, what's the protocol here?*

I leaned in next to Lexia's ear. "Don't wander away from me. Just stay by my side and don't do or say anything to anyone. And yes, the city stinks. I know."

After Lexia nodded, I gave the same message to the other beastkin. Allen led the way through the gates but stopped everyone just as we entered.

"Brilliant Crusade, you are dismissed, except for you, Gordon. I want you to go get the captain of The Maidens and bring her to the oracle stone. Omega Gamma and the beastkin, come with me." Allen's voice boomed over the inane chatter of the populace.

I guess that makes things easy.

Mark and Dinar took over carrying Penny, and then Allen led us through the streets.

I don't remember much of the stares I received when I first arrived in this city, but there's no way I received this many. I guess four beastkin walking through the streets makes a bit more noise, especially when we're with several humans, elves, and a half-elf.

Lexia clung close to me while the two guys flanked us. Fina kept close too. *I hope things don't get out of hand. Since they've been dealing with me for the last eleven years, they won't be too hard on the others. This whole situation is hard not to get anxious over.*

An angelic voice reached my ears. "Lucia? You're home!" That was a voice I'd missed so much.

I turned to see Mom running towards me. I couldn't hold back.

After slipping out of my sister's grasp, I sprinted towards my adoptive mother and hugged her tightly.

"Uh, honey. You're crushing me," Mom said in a breathless voice.

I eased up on the hug, but I didn't let go. I even nuzzled my face against hers. "Sorry, but I missed you."

"Welcome home, baby." Her voice sounded sweeter than ever. *They say absence makes the heart grow fonder. Boy, is that true! I guess I'm Mommy's little girl after all.*

"Do you want to explain why there's someone who looks almost exactly like you?"

I laughed nervously. "Oh, right. Funny story..."

48

LIMITS

I wrapped my tail around my leg and quickly glanced back at Lexia. "Can I tell you the whole story later? Maybe someplace quieter?"

"Okay," Mom said, drawing out her response. I could feel her gaze boring holes in me. "Can I at least have a name?"

"Hello, Nora. My name is Lexia. I'm Lucia's twin sister." Lexia walked up and extended her hand.

Mom arched an eyebrow. "You know who I am? Sister? How much has Lucia told you?"

Lexia smiled mischievously. "Only her entire story."

Mom turned her attention to me. "The entire story?"

How do I put this? "I told her everything that happened to me from the moment I woke up without any memories of who or what I was." *She should find the hidden meaning in my words.*

Her nod told me she did.

Allen stepped in between Mom and Lexia. "I imagine you two have lots you want to talk about. But right now, we need to debrief your daughter and the others."

Mom glared at the captain. "Then may I join?" Her question didn't sound like a request; it sounded like a statement of fact.

"As you wish," Allen said as he waved towards the courthouse's doors.

Almost everyone gave my mother a look of shock and awe, but Anna and I simply giggled. We knew she always got her way.

Lexia took the moment Mom walked in front of everyone to latch onto my arm again. "She's pretty," Lexia whispered. "And how is she so intimidating?"

I chuckled. "She is, or at least was, the most powerful magic user in this entire kingdom and, at one time, the entire world. When you have the power to wipe out an army, most people let you do what you want. After they get you to join their side, of course."

"Oh." Lexia just stared at my mother, her tail wagging.

Yeah, those two will get along just fine.

We all marched through the building. Allen carried Penny. *She doesn't have a problem with him. Maybe it has something to do with how likeable Allen is.* He sat us around a long, rectangular table before taking us, one at a time, to the oracle stone for our report. Since Aenwyn hadn't arrived yet, Allen took Daric first.

"How often is debriefing done like this?" I asked Mom.

Mom leaned back in her chair and looked up at the ceiling. "The oracle stone is only used for debriefing when someone returns from another kingdom. And sometimes if it's someone from another kingdom. Given what I heard about what's happening with the Wild Kingdom, I almost went out to look for you. Your friends... They are your friends, right?" I nodded. "They'll be given the standard questions to root out spies. Then they will be free to do whatever they like."

So she knows about what's been going on. Does the entire kingdom know, or did someone tell her because of me? She was going to find out anyway, so I guess it doesn't matter. But there's something I never thought about.

I turned to Lexia. "So, what are all your guys' plans?"

The other beastkin exchanged glances before they returned to focusing on me. "We were following you," Lexia answered.

"You aren't all planning on living with me, are you?" My voice trembled.

"It's alright if your sister joins us," Mom added in her sweetest voice.

"Where my mate goes, I go." Gifford crossed his arms as he stared at my mother.

"Mate?" My mother didn't bother hiding her surprise.

I shrugged. "Think of them as married."

Mom turned to glare at Lexia. "And how old are you? You said you were her twin sister. Doesn't that mean you're fifteen, too?"

Lexia flattened her ears as she growled slightly. "Is that a problem?"

"Aren't you..." Mom shook her head and pinched the bridge of her nose. "No, technically, you're an adult." She took a deep breath, and then her eyes nearly exploded as she turned to Victor before snapping her focus back to me. "You didn't, did you?"

I pouted. "If you're asking whether I've accepted him as my mate, no. Not yet, at least." I could see the words about to flow out of my mother's mouth. "I've considered it, but now isn't a good time. Especially given what Lexia, Anna, and I saw in that town."

Mom must have ignored the last sentence, because she went back to staring at Victor.

Victor locked eyes with my mother and started growling.

I growled louder at Victor and gave Mom a nudge with my elbow.

He stopped and pointed at me. "Why are you telling me to stop? It's her challenge."

"This is not the place or the time." My voice was flat. Victor wilted under my glare. "And she wasn't challenging you, just studying you. Trust me, her challenge will come later."

I watched the bear's heart drop.

"Animals," Penny spat under her breath.

I and all the other beastkin directed our attention to the rude elf. Mom joined us after she saw us all react to something. Penny's mouth tightened as she looked at the door of the exit. I dug my claws into the wooden table.

"You need to calm down, Penny." Dinar's voice broke the silence.

"Easy for you to say," Penny said as she crossed her arms. "While I was busy being crippled by the demon, you slept like a baby."

"If I hadn't magically exhausted myself, you would have died before that." Dinar leaned forward in her chair. "You're the one who turned on us first. Be glad we didn't execute you like the traitor you are. Daric seems to think there's something redeemable in you, but I don't see it."

Tears leaked from Penny's eyes. "How can I be a knight now? A crippled knight? I'd be the laughingstock of the entire kingdom."

"You'll be lucky if they let you stay in the kingdom." Dinar's voice was full of venom.

Penny looked up at Golditress with bloodshot eyes. "You've got to have recovered by now. Why haven't you used your healing magic to heal me yet?"

Golditress shrank in her seat. "I don't know how," she whispered.

Penny slammed her hands on the table. "What? Just use your magic."

Golditress jumped. "It's not like that. Your bones are shattered. My magic will only make things worse for you. If I don't heal them exactly correctly, you'll be in unbearable pain for the rest of your life. You still wouldn't be able to walk. And my magic won't do anything with the shards of bone still in your legs. There are limits to healing magic. I'm sorry."

Penny's jaw dropped.

I looked at my mother, who sat watching the exchange without an ounce of emotion on her face. *She's been awfully quiet. She also hasn't asked any questions about what happened. Is she waiting for my turn once Captain Aenwyn gets here?*

Just as I thought about her, my captain walked through the door. She stared at us and blinked several times as she looked at us sitting around the wooden table.

"There are more of you than who left." It sounded like she was talking more to herself. "But there's someone missing."

Everyone went quiet. I could hear Daric and Allen walking back down the stairs. When they entered the room, Allen waved for Daric to take a seat.

"Good, you're here. Would you like to get Lucia done now?" Allen asked Aenwyn.

"If it's alright with you. Keeping her cooped up will only make things worse later." Aenwyn turned to my mother. "I assume you wish to join. Is that correct?"

"It is," Mom said with a nod.

I turned to my sister. "I'll be back. This is something I have to do without you and you'll have to do without me."

Lexia pointed to my mother. "But she gets to go with you? Why can't I?"

"One of the stipulations of Lucia becoming a knight at her age is that her mother is present for her debriefings," Aenwyn interrupted.

"But I'm her sister."

Aenwyn's eyes grew wide at Lexia's comment. She rubbed her temples. "I'm getting too old for this."

I put a hand on Lexia's shoulder. "Remember what I said. Humans have different rules, and you have to follow them while you're here." My sister looked like she was about to cry. "We'll have plenty of time together once we satisfy the bureaucrats."

"The what?" Lexia asked.

"The government. This is one of my responsibilities." I put on a smile for her.

Wordlessly, Lexia leaned back in her seat, staring at the table. I took the action as her letting me go, then followed behind my mother and the captains upstairs.

They led me to the oracle stone. It was in the same small room that I visited all those years ago, but this time there was a small desk and a female elf sitting in the corner with a stack of papers and a pen in her hand. The woman was familiar, but I couldn't remember where I'd seen her before. She stood up and walked to the other side of the table.

The auburn-haired elf was thin, but not unhealthily so. She wore a thick black dress that went to her ankles. She followed me with her emotionless eyes and pointed to the featureless stone slab on the other table in the room.

"Please stand next to the oracle stone as we prepare to get started." Her voice was just as emotionless as her eyes. "And please place your hand on it and don't let go until we tell you to."

Why is she so familiar?

I followed the instructions the lady gave. After I placed a clawed hand on the stone, I tried to imagine waterfalls to calm myself down. "I'm ready whenever you are."

The elf raised her left hand and pointed her palm towards the stone. I could see magic gathering in her palm. "Judge." As the word left the elf's mouth, the stone next to me flashed as it reached out and collected the magic from the elf. I nearly jumped at the sight.

Okay, this is a totally different experience when you can see magic. Given the number of times I've gotten myself in trouble, it's a wonder I never had this thing used on me. Even during the incident with the Crimson Tide. They questioned them with the stone, but Aenwyn talked to me without it.

The elven woman lowered her hand and the pen on the desk started glowing with magic. It stood up and floated over a piece of paper without being touched.

Is she really using magic to manipulate a pen?

"Let's start with your name, age, and affiliation."

The woman's monotone voice snapped me out of my fascination with the floating pen. "Lucia Silverbreeze. I'm fifteen. I'm a knight for the company The Maidens."

As I talked, the pen matched my words. I turned to look at Aenwyn.

"Yes, this is being recorded," she said. "Arsane can write faster with magic than by hand." The scratching of the pen on the paper matched my captain's words. "She just writes everything down. But please be honest. The oracle stone will react if you lie."

Now I remember. She's the lady from when I first signed myself up to live at the orphanage.

"How did you get a title when you're so young?" Arsane stared at the stone with unabashed shock.

"I killed a sin of gluttony and helped save Princess Evalana's life."

The stone didn't react. I watched as more emotion broke through the woman's stony persona.

"That's not relevant to the current situation," Captain Aenwyn interrupted.

"Sorry." The elf straightened her shoulders and cleared her throat. "Anyway. What is your relationship to Daric and the Omega Gamma?"

My tail swayed behind me. *This is going to take forever at this rate.* "They hired me to guide them through a patch of forest that I claimed as my hunting grounds. They also wanted me to travel with them to show them how to live off the land and hunt food for them. Someone had asked them to take Anna to investigate the blood anchor that happened to be in the Wild Kingdom. I—"

"Stop." I flinched at Arsane's shout. "What are you doing?"

"I'm trying to speed things along. Do you think I want to be here all day?" I waved to my mother and the captain. "They probably want to hear the entire story, and there are parts in it that the kingdom might find important."

Mom wrapped her arm around my shoulders. "I know you're getting agitated, but we need to do this." She scratched my back in between my shoulder blades. My tail wagged as I leaned into her scratches. "Take your time and stay calm. I'm here for you. There's no rush."

"Can we continue?" Arsane asked as she tapped her foot. Mom nodded. "If you want to tell your entire story, then we will do it your way. Now explain the events that led up to you leaving the Wild Kingdom."

I gave Mom a nervous smile before I closed my eyes and took a deep breath. "I was afflicted with the frenzy and attacked the beast king. Lexia, my sister, traded her freedom to the sin of lust so they would spare my life." Mom stopped scratching my back. My voice caught in my throat slightly. "We followed the sin of lust and the beast king back to the kingdom to a town I can't remember the name of. The beastkin were attacking it. I killed the beast king and the sin of pride that was with them when we caught up. The sin of lust escaped." Tears started flowing from my eyes.

"What happened in the town?" Arsane's voice boomed.

My claws dug into the oracle stone. "I became the beast queen because I killed the beast king. The demon injured Lexia in the fight. Afterwards I commanded all the beastkin in the town to run away and return to the Wild Kingdom. I also gave them the order to pass on the title of beast king to someone named Grant. There were people still alive in the town when I left it."

Mom held me tighter. "Give her a moment. She needs to calm down."

"Keep going," Arsane barked.

"After the beastkin ran away, the Crimson Tide showed up and accused us of killing everyone in the town. Their leader even bribed Penny to join them. Dinar put everyone to sleep except Barney and me. I killed him when he attacked me. Then..." My heart pounded in my chest. I don't know why, but the words flowed from my mouth. I needed to tell the story. "Then the Rider of Pain arrived. We attacked him. He killed Anna's angel and Silver, and he crippled Penny in the fight. He stabbed Daric through the stomach and nearly drowned me. I was about to die..."

All words died in my throat as I fell to my hands and knees, sobbing.

"Enough!" Mom's word shook the room. She sat on the ground next to me. "It's okay. I've got you now." She pulled me into a hug, where I wept on her bosom.

"We're not done yet." Arsane stomped her foot.

"Yes, we are," Aenwyn said in a cold, threatening voice. "We'll finish hers later. But I think that should be enough for you as it is."

The scratching of pen on paper finally ceased, but I hugged my mother as I continued to shed tear after tear.

MORAL COMPASS

Mom lifted me off the floor and carried me out of the room and into another one. Aenwyn followed behind us. The nameplate on the door said, "Arsane."

"She won't mind if we borrow her office for the time being," Mom whispered as she sat me down on a chair. "How are you feeling, honey?"

I trembled in the chair, unable to focus on anything specific. "Scared."

Two chairs slid next to mine. "That's a completely normal reaction." Aenwyn grabbed my hands and pulled them towards her as she sat down across from me. "I was hoping to have this conversation with you in a couple of years."

"What conversation?" I sniffled as I looked at my captain.

Aenwyn frowned. "The near-death experience talk. And the fallen squad-mates talk."

Mom sat in the chair next to me. "It's a talk every knight has at least once. Those that don't have this talk usually raise other warning signs."

I wrapped my tail around my waist and flattened my ears. I pulled my hands away from Aenwyn and hugged my legs to my chest. "It's...

I don't know." My mind went in every direction without letting me catch up.

"Dying is terrifying. You stood up against the sins of wrath, gluttony, lust, and pride. You were injured by the sins of wrath and gluttony, but you recovered. And both times you didn't have time to see your death coming." Mom scratched my back again. "I've experienced something similar. It was when I met Midas. You remember that elf I told you about that dueled me to a stalemate?"

I nodded. *I don't remember what you said her name was, but you said she was one of four magic users on your level while you were at your peak.*

Mom moved her hand to scratch the base of my neck. "Well, that fight left us both magically fatigued, bordering on magical exhaustion. As it happened, we fought near the throat of the world, and—"

"What caused the fight?" I interrupted.

Mom shook her head. "That's not important. Just know that it was one of my many youthful blunders." She paused scratching me for a moment to look past me with hurt in her eyes.

I shouldn't have asked. My ears drooped as I lowered my head. "Sorry."

Mom smiled softly. "You don't need to apologize. It's in the past." She ruffled my hair in between my ears. My heart slowed to a normal beat. "As I was saying, the state of the mountainside after our duel was precarious, at best. A rock slide started, and we couldn't run away fast enough. It didn't kill us immediately. Massive rocks trapped us, and we couldn't use magic to move them. The two of us also got several broken bones."

"How did you get out?" I released my legs and leaned forward, my tail wagging.

"After three days of lying trapped, we recovered enough magic to free ourselves. But neither one of us could use healing magic. So while we were free, we were exhausted, starving, and dehydrated." Mom's voice never wavered. "The rocks destroyed our supplies. Midas and his company were headed to the monastery near the top of the mountain, where they happened upon us after we sat there for another two days. We thought we were going to die there because we needed to feed our egos. They nursed us back to health, and we followed them up the mountain as thanks for saving our lives. The other elf went back to the Osarin Kingdom while I joined Midas's company."

"So you two never fought again?" My tail hit the back of the chair as I wagged it vigorously.

"That's not the point of the story." Aenwyn poked the top of my head. "She said she was starving for days, unable to do anything but face her mortality."

"Oh." *I guess I got caught up in the story.* "That sounds terrible. How did you deal with it?"

"Up to that point, I thought I didn't need anyone else. But the experience put everything in perspective for me. And the bonds I formed with the Excelsior members became irreplaceable." Mom scratched behind my ear. "Having others to lean on is the most important thing you can ever have as a knight."

"Thanks, Mom." I hugged her. "I guess I failed to earn that bed, didn't I? Silver never made it home. There's a pit in my stomach. He was nice and smart, and I wish I'd gotten to know him better."

Mom's smile disappeared. "That's something I can't help you with."

"I'm going to finish up the debriefings for your friends as quickly as possible. Then I'll bring them here so you can talk about it." Aenwyn stood up and placed a tiny bag on the chair. It jingled with the sound of metal coins. "When you guys are ready to leave, I want you to go get her some fresh bacon and take her fishing. Don't bring her back until she's ready."

"How long do we get?" I asked.

"How long do you need?" The elf turned and put her hands on her hips.

I scratched the back of my head. "What if we don't come back until the end of the water season?"

Aenwyn smiled as she relaxed. "Then you come back in the fire season. We'll make sure your training is still up to par and then let you deal with what you need to. You're fifteen; don't rush this." A look of concern replaced her smile. "And if you come back and decide that you don't want to be a knight, then we can talk about that, too. I would much rather you learn that this life isn't for you now rather than later, when you'll regret everything. Take this time to think and talk things over with your family and friends. Let them help you."

"Whatever decision you make, we'll do everything to help you." Mom lightly squeezed my knee. "Will you be alright if I leave you alone? I want to sit in on your sister's debriefing. Just to ask her some questions."

"Yeah, just send her here afterwards." I wiped the tears from my face. "I imagine she's getting pretty antsy with me being gone for as long as I have. She's a bit clingy."

Mom stroked her chin as she looked at the ceiling. "I wonder if that's a family trait?"

"Hey!" I glared at my mother and captain as they giggled and stood up.

Mom leaned over and kissed my forehead. "I love you, sweetie."

"I know, Mom. I love you too."

I watched the two women leave. After they closed the door, I picked up the coin pouch and gave it a testing toss. It sounded like there were plenty of coins to cover my pay while I was gone. Opening it up and counting them proved that there was ten percent extra.

She really wants me to go on that fishing trip. I really want to go on that fishing trip. After I put the coins back, I noticed a basket in a corner of the room with rolls of paper in it. *Silver's aptitude was basket weaving.* Tears flowed down my face.

Silver will never go on a fishing trip again. He died, and I could have joined him. Daric should have joined him. But I told Victor to bring Golditress to save him. Why? Why did I suggest that we save Daric? Was it all the heat of the moment? Do I really care about him? He really isn't all bad, just misguided. He tries his hardest to follow his morals. We really are two different people. He's able to forgive, and he does it so willingly too. Me? I'm quick to kill for any infraction.

I buried my face in my hands. *I'm a hypocrite. All this time I've been afraid of people killing me, and now I have the audacity to kill so eagerly. If I'm going to kill someone, why shouldn't I expect them to defend themselves just as fiercely? It's a dog-eat-dog world.* I looked at my claws. I admired their sharpness and recalled their reliability as I flexed them.

Something stirred in my soul. *If people want to kill me, I'll kill them back. If anyone wants to hurt me, my friends, my family, or my pack, I won't give them an option. They will die. Man, woman, beast-kin, elf, orc, demon, rider or the demon king himself. It doesn't matter. I will protect what's mine. Daric can forgive, but I cannot—I will not.*

I could still smell my mother's scent on the chair next to me. *But I just can't be a mindless killing machine. There are others like Fina out there. There are people in the world worth being nice to. For every person like Avollea, there's a person like Mom. Why do people have to be so complicated?*

I picked up the chair in front of me and slammed it to the ground. Several larger pieces remained intact, while the legs splintered and scattered tiny pieces of wood across the floor. *Why can't life be more simple?* I grabbed what was left of the chair. Growling, I repeatedly bashed what was left against the ground until it was nothing more than splinters.

I panted and growled at the pile of debris.

The door opened. Lexia and Mom were standing in the doorway, staring at me.

I looked back at the remnants of the chair. "Sorry," I said as I flopped into the chair behind me.

Mom sighed and guided Lexia in. "No more." I looked up at her. "You're not to be left alone again. Not until I know you're fine. And I mean completely fine."

Lexia swiveled her head between my mother and me. "What are you talking about?"

Mom pointed to the pile of debris. "That was a chair when I left. I know you heard her growling on the way here. Your sister needs help. Something is eating at her. Hopefully now she sees it too." She gave me a sad look. "Honey, if you didn't want me to go, you just needed to say so."

Lexia sat next to me. "What's wrong?"

I turned to look out the window. *Can they understand? Do I know what to say?*

"Talk to us," Mom said. She used her magic to pull the last remaining chair towards me and sat down.

Here goes nothing. "I'm torn." I took a deep breath. "Every time I think about how to deal with people, it always frustrates me." I curled up in the chair as much as I could. "My instincts want everything to be simple. One half of me wants to kill every threat, then proceeds to view almost everyone as a threat. The other half wants to believe that there are others like you, Mom. People like Fina, Aenwyn, and Daric." *I can't believe I just said that.*

"Daric?" Mom flinched slightly.

"He's a good guy, underneath it all. And I don't mean that he's someone I want to mate with. No, he's moral. He's someone who will do the right thing because it's the right thing and for no other reason. Sure, if you showered him with praise, he would accept it, but even without fame and wealth, he would do the right thing. It's like he can't do the easy or wrong thing." My ears went flat. "Not like me. I'm quick to kill. And honestly, I enjoy the kill, the rush of proving my superiority. It's not as bad as my addiction to hunting, but it's there."

"What are you saying?" Lexia's voice quivered.

I looked at my sister. "My moral compass is broken. Or at least I can't read it. I need someone to help me."

"Are you suggesting that you stay with Daric? It sounds like you admire something about him." Mom pushed the chairs side by side with her magic. I could feel the chair beneath me shift, and the sides of the three chairs folded downward. After she turned the three chairs into a bench, Mom pulled the two of us close. "There are good people and bad people out there. Nothing will change that."

"I will always be there for you, Lucia." Lexia nuzzled my arm. "If you need me to help you see right from wrong, I can do that."

I took a deep breath. "Unfortunately, Lexia, you can't. You're too biased towards me. You sold your freedom for my life. Because of that, I had to fight you. Don't make me go through that again."

Lexia slumped against me. "But why Daric? It looked like you couldn't stand him."

I carefully petted my sister. "It's because I can't stand him that he's better suited to the job. Since I destroyed any dreams of him becoming my mate, our relationship can be strictly professional. Feelings and biases won't interfere with his judgment."

My stomach growled, and I stared at it. *Now isn't the time.*

Mom laughed. "I see something still hasn't changed." She pushed Lexia and me into a seated position. "We can continue this talk later. How about we go get you some bacon? When's the last time you've eaten?"

My tail wagged at the mention of bacon.

Lexia glanced at my tail and back at me. "What's it about bacon that you like so much?"

"It's the best meat there is," I said with a grin.

Lexia pouted for a moment before smiling. "I guess I'll have to try some of this bacon of yours, then."

I jumped up. "You're going to love it." I ran out of the room and got halfway to the stairs before I noticed they weren't following me.

When I neared the doorway, I heard Lexia talking. "Why did you do that?"

I stopped and focused on listening to them. "She needs a distraction," Nora replied. "The healing process won't happen in a single sitting. It takes days or even weeks. A sense of normality helps ease the pain."

"You make the perfect mother for her," Lexia mused. "It's easy to see how much you care for her. Our mother can rest easy knowing you treated her as if she were your own. I guess her living here wasn't a true waste. But it seems I have a lot of time to make up for."

"She may not have been born to me, but I don't see why that should make a difference."

Alright, enough of the mushy talk. I ran into the room and grabbed both of their wrists. "Come on. Let's go."

As I pulled them out of the room, I saw Mom wave her hand at the chairs, and they returned to the way we found them, except for the one I obliterated. *My bad.*

I turned my head to glance at my mother. "Thanks, Mom."

"Any time, honey." Mom let a single tear run down her cheek.

50

MORE BACON, MORE FAMILY

As we walked downstairs, we saw everyone else still sitting and waiting to be debriefed. Daric looked as melancholic as ever while he ignored everything around him and stared at the table. Gifford was missing, so I assumed they were debriefing him.

I froze as I saw everyone. Mom and Lexia ushered me out the door after they told the other beastkin to wait where they were until we came to pick them up.

"We're getting you bacon, remember?" Mom nudged me down the street. "Do you have the money?"

I handed Mom the pouch of money. "Here." *I'm never any good at holding on to money.* Lexia stared at the pouch. "Remember, things are different here. If you want to stay, you'll need to follow the rules."

Lexia flattened her ears. "So everything I've known about how things should be done is wrong?"

Mom arched an eyebrow. "That's an odd way of saying it, but I imagine this is going to be quite the culture shock for you. And I hope you never have to experience it again. But you can look to your sister for motivation. She learned the rules"—she gave me a wink—"after some adjustments. If she can do it, so can you."

Culture shock is a mild way of putting it. And it was only a part of what I was dealing with. The culture was the simple part.

I grabbed my sister's hand. "It's okay. I'll guide you through the streets. Just ignore the stares as best you can. Mom was right, they go away eventually."

Lexia glanced around. I could see her noticing the stares I'd grown accustomed to years ago.

"Focus on me. They won't do anything. You're just new. And new attracts attention."

"Are beastkin rare in this kingdom?" Lexia locked eyes with me.

I shrugged as I started leading her down the street. "When I first arrived, everyone said that I was the only beastkin in the entire city. So, very rare."

Lexia walked even closer to me. She grabbed my elbow with her other arm. I could hear Mom following us. I kept everyone moving towards my favorite butcher shop. The orange in the sky told me the sun was about to set, but the streets were still bustling. Thankfully, everyone stayed out of my arm's reach, and eventually we made it to our destination.

"Lucia, good to see you again," a familiar raspy voice called out as I entered.

I turned and saw the grizzled butcher with his arms out wide. His face looked like he hadn't shaved in a few days, which meant he had a full, bushy beard many men would envy. He wore his usual leather apron, and I could smell the blood on it.

"Afternoon, Hugue." I gave him a toothless smile.

My sister followed me in, and Hugue's eyes went wide. "There are two of you?"

I presented my sister. "This is my sister, Lexia. Lexia, this is the man I sell my extra meat to, Hugue. Don't worry about him. He's nice." I waved my hand at the man. "Mostly because I'm both his best supplier and customer."

"Hi." My sister released my arm just long enough to wave her hand at the man.

"Am I right to assume that she's of the same dietary disposition as you?" The butcher rubbed his hands together. The greed in his eyes was unmistakable.

Lexia's tail flicked back and forth behind her. "My sister is a primal. I'm not."

Hugue stared at my sister without blinking.

She sighed. "While I enjoy the taste of meat a lot, I don't require it like my sister."

Hugue deflated. "Oh."

Mom walked in and held up the coin purse Aenwyn gave me. "If it makes you feel better, how about some bacon for Lucia? She just returned from her first mission, so we're going to celebrate a little tonight. How much do you have?"

"One moment, I'll go check." The butcher jumped as he took off for the back room.

I smiled and winked at my sister, then I turned to my mother. "How much of the bear meat did you sell to him?"

"About half," Mom replied as she shrugged. "I don't eat nearly as much as you do. Even when I was younger, I couldn't even come close to your appetite."

"What can I say? I'm a growing woman."

My comment earned a chuckle from Lexia. Mom shook her head. "Don't give me that. You're done growing. I know better. It's hard to remember sometimes, but looking at you, you can't possibly grow up anymore. You're probably taller than everyone else in this city."

I tilted my head to the side. "So? Maybe it's my aptitudes that give me such a high metabolism."

"Metabolism?" Lexia interrupted.

I flinched. *Oops. That's a no-no word. Deflect, deflect.* "I eat a lot because I need to eat a lot."

"You're different." Lexia leaned in closer to me. "There's something different. It's like you're more relaxed. You didn't act like this while you were in the Wild Kingdom."

I glanced at Mom. *Help me, please?* I hoped she would see my wordless plea.

Lexia turned to face my mother too.

"I wish I knew," I said. "Honestly, if you hadn't pointed it out, I would never have guessed that I'm acting differently."

Mom smiled softly as she reached up and stroked my hair. "You're relaxed here. This is your home. To you, nothing here is dangerous. Even now, I can see the difference between the two of you. Lexia's eyes are constantly moving and her tail is stiff. You're the opposite. Your eyes aren't moving much while your tail is constantly wagging."

I turned to look at my tail and saw it wagging slightly. "When did you pick up on that?"

And I guess I really missed home. Anna was right, I was homesick. Absence makes the heart grow fonder. Now I see that I really don't have it that bad here. Now Lexia's in my place. So I'll have to make sure she knows that I'm here for her at all times.

Mom glared at me. "I'm your mother. If I hadn't learned that your mood is tied closely to your tail, then I'm a terrible parent. Your emotions have always been easy to read. It's something I saw fairly quickly."

"It might have something to do with the fact that I was working too," I mused.

"I have three whole pigs' bellies." Hugue interrupted our little chat by bursting into the room carrying three large slabs of uncut bacon. "Oh, did I interrupt something?"

I drooled instantly as the wonderful scent of pork belly filled the room. "Give me." I held out my arms as I walked towards the meat like a possessed woman.

"How many?" Hugue smiled.

"All of it." I wasn't thinking about anything other than my stomach. My stomach demanded food, and I was happy to give it bacon.

Mom jumped in front of me. "We'll take them. Now quickly take them to the back and wrap them up before she loses control."

As Hugue retreated to the back, Lexia's laugh halted my movements. Mom and I turned towards her. She was clutching her stomach and bent over, laughing harder than I had ever seen from her. Tears started flowing from her eyes.

I looked at Mom and shrugged.

"You're something else," Lexia said in between laughs. She gasped, only to resume laughing again. We stared at the woman until she calmed down. "I didn't know you could act like that."

"Why couldn't I?" I asked.

Lexia wiped the tears from her eyes. "All this time, I thought you were just a serious person. You were caring, but always more serious than anything else."

Mom looked at me and giggled. "She's always pulling a stunt like this at least once a week. It's refreshing to see in between her bouts of rage."

"Hey!" I stomped my foot. "Whose side are you on?"

"So is this what having a family is like?" Lexia's voice was quiet. "Darmin and Maggi weren't like this. This is nice." Mom and I stared at her. *Right, she was orphaned too. Others raised her. I never asked about how she was brought up.* "Can I join?"

A tear escaped my eye. "I already consider you my family."

Lexia turned to my mother. "Can I call you Mom?"

She's jumping head-first, isn't she? If it makes her feel safer, then I support this decision.

Mom burst into tears and ran to hug my twin sister. "I would be happy to accept that responsibility."

Mom and Lexia hugged, so I joined in and gave them one big hug. Mom and Lexia just kept crying. We enjoyed our first family hug.

I heard Hugue walk into the room. I glared and bared my fangs at him, but I didn't growl. *Don't ruin the moment, you idiot.*

He gently placed the wrapped bacon on the counter, clamped his mouth shut, and stood quietly.

Good boy.

5 1

PERCEPTION CHECK

We ended the family hug when a human couple walked into the shop. They gave us strange looks. Mom paid for the bacon and handed the three slabs off to Lexia. *I'm not trusted with bacon. Not after that one time I ate the whole thing before we got home.* Mom told me to lead Lexia home, but she wouldn't let us leave until I promised her I wouldn't leave Lexia's side.

She went back to the courthouse to get Gifford, Victor, and Fina.

Our walk through the streets was easing up as people filtered out and settled in for the night. While we were getting close to the north gate, something in the air caught my attention. I stopped Lexia midstride.

"Do you smell that?" I took another sniff. "It's some kinda perfume. A sweet and smoky one."

"I don't know how you can smell anything here," Lexia grumbled. "Everything stinks and everything is so loud."

I gave my sister a sympathetic look. "Yeah, blocking it out took years. Although it's impossible to ignore entirely. But there's a perfume smell in the air. I've smelled it before, but I can't remember where."

Lexia looked around. "Do you know where it's coming from or where the scent went?"

I scowled at my sister. "That's easy enough to do in the wilderness. But in the city it's impossible."

"Do you just want to ignore it? Maybe it will come back to you later." Lexia's eyes still darted around.

Mom was right; Lexia is very uncomfortable here. How did I miss that? "Come on, let's get you someplace quiet." I hooked my arm with hers as I led her down the street. "It's going to bug me all day. Perfect memory must be nice."

"Not as cool as being super strong and fast," Lexia said as she huddled as close to me as she could.

"You're the brains, I'm the brawn. Together, we're unstoppable." I laughed at my statement. Lexia joined in as we walked home.

A man was walking down the street, his cane clicking against the stones of the city road. I recognized him as Tobey. Perfectly tailored clothes in pristine condition made the man stand out in such a location. But he leaned heavily on his cane, something I didn't remember him having before. His face also looked like it hadn't aged in the years since he gave me my first job.

How he survived being investigated when the sin of wrath was summoned in the city years ago, I'll never know. After all, it was his henchman that hired the goons to sacrifice me as a means to summon the demon. *He probably bribed someone. No, they would use the oracle stone to find out.*

I held up a hand to stop Lexia. Tobey stopped at an edge of an alley and looked around. *He's trying to hide something. I'm really curious what.* Tobey disappeared into the alley, and I moved to follow him.

"Do we have to do this here?" Tobey asked in an agitated voice. "I would prefer if we weren't in the open like this."

It sounds like he's up to something interesting. The walls of the alley made hearing him so much easier.

I turned to my sister and put a finger to my lips. "Stay quiet. There's something going on over there." I pointed with my thumb down the alley.

"But Mom said you need to stay with me," Lexia responded in a harsh whisper.

I heard a second voice. It was deeper while carrying a feminine feel. "I'm not going into your buildings and separating myself from my power. Not after seeing those girls in this city."

Now I have to know. But Lexia's here. I pursed my lips. "Fine, but stay behind me and keep quiet. If I say run, run. Got it?"

Lexia nodded.

We moved towards the alley. I poked my head around just enough to see two figures facing one another. A woman stood half a head taller than Tobey. She dressed in loose silks that flaunted her attractively athletic body. Her dark skin matched well with her long, flowing locks of slightly curly black hair. My instincts tried to push me into attacking her the moment I saw her.

"You've been useful for some time now, but it seems your time is coming to an end." Her voice was full of contempt. "My plan worked thanks to you keeping the knights away from that town. But you didn't warn me there was a pair of dangerous beastkin living in this city."

Tobey flinched. He lifted his free hand. "There's only one beastkin in this city, and she went to the north. There's no way she had any reason to be in Alelry while you attacked it. The plan should have worked. You assured me your allies could get the beastkin to attack."

"The plan did work." The lady poked Tobey's chest, and each time she poked him, he took a step back until he hit the wall. "But there was a problem. As soon as your people summoned the rider, a group of your humans attacked him. They were joined by a wolf beastkin. I thought I sent the silver-furred beast away when she claimed to be the beast queen. But no, she followed the humans. The rider almost dealt with them until another beastkin killed him with the largest spear of ice I've ever seen. I doubt the sin of sloth could make something that large. It was a second beastkin that made it. She looked almost identical to the other. Now both beastkin are here, so I have yet another complication to plan around."

"I leaked the information about the blood anchor, just like you wanted." Tobey attempted to make himself even smaller. "Midas acted just like you said he would, and they even took Lucia and kept her busy. How could she even be that far south? Why?"

Alarms rang out in my head. *I've never seen that lady before. How did she send me away? I talked with an old lady... She's not human, is she?* I turned to Lexia. *I can't just let this go. If I try to find another knight, they may leave the city. Lexia can't fight; she's still recovering.*

The woman started pacing. "I didn't bother to ask. Because if I did, that would have been stupid. I'm not like Lust. I can't make myself disappear. I'm capable of only changing my appearance."

Yup, that confirms it. She's a demon.

"It has to be someone else. There's no way it's Lucia." Tobey quivered against the wall. "I've done everything you've ordered, and I've told you everything I know. There's nothing else I can do."

"Then I think it's time you were retired. Loose ends and all that." The woman leaned back and smirked. "Maybe I'll find someone more important. Maybe this time they'll have a backbone. You were greedy enough to get my attention, but you lack the spine to be of any long-term use."

I have to save him so he can tell me more of his secrets. If he's been involved in dealings with demons, he'll know something about their plans. But now they're about to turn on him. I definitely don't have time to get help.

"Wait!" Tobey held his arms over his head. "I can still be useful. You still need me."

The woman laughed. "No, we don't. It feels like Envy has completed her mission. So that means we only have two anchors left to create. I think we'll manage."

The woman lifted her arm to punch Tobey.

Time's up! I pushed Lexia back as I sprinted towards the demon. She didn't act like she heard me, but as I pounced to tackle her, her head snapped towards me. Panic filled her eyes.

While I was midair, the woman and Tobey switched places with neither one moving their feet. My claws dug into Tobey's chest. His shout likely alerted everyone in the area.

I saw the woman look down the alley to see Lexia standing at the entrance, still holding the bundle of bacon. "I'm not returning today," the woman mumbled to herself.

I ripped my claws out of Tobey, causing him to shout again, and pounced towards the woman. She dropped below my attempt to catch her. I looked down as I sailed over her. It seemed like the ground melted around her as she sank into it.

When I touched the ground, I turned and reached my hand out to grab her hair. I grabbed nothing but the air as she finished submerging herself.

I growled as I slammed my hand where her head had been moments before. The woman didn't come back up, and I couldn't hear her moving underneath me. There was an unmistakable scent of perfume in the air.

She was definitely that old woman. Is she a sin? If so, which one?

"What happened? Why did you do that? Who was that woman? Who's he?" A torrent of questions flowed from my sister's mouth as she strode towards me.

The corners of my vision turned red as I stood up. "That was probably another demon. As for what it was doing in the city? I don't know." I growled as I looked at Tobey. "Him? Oh, he's someone who is in for a world of hurt."

"There really are two of you," Tobey moaned as he clutched the spots my claws had dug into.

"He knows you?" Lexia eyed the man cautiously.

I turned to face my sister. "Yeah, I kinda worked for him for a day."

"And then you ruined everything," Tobey grumbled under his breath.

I'm going to enjoy this.

The sound of Tobey's cane tapping the ground and his grunting as he stood up was my signal. Without looking, I kicked my leg back into his gut.

He collapsed in a heap, wheezing as he tried to fill his lungs with air, his cane rolling on the ground.

That felt good. "You're under arrest for colluding with demons and conspiring to commit treason. Let's throw in resisting arrest while we're at it." As I listed the charges, I heard Tobey collapse to the ground, likely unconscious. "If anyone asks, he resisted arrest. Okay?" I gave my sister a wink.

"Okay." Lexia looked between Tobey and me. "Are you going to tell me what that was about?"

I shrugged. "The short version is because I'm a knight, I'm responsible for the safety of everyone in the kingdom. Tobey's actions"—I pointed to the man in question—"have and would have endangered many lives. So I put a stop to it before he could implement them."

"It didn't sound like he was planning anything." Lexia tilted her head as she looked at me. "It sounded like the demon did all the planning."

I slumped my shoulders. "Okay, maybe there were some personal reasons too. Because he's such a high-profile member of the city, I need something serious to charge him with. Questioning him would be impossible otherwise." I hooked my toe-claws around the cane and kicked it up behind me. Without looking, I caught the stick with one hand. "He served the demons, and he can tell us everything they're planning. Now I have proof and a witness: you."

"That doesn't make any sense." Lexia pouted. "What do you have to do now? Weren't we supposed to go to your home?"

"Yeah," I lamented. "It's alright if this doesn't make sense. Just know that he's a bad man who did bad things, and now I have proof to get him punished." I scooped Tobey up and threw him over my shoulder. "We just have to go back to the courthouse one last time."

"Okay. If you say so." My ears itched at the sorrow in Lexia's voice.

"We'll have some alone time together. Don't worry. This will be the last thing, I promise." I gave my sister a toothy grin.

Lexia pouted. "I'll hold you to that."

52

QUESTIONS, QUESTIONS

The stares we'd received to this point paled beside the ones we received as I carried Tobey over my shoulder. *It's my first day back and I'm making a scene. By the looks of things, people remember me enough not to stop me.*

We walked into the courthouse with Mom and the other beastkin staring at me. I didn't see the others from Daric's group or Captain Aenwyn. Although the shocked look on Mom's face was entertaining enough to earn a giggle from me.

"What's going on?" Mom hurried over and grabbed Tobey. "Who's this?"

I tapped Tobey's back. "I overheard Tobey talking with a woman, whom I believe was actually a demon. They were talking about the city that was attacked and how everything was planned, including the summoning of the rider. He's under arrest for conspiring with demons and treason."

The other beastkin stood back, watching with indifference. Mom's mouth opened and closed repeatedly, soundlessly.

I heard footsteps coming down the steps. Aenwyn walked in with a stack of paper in her hands.

She stopped and stared at me the moment she reached the bottom of the stairs. "Are they alright? What happened?" Her expression changed from shocked to a more sour one. "What did they say to you?"

I glared at my captain. "Tobey is under arrest."

"Tobey? As in Tobey Coinwhisper?" The shock returned to Aenwyn's face.

"Why is he unconscious?" Mom asked as she inspected his face.

"He resisted arrest," Lexia answered before me.

I rolled my eyes. *Thanks, Lexia. You were really eager for that one, weren't you?*

"You understand what you're doing, right?" Aenwyn asked.

I growled. "Have I ever brought anyone in who didn't deserve it?"

My captain stared into the distance for a moment. "No. However, you have brought them in worse condition than should be expected."

I could feel Tobey stirring on my shoulder. "Well, it looks like someone is waking up."

Tobey woke with a jerk. "What? Put me down!"

He flailed and started rolling off my shoulder. Before I could stop him, he grabbed my hair. I screamed and put a hand on the base of the hair he was pulling, and Tobey swung down. After I lowered myself to allow Tobey's feet to touch the ground, I grabbed his hand and crushed it. I could hear the bones snapping and grinding, even through Tobey's howls.

"Don't pull my hair." My teeth were inches from the man's face as he collapsed to his knees. It took every bit of my control not to bite his face off.

I threw Tobey's arm back at him, and he cradled his disfigured hand like it was a baby.

"Alright, let's get him in a cell," Aenwyn said as she pointed to the doorway leading to the temporary cells. "This can at least wait until tomorrow."

Mom waved her hand, and Tobey rose from the ground with her magic. "You've done enough. I'll take care of this. Go home. Take everyone with you. You're not supposed to be working right now."

Tobey looked around frantically. "Cells? Why? Do you know who I am? I'm not some common criminal."

"You're right. No, you're so much worse, traitor." *I might as well make this as official as possible. The captain's watching.* "As a knight in the service of the Kingdom of Rophmna, by the power granted me by Captain Aenwyn of The Maidens, Tobey Coinwhisper, you are under arrest. I, Lucia Silverbreeze, am charging you with colluding with demons and conspiring to commit treason."

"And resisting arrest." Lexia hopped up and wagged her tail.

"Thanks, Lexia." I gave my sister a soft smile. *She's adorable.*

Tobey's jaw clamped closed so hard that his teeth clicked.

He knows he's done for. I gave the man a toothy grin as Mom used her magic to carry him to a cell. Something in me wanted to see him placed behind bars, so I followed them.

Tobey hung his head as Mom placed him on the simple bed. Aenwyn closed the door and locked it. She gave it a quick pull to test it, and the door didn't budge.

"Well, I guess that means your usefulness is forever spent." The woman from the alley's voice sounded from every direction. Tobey stiffened as he looked around for the source of the voice. "We can't have you spoiling all our plans now. Loose ends are such a problem."

The stone wall at the back of Tobey's cell parted like a pair of doors opening. The dark-skinned woman strode in confidently. I could see Mom charging up her magic as Aenwyn scrambled to open the door. The woman in Tobey's cell grabbed him and hauled him to his feet with a flick of her wrist.

"Move!" Mom threw her arm forward.

Aenwyn turned and dove to the side. I rushed behind the magic and grabbed the door. Growling, I pulled on it, the metal locking mechanism groaning as I did.

The woman half spun backwards as Mom's magic struck her.

I froze as I saw the woman's face. A chunk of her head had gone missing as she wrapped her arms around Tobey, who stood whimpering. The blood and bones that I was expecting to see weren't present. There wasn't even exposed flesh. Instead, it looked like the woman was made of light-brown rock, but her skin clearly covered the rock.

She stared at us with one eye and half a face, grinning. "Nice try,

Nora." Her voice gained a grating quality to it. "But this one's mine, and I always keep what's mine."

A swirl of reddish-purple smoke flowed from behind the creature. Tobey screamed as both beings in the cell were pulled into the rapidly forming cloud. And just as quickly as his screams began, they ended. The cloud then went from swirling like an egg standing up to collapsing and spilling out in every direction. Mom pulled me and the captain away from it.

"What is that?" I asked. "What was she?"

Mom continued to stare at the smoke as it slowly thinned out. "I don't know what that smoke is, but I don't want to know what it will do." She took a deep breath, her shoulders slumping slightly. "That woman was a demon. The sin of greed, specifically. She likely took Tobey to the demon realm."

As the smoke thinned out entirely, I could smell the distinct scent of cherries. *That's an odd scent for a demonic portal. Shouldn't they smell like fire or brimstone?*

"She knew your name." Aenwyn turned to face Nora. "She also said she had plans. What could she be doing?"

I scratched the floor with a toe-claw. "They're bringing the demon king to this world." I could feel my captain's gaze lock on to me. "What's worse is that she said they needed two more anchors and they'll be done."

Aenwyn turned my head to face her. "How much did you hear?" My ears twitched at the urgency in her voice. "Tell me everything."

I nodded my head towards the entrance, where my sister was standing. "She's better at it than me. She was there." Aenwyn let me go, and we turned to Lexia. "Lexia, can you please repeat what the woman said in the alley? Try to summarize it if you can."

Lexia stepped up with a blank look in her eyes. "She said that the man was no longer useful; he didn't warn her about two dangerous beastkin living in the city; their plan worked; a group of humans accompanied by a silver-furred beast she thought she'd sent away killed the rider they summoned; she doubted a sin of sloth could create a spear of ice as large as I created." *Okay, maybe I shouldn't have worded it so loosely. She's repeating everything.* "Then she talked about finding someone else; he was greedy but didn't have a spine; someone named Envy completed their mission and they had only two anchors left; she wasn't going to return today—"

"Alright, that's enough." I held up my hands to stop my sister's rambling.

Captain Aenwyn stared at my sister, blinking several times as her mouth hung agape. "I will never get over how emotionlessly a person with the memorization aptitude recites information." Her words were barely audible.

Mom crossed her arms, looking deep in thought. "We have a problem."

"Yeah, several." Aenwyn flopped in the chair. "The demon knew who you were. That's probably only the beginning of what Tobey told her. And now we'll never know how long he's been feeding them information or how much. When things go wrong, they all go wrong at the same time."

I turned my head and flicked my ears toward the captain. "What do you mean?"

She rubbed her face with a hand before giving me a forced smile. "You're going on leave. This isn't something for you to worry about. Leave this to officials and those in charge. You've done something incredibly important. Let others take it from here. Enjoy your fishing trip. That's an order."

I could see the tired look in her eyes. "Will you do me a favor?" Aenwyn nodded. "Tell everything to Daric and Midas."

"Why those two?" Aenwyn asked. "Midas is retired. And why Daric?"

"Please?" *I don't want to explain it.*

Aenwyn smirked. "Only if you go home now."

I tapped my toe-claw as I crossed my arms. "Aren't I the bargainer?"

Mom placed a hand on my back. "How do you like the taste of your own medicine?"

I laughed as I gave Mom a hug. I turned to see Lexia staring at us with longing and excitement in her eyes. "What are you still doing over there? Get in here. You're family too."

Lexia gasped before she bounded over, tail wagging, and joined in the hug.

Mom waved her hand, and the opening the demon had made in the wall closed itself. "Let's go, girls." She ushered us towards the exit. "We should get home before dark."

"Why?" Lexia looked up at Mom as we walked into the entryway.

Mom ran her finger through Lexia's hair. "Because you've had a long day, and I can't see in the dark like you can."

"Uh..." Gifford stared at us, dumbfounded. "Did I miss something?"

Lexia's tail wagged behind her as she looked about to burst from excitement. "We're staying with my sister and new mother."

Gifford's left eye started twitching as his breathing stopped.

Lexia bounced over to him and scratched his chin. "Come on, it'll be fun. Even you know that it's not a bad idea."

Gifford slumped his shoulders as he sighed. "I guess you're not wrong."

Lexia giggled at her mate's surrender.

"I adopted Lucia years ago. Since Lexia wanted to be part of a family, she joined this one." Mom held a hand out towards Gifford. "It makes sense that my daughter's sister wants to be part of the same family. If you aren't comfortable, you can just call me Nora. There's no need to worry. Am I to understand that you two are already married?"

"We're bonded." Lexia nuzzled Gifford's shoulder. "He's my mate." She threw the bacon into his arms. "Can you carry these, love?"

"Sure," Gifford answered absentmindedly, not taking his gaze away from Mom.

"We can talk more in the morning. I imagine you, Fina, and Lexia are tired." I waved towards the door. "For tonight, we'll work something out so that everyone is comfortable."

Victor and Fina followed us at a short distance as we traveled through the town uncontested. The sun barely tipped over the horizon and turned the sky a beautiful orange that slowly shifted to purple the farther away from the sun it got. Victor watched the sky more than he watched the people in the city.

We exited the town and headed to the farmland where our home was built. I ran ahead and opened the door for everyone. "Single line, everyone. Please make yourself as comfortable as possible. We'll get some food for dinner, and then we'll work out sleeping arrangements."

Everyone filed in except for Victor, who stood at the doorway. His eyes darted around while he fidgeted with his claws.

"You alright?" I asked as I tried to get him to look at me.

The bear continued to fidget and not look me in the eye. "Can I... I..." He took a deep breath and clasped his hands together. "I don't do buildings very well. Can I stay outside?" His voice was soft and didn't carry its usual rumble.

Is the big man claustrophobic? I guess when you barely fit in doorways, buildings don't have the same appeal to you as they do to everyone else. "Are you scared of small spaces?" I turned the bearkin around and pushed him away from the house.

"I'm not scared," Victor said as his legs locked. "No, I'm... I just really like to see the stars at night. They're always a magical sight." He looked up at the night sky. A few of the brighter stars glimmered in the night sky as the sun finished tucking itself behind the horizon. "All my life, the stars have been there for me. Not seeing them just feels like something's missing. Do you understand?"

I gave him a slight smile. "This is about Cirra, isn't it?"

He nodded.

That's actually sweet. He's still not forgotten her. Some things are hard to forget.

"I've always found glowbugs fascinating. The way they glow from their butts. How do they do it? It's not magic. It's natural, and like the glowbug, there's nothing magical about the stars." I saw Victor's mouth open, but I continued before he could get a word out. "That doesn't make it any less majestic. Actually, it makes it more mesmerizing because it's done without magic. Hold on to that feeling. Let that be an anchor to keep you tethered to reality."

"You must think I'm a coward." Victor lowered his head.

I shook my head and grabbed his hand. "Far from it." Victor's heart was beating so hard I could hear it. "When we faced that demon, you did the intelligent thing. Running away doesn't make you a coward. You came back with help. That takes more courage to return than to just keep going. Your actions saved my and Daric's lives. There's nothing I can say to tell you how thankful I am."

Victor stepped in front of me and opened his mouth, but I put a finger on his lips before a word came out.

"I know what you want to ask." I closed my eyes as I squeezed his hand just a little more. "But the answer is no. Not yet. The demon we saw today said that the demon king is almost here. If I brought a child into this world now, I wouldn't be able to help those who need me the most. My instincts really want me to have children, and the rest of me is starting to want them too. But not now. The world is too dangerous. I can't put my children in such a situation." Tears leaked from my eyes.

Victor lifted my chin with a gentle hand. I opened my eyes and stared at his blurry visage. "That's why I wish to be your mate. You are noble, caring, and strong, and your devotion to family is without equal. If you wish to wait, then I will wait however many years it takes."

Victor dropped his bag and pulled out two silver bands. He clasped one around his wrist before handing me the other.

"When you're ready, will you do me the honor of wearing this band and being my mate? I will be yours."

You're really persistent, aren't you? My inner wolf nudged my back with her snout. She walked in front of me and sat next to Victor. *You really like him too, don't you? The fact that I can see you and this isn't a dream must mean I'm going crazy doesn't it?* She shook her head. *Whatever the case is, you're going to really want kids in the future. You're pretty insistent on it already, and I haven't agreed to a mate yet.*

I looked at the bearkin. *But I guess Victor's not that bad. He's kind, honest, and it doesn't feel like I need to prove myself to him. I could do a lot worse than him. He says he was a coward, but I feel like he's more intelligent than he gives himself credit for. If I can only pick one... I* looked down at my inner wolf again. She pawed at Victor's leg, yet never touched it. *You win, again.*

I grabbed the bracelet. "You know what? Forget what I said earlier. I'll be your mate."

He just proposed to me and I said yes. I lost all control as I hugged the bear with everything I had. Tears soaked the fur on his shoulder while I wept.

Mom's going to kill him.

DINAR LET a single tear roll down her cheek as she watched the wolfkin hug the bearkin. In two hundred years, she had only married once: to her career. Being an assassin meant she couldn't afford to have a regular life. Her enemies would use such attachments to retaliate against her. This was the closest she'd ever been, watching others have normal lives, laughing, finding happiness and love.

Lucia was special. Dinar knew that. Now she knew why Midas Bloodless had ordered her to keep Lucia alive, no matter the cost. If anyone could defeat the demon king when he came, it'd be her.

Dinar turned and walked down the road to report her mission's success to Midas. A hole burned in her heart as she missed her home. One day she would go back, and she now knew someone who could help her get there.

There was just one problem. She needed to find out how extensively the demon king's cultists had infiltrated each kingdom. Given the events at the courthouse, Rophmna wasn't too bad yet. The cultists were here, but the upper government should still be clean. Brentiveil, the kingdom of dwarves, was an unknown.

Dinar placed a hand on her head as she pulled her hood up to hide her baldness. She knew exactly how corrupted Osarin was. Every time she looked in the mirror she was reminded how bad things had become before she'd found the truth. A truth she almost died for.

I've done you a favor, Lucia, and now you owe me. I'll collect one day, and you'll save the world, just like you're meant to.

53

FIRST STEPS OF HEALING

I took the band after I finished crying on Victor's chest. He didn't say a word. *Thankfully.* When I turned around, my eyes bulged and my face heated up. Mom stood in the doorway with her arms crossed. I couldn't tell who she was angrier at, me or Victor. Lexia was leaning out a window with a massive grin on her face, and her tail wagged almost as fast as my heartbeat.

How do I explain this to Mom?

My claws dug into the ground, and it was impossible for me to take another step towards my mother. My instincts poked in the back of my mind, telling me to grab Victor and run to my territory. I knew my instincts were overreacting again, but the unreadable expression on my mother's face made it hard to discredit them completely.

Mom extended an arm and curled a finger, beckoning me to come closer. My tail wrapped around my leg as my heart slammed against my chest.

She lowered her arms and stepped towards me.

"You're not in trouble... yet." Her voice was almost as emotionless as her face. There was only the slightest hint of curiosity in her tone.

Everything that scared me just disappeared. *She doesn't know what the armband means.* I walked towards her and met her halfway.

"You left wanting nothing to do with men, and now you've got one giving you jewelry." Mom smiled and held out her hand. "May I see it? And what's changed?"

I placed the silver band in her hand. "It's a promise... a promise for the future. I would be lying if I said my instincts weren't influencing me right now."

Mom gave me a quick glance before studying the bracelet. There weren't any engravings or identifying marks on it. "Believe me, I know how your instincts get about wanting to be a mother. You going into heat is an unforgettable experience." She handed the bracelet back to me. "I just don't want you rushing into it. You're not ready."

I laughed. "I agree, wholeheartedly. Getting pregnant now would be the dumbest decision I could make this year." Mom gave me an inquisitive look. I held up a finger. "After the things we heard today, and seeing how desperate the demon was to keep us from learning what Tobey knew, I need to be ready at all times." I glanced at Victor. "The demon king is coming. There's no doubt about that now."

"What makes you say that?" Mom asked.

"The demons have beaten us at every turn. Yeah, we won the first time. But they're too close to their goal and have a head start." I turned to look at Lexia. Her tail wasn't moving anymore, and she was staring at the ground. "Even though I defeated two demons and Lexia killed the rider, I don't feel like we slowed them down at all. They manipulated an entire kingdom to attack another. The sin of greed has been hiding in this kingdom for an indeterminate amount of time."

"I see." Mom looked proud. "You want to help, don't you?" I nodded. "You're not ready yet. You've been through a lot and you need some time to relax. Trust me, if the opportunity presents itself, take the time to stop. It won't do you any good to keep going as you are now."

"But—"

"What do you plan to do?" Mom interrupted me. "You've already told Captain Aenwyn everything. She's handling it. Trust her. Let others help you carry the burden. They don't want this world to suffer just as much as you. It isn't a crime to take some time off when you need it. It's obvious you need it." She smiled. "Don't you want to go fishing?"

"I'll try." My voice dropped like my head.

"How about we start with some food? Don't tell me you aren't hungry. You're always hungry." Mom led me towards the door. "I'll leave your bacon raw. Oh, does your sister like her bacon raw too?"

"You can ask her. I know she can eat raw meat, but she has tastes of her own." A smile grew on my face. I turned to Victor. "Hey, Victor. Come on in and eat. The house is big enough for me, so you'll be fine. We can figure out someplace for you to sleep outside after dinner. If that's what you want."

"Since you asked, I will." Victor rubbed his hands together as he took small steps towards the building.

"He isn't staying during the rest of the water season, just so you know," Mom whispered in my ear.

How much did she hear? Nah, it should be fine. He'll be fine. My tail wagged as I walked into the house.

With everyone in the house, everything was a bit more crowded than I remembered. Victor relaxed once he realized he wouldn't hit his head unless I threw him upward. We scrambled to get seats for everyone while Mom used her magic to stretch the table out so we'd all fit. *I guess we did only have furniture for the two of us. So are we going to need furniture for three or four? Five? I'll worry about it later.*

Lexia and I made chairs of ice while Gifford roped together some firewood to make a stool, one for him and another for Victor. Mom and Fina would sit in the chairs we had. Fina went to work in the kitchen. Mom followed her after she finished with the table. She warned us not to hit it too hard or it would break with how thin it was.

The rest of us who didn't know how to cook—*I didn't know Fina knew how to cook*—sat around the table, staring at each other awkwardly. I stashed the bracelet Victor had given me in my room next to the toy unicorn Nick gave me. That left me fidgeting with my claws as I avoided eye contact with Victor. Something about looking at him made my heart beat faster.

Lexia and Gifford sat on one side while my mother and Victor would sit at opposite ends. Mom would sit with a daughter on each side. Fina sat between Victor and me.

Once the food started coming out, it was hard to keep everyone from devouring the dishes as they came. Dinner was simple since half of us had specific diets. Victor's diet was much less restrictive than Gifford's and mine. He just needed to eat his food raw.

Lexia and Fina and their preferences for meat led to our table looking a little nutritionally one-sided. We didn't waste time talking. Everyone was too busy stuffing their faces. Mom stared at everyone, her look of concern growing with each bite we took. At one point, I was worried that we wouldn't have enough to eat.

One by one, everyone stopped eating, starting with Mom. Victor and I were the last two eating, and I even ate the last few pieces of bacon. All the blood in my body migrated to my belly to begin the colossal task of digesting the largest meal I'd had all season.

As I looked around, I noticed I wasn't the only one. I could see the look of tiredness in everyone's eyes except for Mom, who just sat there in an almost shocked state.

"You ate everything," Mom whispered as she propped her head on her arms as she rested them on the table. "When was the last time you all ate?"

"I've never been able to eat like that." Gifford patted his stomach as a grin grew on his face. "That bacon... how has something like that not found its way to the Wild Kingdom?"

I giggled. "Well, to be fair, they all came from a kingdom that's been struggling with food for the last few years."

Without moving her head, Mom glared at me. "You, what's your excuse? Even you don't eat that much after some of your most active days."

"Yeah, those last few bites may have been a bit too much." I flattened my ears and curled my tail around my waist. "But they were too good to save for later."

Mom smirked. "You would say something like that." She clapped her hands and wiggled her fingers. Then the plates all started stacking themselves in the middle of the table. "So, what are you planning on doing for sleeping arrangements?"

I curled my fingers in my tail fur. "Okay, I didn't think this through. But I couldn't just leave them without trying to help them."

"That's fine sweetie," Mom cooed. "How about Fina takes the couch?" Mom put a finger to her chin.

"Lexia and Gifford can use my bed," I announced. I lifted a finger and pointed at Gifford. "No sex. I don't want to smell that for the next few days as I'm trying to sleep. Victor wants to sleep outside." I turned to him. "There's an apple tree you can sleep next to. It should keep any snow off you if it does snow tonight."

"Where will you sleep?" Fina asked.

I shrugged. "I'll make an igloo and tough it out one more night. It's not like I need as much sleep as the rest of you, either."

Mom had a knowing grin on her face. It looked like she was trying to hold in a laugh.

"What?"

Mom's smile grew. "Your sister and her mate can keep your old bed."

"Old bed?" I stood up and knocked my chair backwards. *I didn't see another bed in my room.* "What are you talking about?"

"Follow me," Mom said as she stood up.

The others looked at each other, even more befuddled than me. I followed my mother into one of the spare rooms. The center had been cleared out to make way for a large bed frame. Being as tall as I was, my beds needed to be larger than most. This one was more than large enough to fit me with plenty of room to spare. Inside the frame was a mattress, but it wasn't made of the usual burlap my old mattress was made of; this one was made of something else.

It looked like someone braided together three different strings— one gold, one silver, and one black—then turned them into a sheet that became a mattress cover. While studying it, the entire mattress looked to be made of a single braid that weaved back and forth. *How long did it take to make that?*

I poked the mattress, careful of my claws. My finger depressed into it. I jumped as I felt almost no resistance, and when I removed my finger, it looked like the bed rippled like it was made of water.

Mom laughed. "I was told it's called a waterbed."

I looked at my mother, not bothering to hide my confusion. *That thing is filled with water?*

"They're the latest creation from the dwarven kingdom, Brentiveil. Some extra enchantments had to be placed on it for you, but it's the closest I could come to making a bed out of ice."

I turned back to the bed and placed my hand against the mattress. I pushed my hand down as far as it would go without excessive force. The mattress compressed to about the halfway point.

"It has enchantments that increase the durability, so your claws don't cut it. Give it a try." Mom waved her hand towards the bed.

Might as well try it now. I wouldn't want to be sleeping and accidentally cut it. I extended one claw and dragged it across the woven fibers. It glided across the material without causing any damage.

"It didn't snag, cut, or anything?" I stared at my claw, wondering if it had gotten dull. *No, it's still just as sharp. It's time to really test it now.*

I jumped on the bed with all my claws extended. The mattress undulated underneath me, which made me take a few moments to balance. When I looked down, all my claws were extended, but none of them penetrated the mysterious weave.

"I didn't expect you to go that far," Mom gasped. "Well, it's good to see it works."

It's durable, I'll give it that much. But is it comfortable? I retracted my claws and sat down on the bed. *This swaying motion will take some getting used to, but it's not that bad.*

Mom touched the mattress with a finger. "It also comes with the ability for you to do this."

I watched as she channeled her magic into the mattress, and I felt the bed's temperature lower. *I can control the temperature of my bed? This is the best bed ever!*

I wagged my tail as I stared at my mother. "Thank you. You're awesome." Guilt crept in. "But what did I do to earn this?"

Mom gave me a sour look. "Does a mother need a reason to spoil her child?" I returned my mother's glare with one of my own. She relaxed. "It's your reward for your first mission as a knight. You were going to succeed, but then you did so much more than anyone should ever have asked of you. You took on a rider and prevented a large-scale conflict. That deserves a reward."

"Wasn't the deal to bring everyone home safely?" Tears leaked from my eyes as I slouched forward. "Silver didn't come home. I don't deserve this. I failed."

Mom joined me on the bed and wrapped her arms around me. "Facing a rider was never part of your mission. You did everything you could, and every decision you made was good. You didn't fail. Not everything is under your control. You're not some all-powerful being." Two more sets of arms wrapped around me. I could smell that Lexia and Fina had joined us. "You're my daughter who saved countless lives with her actions."

My sobbing worsened. "But I couldn't save one that mattered."

"All lives matter, even the ones you'll never meet." Mom laid her head on my shoulder. "Silver didn't lose his life. He gave it. You didn't need to save him. He knew the risk that he might not come home, but he fought anyway. He gave his life so that others who weren't ready to give theirs wouldn't have to. He's a hero too."

"Will his family be fine without him? Did he even have a family?" More guilt wracked my heart. "I didn't know that much about him. I didn't even ask. Now I'll never get to ask. The others too. I didn't bother learning about them either. Even my own sister. I'm a selfish—"

Lexia slapped her hand over my mouth. "No! I don't want to hear it." Tears rolled down her cheeks.

"You care." Fina's quiet voice echoed in my head. "You help others too much."

"If you were selfish, would you have given up being the beast queen? Would you have run so hard to catch up and save me from my own stupidity?" Lexia's voice held a slight rumble. She stared at me with bloodshot eyes. "I will not believe you are selfish."

"You have time to address the guilt in your heart." Mom stepped back and waved her hand towards Lexia. "You can still talk to your sister and ask her. Just because you haven't done something doesn't mean it's too late to try. You know someone who can tell you about

Silver. All you have to do is ask Daric. I'm sure he would love to tell you more about Silver."

I sniffled as I wiped my face on my sleeve. "Thanks for helping me." Lexia and Fina released me from their embrace. "It still hurts, but not as much."

Mom smiled softly. "It's going to. I won't lie. Wounds like this take time to heal. That's why your captain gave you so much time to work through this. This is one thing your recovery aptitude can't fix overnight."

Lexia poked my side. "You need a distraction. You mentioned a fishing trip, maybe you should go. Tomorrow maybe?"

My mother glanced to the two girls sitting on the bed with me and put her hands on her hips. "If we're going tomorrow, it's going to be a busy day. We have a lot of laundry, shopping, and packing to do. So it's best to get ready for bed now."

Fina and Lexia looked at me with perplexed faces. I wrapped my tail around my waist and lowered my head. "I hope you don't mind, but do you two want to go fishing with me? We can bring the boys too."

Both of their faces softened. "Of course," Lexia answered.

"I'll help." Fina wagged her tail.

"Alright, get your stuff, girls." Mom waved to the door.

As Lexia and Fina got up from the bed, I felt an emptiness in my gut. I grabbed Fina's wrist. "Um..." I couldn't look her in the face as I asked, "Can you come back? I don't want to be alone."

"Yes. I'll return." Fina gently removed my hand and placed it on the bed.

Mom stepped next to me. "I'll stay here until she gets back."

"I'm a mess, aren't I?" I asked absentmindedly.

Mom ran her fingers through my hair. "You are. But I still love you all the same. I'll be here until you sort yourself out." She started scratching behind my ear. "Don't forget you've got two others as well. Fina and Lexia will be here for every step along the way."

54

AN UNDERSTANDING

I woke up with Fina sleeping on the bed next to me. She'd wrapped herself in an extra blanket after I'd made the mattress as cold as I could. Strangely enough, it didn't freeze solid. There was a healthy level of frost on the mattress where our blankets and pillows didn't cover.

She's fine with the cold, just not to the level I like it. I wonder if Lexia likes things as cold as I do. Hopefully Victor slept well.

I smiled as I let the lynx sleep. Her body stirred slightly as I rolled off the bed, but I could see she was still in whatever dream she was experiencing. After putting on some clean clothes, I strolled outside to check on Victor.

I can't get him out of my head. So did I fall in love with him? I wish I remember what love felt like in my last life. I slapped myself. *Wake up, Lucia. It doesn't matter what my last life felt like.*

The moon poked through the clouds, illuminating just enough to see. I eventually found Victor still sleeping under the tree I'd suggested. My chest tightened as I saw a blanket wrapped around him and a pillow cradling his head.

I'm in love. I don't know when it happened, but it happened. Since beastkin mate for life, that means I won't find anyone else. How does that work? Will I not find them attractive, or will I constantly keep him on my mind? Considering what my first thoughts were this morning, probably the latter.

I let the sleeping bear lie and headed out to my territory. I could feel a tightness in my limbs, so I decided some exercise was in order. And there was no better exercise than a good hunt.

As I wandered through my territory, I found that everything was as it should've been. After knowing everything was secure, I went looking for prey. I caught the scent of something, so I followed it. It wasn't something I had smelled recently, but it felt familiar.

The scent led me to a pond just outside my territory. It had a layer of ice over the top. But the bulge in the center caught my attention. I stalked towards it and saw a giant toad hibernating in the ice.

This is too easy. I left the frog to its slumber. *I'm here for a hunt, not to kill.*

I picked up the scent I'd followed earlier. This time it led me farther north, to a small clearing. On the far side, a deer grazed on the branches of the trees. A smile marched across my face as a growl grew from my throat. The deer turned its head towards me. I wanted it to hear me. And just like I wanted, it took off running.

I chased. I caught. I killed.

I removed the worst organs and licked my claws clean. After I hoisted its corpse onto my shoulders, I began my trip back home. I had a bounce in my step as I walked.

It's good to be home.

The silent walk home was pleasant, and as I left the woods, snowflakes danced in the surrounding air. I couldn't help but wag my tail. *More snow, yay!* When I arrived by the tree Victor had slept under, he was nowhere in sight. The sun still had some time before it rose, but it was getting close.

Mom leaned in the doorway. The smirk on her face was all the greeting I got. I placed the deer on the butchering table by the door.

"Why is it every time we're getting ready to go someplace, you have to go hunt for something?" Mom didn't hide the amusement in her voice. "We're going to need to sell that before we leave. You know that."

I shrugged as I turned to face her. "Yeah, I do. But I needed to get that out of my system." I tilted my head as I stared at her relaxed attitude. "I'm surprised you haven't yelled at me for going out alone."

Mom giggled as she stood up straight. "I know how you get when you hunt. Nobody can keep up with you. More importantly, you don't think of anything else while you're at it. So it was fine."

"It's fun. I'm never going to stop hunting." I looked at the deer. "Maybe my instincts were craving normalcy." *Or maybe it was me.*

Mom placed her hand on my shoulder. "Finding and following what's normal helps." She started laughing. "Besides, if you stopped hunting, there's no way I could afford to feed you."

I couldn't suppress a laugh of my own.

We gathered everyone's dirty clothes as they woke up. Mom took Lexia, Gifford, and Victor to the city to sell the deer I'd hunted and pick up some supplies and new clothes for everyone. Fina and I were left doing the laundry for the clothes that survived the mission.

The snow flurries upgraded to full-on snowfall as it accumulated on the ground and coated everything. We had to work fast because even though I could keep the water from freezing completely, it took a lot of extra effort. After wringing out the clothes as much as possible, Fina hung them on racks by the fireplace to dry.

We finished just as the weather turned heavy. The visibility was dropping as the snow fell harder and harder. *It looks like we aren't leaving today. We won't be able to see where we're going. Oh well. Hopefully the weather will improve tomorrow.*

After getting all the snow out of our fur, the two of us spent time brushing ourselves. Fina's fur was finer than mine, but there was so much more of it. *She's oh so fluffy.* While we were complimenting each other's fur, a knock at the door ruined our fluffy moment.

I opened the door and saw Daric, bundled up and covered in snow. "What do you want?" I asked as I prepared to slam the door in his face.

"It's cold. Can I come in and talk?" Daric's teeth chattered.

"Fine." I rolled my eyes as I made room for him to come in. "It's not that cold. Actually, it's almost perfect."

Daric tried to shake most of the snow off himself before he stepped in. "Says the wolf girl covered in fur."

I looked at Daric's footprints and saw that the snow was about five inches deep. *I hope Mom and the others are fine. Mom doesn't like the snow.*

Daric shivered as he stood in the entryway, and I closed the door. "Are you jealous? Be warned, it takes a lot of upkeep to keep it looking this nice. And don't get me started with the fire season." I channeled my magic to pull the remaining snow off him. *I don't want him to leave a puddle of water in the entryway. He's not the one who will have to clean it up.*

Daric watched my magic. "No, I'm more jealous that you can use magic. Why do you get to use magic and not me?"

I wagged my finger in his face. "Do you know if you can even learn magic? Not everyone can use it."

Fina poked her head in the room. "Daric? What are you doing here?"

"I came to talk to Lucia." Daric smiled at the other girl's entrance. "My tutors told me I'm capable of learning magic, but I've never succeeded in channeling any of it. Nobody has been able to explain it in a way that makes sense. How do you do it?"

I scratched the back of my head. "Well, I sort of just feel it. It's kinda hard to explain." I extended my hand to him. "What does it feel like when people use magic on you?"

Daric shuddered, not from the cold, and there was a disgusted look in his eyes as he stared at the ground. "Like there's this sticky, oily feeling crawling under my skin."

I flinched. "That's not what I feel at all." Daric snapped his attention to me. "I get this tingling sensation, kinda like an itch."

"Oh." Daric slumped his shoulders, defeated.

We need to change topics. "You said you wanted to talk, so what did you want to talk about? I know you didn't brave this blizzard just to talk to me about magic." I extended a hand towards the fireplace in the next room. "You can sit by the fire to warm yourself up."

"Thanks," Daric said as he removed his outermost cloak and hung it on a rung by the door. He looked at Fina and then back at me. "But what I want to talk about is private. It's about you-know-what."

He still wants to talk about our reincarnation? I flattened my ears as I looked at Fina. Her tail swayed behind her as she gave me a curious look. "Could you give us some space? And please don't try to listen in." I could see she didn't understand. "Daric is coming to me in confidence. Please respect his wish."

"I want to help." Fina lowered her ears and wrapped her tail around her waist.

I shook my head. "Not this time. Please?"

"What about what Nora said?" Fina leaned towards me. "What if you need me? You aren't allowed to be alone."

"I won't be alone. Daric will be with me." I gave the man a hard look. *He won't be of any use if I slip up. Besides, I really don't want him to see me like that.* "If I need you, Daric will come to get you. I promise."

Daric's eyes darted back and forth between me and Fina. "How will I know you need her? What are you talking about?"

"You'll just know," I said with a growl.

Fina gave me an annoyed look. "She says bad and wrong things about herself."

Daric gave me a sad look.

I growled and bared my fangs at him.

He raised his arms up defensively. "Maybe now isn't the best time for this talk then."

"If we don't do it now, it won't be for a week or two. Besides, do you really want to go back out there?" I pointed to the door behind me with my thumb. "Also, now that I think about it, there's something I wanted to talk to you about."

Daric glanced at the door. "No, I guess not. At least not until it stops snowing so hard." He turned to Fina. "If you need to stay, I can adjust what I say."

"I will go," Fina said. "If going helps, then I will go."

I walked over and hugged Fina. "You're a great friend. More than that even. But this time... this time I have to do my best on my own." I gave the woman a soft smile. "Just don't go too far. I may need your help afterwards."

Fina nodded. "Please call for me if you need me."

I patted the lynxkin's head before she padded off to the room we'd slept in last night. Daric followed me to the fireplace. I invited him to sit next to it while I kept my distance.

"You really don't like fire, do you?" Daric eyed me as I sat in a chair I brought from the dining room.

I scowled at him. "I was serious about that. Something about fire sends my instincts into a panic."

"Was that something from your past life?"

I carefully rubbed the corners of my eyes. "As I told you already, I don't remember. Lexia said I wasn't always afraid of fire. So maybe."

Daric crossed his arms as he stroked his chin. There was noticeably more facial hair there.

"How many years did you lose?"

Daric almost jumped in his seat. "Oh, uh, you're talking about when Goldy used her healing magic on me, right?" I nodded. "It was a year. I'm eighteen now, according to the oracle stone."

I arched an eyebrow. "The stone told you how old you were? It can tell you how much you age after receiving healing magic? When's your birthday?"

"My birthday isn't until the third to last day of the fire season. And apparently, yeah. I didn't know that the oracle stone could show that. It was something that the elf lady said when I mentioned that healing magic was used on me." Daric sounded distant.

I glared at him. "Evalana had healing magic used on her when she lost her arm, and she lost three years. How did that only cost you a year? You nearly died."

Daric shrugged. "Maybe it has something to do with my recovery aptitude." He shook his head. "That's not what I came here to talk to you about." He stared at the ground, expressionless. "I wanted to tell you that you were right."

I leaned back, blinking a few times. "Uh, care to elaborate?"

"I can't save everyone. There are those in this world not worth saving." Daric clenched his fist. "All these years, I thought I was the hero. But now, I don't think so. You were also right that I had been treating this like a game. When I was sent here, it was like a dream come true."

I can't say I'm surprised I was right. But admitting it is a big step for him.

Daric turned to the flames dancing on the logs in the fireplace. "All my life before this one, I read stories where someone was sent to another world to be a hero. They became heroes. They saved the day, they got the girl, or girls, and they never gave up who they were. People followed them because they were right and just."

I crossed my arms and flicked my tail back and forth. "Let me guess, they all stayed human in those stories."

"They did," Daric answered with an apologetic voice. "I stayed human too. Even my two aptitudes felt like my cheat power." *I smell a "but" coming.* "But after seeing you take charge like you did and everyone following you while I stood back and did nothing, I know I don't deserve to call myself a hero. You're the hero."

"I'm not a hero, and neither do I need to be one. At least not in the way you think of a hero." I took a deep breath. "I chased after my sister because I needed to. There's no way I can leave someone in my family in the hands of the demons. Those close to me are all I care about. Fina, Gifford, and Victor are all special to me now. Silver, Dinar, and Golditress, while not as close as the other three, still became close friends to me."

"What about Mark and me?" Daric leaned forward towards me.

"Mark, I couldn't care less about him. You, on the other hand, I think I need you." *This is hard. I never thought about what I wanted to say to him.*

Daric jumped in his seat as he looked astounded. "What—what do you need me for?" he stuttered. "I'm nothing compared to you. You're decisive, confident, and you're..." The words died in his throat as he slumped in his chair. "I wish I could be more like you."

I couldn't help but smile. "What, female and covered in fur?" I waved my hand at myself. Daric opened his mouth, but I held up a finger. *I know that's not what he meant. But I couldn't help myself.* "I'm short-tempered to the point of excess. I'm happy to kill someone. I'm eager to kill. My instincts and I make snap judgments constantly, and there are times I'm wrong." I started picking at my claws. "What I'm trying to say is, I'm not a saint either. Making the right decision is hard for me when every part of me wants to take the easy route. Being me isn't the dream you think it is."

Neither one of us said any more. The crackling of the fire was the only thing that kept total silence from reigning.

Daric finally broke the silence with a chuckle that turned into a laugh.

He lost his mind, didn't he?

Slowly, Daric stopped laughing and smiled at me. "We just had one of those 'grass is always greener on the other side' moments, didn't we?"

I chuckled. "We did. We're acting like a pair of children. I'm fifteen. What's your excuse?"

"You got me; I'm childish." Daric shrugged. "You mentioned that you think you need me. How?"

"Over the years, my moral compass has slowly tilted towards ruthlessness." I looked down at my claws as I flexed them. "What I need is a set of morals. Someone to stop me from killing anyone and everyone for the most trivial reasons. I can't just go around killing everyone."

Daric sighed. "But there are those out there that need to be stopped. I see that now. Sometimes killing someone is the best answer, and you have no other choice. You showed me that with Barney. Sometimes you can't spare the resources to take someone to trial." He rubbed his hands together. "Allen told me that there are times I have to be the judge and executioner. That's a responsibility I don't know if I can handle."

"Then don't."

He gave me a confused look.

"Mom has been telling me recently that I need to work on letting others help me. So you help me, and I can help you. When the situation calls for it, I'll let you judge. Your sense of right is something I need you to keep. In return, I'll be your executioner."

"I guess it's a good thing that I disbanded Omega Gamma so I can follow you around." Daric's smirk turned into a scowl. "Can you really do that? Will you?"

"You know you can't join The Maidens. Captain Aenwyn's adamant about only allowing women." I crossed my arms. "What are you going to do while I'm in between missions? I'm sure Aenwyn and you can come to some kind of agreement to accompany me on missions."

Daric waved his hand dismissively. "I'll just freelance it. Besides, I imagine that my current father is going to give me an earful when I get back home." He stood up.

I stood up too. "Where are you going?"

Daric headed for the door. "I'm going to go back to town. I have a room at an inn. You already have a full house."

I flicked my tail back and forth. "It's a blizzard out there. Are you really going to go out in it?"

Daric stopped and turned to face me. "Are you concerned about me?"

I shook my head. "Don't flatter yourself." *Besides, Victor has already taken the role of my mate. That's weird to say. My mate. That's going to take some getting used to.*

"Hello?" Daric waved his hand past my face. I grabbed his wrist and growled at him. "Sorry. You just started spacing out there. I didn't know if I needed to get Fina or not."

I let his arm go. My cheeks warmed. "Sorry, I was lost in thought." I turned around. "Just don't get yourself sick or worse. I'll need my moral compass later."

Daric laughed. "It sounds like someone's falling for me. You really have that hard-to-get act down."

I whirled around to grab his throat, then slammed him into the wall. "There is no way I'm falling for you." The panic in Daric's eyes was intoxicating. "Victor is more of a man than you will ever be. I've already decided on my mate." I leaned in and put my fangs right next to his ear and whispered, "And it isn't you. Don't ever think otherwise."

I gave him another shove into the wall and left him. There was nothing he could say that I wanted to hear.

Daric's feet shuffled out the door.

Men. I hope that when I was a man, I wasn't remotely as bad. I looked around the room. *Great, now I'm all worked up and there's nothing for me to vent on.*

I heard the door open. "What did Daric want?" I heard Mom's voice as she walked inside.

"To talk." My voice still carried a rumble.

Mom stepped into the living room. "Are you okay? You sound agitated."

My tail lashed behind me. "It's because I am." I turned to see Gifford and Lexia walk into the room. "Where's Victor?"

"He's outside moving the cart to the back." Mom grabbed my hands. "I know I said that we were going to leave for the fishing trip today, but the weather is too rough. Hopefully it stops snowing tomorrow. I hate these late blizzards."

"That's fine." I eyed Gifford. *You know, I believe I have someone to vent on. Lexia will understand.* "Gifford, how about we work on your knight training tonight?" A toothy grin spread across my face.

Gifford tucked his tail in between his legs as he shivered.

55

FISHING FOR FORGIVENESS

I woke up the next morning and everything felt lighter. *Maybe because I went to bed not sobbing my eyes out.* Like yesterday, I woke up before Fina. *Her face is adorable while she sleeps.*

I let her sleep after changing into clean clothes. I grabbed my hairbrush, then headed to the dining room. A subtle rumble disturbed the blissful silence as I walked through the halls. When I poked my head into the living room, I saw Victor sleeping on the floor by the couch that wouldn't fit him. The coals in the fireplace barely glowed as the last embers fought against the cold.

I worked him pretty hard yesterday, didn't I? At least he didn't complain like Gifford did after I sparred with him. It's not like I hurt Gifford that badly. Besides, Lexia made it up to him with all her fawning over him. I don't know if she's doing that simply because she loves him or if she's doing that to help motivate him to train. If it works, it works. Who am I to judge what motivates people? I'll do most anything for bacon. I shrugged my shoulders as I went to the dining room to brush my fur and get some morning stretches in.

After finishing my stretches, I poked my head out to see if the weather had cleared. All three moons were visible in the sky, illuminating all the fresh snowfall from yesterday. I wagged my tail at the sight. I couldn't help myself, so I jumped into the snow banks and ran through them, grinning the entire time.

After enjoying myself until just before dawn, I flopped into the snow to stare at the last of the stars. The snow rose up around me, making me believe it was about twelve inches deep. *Wow, that was the heaviest snowfall all year.*

I let my mind drift off to nothingness as I watched the sunrise from my bed of snow. As the sun climbed the horizon, I stood up and shook off. What snow stubbornly clung to me I used my magic to remove. I then used my magic to clear the snow from the doorways into the house and around the firewood storage shed. *Magic makes clearing snow so much easier and faster.*

One by one, everyone else woke up, and I found out that Victor had been watching me play in the snow. Mom got food together for breakfast while Fina helped her. Lexia clung to Gifford again, but after she saw the snow outside, she dragged him outside to have her turn running through it. *So I'm not the only one.* Gifford didn't run with her, just watched her playfully dive from snowbank to snowbank.

Watching my sister drove me to join her. We played around, chasing each other. I took it easy on her and let her catch me a few times. We even got Victor and Gifford to join us eventually. Poor Victor couldn't keep up with any of us; we were far too agile for him.

You know, sometimes you need to let your inner child out to play. My inner child is more like a wolf capable of brutal slaughter, but that's nothing to worry about... most of the time. Things just feel different now that Lexia's in my life. I feel different. Since I've accepted Lexia as my sister, I've wanted her to be happy and safe. Evalana and Zenny have been important to me, but this is more. And now I want to feel it more. I miss those two. I'll have to see them after I get back from fishing.

Mom giggled when she called us in for breakfast. After we ate, we packed up, cleaned off, and loaded up the cart Mom rented yesterday for the trip. Mom led the way with her magic, clearing the snow so the cart didn't have to plow through it. I pushed the cart most of the time, much to Victor's disappointment.

I think he still struggles with the fact that I'm much stronger than him. He's stronger than most people, but my physical aptitude changes everything. It's sweet of him to want to help me. I'm just glad that everyone isn't giving me a hard time about needing to find a mate now. I'm not looking forward to having that conversation with Mom later, because there's no way I'm going to be able to hide it while I'm in heat.

Victor and I kept taking turns, but he would tire out quickly and recover just as fast. But I could pull the cart almost nonstop. Mom kept clearing the snow with her magic. She even had Lexia, who really wanted Mom to teach her some more about magic, spend some time removing the snow after the first few days when her magic completely recovered.

It took seven days to get to the river where Mom and I fished. We kept the trip light, making sure no one got tired with plenty of breaks. After all, this was supposed to be a vacation, not a forced march. Fina didn't take to the snow like Lexia and me. She preferred to walk next to me while I pushed the cart and walk behind the cart when I didn't. Because when I wasn't pushing the cart, I traipsed through the snow with Lexia. Traveling as we did was much more fun with everyone than when it was just Mom and me.

We stood near the riverbank. The edges of the river were frozen, but at two and a half arcs wide and two arcs at its deepest, even the ice season could freeze the flowing water completely. I left the cart and was the first to take off for the river.

I dove into the river without hesitating. I had to admit the water was cold, but that meant it felt nice. Almost immediately, four fish scattered around me as I looked for something to stick my claws into. *It looks like it's going to be a good day for fishing.*

The wintry water was exceptionally clear and allowed me to track the fish's movements easily. After seeing the fish split into pairs, I reached out for the closer set. They were able to avoid a few of my swipes. But just as they were almost past me, my claws latched onto a tail. Red wisps flowed from it as I pulled it closer. It squirmed, trying to escape my clutches, but when I got my other hand on it, its fate was sealed. I bit into the spine just behind the head to hang on to it while I swam to the surface.

I dug my claws into the ice and pulled myself ashore. Water poured from my fur as I eventually found my footing.

"What kind of fishing is that?" Gifford's voice carried through the open air. "That's no way to fish."

Mom put a hand on his shoulder. "That's how she is. Always jumping all-in without a single concern about the consequences. At least not until after the fact."

I bit down completely, severing the fish's spine and putting it out of its misery. Then I savored the meat as I worked the scale-covered skin away from the delightfully soft flesh. "I can hear you," I called to my mother after I spat out the skin.

She gave me a knowing smile before she went to set up our campsite with Victor and Fina.

Lexia and Gifford joined me by the river. I took the time to inspect exactly what I had caught. The fish was about twenty inches long and covered in near-reflective silver scales with a red stripe on each side. *Mm, a steelfish.*

"That's such a waste of energy when you dive in like that." Gifford shook his head. "Now you're all wet and will need to dry off before your fur freezes."

I scowled at the foxkin. But it was Lexia who said something first. "But she looked like she was having so much fun. Not everything has to be about efficiency." She gave him a mischievous smile. "You should try it, love. It might be fun."

I couldn't help but grin as Gifford stepped away from my sister. "Oh no. I don't know how to swim."

"Then it's a good time to learn." I grabbed his shirt and gently threw him into the river.

Gifford hit the water in an unceremonious splash. He did manage to come up for air, but his floundering was almost comical. His arms and legs flailed as he tried to keep his head above water.

"You two... are bad... influences... on each... other," Gifford said whenever his head crested above the water enough to get any words out.

I turned to Lexia, who gave me an innocent smile. "I see someone's starting to relax. But I'm guessing you want me to go get him before the current takes him away."

Lexia leaned forward and batted her eyes at me. "Would you, please?"

I rolled my eyes and smiled. *She's definitely trying to mimic me.* "Fine, but hold this." I handed her the fish. "And don't eat it. That's mine."

Lexia nodded as she held the fish by the tail with both hands.

I dove into the water and swam up next to Gifford. I grabbed the back of his shirt and pulled him closer to the shoreline. "Alright, calm down and put your feet down." *He should be tall enough to stand here.*

Gifford followed my instructions and started panting as he headed for shore. He sat on the frozen bank, water pouring from his fur. "How do you make it look so easy? Is your aptitude making it that easy for you?"

No, apparently I remembered how to swim from my last life, but only the basics. The rest I figured out along the way. But that's not the version I'm going to tell you. "No. The most important thing you need to do is not panic. Swimming isn't that hard even though our fur weighs us down."

"Easy for you to say," Gifford said through his clenched jaw.

I glared at him. "How is it that your aptitude is fishing and you don't know how to swim?"

Lexia skipped through the snow to join us. "The few rivers we've seen were never this deep." She stopped and looked like she was thinking about something. "I guess calling them rivers isn't quite right then. Streams, maybe?"

We spent more time fishing. Gifford stayed in the shallows while Lexia joined me in the river to learn how to swim. She had the basics down by the time lunch was ready. I knew she could get to safety if she needed to. Victor joined Gifford's style of fishing, while Mom and Fina watched. When I asked Fina if she wanted to join, it was the first time I saw her refuse to do anything.

I guess she's kind of a cat, and cats don't like water. Fair enough.

Mom used her magic to dry everyone off before we ate. There was plenty for everyone. The guys caught a few bluegills that slipped past Lexia and me. Their scales were a vibrant blue, and they were only about seven inches at their longest. But the sight of the blue scales reminded me of Silver, and the guilt resurfaced.

I stared at the fish in my hands, unable to look away.

"Does time really heal all wounds?" I didn't direct the question to anyone in particular.

"Yes, but not without scars." Mom's voice cut through the fog of doubt. "What are you feeling?"

"Guilty." The word flew out of my mouth before I could consider my feelings, but it felt like the right word.

Mom sat next to me and placed a hand on my forearm. "Why?"

I closed my eyes when I felt tears building. "Here I am, having fun like my friend never died. I even gave the order to have him buried in an unmarked mass grave with other beastkin. He didn't deserve to be abandoned like that." The tears broke through my eyelids and trickled down my face. "I know it was better than nothing. If he had loved ones, they'll never have the chance to say goodbye. It's not fair."

"No, it's not fair." Mom pulled me close and let me cry on her shoulder. "Life never is. But life always goes on. I'm not saying you shouldn't feel anything. But do you really think Silver would want you to put your whole life on hold because he no longer has his?"

"Probably not," I answered.

Mom started rubbing my back. "You need to find a way to forgive yourself. Nobody can tell you how to do it. It's something you have to find on your own. I'll be here anytime you need me."

Someone else sat behind me and joined the hug. "I will too," Lexia added. "Even though I don't understand what you're feeling, I'll do my best to help you however you need me to."

"Thanks, you two." I pushed Mom and Lexia away as I stood up.

I stared at the fish that was still in my hand, then up at the campfire Mom was using to cook her fish. I stepped as close as I could before my phobia stopped me.

I know you'll likely never hear this, but I'm sorry. You deserved better. You were a hero, and people should know about it. Somehow, I'll make sure you're remembered for your sacrifice. Maybe you'll get a second chance at life, like me. I know you deserve it. Please, forgive me.

I tossed the fish in the fire. As I watched the flames consume the small fish, everything felt a bit lighter. My tail didn't reach for the ground anymore. Instead, it started swaying behind me. My ears flicked around easier, and where I felt a hole in my heart, it felt somewhat filled.

I turned towards my seat.

"Are you going to be alright?" Mom asked.

I smiled. "Yeah." I took one last look at the fire. "I think I will be."

For Silver.

EPILOGUE: MOSTLY DEAD

Blood dripped from the sin of lust's wounds as her skin cracked from the burns. She limped towards the rider. The pillar of ice embedded in the powerful demon impressed her.

"You can fool the mortals, but you can't fool me." The succubus's voice cracked as she stared up at the disfigured face.

The demon's one remaining eye snapped open and locked onto the demon woman. An indecipherable gurgle came from the remains of the humanoid mouth.

"Shh. Don't speak. I would never have guessed the humans would be able to do this to you." Lust smirked. "You are in no state to serve the king."

The rider stabbed her with his spear-arm. She cried out as he pierced her thigh. But the pain of the attack was only the beginning. There was a tugging sensation in her magic. In a panic, she jumped away, stumbling to the ground.

The tugging sensation left her as she dislodged herself from the rider. She stared at the wound with fascination. When she turned towards the impaled rider, she could see his fury. He constantly reached for her with his spear-arm, but she was just out of his reach.

Thoughts ran through her head like a whirlwind until one idea clicked. "You were going to take my power to strengthen yourself," she thought out loud.

All the souls she claimed in the demon realm were hers. She used them to gather her strength. But with what the rider had just shown her, everything changed for the demoness. There was a shortcut to power, and someone had conveniently handed it to her on a platter—or a kebab, in this case.

If more demons learned that they could claim each other's power, the demon realm would collapse into chaos. It was a secret the sin of lust needed to keep to herself, but it was one she would use for her own gain. Especially now.

One problem: The rider looked like it wouldn't forfeit its power to her.

The sin of lust circled towards the rider's back. His attempts to reach her became more frantic with each step she took towards his vulnerable back. She didn't need to see the fear in his eye to know he knew his time was running out.

The rider tried to turn, but the icy pillar pinning him ended such attempts.

With her opening secured, the demoness marched to collect her prize. She grabbed the demon's head and twisted it around, knowing that wouldn't kill the Rider of Pain.

She planted her lips on the spot where the rider's mouth should have been and focused on doing the same thing he had done to her moments before.

The rider resisted and fought back, pulling at her power. Reluctantly, the demoness broke the connection after she admitted they'd hit a stalemate.

The succubus extended her fangs and bit into the demon's flesh, injecting every bit of venom she had. Its effects weren't as potent on demons, but the demoness hoped it would be enough to tip the scales of control in her favor.

After she emptied her venom sacks, she returned to her attempt to wrestle the rider's power away from him. Their struggle for dominance grew with intensity with each passing moment. But to any onlooker, they would have seen nothing more than the sin of lust kissing the Rider of Pain.

Bit by bit, the succubus could feel her opponent's will wane. Like a dam breaking, power flooded into the sin of lust the moment her opponent couldn't fight both her and the venom.

She drank the power greedily. And as power filled her body, her wounds healed. Her scorched skin flaked away to reveal new, supple skin. The wing that was ripped off grew back at an alarming rate. But there was more power to be had, and the sin wanted it all.

After her wounds finished healing, her muscles rippled and expanded. As her strength grew, her skin shifted from milky to a soft shade of pink and then darkened until it was a vibrant cherry red. Her body grew in all directions, adding several inches to her height. The last change settled in her feet. Her toes fused together, turned black, and shifted into hooves.

When the last drops of power left the Rider of Pain, his body lost all color and disintegrated into a pile of ash.

The demoness stepped back, nearly tripping on her new hooves. "Oh, this is unexpected," she said as she looked down at her appearance.

The shape of her body remained unchanged. She was still an unrivaled beauty. Now, though, she had visible muscles and a change in skin color. The hooves were annoying, but she had never liked walking in the first place.

The demoness looked for her pet, but noticed the loss of connection to her. She shrugged. It wasn't a big loss. The power she had received was so much more intoxicating. For the first time in a long time, she felt satisfied. Yet a new hunger blossomed.

"I have one rider's power, but what if I had another's?" the demoness mused to herself. "What if I had them all? I could challenge the demon king himself." She started laughing. "Then the demon realm would have a demon queen, one fit to rule."

There was an interesting recent addition to her usual senses. She could feel other demons, like the sin of greed, watching her now. The demoness grinned as she turned towards the dijin. She felt the other demon flee and couldn't help but laugh again.

"Let her keep her foolish plans. I've got something far more inter-esting coming." The demon flapped her wings as she took to the sky. "Is that another rider in the distance? Is that the Rider of Death? I think it is. But I don't think I can defeat him as I am now." A grin spread across her face as idea after idea ran through her mind. "But why do I have to do all the work? I know exactly who can help me weaken it. And if she fails... Well, that's one less problem for the future. But I'm going to need a bargaining token first."

The new Rider of Pain cackled as she flew towards the north.

NEWSLETTER SIGNUP

Do you want more? More is coming. If you want updates about this series and possibly more, please consider joining my newsletter here:

subscribepage.io/13PBC

I will keep you posted on my progress on future books and projects.

Whatever you choose, I hope that you find it in your heart to leave a review on whatever platform you purchased this book from. Authors—including me—love to receive feedback. There is something about algorithms, but that is just a bonus.

It doesn't have to be complicated. Just say what you liked, what you didn't like, and/or your favorite scene or character(s). Or you could simply just hit the rating button. One click and you're done.

If you don't mind doing some alpha reading, come find me on Royal Road:

https://www.royalroad.com/profile/241783/fictions